Debbie Carbin is the author of *Thanks for Nothing, Nick Maxwell*. She lives in Kent with her husband and two children.

D1454635

www.rbooks.co.uk

Also by Debbie Carbin

THANKS FOR NOTHING, NICK MAXWELL

and published by Black Swan

THREE MEN
AND A MAYBE

Debbie Carbin

BLACK SWAN

TRANSWORLD PUBLISHERS
61–63 Uxbridge Road, London W5 5SA
A Random House Group Company
www.rbooks.co.uk

THREE MEN AND A MAYBE
A BLACK SWAN BOOK: 9780552774192

First publication in Great Britain
Black Swan edition published 2009

Addresses for Random House Group Ltd companies outside the UK
can be found at: www.randomhouse.co.uk
The Random House Group Ltd Reg. No. 954009

The Random House Group Limited supports The Forest Stewardship
Council (FSC), the leading international forest certification organisation.
All our titles that are printed on Greenpeace approved FSC certified
paper carry the FSC logo. Our paper procurement policy can be
found at www.rbooks.co.uk/environment

Typeset in 11/13pt Giovanni Book by
Kestrel Data, Exeter, Devon.
Printed in the UK by
CPI Cox & Wyman, Reading, RG1 8EX.

2 4 6 8 10 9 7 5 3 1

For Richard. My one.

Acknowledgements

As ever, I am deeply grateful to those harrassed and slightly twitchy members of my family and friends who read this as it was coming along and gave me such valuable feedback, particularly Lois Whipp, Irene Carbin and Lucy Coates. And of course Tom and Beth, my biggest fans.

Special mention must go to Suzanne Allen, for that mammoth session in the Mayfly on Luke's birthday; and Tracey Owen – without you, I would never have sent it off. Thank you so much.

Many thanks again to Laura Morris: agent, editor, friend. And Lydia Newhouse, who has given me a metaphorical hand-hold for two years. Thank you.

One

Welcome and Introductions

Short-term Goal: Be the best training presenter this town has ever seen.
Obstacles: None really. The town is sadly lacking in good training presenters. It's not even a challenge.
Long-term Goal: Find true love and happiness with my one and only soul mate, Richard.
Obstacles: Richard is (actually) out of the country.

Don't you just love it when things change? We all need change in order to progress, don't we? Without change there would be no wheel, no penicillin, no hair-straighteners. We should welcome change, embrace it, encourage it, because it gives us all a chance to start again, like spring after winter. The seasons change: life starts anew. There is no death, no ending, only change.

What a complete load of cretinous bollocks.

I mean, seriously, who really likes things changing? Who is genuinely happy with everything they have worked for and got to know and trust suddenly collapsing into chaos like a cheap Swedish table? Does anyone, on returning to their home from three weeks on holiday, think, Oh look, squatters have moved in while we were away, how marvellous, this will give me a chance to develop my negotiating skills? No. They don't.

But I've got to sell it like I mean it, like someone who can clasp their hands together and beam in heartfelt joy at the start of each new beautiful, God-given day, and isn't a pathetic, over-enthusiastic saddo. I've got to sell it because that's my job. No, I'm not an estate agent. What I do is far more significant than people's homes. I work for Love Learning, this town's best training provider, and I am Beth Sheridan, Love Learning's best training facilitator. Today I'm doing Change Management, and in about three minutes I've got to walk into a room full of cashiers and tellers and lending advisers from the bank in the high street and present 'Day One – Preparation'. This means that I have to convince them all of how marvellous and peachy change is because it means evolution, revolution, and we all have fantastic new experiences and learn new things.

It's utter bullshit.

The manager of the bank has probably booked this course for his staff because the branch is closing down in three months and he wants them to see it not as *redundancy* but as *opportunity*.

No, no, I mustn't think like that, they'll see it in my face. I have to be positive, upbeat and passionate so that after five days of listening to me they can go back to their workplace enthused and excited, eagerly anticipating the next God-awful change so they can have the chance to manage it . . . before they pay an unexpected visit to the Job Centre. I'll just have to cross my fingers behind my back.

Three months ago, I didn't feel like this at all. Three months ago, I still believed in change, and was sitting in my flat in a negligée and baby oil, anticipating, waiting – no, *hungering* – for a change to happen. My boss, Richard Love, the owner and founder of Love Learning, was coming over at eight o'clock that evening because he had something to tell me – something important that couldn't be said over the phone. He wanted to say it to my face. I knew what it was going to be.

Richard and I had been in a relationship for eight years. Not, you know, technically boyfriend and girl-friend, but it was definitely a relationship. It started when I was taken on at Horizon Holidays, which is this massive company on a roundabout in the town centre where they sell holidays and flights and travel insurance. Apparently the owner, Rupert de Witter, didn't want to take up space in the town – something about the environment – so he had it built on a roundabout, which I think is incredibly short-sighted. No matter which way you went out of the building, you always had to cross a road. It was really annoying, particularly if you were just popping out to the chemist or something. I mean, it wasn't my fault it took so long to get there and back.

Anyway, I was going to be the training manager's assistant, and at that time, Richard Love was the training manager. I was twenty, had left school two years earlier and this was going to be my first proper job. He was twenty-seven, my boss, and had been working at Horizon Holidays for five years. He was a manager; he told people what to do, and they did it. So did I.

11

The first thing I noticed when I was led into his presence was his height. He was standing on the other side of the desk with his back to us, arms folded, blocking the light from the window so all we could see was a tall shadow. The bloke from Personnel had to look up just to stammer nervously to the back of his head.

'Er, Mr Love, sir, I've brought your new assistant up.' Richard turned round at this point and looked at me. And that was it. His hazel eyes met mine and an unbreakable link was forged. Electricity zipped through my veins and a force on my body began inexplicably trying to pull me towards him, like a tractor beam. Our eyes were locked together for only an instant, but in that brief moment, we saw into each other's souls and recognized a kindred spirit. I stopped breathing, clocks stopped ticking, the traffic on the street fell quiet. The magic of the moment held all in the room spellbound.

'She got a name, then?' Richard barked suddenly. He was no doubt just trying to hide his confusion.

'Oh, er, yes, sorry, this is Beth Sheridan.'

Two years later, we walked out of there, hand in hand. Not literally, you know, physically holding hands. It was a metaphorical hand-hold. Actually, I would have held his hand if he had walked out a little more slowly. And hadn't been carrying armfuls of stolen stationery. He marched out of there in protest at the crapness of Mr Rupert de Witter and his crackpot training policy; I scuttled out behind him to show my support.

Horizon's training policy was to put every member of staff through every training course, regardless of what department they worked in or whether or not they would actually benefit from it. The sheep-dip approach, Richard called it. So even the girls who worked in Telesales were given courses on Excel and PowerPoint, just like everyone else, although they were never likely to use them discussing painting holidays with old ladies in Llandudno.

'It's a stupid waste of resources!' Richard would shout down the phone to Rupert de Witter, rolling his eyes at me and lobbing hole punches around. Sometimes, in quieter moments, we would spend ages – as much as five or six minutes – dreaming of training that was tailor-made to the needs of the delegates.

'Wouldn't it be great, Bethy,' he would say, gazing at me with his chin on his hand, 'to give people only training they could actually use?'

I'd nod, captivated. I never felt closer to him than in those moments.

Eventually, Richard himself was invited to attend a course called 'Introduction to Using a Mouse', in spite of the fact that he has a degree in IT. He was a bit disappointed about that. I think he said something like, 'You fucking *what*?' That's when he did his Jerry Maguire and walked, taking with him nothing more than his sense of what was morally right, and the bedazzled girl who worked for him (me). It was exactly the same as the film apart from the fish (there weren't any). Richard was determined to do what was best for his clients, just like Tom Cruise; and, just like Renée, it was me with stars in my eyes who went with him. He had me at 'Are you coming or what?'

I went.

That is probably my all-time favourite film now.

Morals triumph over money, and love triumphs over all. Jerry gets his own back on the people who let him down by being better than them, with no one but Renée Zellweger to help him, and falls in love with her in the end. It's exactly what happened to us. Except that Richard wasn't sacked. Oh, plus he's taking a bit longer to fall in love with me than Tom took with Renée. Unlike her, I'm prepared to wait.

It's six years since we left Horizon together, and in that time we've set up Love Learning and worked bloody hard to make it the best training provider this town has ever seen. Our pledge to our clients is that the training we provide is so good, employers will notice a difference when their employees return to their jobs after attending a course. Our training is tailor-made; Richard's dream is reality. I have slogged for six years to make sure of it.

Richard is brilliant with money and premises and tax returns and all that, so he focused on that and left me free to concentrate on bringing in the work. I came in early, stayed late, worked weekends, trawled round the town looking for inspiration, infiltrated local businesses to find out their training needs, researched on the internet, visited libraries, conferences, meetings and workshops, mostly in my own time. After four months of seventy-hour weeks, insufficient sleep and too much coffee, all that delving, spying, snooping and browsing really started to pay off. I was lucky enough to be the first one in the entire town to notice a teensy article in an industry magazine that had a teensy insignificant quote in it from the head of a chain of restaurants about bringing his establishments into the twenty-first century.

'Of course,' he had said, probably nodding wisely, 'all my workforce will need retraining, too.'

I stared at those words while bells rang, lights flashed and fireworks went off around me. It was probably lack of sleep.

I acted. Well, it was midnight so I went to bed first. But I acted first thing next morning. I went to see the local branch of this chain and persuaded the manager that if he was looking for training for his staff, Love Learning could provide everything he needed. He went for it.

That was the beginning. From then on, there was no stopping me. I realized that the most lucrative contracts were the ones that got Richard's attention, and they were the ones where other training providers weren't bidding. That meant approaching businesses with our prospectus before they made it public that they were in the market. Which meant finding out they were looking for training before they announced it.

I had a knack for it. It must have been the four solid months I spent completely immersed in training literature, but somehow I was able to spot the potential in an irrelevant throwaway remark in an unconnected article. When the manager of the Seahorse Hotel was in the local news because a minor celebrity had stayed there and complained about the room service, I went to see him and wondered if some Customer Care training might be useful. And when a restaurant out in the business park was threatened with closure because of poor hygiene standards, I couldn't help but observe, when I was there, that if the staff had a bit more time available, they could put more into their hygiene routine. The manager was very interested to hear about our new Time Management programme.

Love Learning grew, and Richard had to take on eight more staff – seven more presenters and Ali, our admin assistant. With one eye on Richard, I managed to beat the other training providers to the signature over and over again, repeatedly landing lucrative contracts. Richard got very rich, very quickly.

'Bethy, Bethy, Bethy,' he said to me once, taking hold of my shoulders. Which made the utter exhaustion, malnutrition and coffee dependency completely worth it. 'Where would I be without you?'

He was gazing earnestly into my eyes, the heat of his hands burning through my blouse and surely leaving ten little scorch marks on my skin as I stared up at him. I started to tremble, and I didn't think it was caffeine withdrawal. My lips parted, my breath stopped and my heart pounded as I waited for him to say that he couldn't live without me, that he loved me deeply and passionately and couldn't bear to spend another day without—

'I'd be broke, that's what. No, don't look like that, Bethy, it's true. Your hard work has made me rich. What shall we do to celebrate?'

'Well,' I croaked, mouth dry, 'we could—'

'I know! Let's go out for tea!' His eyes were shining, his face ecstatic, and it was totally clear that it was my hard work and dedication to the business, born of loyalty to, and admiration for, him that had made him so happy. 'God, I am so happy about all this money!' he said, pulling his jacket on. 'I love being rich!'

Well, anyway. I liked spending time alone with him. All those impromptu celebration pizzas and curries were the high spot of my life.

'Gratitude isn't love,' my flatmate Vini likes to say, with a slow, knowing shake of her head. Well, she's wrong, and even if she's right, it's very close. And even if it isn't close, it's definitely better than nothing. You get smiles, food and sometimes even physical contact. Sounds exactly like love to me.

So by seven o'clock that night three months ago, I'm scrubbed, shaved, scented and oiled and was sitting on my sofa, trying to get comfy. A change was coming, I could feel it. I knew in my hammering heart, in my tingling skin, in my fluttery tummy, that after eight years together Richard was finally about to realize that he had fallen in love with me at first sight. All right, I hadn't expected it to take eight years, but it didn't matter. The moment was finally here.

Actually, I wasn't really thinking about comfort on my sofa three months ago. I was thinking about seduction. I needed to be able to flop down – no, descend – onto the sofa as if I was just casually doing it, while neatly arranging my limbs into the position that achieved maximum seduction potential. I'd brought the tall mirror out of my bedroom and propped it against the telly so I could see how I looked each time. I needed to accidentally expose a fair bit of flesh, without doing a full Britney Spears, and it wasn't easy in that tiny nightie. The first three times did not go too well for reasons I won't go into, and just as I was smiling coyly into the mirror for the fourth time with the words, 'Why, Richard, whatever do you mean?' the doorbell rang.

He's an hour early. A whole fucking hour. I am frozen where I stand, staring at my horrified face in the frankly fuck-off ENORMOUS mirror that is completely out of place in the living room. I should move it. He is going to wonder what on earth it is doing here in the living room. I take one step towards it, but I know I don't have time. It's incredibly heavy and I only got it here this afternoon by walking it, corner by corner, along the hallway. It took half an hour and the skin off my big toe to do it. The doorbell goes again. Stuff it, it will have to stay. Thank God I overestimated how long it would take to light all the candles, and started doing it at half past five. I was intending to blow some of them out as twenty-eight – one for each year of my life before this moment – doesn't seem such a good idea any more, but it's too late now. I walk languorously to the door, feeling like a leopard stalking her prey, sinewy and seductive, knowing I look fantastic, knowing this is the moment everything changes.

'Power cut?' is the first thing he says, striding into the living room in his jeans and so-familiar camel coat. I close the front door and follow him into the room. As I enter he looks at me properly and I feel my stomach flip over. I smile seductively and drop down onto the sofa. It goes perfectly. The mirror is still there so I grab a quick peek and – yes! I look great – lots of leg and cleavage, but no actual . . . Britney. Perfect. I look up at Richard through my lashes – he's still standing – and I can see his face is covered with confusion. His eyes are darting about, his hands in his pockets are jumping, fiddling with his keys and loose change, he's slightly flushed and he's biting his bottom lip in that uncomfortable way I adore so much. He is clearly completely besotted and can't find his voice. It's fantastic. I don't move, savouring the moment,

18

maintaining my perfect pose, even though my left foot is starting to go numb, and stare at him, my lips slightly parted, my heart pounding in my chest.

And then he says, 'Oh shit, Bethy, have you got someone here?' He puts his hand over his mouth and his eyes widen as he takes in my outfit, the candles, the mirror . . .

'No, no one. Of course not.'

He smiles. 'Oh come on, Bethy, don't be silly. You don't have to hide it from me.' He flicks his eyes to the mirror, and raises his eyebrows with a knowing grin. 'Filthy bitch.'

I start to stand up, but I haven't practised this and it's very hard to preserve my dignity. In the end I have to hold the nightie down with one hand while I shuffle to the edge of the sofa, then push myself up with the other. From the corner of my eye I catch sight of myself in the huge mirror, lumbering to my feet like an ancient creature awoken from a thousand-year-long sleep by a nuclear bomb test. In a baby-doll nightie.

'No, Richard, honestly. It's only the two of us here.'

He looks at me intently, from my bare feet to the almost bare rest of me, then, after what seems like an age, he says, 'OK. Well, look, Beth, there's something I need to tell you. Something's happened. It's this amazing, unexpected . . .' He's staring at me and I can see his eyes are shining, his mouth is smiling and there is a barely contained excitement moving beneath his surface.

'Yes?' It comes out as a whisper.

'I'm in love, Bethy.'

'Yes.'

'Deeply, madly, passionately in love.'

'Yes.'

'Her name is Sabrina.'

'No.'

'What?'

'Nothing.'

'Oh. OK. Well, look, Sabrina's Portuguese, so guess what? I'm moving to Portugal. Tomorrow! I'm starting a whole new life!' He moves nearer, staring at my face. 'I can see you're worrying about Love Learning. Typical Bethy, always conscientious. But it's OK; I've sorted it all out. My brother-in-law, Chas, will manage the place for me when I go. Here are the keys to the office. Chas will be arriving about ten – can you give them to him when he gets there?'

Anyway. No need to go into that too much. Suffice to say that Richard left the living room, my flat and the country, at top speed, and I haven't seen him since. That was me, three months ago, longing for a change. A change came all right, just not quite the change I had in mind.

So now I am going into this training room to tell these people from the bank that change is good, change is great, change is a fabulous, desirable, seductive idea, and behind my back my two fingers aren't crossed, they're in a 'V'. A little salute to absent bastards.

Two

The Need for Change

**Short-term Goal: Convince the bank people that they
should love, welcome and embrace change.
Obstacles: God will probably strike me down in the
middle of Action Planning.
Long-term Goal: Still the same – marry Richard, or
someone else.
Obstacles: He's still in Portugal. And there's no one
else around worth bothering about.**

I'm a professional, so I don't give away my true
feelings. I don't even accidentally betray them by
sneering unintentionally. I am in total control of my
facial expressions and other non-verbal signals all
the time, and make sure I always present a pleasant
countenance to the world. I do this for two principal
reasons. Firstly, absolutely everyone has heard that
saying: There's nothing so unattractive as a woman
scorned. I refuse to be bitter and twisted like that. To
spend my entire life miserable and warped because I
was let down once is a complete waste. Plus it could
seriously undermine my chances of attracting someone

else. Although that's largely irrelevant at the moment. As the first part of 'Day One – Preparation' comes to an end ninety minutes after it started, I have realized that yet again there are no decent blokes on the course. It's so depressing: who do all the female bank employees flirt with?

I switch off the lights and the coffee machine and head back to the office, leaving the delegates to get to know each other over a mind-map and a coffee. It used to be a custard cream too, but we've had to stop buying them. Little economies here and there, Chas says, will make all the difference. It seems money is much tighter with Richard gone.

Back in the office, I stroll seductively to my desk and sit down, folding my legs under my chair like the Queen, maintaining serenity and elegance at all times. You wouldn't know how completely pissed off I am to look at me. As I log on to my computer I am focusing hard on looking preoccupied, to give the impression that I am deep in thought about something. No one is watching me while I do this, so you can be forgiven for thinking that I really am deep in thought about something. I am still maintaining a teensy smile, as if what I'm thinking about pleases me; my feet are tucked neatly to one side under my chair and crossed at the ankle (you're never too young for varicose veins); my hair, shoulder length and light brown, is tucked sweetly behind one ear; lips are glossed but not overdone, make-up nude. I am sure, as I sit here, that I look quite adorable, in a girl-next-door kind of way, and that is exactly what I am trying to achieve.

'Look at her,' Richard said to me once, when we were out for a pizza. 'Now that's what I call attractive.' I turned round to see who he was talking about. It was a girl of about twenty sitting behind me, with shoulder-length brown hair, hardly any make-up on and her feet tucked under her seat like the Queen. 'Look at her skin – completely flawless. Not done up like some dog. That's natural beauty, that is.' He was smiling away at her, gazing right over my shoulder, apparently unable to look away. Until I started choking really badly on some pizza and nearly died.

So I know what Richard considers beautiful, and that is the image I have perfected. All I need is for him to come back and see me. And when he does, I will be ready. Which is my second reason for always looking cheerful and sweet.

Have you ever noticed how, whenever the hero is secretly observing the girl through a nearby window or across a crowded room, she's never picking her ear or scratching her armpit or even staring into space looking heartily fed up? She's always laughing with a friend or helping a disabled person or giving away food. When Superman looks through the walls to watch Lois going up to the roof in the lift, she just stands there looking sweet, her hair all perfect, her feet nicely placed, completely motionless. I mean, she's in that lift on her own, for God's sake, why doesn't she adjust her bra strap, or pull her tights up, or get that annoying bit of celery out of her back tooth, like everyone else does? But she doesn't. She still manages to look attractive, when there is absolutely no need to. Thank goodness she does, because of course her man can see her wherever she is, whatever she's doing.

I don't harbour a secret belief that Superman is watching me through walls all the time, and is one day

23

going to snatch me from certain death as I plummet all the way down from the third floor in a faulty lift, then carry me lovingly away for a moonlit flight over the town, dropping me off at my front door before reluctantly departing to save another life. Of course I don't; that's completely ridiculous. But what I am sure of is this: Richard is coming back. One day. In ten minutes or six weeks or a year, I don't know, but it will happen, and when it does I intend to look nice. He may have been temporarily sidetracked by the transparent and frankly rather cheap exoticism of some foreign bimbo instead of falling for me, but that doesn't mean he's not in love with me.

As soon as he realizes he's been in love with me for years, he is going to walk back into this office like Richard Gere in *An Officer and a Gentleman* looking for Debra Winger. He'll stride around searching for me and then see me before I see him. With his eyes fixed on me, he will soften, a smile will appear as he watches what I am doing, and he will know, in the depths of his heart, that he has come home at last. Or he might text. Anyway, the point is that I have to be ready, at every moment, with a lovely expression on my face or doing something worthy, because it will be unannounced and I will have no time to arrange my features into an attractive expression or put on lipgloss.

I'm not ruling out meeting a gorgeous bloke on a training course, or in the supermarket, or in a queue at the bank, on the street, in a car park, pub, shoe shop, library, petrol station, whatever, in the meantime. Those sorts of Chance Encounters happen all the time. And then when Richard does come back, I'll be able to say, 'This ship has sailed, baby.' I'd love that.

So at my desk, I appear to be deep in thought to anyone who might be looking. I gently rest my chin on my hand. Well, I don't actually rest the weight of my entire head on the hand as it would squash up the flesh under my cheek, but the gesture gives me an interesting, thoughtful appearance.

At the moment, there are seven training facilitators at Love Learning, plus Ali, our assistant. I sit next to Fatima, back to back with Grace, facing Derek. My desk is the one with the newspaper clippings, magazine articles, print-outs, interviews, reviews, reports and charts all over the partition. Under one of the full-page articles is a little photo of Richard that I took with my phone once when he wasn't looking. It's a bit fuzzy and quite small but it's the only picture of him I've got. He's standing by his desk, looking down at something, one hand in his pocket. I'm the only person who knows it's there, so don't tell anyone.

Next to me, Fatima stands up. She's wearing a T-shirt that says in large letters:

WHY ARE WE HERE?

and underneath in much smaller letters, WE COULd bE IN a baR. Obviously she's not presenting today. She leans over the partition towards me.

'Hiya, Beth, your hair is lovely today. How's the Change thingy going? You're dead good at that one, you make it look so easy. Me, I always get so blooming nervous, get all my words jumbled up, don't I, with everyone watching me and listening to my voice, waiting for me to make a mistake. Anyone dishy for us to drool over?'

Fatima is in the wrong job.

'Fatima,' I answer with a serene smile, 'there is so much more to a group than what the blokes look like. Honestly, is that all you think about?'

Her smile drops a little as she sits back down. 'No, no, I didn't mean that, of course I know what . . . I mean, I'm not . . . It's just . . . Do you think you'll get on with them, anyway?'

'It's difficult to say at this point. But they do seem to be interested. So far.'

'Oh well, that's good then, that'll make it much nicer for you, won't it? Nothing worse than trying to deliver sessions to people who aren't interested, can't get through to them whatever you try, just a waste of time. Fancy a cuppa?'

I suspect that Fatima's delegates would probably lose interest even if she was explaining how to spin straw into gold, but I don't say it. 'Yes please, Fats. Thanks very much.' She heads off towards the kitchen and I turn back to my computer. I've got a fifteen-minute break now, which will involve looking interestedly at my computer while sipping a hot drink. I risk a surreptitious glance at the external door, just in case. Nope, still in Portugal.

Fatima is taking ages with that tea. It can take me a while sometimes because I am always distracted by thinking about something that's making me smile, or gazing serenely at a rainbow, or feeding the birds; but Fatima will be routinely pouring the hot water into the mugs, with no adornments. I glance at my watch, working out how long each part of the tea-making process should take. Put tea bags into mugs – four seconds; dispense hot water into mugs – eight seconds; wait for it to brew – two minutes—

From the kitchen comes the sound of screaming.

The reaction in the office is instantaneous. As one, every head snaps round to face the direction of the screams, then turns back to peer around the room and see if someone else is going. Opposite me, Derek immediately coughs and clears his throat loudly without raising his head, the idea being, I suspect, that he didn't hear the scream because he was clearing his throat at the time. Hmm.

It's a good job these guys aren't on Skull Island. When that poor girl screamed at first sight of King Kong, they'd all be closely examining a rather interesting rock formation, or leafing through a magazine.

'It's all right,' I say, standing up quickly, 'I'll go.' My expression is one of shocked concern as I make for the door. They should all be bloody well grateful, though. Fatima injures herself at work about once a fortnight, and no one in the office goes to her aid as much as I do. If she times it right, and I go to help her every time, there's a good chance I will be tenderly nursing one of her injuries the moment Richard marches into the office demanding to know where I am. Tending to an injured friend is one of my top five things I want to be seen doing by Richard when he returns.

Don't get me wrong. I am not glad that Fatima has been hurt. Of course not; Christ, I'm not a sadist. When I arrive in the kitchen, I can see immediately that her left hand has an angry red mark on the back, which spreads up her wrist onto her forearm, and looks terribly painful. But it's an ill wind, as Chas likes to say.

27

I'm sure that Fatima would be delighted to know that there's an upside to her agony. She won't have suffered in vain, then. And when I say my face is showing shocked concern, please don't think that means that I don't feel shocked and concerned, because I do. I just have to be sure that it is plainly obvious on my face, so I exaggerate it. Just a little.

Fatima is sniffing a bit, looking from her injured arm to the evil hot-water dispenser, as if trying to make it feel guilty. Or, let's be honest, more likely trying to fathom out exactly what happened. 'Hey, Fats, are you OK?' I say, looking down at the wet paper towel that she is folding over her left hand.

'I'm fine,' she says wetly. 'Scalded myself, that's all. Stupid me.'

I tilt my head on one side and look at her with a sympathetic smile. Not only does this look good, it also stops me from nodding. 'Well, anyone can make a mistake. Look, would you like me to make *you* a cup of tea now? Seeing as you're a bit incapacitated for the moment.'

She nods and smiles at me gratefully, so I turn round and pointedly wash up a couple of cups under the hot-water tap, but she has already hobbled away.

I take Fatima her tea. I'm walking slowly, my face still solemn and anxious, my hair tucked back behind both ears now because it's more serious. When I get to her desk, I put my hand on her shoulder and smile reassuringly. My reassuring smile is a good one, so I try to use it whenever possible.

'Oh, thanks, Beth, that's lovely,' she says. 'You really didn't have to, you know, honestly, I could have done it myself, I'm not totally incapacitated. Mind you, knowing me I probably would have poured the water on my hand again, or tripped over the coffee table, or dropped the cups, or knocked the telly over . . .'

She's not exaggerating; they've all happened.

Mike, who sits opposite her, has pulled his chair up alongside hers and there are pieces of paper and forms spread out across her desk.

'"Describe the environmental conditions on the day of the accident,"' Mike says, looking up from one of the forms. 'What do you reckon today, Fats? Shall we put "Grey and dull"?'

I open my mouth to make a joke about the décor in the kitchen, but think better of it. I will save those words and use them later in my life.

The only other interesting thing that happens for the rest of the day is Chas coming out of the wood-panelled door and appearing unannounced in the main part of the office during my afternoon tea break. He comes into sight about as frequently as Halley's Comet, so we all stop what we're doing and turn to take in the spectacle.

The day that he started here, when Richard had asked me to give him the keys, I stood by the door and watched him arrive on a bike. I'm talking about a push-bike, not a motorcycle. Can you believe it? On a bike in a three-piece suit, with a briefcase in the basket on the front and bicycle clips holding his trousers in. 'Ah, I see you have noticed my environmentally friendly, economical and life-saving mode of transport?' he said to me as he flung his leg up and over the saddle, then scootered on one pedal towards me. He banged his chest. 'Excellent workout for the heart, you see. This little beauty is going to keep me alive.'

Not if he gets flattened by a cement lorry.

In the office, he stands there blinking for a few moments, disorientated, then clears his throat to get our attention, oblivious to the fact that we're all gawping at him already. Finally, he starts with the announcement that we have a need for change. For once, I agree with him and actually start to get up, smiling, to wish him well in his new career. But he goes on. He tells us that we have three working weeks left before we close for Christmas on the twenty-second, and that he wants at least one new contract from everyone before then because with Richard gone the high turnover and success that we've all become used to has started to drop. He makes it sound like it's our fault because we have been 'resting on our laurels' and now we need to 'put our best foot forward' and 'take the bull by the horns'. He finishes by giving a rousing speech about a phoenix and some flames, adds very quickly that if we don't, at least four jobs will go and the business might even fold, then disappears back behind the door. We barely have time to turn open-mouthed to each other before he reappears.

'And while I've got your attention,' he says, pointing at us all, 'please remember what I told you last week. I am still finding lights and electrical appliances left on when they're not in use. You must switch them all off when you've finished with them. I am not joking – this is crucial, people. It will save money, and that will save jobs. Take heed.' And with that he disappears again. Like the comet, we know he is out there somewhere, but we know he's not coming back for quite a while.

It seems to me that he is heroically ignoring the fact that we have already undergone one of those deeply fulfilling, life-enhancing, God-given, peachy little changes I was talking about. Richard out, Chas in. Result: fucking disaster. See what I mean?

Fatima grabs my arm suddenly, making me jump. 'Oh, Beth, did you hear what he said? Four people to go. Who do you think will go? Do you think it means I'm going to lose my job?'

I smile at her. 'Fatima, you really shouldn't worry about it.' No point because sadly it's a dead cert. She might as well empty her desk now.

Her face brightens a bit and a flicker of hope is there. Just like that. 'Really? Do you think I'll be all right? Because I don't know what I'd do. I can't lose my job. I've got a cat and guitar lessons and satellite telly. I can't lose my job.'

Today is Monday, 4 December, so after work I am meeting Vini in town for some Christmas shopping. I am so looking forward to it. I am already trembling with excitement about the possibility of a Chance Encounter with someone who turns out to be my soulmate. My other soulmate. And, of course, Richard could have just touched down at the airport and quickly popped into town to get me a gift – or a ring! – before zooming straight round to the office. Feathered or sparkly items will look particularly sweet in my hands when he sees me, I think, particularly if one of the feathers gets lodged in my hair. Then Richard, or whoever it turns out to be, can gently extract it, or blow it away, smooth my hair down gently with his fingertips and say, 'Will you have a cup of coffee with me?'

Also I need to get a dressing gown for my Uncle Colin.

'Going out?'

It's all right, don't panic. It's a woman's voice. Which of course it should be, as I'm standing in the Ladies brushing my hair and touching up my lipgloss before I head off to town. This is one of the few places where I know it would be impossible to be secretly observed by Richard. Although I'm not ruling anything out. When he does finally come back, he might be so anxious to see me, he could very well burst in here. In the mirror, though, I see it's not him. It's Grace.

Grace is my arch-enemy. She's like the opposite of me. She so doesn't give a damn about good presenting or thorough research and looks like the sort of person who would sleep with her sister's fiancé the night before the wedding. She's a total fake. Just like the colour of her hair. Hair that blonde and shiny just doesn't occur in nature. And it doesn't matter how long you lie on a beach, no one tans that evenly. It's so out of a bottle, but she'll never admit it.

Not that there's anything wrong with using bottletan. I dab a bit on my face and arms during the winter, just to keep the pale at bay. It's more out of kindness for everyone that has to look at me, really. The trainees certainly don't want to be staring at Snow White during their courses. The difference between Grace and me is that she covers herself in it, top to toe, winter and summer, and then goes around saying she spent two weeks in Dubai.

I smile sweetly at her in the mirror. 'No, just shopping.'

She approaches the mirror. 'Oh, that's nice. Better than going out chasing boring old contracts, anyway.'

She tuts and rolls her eyes exaggeratedly. 'What a load of saddos.'

I frown. That's so immature. I mean, I know that I'm not going contract hunting tonight, but that's only because I have a prior engagement. Anyway, I've no doubt that my imminent immersion in local retail outlets will give me an inspirational idea about whom to go after for a contract. But Grace, it seems, isn't giving it a second thought.

'What do you mean?' I'm trying not to look directly at her face as I ask because when I look back at my own reflection afterwards, it's always a bit of a let-down.

Oh, she's not prettier than me. God no. It's just that her perma-tan and peroxide hair make me look pale and mousy by comparison. Although next to Cath Parson, whose desk is opposite hers, my face could launch a yacht or two. Beauty is in the eye of whomever you're standing next to. If only Cath were here now.

Grace leans towards the mirror, opening her mouth to put on mascara. 'Oh, you know, everyone else in there rushing straight out after work to try and get contracts. Like it's life and death. You know?' She glances at me in the mirror and shakes her head with a little smile. 'Sad.'

'So I take it you don't think it's important?'

'God no. Why would I? Not yet, anyway.' She pauses, mascara wand mid-air as if she's about to cast a spell, and turns towards me. 'Do you?'

She's clever, isn't she? I can't violently disagree with her and tell her she's being short-sighted and imma-ture and pathetic, not to mention vain, and ought to be doing more to save the company and everyone's jobs,

33

because that will lump me in with all the others in the office who, according to her, are saddos. But if I agree with her, I'll be . . . well . . . agreeing with her, which I hate doing, on principle.

In the end, I shrug non-committally. 'Each to his own,' I say, which I am dead pleased with. It just about covers every option. I am adult and serene, whilst not accepting that not going after contracts tonight is OK. Brilliant. I have to stop myself from smiling as I turn back to my own reflection.

'Absolutely,' she says, going back to her eyelashes. 'I have got much more fun to be having. See you tomorrow.' And she swings her bag onto her shoulder and leaves.

Of course, she didn't hang around to learn about all the fun I am just about to go and have. I am tempted to leave too, so I can fill her in on that in the lift, but common sense wins and I stay to finish touching up my make-up. I don't know it yet, but I will be bloody glad I did later.

Three

Awareness

Short-term Goal: Have loads and loads of fun Christmas shopping with Vini.
Obstacles: None. This will be easy because we always have incredible fun when we're out together.
Long-term Goal: As before. Plus have fun all the time.
Obstacles: Too busy having fun to think about it.

Aah, Christmas shopping. It's such fun. It's chilly, and dark early, but it doesn't matter because the whole town is bedecked with gorgeous twinkling lights shaped like swans and soldiers and pear trees. Everywhere you look there are joyful, rosy-cheeked families in woolly scarves and mittens carrying armfuls of beautifully wrapped parcels as they glide effortlessly from shop to shop, finding perfect gifts from a huge variety of tasteful knick-knacks. Jovial vendors are selling hot peanuts and mulled wine from a stall in the precinct, Santa is ringing a bell for charity on the street corner and a group of children is standing around the huge tree in the centre singing 'Good King Wenceslas'.

Oh, no, wait. That was a Christmas card. This is more like a scene from *Dawn of the Dead*.

I have to walk through the town to the Post Office, where Vini is waiting. I say 'walk'; what I actually have to do is bump my way, sideways and in tiny steps, through surging crowds who, apparently, are all walking zombies, intent on feasting on my flesh. Well, no, they're not, but they aren't being very nice.

'Oops, I'm sorry, did my ribs hurt your elbow?' I say, as a woman pushes past me, but she is gone before she has a chance to repent. A booted foot crushes down onto my toes – 'Oh, I didn't get blood on you, did I?' – and something long and sharp that I assume is either a Teletubbies kite or a sawn-off shotgun, jabs me in the face. 'Ow!' I yell. 'For fuck's sake!' But in the precinct, no one can hear you scream – the man with the glockenspiel is making far too much noise.

Vini is waiting by the one remaining phone box in our town centre. It's late-night opening tonight, so we've got plenty of time, and she likes standing around in crowded places, anyway.

As I approach her I see she is talking to a very thin blonde woman who takes a card from Vini before walking away.

'Hi, Vin. Have you been waiting long?'

'It's OK, I was a bit late myself. Anyway, it gave me a chance to have a good look at the lovely people of our delightful little town.'

'And?'

'Well, did you see that woman I was just talking to?' I nod. 'She could easily do Keira Knightley.'

'Blimey. That's a good one.'

'I know. I have been after Keira for months.'

Vini runs her own look-alike agency called Fake Face. She's been going for over five years now and it's a huge success. You'd be amazed how many losers there are out there who think that their parties, birthdays, meetings, even lives, will be miraculously enhanced if they have a total stranger wearing a Catherine Zeta-Jones wig or a Tom Selleck moustache present. Not that I'm criticizing. Thanks to those inadequate saddos, Vini has made a lot of money. She is really good at it, actually. She can spot a Paul McCartney in the queue at the petrol station, or a Grace Kelly having a crafty fag outside the bank at lunchtime. She's got over forty clients.

'Right,' she says grabbing my arm, 'let's get shopping. I am fucking ready for this.'

And so we plunge into the crowds. Our first stop is a department store called Whytelys but we're immediately separated by a woman with a double buggy who looks like she might have *My First Weapons of Mass Destruction* concealed in her nappy bag. Vini is doing that peculiar tiptoe running that people do to avoid being rammed on the ankles by a buggy, and I catch a glimpse of her wild eyes as she legs it round Aromatherapy Oils.

After a moment's deliberation I decide to plough on without her. Well, she'll be OK. I'm sure she can hold her own in a busy department store. And we'll meet up later at Pizza Hut.

I head further into the store, then stand and gaze around me, rapt. Sparkly Christmas trees, felt Santas and rigid, glassy-eyed deer are so dense here, there is barely enough room for merchandise. Shoppers are tiptoeing amongst them as if lost in an enchanted forest. I'm keeping a look of childlike delight on my face because childlike delight is one of my top ten facial expressions to be seen doing when Richard returns. I'm sure it looks adorable. Also, it will disguise the fact that I have actually stopped here so I can narrowly scrutinize all my shopping companions. Camel coats like Richard's in particular grab my attention, but anything in trousers is good.

That makes me sound terrible, doesn't it? I only mean I am not interested in the women, that's all. Or the men in dresses. Not into that.

'Are you all right?' says a voice behind me. It's a man's voice, and I feel a thrill of excitement surge through me. It's Richard, asking me how I am after our three-month separation! At least, I didn't hear the voice for long enough to be sure that it wasn't him. Oh my God, this could be it. How do I look? Quick mental check: I know my stance is good as I am still doing childlike delight, which is great; hair – maybe a bit dishevelled, but charmingly so; make-up – good, only touched up at work forty minutes ago; clothes – fine, as nothing except my gorgeous brown boots is visible under my cream, belted jacket. I am looking good. My heart rate moves up a couple of notches, while outwardly it is plainly obvious that I do not care that he went off to Portugal three months ago and am now cheerfully and excitedly getting on with my life, oblivious to his absence.

'Only, you've been standing here not moving for a while,' the voice goes on. 'I wondered if you were feeling OK?'

Dungheaps. It's definitely not Richard. I feel a momentary drag of intense disappointment, then perk up again. There's a man talking to me! I'm having a Chance Encounter, just as I imagined. God, I wish Vini were here to see just how wrong she was about that.

Only, now that he's spoken a second time, I feel I should definitely react in some way. At the very least I need to acknowledge the fact that he's spoken to me, which is suddenly very difficult. I should have turned as soon as he spoke the first time, but I was too busy trying to work out if it was or wasn't Richard. Now it seems odd that I didn't. Bloody hell, should I turn and smile? Turn and look curious? Bewildered? Startled? Or not turn at all?

'In fact,' the voice goes on, 'I hesitated before speaking to you because I wondered if you were a mannequin.'

He's cracking jokes. That's a really good sign. It means he wants to make me laugh, which means that he . . . well . . . wants to see me laughing. I should just laugh, and turn. Or maybe just smile a bit, and turn.

Oh God, what if he's taking the piss? I smile a bit and turn my head slightly so that I am looking down at his shoes. They're black.

'But then I realized that mannequins don't usually write "dressing gown" on the back of their hands in felt-tip pen.'

Oh shit, shit, shit. The dressing gown. I'd forgotten all about that, and he spotted it. How the hell did he spot it? Well, that sure makes me look sophisticated and elegant, doesn't it?

'Or maybe someone wrote that on your hand to tell the porters where in the store you were to be placed. Maybe it simply means you should be dressed in one, and I am making a complete tit of myself

39

having a very one-sided conversation with a giant Barbie doll.'

I giggle a bit through closed lips.

'And now that I've started, I've got no choice but to carry on talking to you until you answer me. Which means, of course, if you are a mannequin, I am in for a long night.' He pauses. 'Well, let's face it, a long year.'

I laugh properly and turn my head at last to meet his eyes. With a shock I realize instantly that I'm looking into the warm, smiling eyes of a man I could find extremely attractive.

'Oh, thank God,' he says. 'You are alive. And I am vindicated.'

'There was never any doubt.'

'Well, that's easy for you to say. You are all right, then, I take it?'

I turn now to face him properly. God, those eyes. I could easily wake up next to those even after he's forty. For a brief moment I imagine this scenario: it's my birthday, he's leaning up on one elbow gazing at me, waiting for me to wake up, a gorgeous diamond and ruby eternity ring sitting in a velvet box on the nightstand. I look lovely lying there – my eyelashes are long and thick, my lips pale pink and slightly smiling as I dream, and I'm wearing silk. I open my eyes, flutter them a bit, notice him gazing at me and my smile broadens—

'Maybe you're not, after all?'

I snap back to Whytelys. He's still there, only starting to look a bit concerned now. Quickly I nod, and say breathily, 'Yes, I am completely fine, thank you.'

'Well, good. I'm very glad to hear that. Although it does leave me somewhat confused. I mean, you were standing very still and quiet in the middle of a department store three weeks before Christmas when I found you. If there was no malady to explain that, I have to assume that you were doing it simply in order to play a cruel practical joke on well-meaning, decent folk as they go about their business?'

I've just realized he's got brown hair. And a long black overcoat. And a briefcase.

'Not at all,' I reply smoothly. 'I was simply dazzled for a moment by all the wondrous sights before me.'

'Ah yes.' He turns to face the same way I'm looking. 'It's spectacular, isn't it? Such a fitting tribute to the day that Christians recognize as the official start date of their entire religion.'

'Winnie the Pooh in a Santa hat. Nothing says it better than that.'

He laughs. 'Yes! Or red, fur-trimmed lingerie.'

We both turn and our eyes fall simultaneously on the see-through negligée that is hanging by my left elbow, then leap away from it immediately to look at something – anything – else. 'Um . . . yes. You're right. The giving and receiving of saucy underwear and soft toys at this time of year is deeply meaningful and represents . . . er . . .'

'Loving thy neighbour,' he interjects with a grin, 'and all of God's wondrous creatures.'

'Yes! Even the fictional ones.'

'Quite. And the massive overeating and heavy drinking binge we're all about to embark on is symbolic of . . .'

'The spiritual nourishment we can receive by accepting Jesus's word.'

He nods sagely. 'Oh, bravo. Thank God at least one person hasn't lost the true meaning of Christmas.'

We both laugh a little. Then he pulls his sleeve back – he's wearing cuff-links! Does anyone wear them any more? – and glances at his watch. Bugger it.

'Well,' he begins, but I don't want him to finish. I can't let it look like I don't want him to finish, though.

'Me too,' I jump in. 'Shopping to do, important symbolic dressing gown to buy.' I indicate the writing on my hand.

'Of course. Right. OK then. Well, in that case—' He stops, pushes his hand through his hair, then says, 'Oh, what the hell. It's Christmas, what better time? I don't suppose, if you're not busy, that you would . . . like to—'

'Fuck me, I thought I'd never see you again!'

We both jump at this and I remember suddenly that I am standing in the middle of a shop. Which is swarming with people. And suddenly very noisy. We look up to see a woman with pink highlights striding purposefully towards us, waving. It's Vini, of course, but I'm wondering if I can pretend not to know her so that I can finish hearing what this man was about to say.

'Where the bloody hell have you been?' she says, walking right up to me. OK, so no chance to ignore her then. I turn from Vini to the man and he's smiling still but now there's something kind of final about that smile.

'Well . . .' he says, at the same time as I say, 'Vini.'

'You'll never guess who I've seen,' Vini says, grabbing my arm. 'This way, hurry *up*.'

'It was nice talking to you,' he's saying, inclining his head towards me and starting to extricate himself from our interaction.

'You too,' I say.

'What?' says Vini, apparently noticing for the first time that I was actually in the middle of a conversation. Her eyes flick from me to the man and back. 'Oh, hell, sorry.'

'Bye,' he says, taking a step back and turning. I want to grab his arm or his coat lapels and keep him from going. My fingers twitch as the scenario runs through my head:

Me: 'Wait, don't go.' My hand is on his arm.

Strange Attractive Man: (He turns back to face me.) 'I have to, don't you see? It has to be this way.'

Me: 'No, it doesn't! You don't have to go. I felt . . . something. Tell me you didn't feel it too.'

S.A.M.: (He takes a couple of steps towards me and enters my personal space. His voice is low and urgent.) 'A . . . connection. Between us?'

Me: (breathily) 'Yes.'

S.A.M.: (He nods.) 'Yes. I felt it too. But you're with someone. I can't—'

Me: 'Oh forget that, it's only Vini, she won't mind. Now, what were you going to say?'

My arm is aching and actually starts to move on its own towards his coat but he is moving out of range and Vini is pulling on my other arm.

'Come *on*.'

He's gone anyway. I turn away finally and follow Vini. She's rushing away into the crowd and it's a bit tricky to keep up with her. Especially as my feet want to stay exactly where they are, and the rest of me agrees with them. Never mind. The scenario would probably have turned out a bit differently if I had gone through with it:

Me: 'Wait, don't go.' (My hand is on his arm.)

43

S.A.M.: *'Get your hand off my arm.'*

I follow Vini as best as I can whilst looking around me constantly to see if I can see him again. Although we have walked away from where he was last seen, so logic dictates that he is somewhere behind us. Then again, logic doesn't matter in affairs of the heart, of course. In a situation like this, he could very easily bump into me on the pavement in half an hour, or be in the queue in front of me at the checkout.

Eventually, we slow down and come to a stop in the menswear department, which always smells faintly of leather. Vini walks back to me and takes my arm again, leading me towards the striped boxer shorts. I'm glancing about me still, half looking for S.A.M. and half looking for who Vini wants me to see. It's bound to be someone who would make a decent lookalike. Must be someone good or she wouldn't have gone to all the trouble of bringing me here. My mind is blank. Who has she been after for ages? Is it that kid who plays Spider-Man? Peter Parker? Oh, no, stupid me, that's the name of the character. What a dunce. God, what's his name? Tony someone, I think. No, not—

'Over there. Look. By the ties.'

I look. It's a man in a camel coat. It's Richard.

'Fall over,' I say.

'What?'

'Fall over,' I say again, more urgently. 'Make it look like you're having a fit.' I can't take my eyes off him, but Vini is not being helpful.

'No.'

Reluctantly I turn to her. 'Why not?'

'Beth. For fuck's sake, I don't want to fall over. I fell over before we came out.'

'Oh come on, Vin. Please. I would do it for you, you know I would.'

'No.'

So after Richard made the dash from his bar in Portugal onto a plane and then broke the speed limit all the way from the airport in his mad rush to find me and tell me that he's been a stupid, blind fool and that he loves me and never wants to be parted from me again, he stops off at Whytelys to check out the cut-price white Y-fronts.

Quickly we squat down behind the lycra cycling shorts. I glance at Vini and then focus back on Richard. I don't want him to see me squatting. Squatting is right up at the top of my list of no-nos, along with scratching, puking, blowing my nose and buying tampons. And I don't want our tearful reunion to play out over a table of reduced underwear. The alternative scenario – me helping Vini up after she had a fit of some kind – is apparently not going to happen, so I am left with only one option.

I turn to Vini. 'I need him to see me somewhere else in the shop, somewhere more favourable. I can't let him spot me down here.' He's moving away towards the tills, so I stand up.

'If you're that bothered, why don't you just go up and talk to him? Christ, this is the man of your dreams, for fuck's sake.'

'That's not the way it goes,' I say to her. I walk over to the pants. His hands touched these Y-fronts; his fingers caressed these seams, pushed through this Y-opening, pulled this elastic. Lucky, lucky pants.

The camel coat is moving further away now, being assimilated by the crowd. If I'm not quick I'm going to lose him. I have planned for months how I would appear to him on his return and I want it to be right. I want him to observe me without me knowing about it, so that I can make sure I present myself to best advantage. I hurry through the rails towards where I last saw him and several people raise their heads to watch me go, like a herd of feeding herbivores wondering if the T. rex is coming.

I come round a corner and stop short. There he is, in the queue at the till, several white fabric items in his hand. The Y-fronts.

The queue is long: he will be stationary, facing the same way, for ages, giving me plenty of time to get in his line of sight. And right in his line of sight – Joy to the World! – are Christmas decorations! Lots of pretty, sparkly things for me to hold up and smile over in childlike delight. It couldn't be better. Quick mental check: hair – oh, fuck it, just get over there.

I don't hurry because, of course, if you're just browsing in a store you don't hurry. I can't anyway; there are nine million people in my way. But my face is serene and happy as I arrive at the Christmas decorations. I pick up a particularly reflective glass bauble and hold it up to the light. Little prisms of multicoloured light dance charmingly on my face and hair, and I let my lips make a tiny, sweet smile that doesn't distort my face, only enhances it. And I know that now, right now, is the moment that he will look up and see me and his heart will stop, his breath will catch and he will be mine. I flick my eyes over to where he's standing.

It's not Richard.

Four

Action Planning

**Short-term Goal: Vini thinks I should get over Richard
but I really feel I should set my own goals. I'll get
over him when I'm good and ready.**
**Obstacles: No point getting over someone who's
coming back.**
**Long-term Goal: Maybe I could find that Strange
Attractive Man again and make a life with him.**
Obstacles: Don't know who or where he is.

For a second there my façade slipped. For just a fleeting
moment my beaming, delighted childlike joy contorted
hideously into bitter, crushing disappointment. I didn't
realize at the time, of course; I was too overwhelmed
by bitter, crushing disappointment. But afterwards,
now that we are home and curled up in the living room
with the tree lights on and a candle burning that smells
of cinnamon, I can look back and say to myself, quite
honestly, that I hadn't looked my best at that moment.
In fact, it was a good job it wasn't Richard buying those
underpants because he would have caught sight of me
looking twisted and unpleasant. Although, of course,

if it had been him my expression would have been quite different. I'm hoping I would have been able to pull dignified welcome with shining eyes out of the bag, although given my complete loss of control when it wasn't him, I'm no longer sure.

Vini is being rather childishly tight-lipped on the matter. I glance over at her but she's resolutely reading an article about North Sea fishermen in the TV guide. It's plainly obvious she's punishing me. I know she thinks I am wasting my time over Richard. I don't know why: he's exactly what we have both sat up late into the night dreaming about – handsome, intelligent, funny and, well, rich. The money thing was one of Vini's criteria. Personally I am not motivated by it at all. The man of my dreams could live in a little shack or something, I wouldn't care. It wouldn't matter if we were in love, would it? And then as we got older I could help him set up his own business and we could move somewhere better.

Vini's quite different to me, though. Maybe you didn't notice but firstly she's got pink highlights, which look, you know, fabulously trashy and punk on her, but aren't right for someone like me. And she always wears these really bright, gaudy colours, like orange boots with a purple suede skirt and a brown and orange paisley blouse or a red vinyl jacket. She says she's expressing her individuality and I always nod and say she looks amazing, so original and so on; but secretly I think she just does it to make people stare at her. Which they do, all the time. Personally, I think that kind of wide-eyed staring or nudging and giggling is humiliating, and there are much more preferable ways of making people notice you when you go out that don't involve freakish outfitting. There's nothing wrong with catching people's attention with a beautiful designer coat, for example, or some stylish well-tailored trousers.

'But you look just like everyone else,' Vini always claims meaninglessly when I suggest this to her. I just don't understand her sometimes.

'Oooh,' she says suddenly from the sofa.

I jerk my head up and look over at her. 'What? Something you're trying to say? Something about forgetting about Richard and moving on? Again. But you don't even know him, Vin. You don't know what we're like together. You're basing your opinion on that one party when he got drunk and accidentally touched your boob, and that isn't representative of what he's really like. I've worked with him for eight years, and he was always a perfect gentleman to me. He is charming, funny, thoughtful and, well, I'm in love with him. That should be enough for you. The fact that he's not technically in this country at the moment doesn't matter.'

There's a brief pause and then she raises her head and looks at me, an earnest expression on her face. 'Did you know that some of these fishermen spend days and days in this awful, freezing weather, with these enormous waves, putting their lives in danger every single frigging moment?' I stare at her. 'Just for a few poxy cod. What?'

'Did you hear a word I just said?'

She pushes her lips out. 'Did you say something? Sorry, I was engrossed in this article. Say it again.'

'No point now. Forget it.'

'Oh, OK.'

'I wouldn't expect you to understand, anyway.'

'Oh really? Why's that?'

'Doesn't matter, you've obviously got lots of reading to do, don't let me interrupt.'

She flings the magazine down and turns in her seat to face me. 'All right, miss, you've got my full attention now. And by the way, Richard isn't *technically* out of the country; he is fucking out. Of. The. Country. And he didn't accidentally touch my boob that time, he full-on frigging groped me. And while we're on the subject, it's obviously escaped your notice that Richard has gone off with his sodding girlfriend, Beth. Girlfriend. It kind of leads me to suspect that he doesn't see himself rushing back to marry you any time soon.'

I pause for a few moments and then say, 'You were listening, then.'

'Yes I was listening. I'm always bloody listening. That's why I pretend to be not listening sometimes. Jesus, Beth, come on. This is so ridiculous, can't you see that? You actually asked me to flop about on the floor in Whytelys like a frigging fish today, just so you could pretend to help me, and Richard could see you doing it. Either he loves you for what you are – a quite pretty, bright training provider without so much as a first-aid certificate – or he doesn't. And no fake emergency scenario is going to change that.'

'Oh, you're just—'

'No, Beth, I'm not. The clues are there, you know, if you would only look.' She pulls her index finger forward with her other hand. 'Clue number one: in eight years, he never made a move on you. And, um, number two: he's got a girlfriend. Oh, and let's not forget the crucial number three: he's in Portugal with

50

her.' She looks back at me and nods sagely. 'That, for me, is the clincher.'

I wish she wouldn't say things like that. It makes me doubt my own mind.

After a long silence, I say, 'All right, you win. I'll give up on Richard and try and find someone else.'

She leaves an exaggeratedly long pause and makes a huge deal out of looking absolutely stunned. 'Really? You mean that? I mean, actively try and find someone?'

I nod. 'Yes, I mean it. I will actively seek out a new man to love. Happy now?'

She grins. 'You know what, Beth? I sodding well am. If you really mean it, I am ec-fucking-static.'

'Good.'

'Excellent.'

She picks up the TV guide again and starts flicking through it listlessly. We converse half-heartedly for a few minutes about what's on tonight and then something occurs to me. Why is it that she thinks she can criticize my near-perfect love life, when her latest habit has been to date a series of look-alikes from her own agency? Just because they look vaguely like someone famous. I narrow my eyes at her, and say, ultra-casually, 'How's it going with Johnny Depp, then?'

She tuts. 'Ugh. It's not Johnny Depp, Beth, it's Captain Jack Sparrow. There's a big difference, you know.'

'Is there?'

'Well, duh. You wouldn't shag Edward Scissorhands, would you?'

We both stare off into space for a moment.

'No. No, you're absolutely right. So, how's it going?'

She sighs. 'Han Solo all over again.'

'Oh no, you're kidding?'

'Nope. Take him out of the costume and he looks just like Martin Hunt, from B and Q.'

'Which is exactly who he is, presumably.'

She nods sadly.

'Oh, poor old you.'

'I know. God, that hat with the eyeliner and the wig . . .' She closes her eyes for a few seconds. 'He was very convincing. But once I got him out of it . . .'

'Martin Hunt.'

'Martin Hunt.' She sighs. 'We were snapped by the paparazzi once, you know.'

'Really?'

'Yeah. Well, actually it was that Adam Beresford from the *Herald*, but even so.'

'Hmm.'

Honestly. And she thinks I am the deluded one! At least the man I fell for is actually who he claims to be, and is not pretending to be an actor pretending to be some rough-diamond fictional pirate in eyeliner.

Vini and I haven't always been best friends. When we were at school, we had nothing to do with each other. She was the freaky one in the thick black eyeliner and Dr Marten's, with a dead mother and a drunk for a dad, living in a trailer and working every evening and weekend in the local diner just to pay the bills. She was the sort who belonged to the maths club, while I was one of the cheerleaders. I mean, we didn't have a maths club, or cheerleaders, but if we had, it would have been like that. And I don't think her mum is actually dead, just in Southampton. But she did live with her dad.

He's a taxi driver, so obviously he can't drink all the time because he'd lose his licence. And she did have a Saturday job in Woolworths. We ended up renting this flat together through Friends Reunited, so it just shows how important it is to keep your membership updated. I got a plumber from there too, and someone to come and sort out the garden. Better than the Yellow Pages.

'Vin, I think the time has come for a change.'

'What do you mean?' She glances around the room, pretending that she thinks I'm talking about the wallpaper.

I sigh. 'Every boyfriend you've had in the past, what, eighteen months, has been one of your clients.'

'Fuck's sake, Beth, I haven't stumbled headlong into an ethical minefield just because I get twelve per cent of all their bookings. Jesus, I'm not going to see close-up photos of my hand in the national papers, or get struck off the look-alike agency register.'

'No, I know. Is there a register?'

'No.'

'Oh, right. Look, I'm just pointing out that you are in fantasyland still. It's like when we were fifteen and were all convinced Richard Gere was going to drive past in a flashy car and ask us for directions to somewhere, but we'd tell him it would be easier if we showed him, so we'd get in, and then we'd go for a really long, romantic drive with him, at the end of which he would be staring in fascination at this gorgeous girl sitting next to him and wondering how he would ever manage to—'

'Yeh, all right, I don't need a *Pretty Woman* précis right now, thanks. Just get to the point, so that I can have children before I die.'

'Exactly my point. You want kids, but you're not even trying to have a serious relationship.'

'Ha, says you! Of the two men in your life, one of them is on a different continent and, oh no wait, there isn't a second one.'

'Technically, it's still Europe, so it's—'

'Shut up.'

I fall silent. We stare at each other. This goes on for almost forty-five seconds, before she looks away with a 'Humph'. Which means she knows I'm right.

'Vin, time is ticking on, you know. We're both twenty-eight. I do not want to be – I absolutely *refuse* to be – single at thirty.'

'But what about flirty, dirty and—'

'No. No way. Not happening. I refuse. So if Richard isn't coming back—'

'Which he isn't.'

'Then I am going to have to start hunting now. I need at least a year to plan the wedding, which leaves me just under a year to find the person I want to spend my life with, get him to realize he can't live without me, march into my place of work, pick me up and carry me out to his waiting car. Piece of cake.'

'Great plan. Can't fail.'

'Well, it's worth a try. I think you should do it too. Cos when I find this guy, I won't need a flatmate any more. See what I'm saying?'

'Well, what choice do I have then?'

'Great! We'll do it together. We know that what we have been doing so far is all wrong, so we both need a drastic change. Don't look at me like that, this is essential and if we get it right, the result will be a lifetime of stable, secure sameness.'

'Wow. I can hardly wait.'

I'm sensing that she's not all that thrilled by this prospect. I've known her a long time and my sensitive nature can sometimes pick up unspoken things about her. 'Vin, if you're not one hundred per cent into this, tell me now. I so don't want you trailing around behind me moaning about everything and trying to get off with the nearest bloke with John Travolta hair.'

She shakes her head. 'No, no, you're right. Things haven't been great: time to try something new.'

'Good. So you are prepared to change everything, including, and especially, the sort of person you have been going for?'

'Yeah, I suppose so.'

'Good, because the first thing I want to do is get you out of those clothes.'

No, it's OK, I'm not harbouring a secret and forbidden love for my same-sex flatmate. Of course not. I'm in love with Richard, remember? Oh, and in case you were thinking that I'd given up on him, I haven't. I mean, eight years together and I simply say, 'All right, you win, I'll give him up.' Did you really believe that? Come on! I thought you were starting to get to know me by now. When I talk about needing a change, I mean Vini, not me.

So my plan of action is this: first, Vini shuts up about Richard. Brilliant. Second, she stops wearing those ghastly mismatched outfits and gets some style. Also brilliant. Third, and this is more of a by-the-by than a significant contributory factor, if Vini and I actively look for someone to fall in love with, I might actually find one. And then I won't have to wait for Richard any more. Because, in spite of the fact that everything I just said to Vini was a lie, it's true that I really am worried about being single when I'm thirty. I mean, of course Richard will be back by then, so it's not really an issue, but still. A tiny, weeny, microscopic part of my brain is saying quietly to the other parts, 'But what if he isn't?' And it's that part that more and more of the other parts are starting to take notice of.

Five

Key Opportunities

Short-term Goal: I am having my hair dyed tonight.
Obstacles: Does intense reluctance count?
Long-term Goal: Fake one: meet a new man, make a
new life with him, live happily ever after.
Real one: wait for Richard and marry him when
he comes back.
Obstacles: Vini.

The next day, Tuesday, 5 December, is the day it happens. I am at work early to prep for the next session in my Change Management workshop. I've been here since just before eight, which means I can watch everyone arriving. Fatima is first, looking worried and bent over slightly as she walks, presumably to protect her upper body from attack. She's holding her scalded hand up against her chest, and is carrying a small Christmas tree in the other. She glances at me and smiles nervously.

'Hi, Beth. All right? Your blouse is lovely. Ooh, I like your shoes, are they new?'

'Thanks, Fats. No, I've had these for ages. How's your hand today?'

She shrugs and tries a dismissive smile, not quite achieving it. 'Oh, you know, it's OK. Throbs a bit but I can bear that. Serves me right, really. Maybe I'll be more careful next time. Look, I've got a tree.' She holds it up, just in case I had missed it.

'Brilliant. Where are you going to put it?'

She glances around the room. 'I don't know. What do you think? By the wood-panelled door?'

'Um, maybe in the corner by the photocopier would be better? People might trip over it if you put it by the door.'

'Oh, yes, good idea. I'll do that.'

I watch her take the bare tree over to the corner. 'Did you go out looking for contracts last night?'

She nods anxiously as she walks back to her desk. 'Yeah, I did. Went straight from work, all round town, every shop I could think of. Didn't get in until . . .' she glances at her watch, '. . . half eleven. Or twelve. I forget.'

'Fats, you weren't out walking round the town at midnight, were you?'

'Well, I lost track of time a bit. And once I'd been going for a few hours, I kind of got into it. I just kept thinking, This next one will be the one, or this next one, or this next one . . .' Her voice trails away and she sits down heavily in her seat.

'But what shops were open at that time?'

She raises her eyebrows. 'Oh, you'd be surprised. Down in the old part of the town, you know, on the other side of the bypass, there were lots of places still open.'

58

I know about those places and they aren't exactly the sorts of places that go in for formal training, if you know what I mean. The skills they use there are the sort of thing you pick up on the job.

'Did you get one?'

'No, no luck last night. Actually, it was a bit . . .' She trails off again and her eyes glaze over for a moment. 'But tonight I will. I am determined.' And she looks up at me with a confident smile. I smile back and nod, but I see her smile slip a bit as she turns to her computer monitor.

Bloody hell, I almost feel guilty, doing absolutely nothing yet to secure new contracts. I was hoping to get some inspiration during my shopping trip with Vini yesterday, but I was so distracted by Strange Attractive Man, and then Richard, and then not Richard, I forgot all about it. Doesn't matter, I've still got just under three weeks. Since my reason for raking in the business fucked off to Faro, I have been a bit listless and lacking in direction, but when I look at Fatima's anxious face, I can feel the old spark flickering back into life. I can probably motivate myself enough to get a contract big enough to save Fatima's job, so she doesn't really need to worry. I glance at her again and notice that she's got a small ladder in her tights, with a pine needle at each end. Good job she's not training today – that would be immensely distracting for the delegates.

No one else really speaks to me as they arrive over the next half-hour, and I don't bother speaking to them. Looking at them, I'm guessing that Fatima was the only one who went out hunting for contracts last night, and she was looking in the wrong place, like the Nazis searching for the Ark of the Covenant. Cath

Parson, the most lethargic woman ever to do up a cardigan, will probably have installed herself next to an ashtray somewhere, and then not budged all night; Ali, our admin assistant, and Skye, our youngest training deliverer, will have spent the evening and all their pocket money down at the arcades; and Mike probably had to see if he had won the giant marrow seeds he was bidding on. I'm not sure about Derek: I really don't know him. Reading a leather-bound volume of historical narratives by an open log fire I expect. But I feel sure that Sean, the fourth person in the other grouping with Grace, Skye and Cath, will have been out drinking or gambling all night, or sitting in a strip club. He's always struck me as the sort of man who would secretly double-cross his two best friends by switching the gold statue with the fake one and then stealing the only horse. If he was ever in that position. I don't think he even knows my name.

Right. I've got about half an hour left before I have to start my session. I go back to practising reading my notes with an earnest expression.

'Morning, Beth.'

Oh God, it's Grace. I arrange my face into a sweet smile and raise my head. 'Hiya, Grace. All right?' Shit, she looks fantastic: red suede jacket, narrow black skirt, red boots. I untuck my foot from under me and slide it back into my pink suede wedge that's on the floor.

'Yes thanks,' she says as she sits down at her desk behind me. She shrugs the jacket off her shoulders and then stands up again to hang it on a coat hanger she keeps in her desk drawer. Then she has to hang it on the topmost part of the coat stand, giving her a chance to stretch up in her tight black polo neck. God, she's so pretentious. Why didn't she just take the jacket off before she sat down?

'Any luck last night?' I ask her. I'm talking about the search for a contract, of course, but knowing her she'll probably tell me she got lucky and shagged some stranger in Halfords' doorway.

'No, no luck. Actually, I didn't even look. How about you?'

I like the way she's left her answer ambiguous, so that she doesn't give herself away.

'No, nothing. How come you didn't even look, then?'

I knew she wouldn't – she hinted as much in the Ladies before we left the office yesterday. She's switching on her computer and turns in her seat to look at me. 'Well, you know, I had other things to do last night. Fun things. Much more important than a stupid contract.'

'More important? What, more important than keeping this place going, and keeping all our jobs?'

She nods and widens her eyes. 'God, yes. A million times.' She swivels back to face her computer and flicks her hair over her shoulder. It's so long it almost hits me in the face. I turn my head away quickly. 'Anyway, I don't have to worry, do I? You're obviously going to land some massive contract somewhere, and save us all. Aren't you?' She swivels enough in her seat so she can glance at me with those last words, then turns back to the screen.

I feel a surge of incredulous resentment, and grip the edge of my seat. Is she actually suggesting – or confirming, in fact, what I have suspected for some time – that she is content to sit and flick her hair around while I slog my way round all the businesses in town and after three weeks of persistent effort, finally land the kind of contract Chas needs to save the company? My fingers start to move towards that incredibly fake hair. It's only just out of reach.

'I'm only kidding, Beth,' Grace says suddenly, turning round to face me again. 'I had plans last night, but I'm going to have a go today. Got to be done, right?'

I nod silently and turn back to my own computer. Jesus, I am a wreck. What is the matter with her?

'Doesn't Grace look gorgeous today?' Fatima leans over and whispers. 'I just love that jacket. She's so stylish.'

At lunchtime, Vini rings to tell me she's got it.

'Got what?'

'The hair dye.' When I don't shriek with uncontrollable excitement, she adds, 'For your hair.'

'Right. Good.'

'Get home as early as you can. We'll do your hair and then we're going out.'

'Going out?' God, here we go. 'Where?'

'There's no need to sound so negative. New horizons, remember? It starts at seven thirty, so be home before six.'

Ever so patiently I say, 'I am always home before six, Vin. Every day of the week, since we have lived together, I have got home before six. And now you've rung me up to tell me to be home before six? It's like ringing me up to tell me to pick up the phone. I will be home around half five, as always. OK?'

'All right, don't tangle your tangas. Just wanted to make sure. See you later.'

I don't like the sound of that. It's obviously not just a pub or club we're going to, it's some kind of event if it has a start time. An event where she thinks we can meet lovely, single men. God, I hope we're not going to a pantomime. They'll all be single dads in crew-necked jumpers . . .

Hang on a minute. Something Vini said is tugging at a small nugget of memory that is gleaming just beneath the surface. It was 'New horizons'. She said 'horizons', and that brings back to mind an article I was reading last week in *Any Port* magazine. I thought at the time that it had potential but didn't do anything about it. I did tear it out, though. Oh my God. I lean forward and start pulling all the clippings off the partition in front of me, scanning them quickly then discarding them until finally the words I have been hunting for leap off the page into the air in front of my face. HORIZON AT SEA? I glance around to see if anyone is looking my way and might have spotted the title, but no one is. Then I lean forward, spread the clipping out between my hands. It's about the falling profits logged by Horizon Holidays for the third year in a row, and the quandary that CEO Rupert de Witter finds himself in as a result. 'What is de Witter going to do', the article soliloquizes, 'to bring his company into the twenty-first century? Whatever it is, he'd better do it soon.'

I stare at the words, my heart speeding up as the implications of the article and Rupert de Witter's quandary make themselves fully apparent. De Witter has got to act, right now, to turn things round. And I am as sure as I can be that his outdated training policy will be one of the first things to go.

Oh my God. I've got to approach Horizon Holidays.

I close my eyes. Snagging a contract with Horizon would be massive – enough to save Love Learning, no problem. But it is going to be very much more difficult than you might think. When Richard walked out of there, I wanted him to know that I supported him, and I didn't hide it from Rupert de Witter. That is, I said 'Exactly' and 'You're so right'. a few times in the background while Richard was shouting down the phone.

Actually, Rupert de Witter may not have heard me. That's possible. But he will have been aware that I left with Richard. No doubt the news of our mutiny reached him within hours, or probably minutes, of our departure. When he heard Richard's name mentioned, he will have nodded in comprehension. No surprise there. But then when he heard that one of Richard's assistants had also gone, he probably stared thoughtfully into his artistic table centrepiece and frowned.

'Who the hell is Beth Sheridan?' he will have said. 'Do I know her? Why did she go? What's her problem?'

'Oh, she's only worked here a couple of years,' he will have been told. 'She's only about twenty-one. Madly in love with Richard, apparently. Follows him everywhere like a sick little puppy. Rather pathetic, really.'

'Isn't it though?' and he'll have laughed cruelly. 'Silly, silly little girl. Doesn't she know that he will clear off to Portugal in about six years' time and all her devotion and hard work will have been for nothing?'

I'll bet they all had a huge laugh about it. And now Rupert de Witter is the man I have to approach about a new contract. Shit. Will he remember me and laugh me out of the office? No, no, of course not, that won't happen, because he won't even agree to see me in the first place, once he is reminded about my mutiny.

This whole uncomfortable situation is complicated by one more thing.

Rupert de Witter is fuck-off gorgeous.

I mean, totally, heart-stoppingly, fumble-your-words, flick-your-hair, attack-of-the-unnecessary-giggles gorgeous. He's got this thick blond hair that sweeps over his brow and sometimes gets in his eyes; and these teeth that are so white and perfect you have to wonder if he was born like that (well, obviously he wasn't born like that, that would look very creepy, no matter how straight and white they were); his eyes are, I think, blue, but it's a bit difficult to tell under the blond fringe and thick eyelashes, which are *not* blond, by the way. And the body under all that beauty is enough to make your nether regions start making preparations to entertain.

I've never met him actually. A mere training assistant had no business mingling with the Top Man. But there's a photo of him on the back page of every Horizon brochure. There's a bit of writing that is supposedly a letter from him, to all his customers, along the lines of: 'Horizon Holidays strives to create the perfect blah blah blah, and I as its Managing Director guarantee that you blah blah.' His signature is reproduced at the bottom, and then there's the photo. He's outside and there's obviously a light breeze because his hair is a bit blown about, but not enough to look messy. Just enough to make you want to push your fingers into it. And then lick whipped cream off his face. He's smiling, of course, showing those beautiful teeth, and he's apparently standing on the deck of some kind of sea-going vessel, in a pale blue polo shirt with a cream jumper slung round his shoulders, one hand resting gently on a white railing.

It's fucking ridiculous, frankly. I have never seen so much fake tan and blond highlights outside of the playground at my old secondary school. And there he is, telling all his clients how he will personally take every care possible to ensure that their holiday is as wonderful as they expect it to be, and he's got fake tan, fake hair and fake teeth. Who would believe him? He looks like an actor.

But he is eye-wateringly sexy. And I was employed by him. And walked out in a loud and obvious demonstration of my disapproval. And nicked some folders. Although he may not have noticed that. And now I've got to meet him and convince him that he should ditch his ancient and impractical in-house training policy in favour of a company that built its foundations on contempt for him and his company.

Right.

What I need is an opener, some kind of clever device to get me into his office without him realizing it's me, Beth Sheridan, Richard Love's sick little puppy. Or some dark glasses. That would work too.

I don't have any more time to think about this now. I have to go and deliver the next part of 'Change Management' in five minutes. Maybe something will come to me while I'm training. Of course there is the fact that Horizon's profits have dropped slightly for the third consecutive year, and the board are worried. Making one or two million quid less this year than he did last year must be extremely stressful for Rupert, and he'll be beside himself trying to find a solution.

He's probably sitting right now in a soft, calfskin leather chair, in a large, glass-walled office, staring out at the cityscape, chin resting on his knuckles, coffee going cold on his heavy oak desk, spotlights glinting on his hair, pondering what on earth can be causing it. And if I'm lucky, his thoughts will return yet again to the training policy, and what Richard Love snarled at him six years ago.

'You are such a fucking ponce.'

No, no, not that. The other thing. The thing about his training policy being outdated and ineffective. Is he wondering if Richard Love was right all those years ago? Is the training policy obsolete? Has he, Rupert, been a stubborn, hard-headed fool?

'You really are a very accommodating boss, Rupert.'

At that exact moment, as I'm heading back towards the training room for the next session, picturing him cursing his short-sightedness six years ago, Rupert de Witter is, in fact, looking out of a window, pondering the view. He's not in an office though. He's having lunch with a friend and associate at one of the best tables in a very exclusive restaurant called Madeleine's, which overlooks the swans on the lake in Fieldwood Park.

This is the place where all the film stars living in our town would come for lunch, if any of them lived in our town. Sadly, the rest of the town, with its pedestrianized precinct and Food Court doesn't quite measure up to Madeleine's, so the film stars tend to stay away, in spite of it.

'Could we have the bill, please, Julian?'

'Certainly, Mr de Witter. I'll bring it right away.'

'Thanks.' Rupert turns to his lunch companion and shrugs. 'Do you think so? Maybe I am. But it seems like a perfectly reasonable request, and I can afford it, so why not? There's only so much profit you can spend, after all.'

His lunch companion sips his spritzer thoughtfully. 'There aren't many businessmen that would agree.'

Rupert nods. 'I know; you're right. We know we're living in a sad, cynical, money-orientated world when most employers would turn down a request for crèche facilities just because it would eat into their profits too much. Why should people be penalized for becoming parents, though?' He shakes his head. 'I hope that when – if – I ever take that step, I wouldn't expect my wife to give up work to look after the children. Why should she? She's got her career, and it's just as important to her as mine is to me.'

'Wife? Christ, why wasn't I invited to the wedding?'

Rupert smiles. 'Hypothetically speaking, mate. I'm sure there are lots of mums and dads at Horizon who feel the same as me. And, from a business point of view, they're the ones that are most valuable because they have got the most enormous incentive for wanting to stay employed. I'd be a fool not to help them.'

'I totally agree. I feel exactly the same about it.'

'Do you?'

'Yep. Absolutely. There are so many mums out there who definitely should be encouraged to go back to work. I mean, you know, intelligent, attractive people who would be wasted just sitting at home changing nappies.'

'Exactly.'

'And if you've got brains, I truly believe that you

should use them. You know, it's criminal to think of all the really sexy people who don't come back to work because they can't afford decent childcare, and haven't got—'

'You mean "intelligent".'

'Hmm?'

'You said it was criminal to think of all the *sexy* people that can't work.'

'No I didn't.'

'Yes, Hector my friend, you most certainly did.'

Hector pauses a moment. 'God, did I really? Huh.' He chuckles.

Rupert leans back in his seat. 'You know, I'm picking up some subtle signals here that you may not be exactly concentrating on this meeting. Am I right?'

Hector looks up frankly into Rupert's widened eyes and slumps his shoulders. 'I'm sorry, Rupe. You're right, I am a bit distracted today.'

'Everything all right?'

Hector smiles broadly. 'Yes, as it happens. More than all right. This distraction is . . . Well, it's the good kind.'

Rupert's glass freezes in mid-air on the way to his lips. 'Fuck me. Hector's found a woman.'

'You don't need to sound so—'

'Well, it's about time. I was starting to think you had given them up, after Miranda.'

'I kind of had, actually. Given up looking, anyway. You know Mum was ill so I wasn't going out much, and I had pretty much decided not to think about it for a while. But this one found me. She just kind of . . . appeared, entered my life, just like that. You remember our meeting here, about six weeks ago? The day Mum died?'

69

'Course I do. You interrupted our meeting to answer your phone, even though it wasn't even your mum.'

'Well, that was her. Rachel. I had to answer it – I couldn't not.'

'You "couldn't not"? That sounds good. So, what's she like then?'

'Oh, God, where do I start? She's so funny, Rupe. The first time I spoke to her, she had found my mobile phone, and I started this little joke about ransom demands. She just played along, straight away. She made me laugh.'

'Well, that makes a change.'

'I know.'

'So when's the wedding, then?'

'Christ, Rupert, give me a chance. We're not even officially a couple yet.'

'Aren't you? Why not? I mean, if she's so great, what's stopping you?'

Hector shrugs. 'It's complicated. But I'm working on it.'

'Really? What, ex-boyfriend hanging around still? Is it Brad Pitt? And he doesn't want to break up with her? Calling night and day, turning up on her doorstep with flowers, begging her to reconsider. You might as well forget it, mate.'

'Thanks for the vote of confidence, Rupe.'

'Nothing against you, Hec. Just, you know, it's Brad Pitt. No one stands a chance against Brad Pitt. I might even turn to the other side if Brad Pitt asked me to.'

'Hmm. Well, as attractive an image in my head as that is, shall we move on? I'll keep you posted. In the meantime, what did you think of my proposal?'

Rupert picks up a glossy blue folder that's lying on the table, then puts it down again. 'Yep, loved it. Perfect. Start straight away. Now, back to the other topic on the table. When you say she kind of appeared, what exactly do you mean?'

'So this system I've designed is definitely what you want at Horizon? It does everything you need?'

'Yes, man, you heard me. We're making losses, so I need to do things differently. I'm thinking about changing our training policy, too.'

'Really? That's interesting. Are you going external, or sticking with—'

'Fuck the training, Hector, answer my question. How did she appear?'

'Aha. I see. I understand. You pretend to be cynical, going on about Brad Pitt hanging around, but really you want to know how I did it, don't you? You like the sound of it, and you want to get your own. I'm right, aren't I?'

'Not necessarily. I might be just interested, seeing as you're one of my oldest friends.'

'OK. Sure. Whatever you say. I believe you.'

'Good. So what's the answer then? How does someone like me find someone like that, without them knowing exactly who I am and going after me for the money?'

Hector raises his eyebrows and presses his lips together. 'I'm afraid I don't know the answer, my friend. I have no idea at all.'

'Great.'

Hector leans forward and raises his eyebrows. 'There is one thing you could try, though . . .'

Six

First Steps

Short-term Goal: Have chemicals poured onto my head and act happy about it.
Obstacles: Dyed hair is so not what Richard thinks of as beautiful.
Long-term Goal: I just want to be married to someone who adores me. Maybe it will be Richard: maybe it won't (probably not, once my hair has become artificially enhanced).
Obstacles: Can't find a decent venue for the reception. Ha ha.

When I finish the afternoon session, having been irritatingly delayed by someone thinking he was clever asking me a lot of pertinent and totally relevant questions, I've got no time to do any research on Horizon, or Rupert, because I have my instructions to be home before six, and it's already five fifteen. The only person left in the office is Chas, and he's standing at the door, playing with the keys. I can just see the shiny top of his head above the desk partitions as he throws them in the air and catches them. Or at least, fumbles, drops them, grabs for them as they roll with a jingle down his belly and eventually stoops to pick them up from the floor. He's so cool.

'Come on, Elizabeth,' he says, having learned my name from the staffing list rather than from actually talking to anyone, 'time and tide wait for no man, you know. Or woman, of course, didn't mean anything by that.'

He's ridiculous but I don't care today. My head is full of Rupert de Witter. Oh, no, don't get me wrong. I'm not dreaming about him shirtless, gazing passionately into my eyes, kissing me and then sweeping me away on his yacht for a weekend in the Mediterranean where he follows my every move with those gorgeous eyes and eventually tells me he wants to spend the rest of his life with me, or anything. He's beautiful, that's true, but a complete knob. I know we never met but I have first-hand knowledge of what he's like from listening to Richard shouting down the phone at him. He's inflexible, childish, arrogant and useless. My head is full of him simply because I need to think of a way to get in to see him. I'm not even thinking about what happens after I get taken into his presence. So far, all I've managed to come up with is sliding down onto the floor giggling helplessly, and I don't think that's going to work.

'Come on, get out, we haven't got much time.'

I look up to find Vini standing at the driver's window of my car. The car is stationary, parked outside our flat, in fact, and I realize with a start that I have no recollection of the drive home. I turn around to look behind me, half expecting to see a holocaust in my wake, the road littered with groaning, bleeding bodies and smoking cars with buckled bonnets, but there's only a small grey dog jogging quietly across the road. I am staggered. This is the first time in eight years that I have had no focus on what I was doing, or what I looked like while I was doing it. Usually when I'm driving, I maintain a slightly dreamy smile in case I'm spotted through the windscreen, but this time I have spent the entire journey thinking about Rupert de bloody Witter. Not good. I will focus more on my driving next time, particularly as it involves manoeuvring a ton of steel, electrical sparks and explosive liquid through a quiet, residential suburb.

I've barely got inside the flat before Vini drags me off to the bathroom and instructs me to disrobe. She's very creative. I mean, in a hair and nails kind of way. She doesn't make picture frames out of old tea bags, or design coffee tables made of pen lids. Thank God for that. But she can do beauty, which is just as well, given the career path she has chosen for herself. She once transformed a scrawny youth with lank, droopy hair she found in Tesco's car park into Marilyn Monroe. It was amazing.

Uh, no, actually it was Marilyn Manson. But still amazing.

So although I'm not entirely in favour of new hair, I put myself in Vini's gloved hands. She loads the stuff onto my head, tucks cotton wool around my hairline and then tells me to sit still on the toilet for twenty-five minutes. Excellent. That will give me twenty-five quiet minutes to think about how to get near Rupert de Witter.

I know! I'll send him flowers, with a card inside that

says, 'From Beth at Love Learning, call me for all your training . . .'

No. Maybe not. People who send flowers are usually trying to say something else. Not that I've had flowers sent to me very often. Twice in my life, in fact. The first one was presented to me at school when I was fifteen because I hadn't won the art competition. I made a beautiful model of Jesus on the cross out of papier mâché and straws, with greying skin, blood clots on the head, and peeling flesh on the hands and feet. He even had protruding ribs because he'd already been up there a day or two. The winner, who got the portable CD player, had done something with a painted egg, which I thought was such a cliché for an Easter decoration. The second time was years later but was basically the same message. John Wilson from the estate agent's in the precinct sent me flowers to tell me he was dumping me. 'Dear Beth, I've tried you out and I've decided that you're lacking in some way so I'm rejecting you. These carnations are to make you feel less of a failure. John.' Well, that wasn't exactly what the card said. But that's what it meant.

Not flowers then. Balloons. Yes! No hidden message there. Balloons are just bouncy air-filled bags of fun, with a poignant, heartfelt message on the outside. They could say something like 'Love Learning, a Centre of Learning and Development' and then I'll put a card in to say they're from me, and my phone number.

That is a completely shit idea. What the bloody hell am I thinking about? Balloons are not serious business marketing tools. He'll think we're a load of unprofessional clowns. He'll be right.

'Right, OK, time to rinse,' says Vini, coming back into the bathroom.

For the next ten minutes I hang upside down over the bath and all the blood rushes to my head making thinking impossible.

After a quick blow-dry, which produces a kind of flicky effect at the sides, Vini leads me to a mirror and then unveils it, like in one of those extreme makeover shows. Except she does it by whipping a soggy towel away with the words, 'Am I good, or what?'

It's blond. I was expecting, I don't know, a mahogany or maybe just a darker brown than it already was. Black, even. Something not trashy, anyway.

But the change is staggering. The paler colour surrounding my face has transformed me. My skin looks brighter, my eyes look bluer, my lips even look fuller. I look alive and vibrant and, well, yes, sexy. As I move my head from side to side, the hair moves slowly with me, like a shampoo advert.

'It's blond,' I say superfluously.

'Duh. So what do you think?'

I turn to look at her, feeling like someone who might wear a top that shows my bra through it. I'll have to get one.

'It's trashy.' I turn back to my reflection. I don't want to take my eyes away from it.

'No-oh, no, it isn't. It's sexy and gorgeous. And it really suits you, I might add. Brightens your skin tone. Knew it would.'

'I look like a tramp. What will the delegates think when they see me?'

She nods suggestively. 'They will think, Fuck me

76

sideways with a board eraser, I never realized our trainer was so damn HOT!'

I flick my eyes in her direction without really breaking eye contact with my reflection. 'But it looks so artificial. Everyone will notice.'

'Uh, well, *yeah*. That's the idea. Where's the problem?'

The problem is that I have spent the past eight years of my life assiduously cultivating a completely natural, fresh appearance because I know Richard prefers it. She has undone all that with this one treatment. I'm not saying that to Vini though. She thinks I've given up on him, remember.

'Vin, I have spent a really long time getting myself . . . ready for this course and a sudden, dramatic change like this' – I touch my hair – 'could have a disastrous effect on . . . the effectiveness of the training.'

She gapes. I can see this out of the corner of my eye. 'Don't you care how fantastic you look?'

'That's not the point, Vin. Although maybe it is exactly the point. If I look too fantastic, no one will take me seriously. Do you think I look fantastic?'

'Yes I bloody do. And so do you, if you'll admit it. Come on, look at yourself. You're gorgeous.'

I frown as I stare. What will Richard say when he sees me? I look completely fake. So my face is lifted, my eyes are brightened and my entire appearance is transformed into an incredibly glamorous and sexy person, so what? None of that matters if . . . I stare harder . . . No, no, it makes no difference to me, if . . . I smile quickly at my reflection before Vini notices. Actually . . .

'All right, Beth,' Vini says, 'you can stop frowning.

It looks fantastic, you are stunning, it's one of the first steps to a whole new life, but you think it's tarty.'

I nod, scowling now, and notice in the mirror that the nodding has caused the hair to dance and shimmer in the light.

'You think I should have told you beforehand that it was blond, so you could choose not to do it?'

I nod again. Diamonds scatter.

'And maybe I should have stuck with something a bit less tarty, like mahogany or rich brown?'

'Yes.' Nod. White lightning glitters off my crown.

'So let's dye it back. Number 001, is it? Natural Sludge Brown?'

'No!'

'Aha!'

'Damn.'

'Gotcha!'

It's not a pantomime. Right now, crossing the car park at the Seahorse Hotel, I actually wish it was. I am nervously eyeing a poster that says in large, terrifying letters, 'Fast Love Speed Dating – 2Nite!' and my stomach clenches a little bit tighter.

'Do we really have to do this?' I say to Vin for the eight hundredth time. She stopped answering me half an hour ago.

When I agreed with her that we would both change the way we had been approaching romance, I didn't mean this. I was thinking more along the lines of, oh, I don't know, bumping into someone on a train and ending up in bed together in the afternoon. Not, and I quote, 'Three minutes of interaction, a lifetime of intercourse action!' I know one thing: my new hair feels right at home here.

The hair was a great bargaining chip, though. Before we left the house, Vini agreed to alter her dress sense, in exchange for the blonde. I've got her in jeans, brown boots and a tan suede jacket tonight, and I watch her striding through the double doors of the hotel. She looks bloody good.

Inside it's just as I thought. The lobby is full of sad but well-dressed people milling about with awkward flowers in their lapels, trying to look relaxed and confident in new underwear. Obviously I can't see that they're in new underwear, but it's evident by the way they move. One woman with a huge, horizontal backside sashays past me with a side-to-side sway that would rival the *Titanic*, some secret lacy thing stuffed between her cheeks erroneously making her feel sexy. Over at the bar, women in their fifties wearing pale blue eyeshadow and hot pink lipstick are holding wine glasses with their fingertips, giggling and trying to look like they're too young to have had alcohol before. The smells that waft past me vary between whisky, cologne and fish, depending on what sort of impression the men are trying to make: Indiana Jones, James Bond or Forrest Gump.

'No way.'

Vini, in the process of hustling excitedly towards the bar, stops and turns to face me. 'You what?'

'I said, no way. Nope. Never in a million. Don't even ask me. No. Never. Uh-uh.'

'What? You are kidding me. I mean, we agreed.'

'Oh, sorry. Maybe I didn't make myself clear. I said—' I turn my back on her and start making my way back to the door. It would have been a good exit, too, if my path had not been blocked by a chicane of balding losers. The nearest one to me catches my eye and raises his eyebrows suggestively with a saucy smile. 'Well, hello,' he says, then throws his head back and violently and noisily sucks all the air in the room backwards up his nose.

'Don't you dare leave,' Vini says, coming up behind me. I turn towards her, relieved to have a reason to move away from Moby Dick. 'Anyway, it's not as bad as you might think.' We both start as the head of a ventriloquist's dummy wearing a Santa hat is suddenly thrust in front of me and says, "Ello, lovely lady, ny nane's Doddy. Will you de ny dirlfriend?'

I look helplessly at Vini who is staring open-mouthed at the dummy. I spread my hands and widen my eyes. 'You think?'

'Not representative,' she says, taking my arm and leading me hastily away from that particular corner of the room. 'Just try it out, OK? You never know, you might enjoy it.'

'Maybe you're right. I only had pulling my toenails out with pliers scheduled for tonight anyway.'

'Great. I'll get us a drink.'

While she's gone, I take another look around, and then wish I hadn't. Near the door is some kind of registration table where excited people are queuing up and being given a sheet of paper. There's not going to be anyone for me in that dole queue. I'm basing this assumption on the man at the front, who is wearing one of those pretend ostrich suits, complete with fake legs down the side so it looks like he's sitting on the bird. I gape at him. This man has obviously sat down somewhere and thought long and hard about where he's been going wrong with women his whole life, and decided that a giant comedy bird costume is the answer. Jesus, I would love to have seen some of the techniques he abandoned in favour of this one.

I have a look at some of the women, wondering which lucky creature will be going home with Bird-Man tonight. One of them is wearing a tartan skirt with a stripey blouse. Perfect. Based on her decisions so far today, she would probably think the ostrich thing was a good idea. I look beyond her to a small, dark-haired woman standing alone by the wall. At last, someone who seems normal and looked in the mirror once before leaving the house this evening. She's wearing ordinary jeans, black boots, brown cardigan, Sooty glove puppet on her left hand. Holy Christ! And Sooty is waving at the man with the ventriloquist's doll. I blink. Where in God's name am I?

I look behind me in panic and spy Vini, head down, walking fast towards me. 'Wrong room,' she says urgently, then seizes my arm and pulls me back the way she has just come.

'What?'

She shakes her head and pulls me hurriedly towards a pair of glass double doors at the opposite end to where we came in. Outside in the corridor we turn to look at the doors we've just used, and above them is a giant banner that immediately clears everything up.

'Puppeteers' Convention?' I say. 'A whole room full of puppeteers? Having a convention?'

She nods. 'Apparently.'

'Bloody hell. What on earth do a whole load of puppeteers talk about? Strings versus gloves? How to

81

make your doll say "mummy" properly? The correct technique to make Punch really cringe in pain and fear?'

'Maybe the puppets do all the talking,' she says mysteriously and stalks off. I hesitate a moment by the doors and watch some of the conversations going on inside. You know, I think Vini is right. The ventriloquist's doll is now in lively debate with Sooty, while its owner is drinking a glass of water; and the ostrich man is checking his watch, oblivious to the fact that the ostrich is attacking a woman holding a small talking donkey. God, it's the Twilight Zone.

I'm following Vini up the corridor towards, I hope, the exit, but suspect not. When I round the corner at the end I find her standing by a glass door that has a sign Blu-tacked to it saying, 'Speed Dating Here 2nite.' My heart sinks. I had been hoping she had got the wrong night and we could abandon the idea. There's a curtain on the inside of the door to prevent you from seeing the misfits inside before you've committed yourself to going in. The glass even has chicken wire embedded in it, presumably to protect the occupants against flying glass in the event of a fight.

'Vin, I'm really not sure about this.'

She's reaching her hand out towards the door, and stops midway. 'Me neither, Beth. What? You think this is my fucking dream date?'

'W . . . No, I mean . . . I wasn't—'

'This is the noughties, you know. This is how it's done now; we are too old for school discos. It's either this or . . . puppeteers.'

'I think I would rather be back there than in here.' I jerk my head towards the becurtained door.

82

'Oh no you wouldn't, Beth. Come off it. Those people were wearing glove puppets.' She makes mouth movements with her fingers. 'Puppets, Beth.'

'Why do you think there's a curtain on this door?'

'I dunno. Cos it's a fuck-ugly door. Now come on.'

'No, it's not that. It's to stop potential speed-daters like us from browsing through the glass before we go in. And you know what that means?'

'I bet you're going to tell me.'

'It means that the people in there are such utter losers, if we could see them beforehand, we wouldn't go in. I mean, speed dating, Vini. Do you really want to meet someone who goes speed dating? They're all going to be either violent psychopathic serial killers or *Star Wars* fans.'

'Beth, you are so—' At this moment, the door opens and a man comes out and bumps straight into Vini.

'Oh, I'm so sorry,' he says, turning back to look down at her. Then he starts to smile. 'Hi . . . Are you all right?'

'Yes,' she says, gazing back up at his face, which is somewhere near the ceiling. 'Perfect, thanks.'

'Yes,' he says, not moving away, 'perfect.'

'I'm Lavinia,' she's saying, holding out her hand, and now I've got a really uncomfortable feeling that she is going to make me go speed dating on my own.

'Hi, Lavinia,' he says, taking her hand. 'I'm Adam.'

'Hi, Adam. Are you . . . ?' she says, indicating the tantalizingly half-open door.

He turns to look. 'What, speed dating? Good God no. I was just in the wrong room. I'm actually looking for the puppeteers' convention. Any idea where it is?'

She drops his hand like it's an earthworm and juts her chin down the corridor. 'That way.'

Interesting how his face is changing, like he is surprised she is put off by the fact that he is a grown man heading towards a puppeteers' convention. I'm checking his hands out for any telltale signs of yellow felt.

'Right. Thanks.' He swings his arms at his sides, waiting for something else to happen. Then he realizes it isn't going to. 'OK, well, it was lovely to meet you, Lavinia. And you,' he adds hastily, suddenly remembering that I'm standing right next to her. 'Bye.'

'Bye,' she says, and as he still seems to be making no attempt to go off and see the puppets, she puts her hand on my shoulder and pushes me towards the door.

And then I'm inside, without really intending to be. Behind me, Vini is closing the door very slowly, her face pressed up against the crack. Presumably the puppet man is still standing outside in the corridor, watching the door close. He's going to miss all the puppet fun if he doesn't get a move on.

Vini joins me and we walk further in. It's smaller than the puppet room, and there are about fifteen single tables, each with a chair on either side, arranged in a large circle. Every table has got a strand of tinsel sellotaped round the edge, and an extremely optimistic sprig of mistletoe hanging above it. In the background is the haunting sound of George Michael singing 'Last Christmas': perhaps not the most appropriate song to accompany people attempting to embark on a new relationship.

One or two of the tables are already taken by fidgety women, fluffing their hair, checking their compacts, pressing their lips together. There is a small bar at one side of the room, where the men are all doing the masculine version of checking their compacts – rooting around in their trouser pockets, presumably trying to find their penises and give them a reassuring pat. 'OK, little guy, are you ready to try sex at last?'

I feel like telling them all not to worry; it ain't gonna happen tonight.

We're each given a sheet of paper with a list of numbers and boxes on it, and a large plastic triangle with a number on it – Vini is five and I am six – and the rules are explained. We will sit at our numbered tables and the men will move around the room. They will spend three minutes at each table, during which time it is recommended that we try to do equal amounts of talking and listening. I hope they're prepared for that too. Somehow, I suspect not – if they could do that, why are they here in the first place? At the end of the three minutes a bell will sound and our companions will move on to the next table, while we are joined by someone new.

Vini turns to me. 'It sounds bloody brilliant, doesn't it?' she says, moving towards the tables.

'Oh yes,' I say quietly. 'Brilliant.'

Our tables are adjacent to each other and a few seconds later a bell rings and the seat opposite me is suddenly overflowing with a large man in a polo-necked jumper. I can feel my neck start to itch, just looking at him.

'I'm Gordon. Number eight.' He points needlessly to the large '8' pinned to his jumper.

'Libby,' I reply, deciding at that exact moment that I need to use a pseudonym, in case he ever stalks me.

He's definitely got serial-killer eyebrows. Or rather, serial-killer monobrow.

'Hi, Libby. God, it's hot in here, isn't it? Christ. I'm sweating like a bullfrog.'

What a great image of himself he's given me in the first two seconds of our relationship. It's difficult to know what to say to that. 'Do bullfrogs sweat, actually?'

'Hmm?'

'I mean, they're amphibian, aren't they? If they get hot, they can just go and sit at the bottom of the pond for half an hour or so, can't they?'

He stares at me. I can see him mentally not ticking my number on his sheet. 'What are you, a zoologist?'

'Yes.'

'Oh. Well then, do horses sweat?'

'Oh yes. Profusely.'

'Great. Cos I'm sweating like that.'

'Oh dear.'

The next guy is just as bad. 'But when I got to level nine,' he is saying, 'there's this fuck-off massive boulder that comes out of nowhere and flattens you. Took me ages to work it out. Do you know what you had to do? You had to blow it up *before* you climbed down the rope ladder. Sh-tupid.'

After forty-five minutes there is half an hour's break and Vini and I go to the bar to compare notes.

'Did you tick anyone?' she says immediately. 'I have.'

'Christ, you haven't, have you? I haven't ticked a single one.'

'Haven't you? *Really?*'

'Nope.'

'What about number ten, with the gorgeous eyes?'

'I didn't like any of them.'

'Not even number eleven, with that sexy voice?'

'You're not getting it, Vin. I didn't like any of them.'

'Well, you're just too fussy,' she says. She's got a point. But when you've spent eight years of your life in a relationship with Richard Love, how can anyone else measure up? Vini leans over and punches my arm encouragingly. 'Come on, don't look like that, it's not so bad. Try and picture them in the pub or something, when they're relaxed and have got more than three sodding minutes to impress you.'

I can honestly say that the best thing about these guys is the fact that they have only got three sodding minutes.

We go back to our tables and that unrelenting bell rings again, heralding the arrival of another freak.

'Hi, I'm Brad,' he says, leaning over the table and taking my hand. His fingers close around mine and as I look up at him I am startled with a jolt of recognition. It's Strange Attractive Man, from the department store. He's left his briefcase at home, and he's dressed much more casually – black chinos, tan sweater – but it's definitely him. I gasp a bit and just for a moment lose all sense of poise. Jesus, I can hardly believe it. As I watch him sit down, his eyes squint a bit and he turns his head slightly as if looking at me through a viewfinder.

'I know you,' he says. 'Have we met?'

I nod. He's still holding my hand across the table, apparently keeping me captive until he's cleared this up. He leans forward and raises his eyebrows.

'Yes, sorry, hi, Brad, I'm Libby. We met yesterday in Whytelys. I am – was – the mannequin.'

He grins delightedly. 'Oh yes, that's it! God, you look . . .'

I'm starting to feel hot, and I can feel my face reddening. He's about to say I look fantastic, and I have to say, so does he. Deep brown eyes, crinkled at the edges, brown hair, lines on forehead and cheeks – from laughing, maybe? My tummy is going all squirmy.

'. . . completely different. You've changed your hair, haven't you? It's lovely.'

Well, all right, not fantastic. But he did say my hair is lovely. And he noticed it in the first place. I went out with a guy once who didn't notice for two days that I had broken my arm.

'Thanks.' It's about all I can manage. Come on, Beth, equal talking and listening.

'So do you . . . ?' he starts, then stops. 'No, nothing. Forget that.'

'What?'

He laughs out a puff of air. 'I was going to say, "Do you come here often?" but given what we're here for, it seemed a bit insulting.'

'Serial speed-dater, you mean? No one fancied me the first seventeen times, so here I am again.'

He presses his lips together with a smile. 'That's not exactly what I was thinking.'

'Oh.'

'Although, now you mention it, I wouldn't have thought you would need to do this more than once.'

'Really? So how do you explain the fact that this is my fourth time?'

He looks genuinely surprised, which is very pleasing.

'Four? Really? Hmm.' He turns away slightly and frowns as he stares into the distance. 'Well,' he says, turning back to me at last, 'after careful consideration I have to conclude that no one ticked you because they were all intimidated by you.'

'Is that right?'

'Yes, that's got to be it. Just so you know, you need to try and look a bit less . . . appealing.'

'Really?'

'Oh yes. It's not going to be easy, given how you look.' He breaks eye contact a moment and glances down at the table. I can feel my face going hot when he looks up again. He smiles, a bit embarrassed. 'What you need to do is, don't wash your hair for a few weeks before you come next time. Make it dull and lifeless, if you can. Maybe wear an old tracksuit, that kind of thing. Much less daunting.'

I smile too. 'Thanks for the tip.'

'It's my pleasure.'

There's a moment's pause, then I say, 'Actually, this is my first time.'

He nods. 'I would have put money on that.' He breaks eye contact again, and clears his throat. 'Ahem. It's actually quite ghastly, isn't it? Having to resort to this partner market set-up, I mean. It's almost like being back at school, having to be told how it's done.'

'I know. It's not so much the skin-shrivelling humili-ation that I can't stand, it's the feeling of incompetence in the adult world, as if I haven't quite made it past my sixteenth birthday.'

'At least there's no mystery, or uncertainty about it this way, though. No second-guessing, no wondering, Oh, does she really like me? Maybe she's not all that keen. Have I misread the signs? Am I making a complete fuck-up of the whole thing?'

I smile. 'Yeah, there's nothing quite so romantic as a tick in the right box.'

He puts his hands up, laughing. 'Yes, all right, you've got me there. There is no romance at all. But that can come later, can't it? I mean, this isn't supposed to be all there is. This is just to see if there's a spark between you, whether you click. Moonlit evenings and boat trips can happen any time, once you've made that connection.' His voice has gone soft and he's gazing into my eyes. An image comes into my head of what an evening out with Brad might be like.

'Wow, moonlit picnics and fireworks over the water. Is that what someone could expect, if they went out with you?'

His eyebrows draw together quizzically as he smiles at me. 'Actually, Libby, I didn't mention anything about picnics or fireworks.'

'You didn't?'

'No. I was thinking of a film and a kebab after. You've put me to shame now.'

'Well, what film would it be?'

'*Nine Dead Gay Guys,*' he says without missing a beat.

'Hmm. Is that a love story?'

'Oh yeah.'

I giggle. 'Well, that sounds romantic. I think the evening has promise. Now tell me about the kebab. Where would it be from?'

'Kev's Kebabs, just round the corner from the library.'

I nod. 'Uh huh. Is there a queue?'

'Not a big one. One or two people.'

'Excellent. So not much standing around. And what will it be like?'

He leans forward conspiratorially. 'It will be hot and steamy, damp in your mouth, your taste buds will throb and the juices will spill between your lips and run over them onto your chin . . .' He stops suddenly and breaks eye contact again, his gaze dropping. 'Erm . . .'

My face is burning and there's a pounding sensation in my belly. I clear my throat. 'Well, yes, obviously Kev does know his business.'

He relaxes visibly and meets my eyes again, grinning. 'Oh, without a doubt. He's the best.'

'Naturally. This is a romantic date we're talking about – of course you're going to go to all the best places.'

He smiles. 'Libby, I am so glad that this evening hasn't been a total dead loss. I was starting to despair if there was anyone out there who wasn't comatose.' He takes a piece of paper out of his trouser pocket and says softly, 'What's your number?'

For a moment I don't answer. Should I give him my phone number, just like that, without the box-ticking exercise that's supposed to precede it? What kind of security does this agency provide, if the person they give your contact details to turns out to be an axe murderer? Will I get a refund if I give him my phone number myself, rather than through them, and then he cleaves my head in two during dessert?

The bell rings and there is a panicky clatter of chairs being pushed back hurriedly. Brad stands up slowly, leaving his hands on the table. 'What's your number?' he says again urgently. 'We need to synchronize.'

And then I realize that he's not asking me for my phone number, he's asking me for my 'Fast Love' number, the number of my table, the number for ticking on the chart. The plastic triangle with my number on it has fallen off the table onto the floor, so I bend down to get it. He's walking away from me now, moving towards the next table, glancing back repeatedly, flexing his extended hand towards me three times: five and five and five. Fifteen. Wow.

Oh my God, where did I put that chart? It's not in front of me so I lean over and look on the floor under the table and then under my chair. Yes, there it is, caught under the leg. I tilt the chair over crazily and manage to extract the sheet with the tip of my boot, dragging it over the carpet towards my reaching fingers.

With the sheet in one hand, I pick up the white plastic triangle with the number on it and hold it up, knowing that for this to work, Brad has to tick me and I have to tick him. If we don't both do it, it won't happen. I look over at him, just as he's about to sit down at the next table, and urge him to look at me. Please, please, just one glance, just one quick look so I can show him my number. And then, miraculously, he looks. Quickly I wave the triangle at him with a smile. His eyebrows raise and he flashes six fingers at me, a question in his eyes, just checking he got it right, just to be sure. And just to be sure I turn the triangle round to check and the number is there, deep and black, number six, so I nod slowly, holding up six fingers myself. Brad takes his pen as I watch and slowly, exaggeratedly, draws an enormous tick on the paper near the top. He turns the paper towards me so I can see that it's there, next to number six, a huge black mark, and while I'm looking I notice that there are no ticks anywhere else on the page. I copy him, drawing a huge tick against number fifteen, drawing circles round it and huge arrows across the page flying in from every direction pointing towards it; then I too turn the page to face him so he can see the tick, the arrows and the circles. I hear him laugh, see him nod, then he sits and inclines his head politely towards his new hostess.

Seven

Evaluate Success

Short-term Goal: Hear from Brad. Immediately. Oh, yeah, plus contact Rupert de Witter.

Obstacles: There aren't any because we ticked each other's boxes. Except I might forget to contact de Witter.

Long-term Goal: Maybe I will dump Richard and focus all my long-term plans on Brad instead. My goal can be to say to Richard when he comes back, This ship has sailed, baby!

Obstacles: He's still not here, so I can't say it to him. Plus I really need to have a proper relationship established with Brad before I say it. Just in case.

I'm reading a book at the moment with an ugly heroine in it. I'm on page thirty-four. It's pretty heavy going because she keeps going on and on about how she avoids mirrors and walks with her head down and dreads meeting new people because she always sees them recoil in horror at the hideousness of her countenance. All very tedious.

It's not really credible, though, is it? I mean, people

who walk around looking at the pavement and never speak or go out or make any effort to appear to best advantage just don't become heroines. Their lives are the sort of pedestrian mundane existences that stories aren't written about. They're the people who end up working in garden centres, or libraries, or theatres or anywhere else where there aren't likely to be many men. There is absolutely no opening for the hero to be transfixed or intoxicated or enchanted by her if she never raises her gaze above waist level. She needs to smile a bit, try and look like she's having a good time. Maybe dye her hair.

This new hair is making me feel more like a heroine. That's not to say I didn't feel like one already. I mean, that's obvious: involved with the lead, had my heart broken by him and now awaiting his return. It's classic. But that feeling has been wearing off a bit since he's been gone. I try every day to maintain heroine status by being ready at any moment for his unexpected return, but it's not been easy, even if it looks it.

But now that I am blonde, I feel renewed. I feel lighter, like a bubble, and I bob around the place, bounding off furniture, breezing through my morning session.

Of course, it could be Brad, not the blond, making me bounce.

It's the next day, my first day at work with this hair, and there was a bit of a sensation when I got here this morning.

'Nice hair, Beth,' Derek said, nodding at me.

'Blimey, you look fabulous, Beth! Doesn't she, Mike? Look at her, she's stunning. God, Beth, it's absolutely gorgeous. What's it called?' That was Grace.

No, sorry, my little joke. That, of course, was Fatima. Grace said, 'Beth, you've gone blonde, like me! God, dyes these days are so good, aren't they? It looks almost natural.' And then she flicked her own hair over her shoulder as if to demonstrate . . . something. Whatever it was, I don't know. I was looking the other way at that point.

The most surprising reaction was Sean, who entered the office, almost walked past me, then stopped and dramatically turned back for another look. It was very hammy, but I liked it. He stared at me a moment then said, 'Wow.' That was it. Oh, and he blew a little whistle out, like Fred Astaire or someone.

Anyway, I don't care about any of that because I am going to get a message from Brad today. I had a dream last night that it was actually Brad Pitt I had met at Fast Love, and when I woke up I couldn't remember if it really was him, or if I'd just imagined meeting someone called Brad. But then I reckoned that Brad Pitt would be far too busy to be speed dating at the Seahorse Hotel. And Angelina wouldn't be too pleased about it, either. Silly cow, what did she expect, that he would stop making public appearances? She needs to wake up and accept that she's with an international sex symbol and he needs his freedom.

But it wasn't Brad Pitt, of course. And it wasn't an imaginary Brad either. The Brad I met last night was a real, flesh-and-blood man who was completely gorgeous. I know this because I asked Vini what she thought of number fifteen, and her effusive and excited reply was, 'He's OK, if you like that kind of thing.' I know she prefers her men bearded, so this is praise indeed.

Since Richard left I have not had much male attention. Well, any, actually. I really only go to work and the supermarket, and the likelihood of meeting an attractive, available and unconvicted man in either place is next to nothing. Three months of enforced celibacy later, I have found myself finding men attractive perhaps a tad too easily. Well, Vini has found me doing it. I was oblivious until she pointed it out.

'Were you flirting with him?' she asked me once as we were coming out of a shoe shop about a month ago.

'No,' I said quickly. 'Don't be silly. Of course I wasn't.'

'So what's all the "Oh, gosh, I'm so sorry to make you go back to the stock room again, you're all sweaty, I might just have to rub you down with a damp towel, tee hee hee"?'

'I did not say that.'

'Well, it was pretty much like that. Offering to go and buy him a fucking ice cream, for Christ's sake. You were flirting.'

'I was not flirting. And so what if I was?'

'So what if you . . . ? Jesus, Beth, he must have been about sixteen! Did you even look past his trousers?'

'Course I did.'

'What did he look like then?'

'Don't be stupid, Vini.'

'No, no, don't brush me off. What did he look like? Come on. Start with his hair. What was that like?'

I don't think I need to repeat the entire conversation. You can imagine the rest. It's just that I was preoccupied with buying the shoes, which is perfectly understandable, especially as they were a pair of beautiful black sling-backs with sequins on them. Or it might have been a pair of boots. It's hardly surprising I couldn't remember a thing about him. And when you're trying on shoes, and someone is standing in front of you to see how you get on, it's not their hair that's at eye level.

So when I've sped through the morning session (Effective Role Models), and then got held up by an annoying bloke insisting on picking me up on every tiny little thing, I hurry back to my desk without actually running and log on to my computer. There's bound to be a message from Brad by now. When we filled in our forms at the beginning, we had to give email addresses as well as a choice of home, work and mobile numbers. I gave my Hotmail address and my mobile number, so one of them is bound to have something from him, or from the Fast Love people giving me his contact details. This is so exciting, I can hardly type my password in properly and end up nearly locking myself out of the system. Jesus, if I do that it will involve a lengthy migraine-inducing phone call to one of the drones at the IT company Richard got the computers from, to reset the password. I am as light and airy as a bubble today, so I feel sure that my answer to their monotone request for the sixteen-digit asset number would be cheery, easy compliance. Or banging my head on the desk, screaming.

So after two failed attempts to type in my password, I carefully remove my fingers from the keyboard and decide to have a look at my mobile phone first. Nope, no texts or missed calls. I've got a good signal at the moment, although it is possible that the signal was interrupted just at the moment a call or text was trying to come through. That can happen sometimes, I've heard. I switch it off and on again but still nothing arrives, so I quickly write a text to myself – 'Hi Beth, how r u? I'm fine c u l8r' – and send it. Sometimes one message coming through forces a load of others through, like toothpaste. It doesn't work, though. In fact, not even the message I've sent arrives. Ridiculous – the phone's right here, the message doesn't even have to go anywhere.

Right, I'll phone Vini at home and see if there have been any calls.

'No,' she says. 'Unless you include Philip from Northern Finance, who wasted the only two seconds I was going to give him by asking me how I was. Moron. I told him I was feeling sad because everything is so fragile and temporary and there is no sense to our existence because we know that whatever we do, we are all just going to die in the end anyway, so what's the point of even trying?'

'OK. So no calls, then?'

There's a meaningful pause. 'Are you . . . expecting a call?'

I hesitate before answering. I didn't tell her about swapping numbers with Brad last night. My anticipation of the awfulness of the evening didn't quite come to fruition, thanks entirely to Brad, but I don't want her to know that. God, she is going to be impossible to live with when she finds out that speed dating actually works. In the car on the way home I was bursting to grin and bounce in my seat and shriek 'I love you, world!' out of the window, but I stayed all monosyllabic and grumpy, just to make sure she knew that the whole evening was a complete waste of time, as I predicted. It's a good job I am so aware of what signals and messages my outward appearance is giving out, because she was absolutely clueless about my real state of mind. But, of course, that only delayed the moment of her finding out she was right; I can't avoid it for ever.

Hang on. Maybe I can avoid it for ever. What if I just tell her that Brad and I had a Chance Encounter in Whytelys, and that's it? He was never at the Seahorse, he never ticked any boxes. Yes! That will work, and she will never need to know where it really happened. The best thing is that it is pretty much true. Everyone knows that if you are planning on deceit, the thing to do is to stay as close to the truth as possible; and this is such a beautiful, perfect plan because it's so close to the truth, there is almost no chance of me being found out.

'You fucking ticked someone last night, didn't you?' she says at this moment.

Bugger.

I pause a moment, then say, probably not very convincingly, 'No.'

'Liar!'

'No, I'm not, because this man is the same—'

'I knew it! I could tell, on the way home last night, you were all fidgety and squirmy in your seat, it was so obvious. Jesus Christ, Beth, why didn't you tell me? Oh, no, wait a minute, let me guess. You didn't want to admit that my plan had actually worked, which makes it instantly better than yours! I'm right, aren't I?'

'Don't be so stupid, Vini. Not everything is about you, you know. Anyway, I've got work to do now. I'll tell you about it later. Bye.'

Bloody hell.

Right. I'm logging on to the computer now, and I've got my password right this time. Actually, I had to write it down because I still can't seem to think clearly, but don't worry, I've eaten the piece of paper I wrote it on. Richard always insists on everyone being very security conscious and just because he is away at the moment is no reason to be slack about it. Although frankly, I can't really imagine someone breaking into my account and putting my 'The Importance of Being Honest' PowerPoint thing on eBay five minutes later. But Richard always says you can't trust anyone.

'All right, Beth?' Sean says suddenly behind me. I jump and turn in my chair a bit too fast so I have to slam my feet on the floor to stop myself doing a full three-hundred-and-sixty-degree spin in front of him. I bring myself to a skidding halt facing roughly the place where he has stopped to greet me as he walked past.

'Er . . . Hi, Sean. Thanks, yes. Thank you.' And then for good measure, I add, 'Sorry.'

He smiles and takes a step towards me, leaning over slightly, as if we're sharing a private joke. 'Let me tell you, you have . . . *nothing* . . . to be sorry for. All right?'

I nod but don't allow my lips to open. The little pauses he leaves before and after the word 'nothing' clearly mean something, and I'm struggling to understand. On top of that, I am stunned that he has decided to stop and talk to me at all. I think this is probably the second time he has spoken to me one-to-one since we have known each other. The first one was: 'Hi, I'm Sean Cousins. Where do I sit?'

He lingers a second or two more while I try to get

him to go away by telekinesis. It might even have worked because finally he turns to go, but not without a little wink at me at the last moment.

My mouth almost falls open in surprise – don't worry, I didn't let it. But I mean, Sean Cousins *winking* at me? This is the bloke who would probably hand his fiancée over to the natives in exchange for a boat to get off the island. What is going on? I look around the room stupidly for a second, checking that I am actually in the right office.

Well I am, of course. I didn't really think I wasn't. But you can forgive me for being a bit mystified. That was about as unexpected as it would be seeing Vini in pearl earrings. She's more Girl With a Skull Nose Ring.

Right. Forget about Sean. Maybe he's having a mid-life crisis. Doesn't matter. I am finally logged on to the computer and am heading straight for my Hotmail inbox to see what funny and romantic message Brad has sent me this morning, having no doubt been up all night thinking about me and the wonderful turn his life seems to be taking at the moment. He will be poetic, affectionate, hopeful, a little anxious maybe, wondering if I feel the same, if he dares to hope that this will be the start of something, the first day of a beautiful, passionate relationship that will seal us together for ever.

Bugger it. There's nothing there.

OK, right, I am not disappointed. In fact, it's probably a good thing that I haven't had contact yet because it would be a distraction from doing the other really important thing I've got planned for today, the details of which will come back to me in just a minute.

Someone like Brad is bound to have a job and probably can't email or phone during the day anyway. He will probably ring me tonight, no need to panic. I can easily wait until then. Or I can check again in a few minutes. For now, I am one hundred per cent concentrating on—

I think I'll just put my mobile on the desk. I never hear it when it rings in my bag.

Where was I? Oh yes, one hundred per cent focused. Now what was it that I was focused on again? Oh yes: finding a way to get the attention of Rupert de Twitter, when he is no doubt constantly surrounded by people who are all trying to get his attention.

I go out of Hotmail and open a new email from my Love Learning account, and in doing so come to the end of my ideas. Fuck. OK, don't worry, just concentrate. What do I know about him? Just about all the information I've got about him is from Richard, which leaves me not looking forward to having to be nice to him. Now I come to think about it, I did meet him once myself unofficially, in Sainsbury's, years ago when I was still working at Horizon. I recognized him from the brochures, although he was looking a lot more dishevelled in Sainsbury's than in that glossy photo. Less square-jawed, chiselled Adonis, more blind drunk. He rammed his trolley right into mine.

'Oops, sorry,' he said distractedly, not looking at me.

'No problem,' I answered, deciding right at the last minute not to add 'sir' or 'Mr de Witter' as I veered off to the side.

'Oh, hey, look, you don't know where anchovies are, do you?' he asked me suddenly, raising his head from the ragged slip of paper in his hand and almost focusing properly on me for the first time.

'Oh, no, I don't, sorry.'

'You know, you're absolutely right. They're completely disgusting. Thanks for the tip.' And he trudged slowly away.

So the only thing I know about the man is that he is an arsehole who likes anchovies. Or thinks they're disgusting. Oh, and he's a multi-millionaire. So quite a shrewd businessman, which means totally ruthless. Shit. The words of my email have got to be so startling, so brilliant, that he will sit up in his chair, smack his head with his hand and say out loud, 'So that's where we've been going wrong! Get me Love Learning on the phone!' But I've got nothing.

I watch the clock tick round from 12.52 until 1.13, feeling exactly the same mounting panicky feeling of being in an exam and not having a clue how to answer any of the questions. Finally, with ten minutes of my lunch-break left, I come up with something. It's not exactly the astonishing, sit-up-and-take-notice message I was hoping to come up with, but it's a start.

Dear Mr de Witter,
Do you ever wear shoes? If so, would you please send me, at your earliest convenience, a description of them?
Yours,
Beth Sheridan
Love Learning

I know, not exactly explosive, mind-blowing, attention-demanding rhetoric. I picture Rupert de Witter sitting in his glass-paned office reading this lame effort and flicking his highlights back as he laughs derisively and bangs out a Simon Cowell type answer:

> That was one hundred per cent average. You should go back
> to the pubs and clubs where your style of email is likely to be
> popular because you ain't gonna make it in this business, darling.

I shake the image out of my head and comfort myself with the thought that a man who sits for three hours in the hairdresser's every six weeks having segments of his hair painted blond and folded up in foil is not a hundred per cent focused on what's important, like Third World debt and good grammar. I expect his assistants have to use words with only one syllable. Well, it's too late to worry about it now, I've sent it. Dear God, let him reply. Amen.

For the rest of the day, the delegates are baffled by a variety of little syndicate exercises, so I can leave the room every half-hour and check my emails and my phone. They probably think I've got a tummy bug, or have developed obsessive–compulsive disorder overnight and am rushing out every few minutes to check the car park for aliens. Or is that schizophrenia? Anyway, it was all a waste of time because I have had no messages from anyone.

At home, Vini is doing housework at arm's length. She likes to keep her distance from menial tasks and dirt generally.

'Hi,' I say dispiritedly, flopping down onto the sofa.

'Hi!' She grins back at me. 'Fancy a cuppa? I've bought some biccies.' And she whips off her Marigolds and skips off into the kitchen.

Oh my God, what's going on? Am I in the wrong flat?

This has never happened before, in all the years we've lived together. She's more likely to be found hunched on the floor over a glass of pomegranate juice painting her toenails black.

'You all right?' I ask, following her into the kitchen. Jesus, she's wearing a red T-shirt that says 'Happy Kissmas' in silver glitter. With jeans. Quickly I grab the counter top to steady myself as the room starts spinning around me.

She nods enthusiastically. 'Yep. Why wouldn't I be?'

I'm staring at her. 'Vin . . . are you wearing . . . pink lip-gloss?'

She fiddles with her hair and presses her lips together self-consciously in a secret little smile. 'Just trying it out. Nothing wrong with that, is there?'

'No, no, course not. I'm just a bit . . . surprised, that's all.'

'Right, well, whatever. Look, I'm off out now. Very important meeting tonight. My whole future could depend on this. I've made a casserole, it's in the oven, just leave it in for an hour and a half, OK? Don't wait up for me.'

I'm still reeling from the casserole news when she hits me with another one. 'Oh, I picked up a TV guide in town. It's on the coffee table.'

And then she's gone. In my tan suede jacket and boots again. She's always going out to functions where her clients are making appearances – that's no surprise. This important, life-changing meeting is probably watching Nicole Kidman open the new car wash on the industrial estate – but she looks so different. There was definitely more pink about her than I could actually see, which is totally unlike her. Maybe she really has decided to make a fresh start.

So I'm alone for the night. Perfect. At last I can get some research done into Horizon, and Rupert de Witter. I get my mobile phone out of my bag and lay it on the desk next to me, just in case it rings and I don't hear it. There's nothing more annoying than ringing someone's mobile and they don't answer it. I mean, what's the point of having a mobile in the first place? Then I log on to the internet.

Horizon Holidays have got a wonderful website. Their IT team have obviously moved beyond 'Introduction to Using a Mouse' in leaps and bounds. I click on various images to move around the site – pictures of beaches take me to the beach holiday page, aeroplanes take me to flights, crutches take me to insurance – but no inspiration comes.

The strange thing is, clicking through every page of the website, including 'About Horizon' and the home page, there are no pictures of Rupert anywhere, other than the same old picture that is featured at the back of all the brochures. I wonder why that is? That photo from the brochures has been the same since I started working there, and that's about eight years ago. Why hasn't he updated it? And why aren't there any publicity photos – him on a cruise ship or handing out prize money, or something?

Well, the website isn't telling me anything useful, except that maybe Love Learning ought to get one. Only we no longer have a manager with an IT qualification to help us out.

I shut down the computer and pick up my mobile. Who am I kidding? I can't focus on Rupert de Sodding

Witter. I'm still getting a strong signal on the phone so that can't be the problem. The landline handset is droning away too, the monotone sound telling me that the line is connected and working and Brad isn't trying to contact me.

I don't get it. I'm sure he was keen yesterday. I mean, there was all that banter and flirty body language, wasn't there? Quick recap of Brad sitting opposite me yesterday at Fast Love: eyes (beautiful shining brown, crinkled at the edges with long thick lashes) focused on me; mouth (top lip slightly fuller, sensuous and sexy) smiling; entire body (unnnhhhhhh) leaning towards me, arms open, hands resting gently on the table . . . A dragging feeling in my belly is pulling me down in my seat and making my breath come faster. Christ, it's been a long time. I sit up and clear my throat. Come on, Beth, get a grip. I glance quickly towards the door but of course no one, especially Richard, is standing there.

OK, so it's plainly obvious to anyone observing me that I fancy him. And I think it's safe to say that he fancied me too. So why hasn't he called me yet? Why didn't his hand leap to the keypad of his telephone the second he cracked his eyes open this morning?

This is obviously the duplicitous nature of men. They smile at you, they laugh with you, they make themselves look lickably delicious so you get all quivery and powerless, and then they dangle you there like a Christmas bauble for weeks until the string breaks. Those bastards – we're definitely better off without them. Unless they call.

A graphic image suddenly grips me: Brad lying prone by the side of the road, trickles of blood on his white shirt, lumps of broken glass strewn around him, his buckled arm outstretched and still clutching his mobile phone, my own number clearly visible in the display, prevented from clicking through to me by the sudden unexpected impact with a cement lorry. Oh my God – he didn't ring me because he had a ghastly accident. This is fantastic! I jump up and start waltzing round the room singing 'Brad crashed on the roadside, whoa-oh!' to the tune of 'Walking on Sunshine', grinning as I hug this wonderful image to myself.

I'm not serious of course. This is just a fantasy and I know that very well. Quickly I change the cement lorry into a small white electricity van – I want him in a hospital bed, not a coffin.

An hour later I'm lying in bed, staring blankly at the ceiling. It doesn't matter how much I try and convince myself that he is grotesquely injured somewhere and unable to dial the phone with his poor mangled fingers, I know it's not very likely. The fact is that he hasn't contacted me because he chose not to, and I really should have known that right from the start because I'm realizing now that speed dating is nothing more than another one of those peachy little changes I was telling you about; and as we know all change is vile and cruel because it promises so much, makes you realize that something else is possible, another, better life is there, waiting, just within your reach, and all you have to do is grab it.

But I know it's a false hope, a cruel joke, because change, just like speed dating, can only be properly evaluated by its success; and lying here in the dark, on my own again, my personal evaluation has to be that speed dating is arse.

Eight

Persuading and Influencing

**Short-term Goal: Be far too busy to think about . . .
whatever his name was.**
Obstacles: Thinking about Brad.
**Long-term Goal: Wait for Richard to realize that he
can't exist without me I suppose.**
**Obstacles: He's taking his own sweet time to realize
it.**

My dreams are filled with blurry images of someone standing behind a mottled glass wall, their hands pressed pleadingly against the surface, their mouth a shadowy hole as they call out indistinct words in anguished, muted tones. I squint and stare but no matter how hard I try I can't make out who it is. It's got to be either Brad or Bungle from *Rainbow*.

But I'm not going to indulge myself by thinking about him today. Or Brad. Ha ha. No, today I am focused on de Twitter and getting this damn contract. Brad is either in traction or a lying, deceitful slug, so if he calls at all it will be after he gets muscle control back, which won't be for weeks. There is no point wasting any more time on checking my phone and inbox every fifteen minutes.

Of course, it only takes two minutes to check my emails when I get to work, so that doesn't really count. There's nothing from him anyway. Tosser.

Or poor, shattered man.

Fatima has just turned up, wearing a hat that looks like a giant felt cake with felt candles on the top and plays 'For She's a Jolly Good Fellow' when you press the rim. The ends of the candles even light up, like little flames.

'What's the hat for, Fats?' Mike says with a cheerful and frankly jaw-droppingly stupid lack of imagination.

'It's my birthday!' she squeals, shedding light into Mike's personal gloom. 'Wish me happy birthday!'

'Happy birthday,' everyone says dutifully.

'What did you get?' I ask her as she sits down at her desk.

'Ooh, look, I got this phone from my mum and dad,' she says, producing it from a pocket. 'It's got a camera and a video and Bluetooth and WAP and plays MP3s.'

'Wow.' I take the phone and turn it over in my hand. 'Do you know what an MP3 is?'

She shakes her head enthusiastically. 'Not really.'

'What about Bluetooth? Or WAP?'

'No, no, but that's why I got this phone, so I could find out.'

'Right. Good plan, Fats.'

'I know! Listen, are you coming to the Bell Pull at lunch for a birthday drink? My treat.'

I hesitate. I know that getting the Horizon contract is going to involve a lot of hard work and commitment,

111

so I've really got to do some research. If Rupert de Witter gets back to me, it would help if I knew a bit about him and his company before we meet. On the other hand, having a drink on a friend's birthday is a great activity to be found doing by someone who hasn't seen you for about three months and walks in suddenly, determined to find you and make you his. It will be obvious I am not missing him at all. 'Well . . .'

'Come on, blondie,' a slow voice drawls behind me. I turn in my seat to find Sean standing very close behind me, his head on one side, regarding me intently. 'Pleeease come for a drink at lunchtime. It isn't Fatima's birthday every day, is it? And she did say it was her treat, so she'll be . . . *very* disappointed . . . if you don't come.'

He's leaving pauses in his speech again, and again I'm struggling to understand what it means. 'Um . . .'

'Oh go on, Beth, please,' Fatima bursts out. 'Even if it's just for half an hour, I really want you to come. It won't be the same if you're not there, please?'

'She's right, it won't be,' Sean says. He flicks his eyebrows up once with a suggestive Mel Gibson grin, turns and moves back to his own desk.

It's extraordinary. Sean has barely acknowledged my existence before, and now he's even got a nickname for me. It must have been a very expensive hair dye. I look from Sean to Fatima, who has wheeled her seat right up next to me and is leaning as far towards me as she can, her hands clasped together. The hat has slipped a bit and is tilting dangerously over on one side, wobbling. I move my seat back a little: I don't want to be under that thing when it comes down. 'OK,

I'll come. But I can't stay long, Fats. I've got this really urgent thing to do.'

'Hooray!' she yells. 'Yippee! Happy birthday to me!'

After a really stressful morning discussing conflict, I decide to have a quick check of my Hotmails, just in case someone has emailed me something really urgent and important, like, you know, details of a nought per cent interest credit card or something. They haven't, and I couldn't help noticing there's nothing from Brad either. But very interestingly, my work account is showing that I have had a reply from Rupert de Witter. This is a surprise – I wasn't expecting anything from him for a few days, at least. But then, he can't be that busy or he wouldn't have time to get his fake tan done every six weeks, would he? I suppose his assistants do all the real work, and just bring him a clipboard to sign every so often, like the captain of the USS *Enterprise*.

'You have the bridge, Number One. I am beaming down to the new planet to get my St Tropez topped up.'

'Aye aye, Captain.'

Anyway, there's a reply. It says:

From: Rupert de Witter
To: Bethsheridan@lovelearning.co.uk
Re: Shoes

Dear Miss Sheridan,
Thank you so much for your kind enquiry. I am delighted to be able to inform you that I do indeed have a leaning towards attire for the lower extremities of my person, and have been known to sport footwear on more than one occasion.

Today, my apparel in that region is a rather dull, size 9 black lace-up.
I look forward to hearing from you.
Mr R. de Witter
Horizon Holidays

I read it again, a smile spreading across my face. Is this real? Is this the arrogant arsehole that Richard moaned on and on about? He seems quite charming and well mannered to me. The whole persuading him to see me and then influencing him to sign a contract with us won't be so hard if he isn't the 'pig-ignorant, fuck-faced titbrain' that Richard said he was. My frankly rather lame idea about the shoes amazingly seems to be working, and far better already than I could have imagined. I tried a humorous approach, and an intriguing one, to get his interest, but truthfully, expecting him to be an arrogant arsehole with probably no real wit or intelligence, I didn't actually expect him to get it.

Although could it have been typed by one of his assistants? He's no doubt a very busy titbrain, so it wouldn't be unheard of to get someone to answer on his behalf. But it does have his name at the bottom, not something like 'Tarquin van Hoople, Assistant to Mr de Witter'. Perhaps Rupert dictated the message, and Tarquin wrote it out. According to Richard, he's an uneducated lout, so I thought that if he replied at all it would be something along the lines of, 'Yes of corse I ware shose why do you wont to no'.

But it's encouraging to think that he is intrigued enough by my message to make sure that his spelling and grammar are correct.

I am desperate to reply but of course we are all going out to the pub in a minute. And at that moment, Chas appears. I drag my eyes away from the screen towards him.

'OK, listen up, people,' he says, clapping his hands. Apparently he's just been watching some cheesy American drama. 'We've got ourselves a bit of a situation here,' he goes on, glaring around the room. At the door, Fats in her hat pauses as she is pulling on her coat and turns to stare at him. 'I think you all know what I'm talking about. I think you're all very well aware of what's been going on. Love Learning is in trouble, and you all know it. And yet some among you are failing to make a satisfactory contribution.' His eyes, which have been roaming around the room, now come to rest squarely on Fatima. Her face drops as she glances around nervously, the giant hat wobbling on her head. 'I will not tolerate anyone who does not contribute,' he says, his voice low and menacing. 'I will not tolerate anyone who thinks it's OK to swan around doing nothing while everyone else is working. I will not tolerate anyone who *does not take this job seriously.*'

By now, everyone is looking at Fatima as she squirms in the hat. Chas's eyes seem to be boring into her and eventually she reaches up a hand and pulls off the hat, holding it by her side. This small action seems to release Chas from his fixation and he looks away at last and addresses the whole room again.

'Now, I want a report from each of you on how you are getting on establishing new contracts. Derek?'

As Derek bumbles on about whatever he's working on, I glance back at Fats. She's crouching down by her desk, stuffing the huge hat as far under it as she

115

can reach, whispering to herself. 'Stupid hat . . . can't believe I wore it . . . should have known better . . .' She's wearing a trembly smile, but I can see from here that her eyes are very shiny. She sniffs quietly once and blinks quickly, dragging one hand across each eye, then pushes her chair under the desk and stands up.

'Beth?' Chas says suddenly.

Shit. I don't want to tell him what I'm working on because then everyone else will know about Horizon and I want to keep the advantage. But I also don't want him to think I haven't been doing anything. 'Oh, er, something in the pipeline,' I say hurriedly.

'Not good enough,' he barks. 'Sean?'

Not good enough! Not fucking *good* enough? How dare he? Doesn't he know that I have been single-handedly responsible for practically all of Love Learning's success so far and that without me, he probably wouldn't even have that job? Well, no, I suppose he doesn't since he's only been here for three months. But I worked here for six years before he appeared – what qualifies him to tell me my work isn't good enough? I clench my fists and grit my teeth, just managing at the last moment to stop myself from snarling. I feel like leaping onto his back and ripping his head off his shoulders with my teeth and spitting it down the stairwell, but I make do with looking deeply affronted.

'And finally, Fatima,' he says, sickly sweet. 'Got anything at all, lovey?'

'I . . . ye– . . . Um . . . The th . . . It's . . .'

'Oh, look, it's all right, poppet, don't you worry about any silly old contracts. Nasty things. You just carry on with . . . whatever it is that you're doing and leave the complicated stuff to the rest of us. All right, lovey?' Fatima's lip shakes and the threatened tears finally start to slide down her face but Chas doesn't see this as he turns his attention to the rest of us and draws his brows meaningfully together. 'Lights off, people. Right? Don't fill the kettle to the top. Print on both sides of the paper. Hot drinks for delegates are now thirty pence a cup. Got it? Little economies here and there will make all the difference. Don't make me tell you again. Right?' He leaves the frown there for a few seconds, then deliberately contorts it into a beatific grin. 'Now, time for birthday celebrations, isn't it? First drink's on me.'

Fatima is rather subdued in the pub later. Turns out she had some little games planned – a music quiz, couple of magic tricks, pass the parcel – and she goes through the motions, but the intuitive, sensitive part of me can tell that her joyous sense of fun has slipped a little.

'For fuck's sake, Cath, just rip it off.'

'I feel sorry for her,' Sean says quietly in my ear later as we're all walking back to the office.

'Sorry, what?'

Sean is unwrapping the box of chocolates that was inside the parcel, then holds it out for me to take one. He's wearing fingerless gloves. 'Fatima. I feel sorry for her. She works hard, tries her best. Not her fault she's not a great salesperson.'

I stare at him, astounded. I mean, I know I don't know him well but I always thought he was the sort of person who could shoot and eat his own dog. Sympathy for a scatterbrained colleague I would not have put him down for. Maybe I've misjudged him.

Now that I come to look at him properly, his slightly unkempt, down-at-heel look, which has always made me think of wily card sharps down on their luck, is actually quite sexy in a dangerous, dirty kind of way. Something about him suddenly makes me want to reach out and cut his hair.

'No, I know. You're right. She didn't deserve to be spoken to like that.'

'No way. Chas is an arsehole.' He is walking so close to me his arm keeps brushing against mine. 'So,' he says, nodding at me as we keep pace. The word comes out of his mouth in a cloud.

'So?'

He grins. 'So, Miss Sheridan. You look really good.'

It's odd but I'm starting to get used to this and my face won't even blush. Probably because it's already red from two glasses of spiced wine. 'Thanks.' I still try to look surprised, though, because that is a much more attractive response than 'Yes.'

'How's everything going with you?'

'Fine thanks. How about you?'

He blatantly looks me up and down, which I really should object to, and then he says, 'Truly fine, Beth. Truly . . . fine.'

'That's good.' I smile at him but I'm not really sure where this scintillating conversation is going.

'How's work going? Your Change Management thingy?'

'It's going well, I think. Nearly done now. Only two more days.'

'I'll bet they can't take their eyes off you, can they?'

'Oh, er, well . . .'

'I'll bet they are completely mesmerized by you.'

118

'Umm . . .' I can't agree with him – that would sound awful. But I really don't want to deny it and protest my own ordinariness either. Fortunately, at this moment I spot some Christmas lights on the roof of one of the houses nearby that would leave a carbon footprint the size of St Paul's Cathedral, and quickly change the subject. 'Look at that! Wow, it's amazing. I think I'll go round there and see if they've got an illuminated Santa. I'll see you back at the office, shall I?'

'I'll come with you,' he says with alacrity. 'I love those lights.'

'OK then. That will be nice.' Bugger, bugger, bugger.

We walk on in silence for a few moments, then turn down the next left.

'Oh, look,' he says, 'there *is* an illuminated Santa!' We stop and gaze at the gaudy display, which includes, for some reason, an illuminated Snow White and seven illuminated dwarfs. 'You've got a real knack for knowing stuff before it happens, haven't you?'

I stare at him. Obviously he's noticed my excellent track record for getting contracts, and has completely failed to notice the hours and hours of bloody hard graft I put in beforehand. Easier for him to believe I've got the knack, rather than admit that I work harder.

'Not really. I mean, that one was obvious. A house with lights as extravagant as that on its roof is nine times out of ten going to have the whole animatronic deer, Santa's grotto, elves and nativity scene going on.'

His eyes really are very, very blue from here. He's peering at me so intently and unwaveringly I feel all the hairs raise up on the back of my neck. I'm frantically raking through my head to find something to say, but I

119

can't think of anything. It's very difficult to focus with him staring at me like this. Come on, Beth, think.

'You're right,' he says, not taking his eyes from my face. 'And very clever.'

'Thanks.'

'No doubt you've already got a killer contract up your sleeve?'

I break eye contact to gaze anew at the wonderful scene before me. In the grass by the shed are three illuminated mushrooms. 'No, not really. I'm looking into something—'

'I knew it! Beth, you're amazing. What is it? Something big?'

I turn back to look into his eyes. It's just after one o'clock but the sky is heavy and overcast and some of the street lights are already flickering on. In this light, it's really hard to read his face. 'All right, Sean, I'll tell you, but you have to promise not to tell anyone. OK?'

He nods eagerly. 'I promise.'

'OK. Well then, I can tell you that . . .' He leans in closer and I can almost see a sparkle in his eyes. 'Yes, it is something big.'

He blinks. 'It's . . . Oh, right, well, that's great. Fantastic, Beth. I'm really pleased for you.'

'Thanks, Sean.'

He looks away, back down the road. Then back to me. 'Oh God, you're shivering. Come on, let's get back. It's nearly half past one.'

You didn't think I was going to tell him, did you? Come on! This guy pays me a teensy bit of attention one day

120

and you expect me to cave in like an ugly virgin and give him everything? You really ought to know me a bit better than that by now.

But I will have to be very careful around him from now on. Of all the people in the office, he is the one most likely to try and get information out of me by nefarious means, probably by tying me up and holding me somewhere until I crack. Somewhere dark and private, out of the way where no one will hear us, pressing himself up against me threateningly, his breath hot on my face. Suddenly I find that my heart is thudding, and as I glance over at him walking along next to me, goosebumps break out all over me.

Before I go back into the training room, I make time to log on to my emails and compose a reply to Rupert de Witter. Not fucking good enough, I think, staring at the wood-panelled door with loathing. I don't think so. I'm only working on a contract with one of the hugest businesses in the entire town. I read over Rupert's message again and find myself smiling as I click on Reply. It's so fantastic that he's entered into the spirit of it. I'm going to rub Chas's face in the contract paperwork when I get it. I mean, literally.

Although, the fact that Rupert has entered into the spirit of it might mean that he thinks I am a joke. I stop typing. Shit.

Well, it's too late to think about that now. I have started it and I need to continue. I resume typing and click on Send. At least he apparently likes my approach, and seems to be interested. But as Fast Love so aptly demonstrated, that doesn't mean anything.

From: Bethsheridan@lovelearning.co.uk
To: Rupert de Witter
Subject: Size 9 black lace-ups

Dear Mr de Witter,

Thank you so much for your prompt reply.

Can I assume that as your shoes are size 9, your feet are also size 9? I'm sure it will not come as a surprise to you to learn that recent studies show that 89% of people do, in fact, choose the shoes that are the same size as the feet, which is why I feel able to make the assumption above. Please correct me if I am wrong.

Yours,

Beth Sheridan, Love Learning

It's not until I've sent the message and am closing down the computer to head back into the training room that I realize I didn't even check to see if there was a message from Brad. Blimey. All that fluster over Sean has driven Brad out of my head.

The afternoon session runs short. It's meant to be three hours, with a half-hour coffee-break in the middle and a fifteen-minute exercise, but I've rushed through it and given them the exercise to do at home. It's not like me to do that, but for the first time in my career I am preoccupied while I'm training. That is unheard of for me. It didn't even happen when the Australian Olympic swim team visited our town. Admittedly, after work I was straight round to the Sports Centre, but it didn't impact on my work performance. Not that the delegates care: they're just glad to get out of here forty minutes early.

The reason I am so distracted is partly down to Sean and partly down to Brad, but mostly down to Rupert de Witter. I am very keen to find out if he has replied again, but before I can do that, I have to walk to my desk. As I pass Sean's desk, he follows my progress with his eyes, so I walk very slowly, apparently preoccupied with the folders I'm carrying. Then I have to reach up to the top shelf of the folder library to put the folders away. They didn't come from the top shelf, but that is where I want to put them. As I stretch up, my blouse comes untucked from my skirt at the back, and even rides up a bit to expose some flesh. Eventually I feel him arrive behind me, the heat of his body enfolding me, his breath just stirring the fine hairs on the back of my neck. He's obviously come to take the folders gently out of my hands and, his eyes never leaving mine, reach easily above me to slide them into place.

'You dozy cow, what are you doing?' says a voice not Sean's. I spin to find Mike standing there, hands on hips. 'Those folders don't go there. They go right here, second from bottom.'

'Oh, silly me. Thanks, Mike.'

I sit down. Well, that's that done. I risk a quick glance at Sean, but he's not looking at me. He probably just was, though, which is excellent. Now I need to see if there is an answer from Rupert.

Incredibly, there is.

From: Rupert de Witter
To: Bethsheridan@lovelearning.co.uk
Subject: Blisters

Dear Miss Sheridan,

Thank you for your email, which I received today.

You can indeed assume that my feet, also, are size 9. I find

it interesting that you refer to most people having feet the same
size as the shoes. Is this a national phenomenon, or confined
only to this part of the country?
Yours in hope,
Rupert de Witter

The first thing I notice is that he has written his name
at the bottom this time instead of just the initials. Then
I notice that he hasn't put 'Horizon Holidays' after
his name. After that, I spot what he's written in the
subject box and I actually laugh out loud. He's funny!
I certainly wasn't expecting that, from what Richard
always said about him.

'That knob-scratch has about as much intelligence
and wit as a baboon's arse,' he was heard to say – by me
– repeatedly about Rupert. Or variations on the theme.
Secretly, I always thought that actually baboons had
really funny arses, if they're the ones that look like
they've had all the fur burnt off them.

Although this is going far better than I anticipated
– which is not difficult as I was anticipating anything
between a curt rejection and a loud 'Piss off!' – the
promptness of Rupert's replies is causing an unexpected
problem. I thought it would take several days for him to
pull himself away from the salon and answer my email,
which would give me enough time, I hoped, to find out
lots of interesting facts about Horizon. And, of course,
compose the next devastatingly clever message. But he's
been replying very quickly, and now I am running out
of ideas. My original plan of likening training to shoes
because they have to fit perfectly is nearly played out,
and the way it's going, it's looking likely that I will be
meeting with him pretty soon to discuss it.

Quickly I log on to the Horizon website again, to see if anything comes to me. Immediately something does: his face. There he is, with his shining gold hair, bronzed skin, white, white teeth. Fuck, he is gorgeous. And a hundred times more witty and charming than a baboon's arse. No, a million times, come on, it's an arse we're talking about. And, let's not forget, very rich. I lean in closer to the picture and gaze at it. I'm so enthralled by it I'm even resting the entire weight of my head on my hand. God, what wouldn't I give to meet you? Crap, I *am* going to meet you. Double crap, what will I wear? I close my eyes as a delicious image comes to me of Rupert standing up to receive me as I glide into his office in a *Pretty Woman* style strapless black cocktail dress. His beautiful mouth falls open as he moves towards me. 'You're late,' I say. 'You're beautiful,' he says. 'You're forgiven,' I say with a wide smile.

I sit up again. Come on, Beth, get a grip. A cocktail dress, for God's sake? You'll be in a power suit because you will be there in a work capacity, trying to convince him to sign you up for all his training needs, not for hot sex and lifelong commitment. Although if I couldn't get the first, I'd settle for the second.

Oh my God, I am incoherent. His luscious face is such an enormous distraction, I don't know how I'm ever going to be able to speak in his presence. Or remain upright. And fully clothed. Quickly I scan the rest of the website to see if anything else can inspire me, and it does. On one of the pages is a small photograph of the telesales office, featuring a couple of smiling telesellers in headphones, and Jean the supervisor, standing grimly behind them, arms folded. It looks fairly recent, and that means that a cameraman has been in there taking pictures, at least once. Which does not make me think of putting a camera round my neck and sticking a fake press pass in the rim of my hat; but I could maybe *sneak* in and have a look round. Maybe chat to someone in the lift about job satisfaction. It's such a huge place, no one knows everyone, not even Rupert de Witter himself. In fact, he probably knows fewer of the staff than most because half the time he's locked away in his office on the seventh floor, and the rest of the time he's having his roots done. Maybe I could even get in to see him and pretend to be one of his employees. I could moan about the training! And then when we do finally meet legitimately, he will recognize me, nod his head and say, 'Touché.' That will definitely make him want to have sex with me. I mean, make a deal with me.

On the drive home I pass the time by imagining all sorts of scenarios featuring me in a crowd of admirers doing something heroic or hilarious and being observed doing it by Rupert. I know, you're surprised that Richard isn't featuring in there any more. Well don't worry, I am still in love with him, this is just a distraction until he comes back to claim me. And if it becomes more, I've always got the 'This ship has sailed, baby' option waiting patiently at the back of my mind.

I should have been passing the time by focusing on the drive because it's not until I'm entering the flat that I realize I have missed the entire journey again. I don't even know if I brought the right car home. I could have got into anyone's car and driven it home. Or anywhere. I could even have committed a crime on the journey. Pointed a sawn-off shotgun into a shop assistant's face;

driven at high speed into a cashpoint machine; or gone the wrong way up a one-way road. I look down at my hands, as if I expect to find a smoking gun there, or blood. But all I have is my own car keys, which is reassuring.

What is it about Rupert de Witter that makes me forget what I'm doing? Oh, yes, of course, he's meltingly sexy. Silly me.

Vini is standing in the hallway clutching a bundle of clothes which she holds out to me the second I close the front door. 'Get these on, I'm taking you out.'

I eye the bundle. It's black for a start and looks as if it's made from old jogging trousers. 'What is it?'

'It's my old jogging trousers. Come on, hurry up.'

'No thanks, Vin. If we're going out, I am going to try and make a bit of an effort. Which means a skirt or some jeans.'

'Not where we're going you're not. Come on, Beth, it'll be fun.'

This doesn't sound good. Last time she made me put comfy clothes on it was a Movement and Music class in the community centre. We had to be trees. I'm not doing that again.

'No way. Forget it. Not in a million, not ever, nada, nyet, non, nein.'

'Look, it's not Earthy Dancing, or whatever that other thing was called. It's just the gym. It's fun and good for you and full of fit, muscly blokes for us to flirt with.'

'Give me two minutes.'

Nine

Fit for Purpose (i)

Short-term Goal: Walk again.
**Obstacles: I can't. Don't want to. No one can make
  me.**
Long-term Goal: Die. Soon.
Obstacles: Can't reach anything lethal.

So I'm not fit. I probably knew that already.

Nine

Fit for Purpose (ii) – Adapting

Short-term Goal: Stagger to Horizon building. Try to move around a bit. Stand stiffly next to Rupert and find stuff out. Get home afterwards.
Obstacles: All my muscles are bleeding.
Long-term Goal: Make the pain stop. Please God, make it stop.
Obstacles: Can't move arms.

OK. Let me tell you something about the gym. First of all, people are wearing sunglasses in there. What's that all about? I mean, it's midwinter, it's seven o'clock in the evening, it's very dark and cold, there is no need for them. In fact, I think that secretly they know there's no need for them, which is why they're all wearing them up on top of their heads.

This, of course, makes running or vigorous exercise of any kind quite tricky because the sunglasses have a habit of slipping down over their eyes, or straight off onto the floor. Consequently, the first thing I'm aware of when I walk in is a lot of well-structured women in lycra, edging very carefully along on the treadmills, trying not to break out in a sweat and disturb their foundation.

'Come on,' Vini says excitedly, pulling me towards the bikes. 'Bikes are easy.'

OK, well that's true. I haven't been on a bike since I was about fourteen, but it all comes back to me as soon as I'm in the saddle. Right, I'm thinking, this is OK, I can do this. I set the timer for a twenty-minute work-out and then have a good look around me.

Very quickly I realize two things: first, there is a huge flaw in Vini's plan for us to flirt with all the muscly blokes here. The room is populated almost entirely by different-sized women. There's enough variety here to suit every taste, if it's women you're after, which makes it incomprehensible that there aren't more men here. I can spot one or two at the back of the room where the weights are, but they are intensely involved with the weights they're lifting, and, frankly, they've got plenty to get on with – there are lots of weights there that need to be picked up and put back down again. They have to do this in front of a mirror, by the way, so that they can imagine how great they would look lifting a car off a trapped child.

Anyway, everyone is wearing headphones, too, so they all go around the room as if they're the only person here. No one even acknowledges anyone else; they just stay out of each other's way like bats, presumably using some kind of gym sonar.

The second thing I realize is that twenty minutes is too fucking long on a bike.

'Cross-trainers then?' Vini suggests, so we head over there.

I'm not going to go into detail here. I am very good at

130

my job. I am intelligent and fairly witty, quite attract-ive, I make a great tiramisu, I'm good at Scrabble, I am smart and clean and can do simple arithmetic in my head.

I can't balance on a cross-trainer. Let's leave it there.

The next day is Friday and it finds me sitting very still at my desk, watching the clock tick round to the moment when I have to get up again. I am focusing hard on getting up without hyperventilating.

This afternoon I am planning to pay a covert visit to Horizon, but after Vini showed me all the amazing benefits a good workout at the gym can give you, like strengthening my heart and lungs, improving my circulation, losing weight and prolonging my life, I have spent the day praying for death. She left the house before I got up this morning. I think she's avoiding me, which is completely unnecessary as she is safer from me now than she has ever been.

It's the last day of the Change Management work-shop today and I'm missing it. And do you know what? I don't even care. I told Derek that I've hurt my back, which explains my stiff, robotic movements (can't admit to being stiff from the gym – that's pathetic at my age), and asked him if he would mind doing the wrap-up today. I knew that he would – he's the sort of person who thinks everyone only just manages to get by without him.

'Happy to step in, Beth,' he said, nodding with his eyes half closed. 'Least I can do.' Which presumably means he thinks he is pulling my workshop back from the brink of failure in the nick of time. No doubt the group will be disappointed, and somewhat mystified, to be sitting in front of a cretin in a cravat instead of me, but I've got a bigger dish to spy.

I thought I might go after lunch, which leaves me with the morning to while away checking my emails again. Fatima isn't here yet, and it's almost ten, which is unlike her, but it means that I can sit here in peace and compose witty, interesting and devastatingly attractive emails to a certain person without interruption.

I reread Rupert's last message from yesterday, which asks whether feet and shoes being the same size is a national phenomenon. I'm smiling as I'm reading it, thinking that he's quite appealing in a callous, cold-hearted businessman kind of way. Mustn't allow my chronic celibacy affliction to cloud my judgement. I click on Reply.

From: Bethsheridan@lovelearning.co.uk
To: Rupert de Witter
Subject: Comfort

Dear Mr de Witter,

Thank you so much for your recent correspondence. I have spent some time conducting extensive research into your enquiry and have found some quite staggering results. It seems that the feet of shoe-wearers the length and breadth of the country are contained within shoes that are exactly the same size as the feet. Indeed, in the entire extent of my research, I found only one person who was wearing shoes that were not the same size as the feet. Her feet were a child size 7, and she was wearing an adult size 6, apparently belonging to another member of her immediate family. I questioned her about this apparent departure from the norm, and her motives for cladding herself thus, but her response was inconclusive. 'I am a princess,' was not deemed a satisfactory explanation for this extraordinary choice. In spite of repeated questioning, the subject provided no insight, and eventually fell asleep.

I have a theory as to the explanation for the phenomenon of shoes and feet being equal, and will be happy to share it with you, if you desire. I will await your further instruction.

Yours sincerely

Beth Sheridan, Love Learning

OK. Now all I have to do is sit here and wait for him to reply. Perfectly still. I'd twiddle my thumbs but the ripping, twisted agony in my muscles makes any kind of movement feel like medieval torture. Well, I should be all right, as long as no one—

'Hey, Beth,' says a voice behind me and I spin round to face the speaker. Then scream, 'Owwww! Shitting bollocking fuuucking *Chriiiist*!' Silently in my head, of course. Outwardly I am Little Mermaid calm, smiling prettily as a million daggers pierce every inch of my flesh. She thought she had it bad just with knives in her feet. She really didn't have any right to complain. Well, technically she didn't complain at all, did she, being mute.

'You all right?' the voice goes on and I realize that I probably look a bit weird, ramrod straight in my chair, hardly daring to inflate my chest, looking straight ahead of me and smiling like a loon.

'Yes, I'm fine thanks.' I raise just my eyes without moving my neck and find Sean bending slightly in the middle, trying to make eye contact with me.

'You don't look fine. No, I don't mean that. You most certainly do look fine. Very fine. What I mean is, you don't look well. Are you sure you're OK?'

'Oh, yes, just hurt my back yesterday. I'll be all right in a couple of days. Honestly.'

He pulls up Fatima's chair and sits down next to me, which is a huge relief. My eyebrows were getting tired. 'Fancy a massage?' He links his fingers together and flexes them out backwards. 'I've been told that I'm bloody good at it.'

'No, it's all right, thanks.'

He drops his hands to his lap. 'I was only kidding, Beth. You don't need to look so terrified.'

Bum, do I look terrified? That's not the kind of message I want to be sending when an attractive man offers me a massage. Quickly I focus on my forehead and eyelids, getting them into a more relaxed expression. 'No, God, sorry, I'm just terrified of the pain, that's all. My back is agony.'

'Fair enough. Are you itching to get on with something?'

I realize when he says this that my attention has been drawn back to my computer, which has just pinged the arrival of a message. I drag my eyes back to Sean. 'Well, yes, kind of. Sorry, I'm a bit distracted.'

'Is there anything I can help you with?'

I face him properly. All these years I've assumed he has a secret agenda, just because he has narrow eyes and a slow, drawly voice. Maybe he is a decent, honest bloke after all, and I let his appearance affect the way I feel about him.

'Erm,' I say, glancing at my computer, wondering if I could take him into my confidence. What harm could it do, after all? He's a colleague, we both want the same thing, surely? And as the old adage goes, two

134

heads are better than one. He might even be able to help me.

And then I come to my senses.

'No thanks, Sean. It's very kind of you but I'm on top of it. I'm going out later so there's not much you could do anyway.' Jesus, that was close.

'Really? Where are you off to then?'

I tilt my head slightly (SHIIIIT!) and smile. 'You're very persistent, aren't you? Why are you so keen to find out what I'm doing? Trying to steal my idea?'

He frowns and recoils from me, sitting up and pushing the chair back slightly. 'Is that what you think? Do you really think of me like that, Beth? That I'm trying to talk to you, to be near you, just to insinuate myself into your life and find out what lousy contract you're going for? Because that . . .' His voice trails off and he shakes his head. 'That is . . .' He puts his hands up in a defeated gesture, shakes his head again, smiles and starts to get up.

'No, look I'm sorry, it was only a joke. I didn't mean it. Of course that's not what I think.'

He pauses, half lifted off the seat. 'Really?'

'Really.'

'OK then.' He sits down again. 'Because the truth is, I do actually want to be near you. And talk to you. And look at you. Not for any ulterior reason, just because . . . Well, it must be obvious. Isn't it?'

'You know, you'd think so, but really it isn't.'

He chuckles. 'Jesus, Beth! I fancy you. Something rotten. Go out with me. Tonight.'

I stare at him. This is not what I was expecting at all. Actually, it might well have been, because I have got no idea what I was expecting. But Sean and I have known each other for a couple of years – why has he asked me out now? Could it be the hair? After all this time, he finally fancies me, because of my hair? Blimey, I wonder how much this dye cost. I'll have to ask Vini where she bought it. 'Oh, I did a dodgy barter for it with a wizened old Chinese man in a dark basement shop somewhere. He said something about three important rules . . .'

I look back at Sean. He has got a pleading, hunted look in his eye, which makes him extremely attractive. There's nothing so sexy as a man tormented by the possibility that you won't go out with him. 'OK,' I say finally, and watch him relax with relief.

'Oh great. Listen, shall I pick you up, or do you want to meet somewhere?'

Hmm. Not ideal. As the man, he should have a night of romance planned, and should therefore be picking me up and whisking me off for the first of our evening's activities. Moonlight skating or a champagne picnic by a lake. But clearly he has nothing.

'I'll meet you,' I say, not wanting to make him think he needs to organize something. I mean, he shouldn't need me to make him think it – he should have thought of that on his own. It's like asking someone to buy you flowers.

'OK, fine. Where?'

This is also not good. The least he can do is suggest some gorgeous venue, so that even if I've got to make my own way there, at least I'll know it will be magical when I arrive.

'How about the Patch and Parrot? On Willoughby Road?'

He nods. 'I know it. Shall we say eight o'clock?'

Even the time is a bit vague, and the fact that it's a question means that he wants me to confirm it. For goodness' sake.

'Eight is fine,' I agree, and he nods, pleased.

'Great. I'll see you there, then.' He grins, then pushes down on his thighs and stands up. 'Can't wait.'

I nod. 'Me too.' Although I don't know what he's expecting to happen. He must know I am spoken for. And I don't think he is the one who will make me tell Richard about the ship. The one that's sailed, remember?

Finally he sidles off to his own desk, shoving Fatima's chair back under her desk as he goes. It brings to mind the image of her stuffing her hat under there yesterday, and I wonder idly where she is today. Maybe she's at home in bed crying. I'll give her a ring in a minute. After I've checked the email that arrived.

Yes! It's from Rupert, again. I feel a bubble of excitement fizzing inside me as I roll my chair right up to the desk and shuffle forward on my seat, as if I can get near to him by doing that. I click on the message, eager to see what he's written back.

From: Rupert de Witter
To: Beth Sheridan
Subject: Relief

Dear Beth,

I am very pleased that you have written back to me at last. I was starting to think I had heard the last from you, and that would have been a great shame. Our little chats about the nation's footwear have become a highlight of my day. Although I have no desire to bring our correspondence to an early end, I feel I must hasten this subject to its finale, so that we can entertain ourselves with talking about something else.

I am assuming that eventually you will arrive at the conclusion that everyone is more comfortable and better equipped to function effectively in the world if they have footwear that is the correct size and fit? And this observation will lead you to the consideration that all things in life should be equally as good a fit as our shoes, like, for example, the training we receive? Am I right? And then, dare I suggest it, you may go on to inform me that at Love Learning, all the training is individually tailored to suit the needs of the delegates, so that no resources – i.e. time and money – are wasted in giving people training they don't need or can't use. And you'll finish by asking me would I like to set up a meeting so that you can go through with me how Love Learning will improve my business's performance so much that I will notice a difference within a year?

The answer is yes. By all means, and as soon as can be arranged. I am very keen to meet you. Please let me know by return which days of the next two weeks would not be possible for a lunch meeting. Days when you're meeting your boyfriend, for example. Or going to your children's nativity play.

I very much look forward to hearing from you,

Yours,

Rupert

Oh my God. Christ. Jesus. He's desperate to meet me. Wow. I can feel hot tingles low in my belly – very low – just thinking about that face. For that face, I could tell Richard about the ship.

But come on, Beth. He's interested in the training, not what you've got in your knickers. Unless it's a hand-out on non-verbal communication, or something.

I'm blushing. God, what's the matter with me?

There is the fact that he answered my last message within minutes of receiving it. Which means either he's got nothing to do all day – and we know that's not true because he's got to go and have his teeth whitened – or he was sitting by his computer eagerly waiting for my answer. And he's obviously asking me if I'm single or not. Why would he do that, if he wasn't interested in more than my portfolio?

But then I start thinking about the message itself. He's sussed out my plan with the shoes, which makes me feel a bit like an idiot. He could obviously see me coming a mile away and probably worked it all out the minute he read my first email asking him if he wore shoes. And since then he's just been playing with me. Bums.

Impetuously I fire off another email.

From: Beth Sheridan
To: Rupert de Witter
Subject: Re: Relief

Are you making fun of me?

And before I have a chance to regret it, Ali shouts that there's a phone call for me. Omigod – so soon? I close down the email screen and lock my computer so no one can infiltrate my Excel spreadsheets while I'm distracted, and put my hand on the phone.

It's so obviously Rupert de Witter, no doubt ringing me up to chat about fire-red sunsets singeing the sky as they explode over black, depthless water; or training. As I wait for Ali to put him through I am subconsciously flicking my hair back with my fingers, and as my blood starts to move a little faster around my body, I smile a tiny, secret little smile.

When it rings, I snatch up the receiver, glancing at Ali over in the corner. 'Don't know what you're grinning about,' Ali says in my ear. 'It's Fatima.'

Fatima was in a terrible state. She was shivering and sniffing and hiccupping so much I could barely understand her. Eventually a man who sounded like an English teacher came on the phone and told me that she had been involved in a raid on certain well-visited establishments on the other side of the bypass at three thirty this morning and needed picking up from the police station.

'Wha—' was all I could manage at first. The idea of Fatima being hauled downtown in a giant felt birthday cake hat with a load of pimps, dealers and crack whores is a bit like opening the velociraptor enclosure and shoving Tinky Winky inside. Time for Tubby Bye-Byes.

'Sh—' was what I said then, because I wanted to make sure that what I had heard was actually what had happened.

'Wh—' was my next enquiry, but of course I knew the answer to that already, so I finished with, 'On my way,' and hung up.

So we're in the car on the way back to Fatima's flat. She's slumped in the passenger seat now, sniffing and rubbing her eyes.

'Trying to get contracts?' I say, because that's what she's just told me she was doing this morning. She nods wearily. 'But why down in that part of the town? I thought you'd already visited there and decided

140

that those places weren't quite what we're looking for.'

'Well, I hadn't decided absolutely for sure not to try there again. Not really. I mean, anywhere that signs on the line is all right, isn't it? It doesn't matter to us what work they do.'

'No, Fats, you're right, it doesn't matter what they do. Unless it's illegal. Then it pretty much excludes them from our programme.'

'Well, how was I supposed to know that what they were doing is illegal? I'm from Taunton.'

She folds her arms and stares straight ahead, as if she has just offered a credible explanation that excuses her from any brainlessness.

Then she says, 'I really can't lose my job, Beth.'

'No, I know, Fats, but you can't spend all your time skulking round the seedy areas of town, trying to get all the druggies, prostitutes and violent psychopaths to sign up for "Handling Complaints". I don't think they're all that bothered about complaints when they've just sold you a bag full of illegal drugs. Their way of dealing with complaints is probably just to stick a knife between your ribs.'

I realize at this point that when she last spoke her lip was trembling so much it was making her voice wobble. You know that feeling when you suddenly notice something forty seconds after it's happened, when it's already too late to stop yourself from making the whole situation worse? Like when the Hero says, 'Oh, yeah, I know all about what happened, and I'm totally cool with it.' So the Best Friend says, 'Oh Buddy, you don't know how pleased I am to hear you say that. I never meant to sleep with your fiancée those eight times, it just happened, but I am so relieved that you finally know because it's been killing me all these months. I am still your Best Friend and I know that Sarah still wants to marry you.' And then he realizes, forty seconds too late, that the Hero was actually talking about the smashed antique watch from his father's will, but by the time he stops talking everything is ruined and the Hero smacks him on the head. Well, I felt like that.

Except when I look at Fatima, I want to smack *myself* on the head.

I pull the car over and turn to face her. 'Fatima, I'm so sorry, I didn't mean that. Of course you won't get knifed in the ribs, that was just a joke. But what is this all about? Why are you so desperate to get a contract that you are putting yourself in the way of vicious knife-carrying psychopaths hiked up on heroin?'

She raises her eyes to meet mine and gives them a vigorous rub. Then she says, 'I've got debts.'

Aha. Of course. It's about money. I raise my eyebrows, waiting for the next bit. I just know it's going to be loan sharks threatening her family. Or some spurious corporation demanding money not to trash her brother's business. Or possibly a secret boyfriend who did a job for some people and accidentally didn't give them all the money, and now they want it back. But she doesn't say any more. I'll have to coax it out of her.

'So is this money that's owing to someone?' She nods. 'Are they asking you for money that they're not entitled to, or is it money that you borrowed from them?'

'I borrowed it,' she says in a small voice.

Well, that's better than 'I creamed it off the top of their extortion profits'. 'OK,' I say. 'Who did you borrow from? A name in a phone box? Someone you met in a club? A friend's next door neighbour's cousin's boyfriend?'

'No.' She sniffs and meets my eyes openly. 'Barclays.'

I blink. 'Barclays?'

She nods again. 'Yeah. It had a really competitive interest rate.'

'*Barclays?*'

'Yes. They've been good so far. But now I'm worried.'

An image pops into my head of a smiling girl with long blond hair and straight white teeth, in a turquoise trouser suit and cravat, standing outside Fatima's front door with a baseball bat. I shake my head a little.

'Right, OK. So why are you worried?'

She looks away. At this point I remember Fatima's love of overreacting and I want to smack my head again. Why didn't that occur to me before? She's probably borrowed a couple of thousand to buy a car or telly or something, and is now panicking.

'If I lose my job,' she says quietly to the lamp post we've parked next to, 'I won't be able to pay it back.'

She's right there, but don't banks offer some kind of insurance to cover unemployment? 'Didn't you take out the insurance?'

She shakes her head. 'I couldn't afford it.'

I gape at her. Jesus. Maybe it's a bit more than two grand. 'Fats, how much do you owe?'

She turns back to me and grabs my arm. 'Beth, I can't lose my job, I really can't. What would my mum say? She already thinks I'm an idiot for borrowing fifteen grand—'

143

'Fifteen grand!' It's out of me before I can stop it.

'Well, my Mini was nine and a half, Beth. I couldn't have bought the plasma telly and my bedroom furniture and my electric guitar if I'd borrowed less, could I?' she says. 'And I've only got another six years to go on it.'

I swallow a few times before asking, 'How much are the repayments?' I almost don't want to hear the answer in case it damages my ears or strikes me dead where I sit. I can feel a drum rolling in the background somewhere. Must not react, must not react. And the winner is . . .

'Two hundred and ninety-five pounds a month.'

'Two hundred and—' I splutter, eyebrows up, slamming my hand over my mouth, staring with wide eyes at poor Fatima sitting there trembling. Whoops, forgot not to react. With an effort, I lower my hand, pull down my eyebrows and bring my eyes back to their usual size. 'OK. So, you have to find three hundred pounds a month.'

'No, Beth, it's not that bad, it's only two hundred and—'

'Ninety-five, yes, I know.'

'But if I don't get a contract Chas will get rid of me and then I won't be able to pay anything. What am I going to do? I'm going to end up in debtor's prison, I just know it.'

'Fatima, no one is . . .' I hesitate. 'Debtor's prison?'

'My mum told me about it.'

'Oh, I see. Right. Well look, I am as sure as I can be that you don't need to worry about debtor's prison.'

'But Mum says—'

'No, I know, but you don't owe enough, I think. It's

144

got to be over, um, sixteen thousand for . . . that.'

Her face opens out a little. 'Do you really think . . . ?'

'Anyway, you just need to sell the Mini, then you can pay off most of what you owe, can't you?'

'I've been trying to sell it for over a month, but no one wants it. I only want to get back what I paid for it, but everyone who's come to see it seems to think that because I have owned it for five months I should be asking less.'

'How do they know how much you paid for it? And that you have owned it for five months?' She opens her mouth to answer, but I put my hand up. 'Second thoughts, don't answer that. I think I can guess.'

'Well, anyway, what if I can't sell it? And then I lose my job here?'

'No one is going to lose their job. I promise.'

'Oh, you can't know that. It's easy to make promises but you can't keep that one because it's not up to you, is it? It's up to Chas. And he hates me.'

'He doesn't hate you.' Actually she's right, he does hate her. 'He's just a grumpy old sod who's horrid to everyone.'

'No, Beth, he hates me. I've seen it in his eyes. He can't wait to get rid of me.'

'Well, whatever. It doesn't matter whether he hates you or not because you are not going to lose your job. I guarantee it.'

'But how can you guarantee it? How can you?'

I hesitate. No, I am not going to tell Fatima about the Horizon contract. Not that I suspect that she would steal the idea but she might accidentally tell everyone else about it. But I can tell her something.

'I can guarantee it,' I say, putting my hand on her

145

arm, 'because I have already got an enormous contract that's big enough not to need any others, and will save the company and everyone's jobs.'

And I am rewarded with Fatima's mouth falling open and a squeal coming out as she throws her arms round my neck and hugs me very tightly.

Ten

Attraction to Change

**Short-term Goal: Oh my God, what the FUCK did I go
and say that for? I must be up a tree with twigs in
my hair, miaowing at the clouds.**
**Obstacles: I have apparently departed from my
senses.**
**Long-term Goal: Have myself committed and spend
my days sucking cutlery.**
**Obstacles: I can't trust myself. Knowing me I'll go and
check myself into boarding kennels.**

It's ironic that when I was so completely preoccupied
with looking after Fatima that I didn't pay any
attention to how I might appear to a secret observer,
someone really did observe me secretly. But I didn't
notice. Obviously. That's why it was, you know, secret.

By the time I've dropped Fatima off at home and
driven slowly and painfully back to work, it's two
o'clock. I am frantic to see if Rupert has replied to my
last message, but only because of my new desperate
determination to get the contract. OK, yes, all right,

maybe also partly because of his charm and wit. And gorgeous bod. But not his yacht. I rush into the office as quickly as I can without muscles and log back on to my emails, not even trying to look interestingly distracted. I mean, I probably do look interestingly distracted, like someone who is rushing to check their emails, but I'm not even thinking about it.

As well as Rupert and the contract and Fatima's tear-stained face, I'm thinking how short of time I am too. I don't know if you remember but I have got a pretty full day today. I'm starting with seducing Rupert – in the business sense, of course – by email now; infiltrating Horizon Holidays this afternoon; and finishing off with a dream date with Sean later tonight. I am allowing myself a maximum of two hours to get the emailing done successfully so that I can be at Horizon by half four and sneak in in time to meet some of the staff on the stairs as they make their way home.

Although now that I'm thinking about it, I'm no longer sure I could sneak in. Rupert is obviously so brilliant and on the ball that he can see straight through everything I come up with. He'll probably be waiting in the entrance hall with champagne and balloons and party poppers. Or dogs.

Plus I don't think walking slowly and stiffly with one hand in the small of my back counts as sneaking.

My emails are open now and I notice immediately that he has sent me two messages. According to the computer, which is never wrong, the first one was received one minute after I sent my last message asking

148

him if he was making fun of me. I click on it excitedly
and hunch forward in my seat.

From: Rupert de Witter
To: Beth Sheridan
Subject: Abject apology

My dear Beth,
I am so sorry. I am such a buffoon sometimes, it didn't even
occur to me that you might have found my last message hurtful
or insulting. Please please believe that I didn't mean to offend. It
was just my rather pathetic attempt at wit, I'm afraid, but I really
should know by now to leave that to witty people. Please write
back and forgive me.
Yours with head held low,
Rupert

Those words seem to be starting a small fire under
my chair. I wriggle a bit and lean back in my seat for
a few seconds to distance myself from the screen, as
if being too near it will make me spontaneously com-
bust.

But I have to be cool and remember that this man
is a ruthless businessman who will probably say anything to manipulate situations to his advantage.

The second email was sent three minutes later.

From: Rupert de Witter
To: Beth Sheridan
Subject: Goodbye for ever

Beth,
As I have not heard back from you for some considerable time, I
understand this to mean that you find yourself unable to forgive

me. For me, this situation is intolerable, so I am quitting this dreary land and going to live in Nepal. Please think of me fondly.
Your friend,
Rupert

I giggle audibly then, so quickly put my hand over my mouth and look up to see if anyone heard me. Doesn't look like they did.

Right. I need to think about this and consider how, and when, it will be best to reply, in order to give the contract the best chance of . . .

Fuck it, I am writing back *now*.

From: Beth Sheridan
To: Rupert de Witter
Subject: Yetis

Dearest Rupert,
I shall certainly miss you on your travels. Do you expect to have much time to study the local wildlife? I would appreciate a photograph of a yeti if you should happen to spot one. I hear they are breeding profusely in that part of the world.
Yours as ever,
Beth

Oh my God. My mouse pointer hovers for ages over the Send button before I actually click it. If I send this one, it is a clear acknowledgement by me that our correspondence has now become about more than just training. I mean, whichever way I look at it there is no way that he could ever think my allusion to yetis was another thinly veiled attempt to get him to sign, like the shoes.

Yetis : myths : facts : training?

Nah. He is going to know I have decided to move up a level with him.

I click. It's sent. That's that.

The rest of the afternoon goes by like *Lost In Translation*. I long for it to end but it just keeps on going. My computer pings a few times, mostly with jokes from Vini and instructions from Chas, and each time I jerk in my seat and turn greedily towards the screen, eyes wide, body tense; then slump when I see who they're from. Once there is a message from Sean, who is out doing a half-day Report Writing workshop in some hotel conference room this afternoon and must be using their wireless network. It says something about looking forward to seeing me later, and although I know I should be excited by it, and I try my hardest to be pleased, I still slump in my seat when I see it's not from Rupert.

I hear nothing from him all afternoon and at quarter to five I pack up and leave. It's later than I intended because I went for a walk to make the time go and ended up much further away than I planned. Then had to Panic Power Walk back in my heels. And now, as I'm parking the car a short walk away from the Horizon building roundabout, my stomach is churning and I am shaking with excitement and nerves. Rupert's beautiful face keeps appearing in my head saying things like, 'I am so sorry, please forgive me,' and in my less lucid moments, 'You are the most amazing and lovely person I have ever met. I can't go on living unless I can kiss you immediately, and then spend the rest of my life with you.' Or words to that effect.

I creep in through the revolving glass doors and

find that the lobby is deserted. Which is just as well because it is impossible to go unnoticed through revolving glass doors. I move further in to confirm what I thought I saw when I first entered – the man at the reception desk is absent. When I worked here it was a lovely chap called Ron. His absence is unsettling. Could he be dead?

Now come on, Beth, get a grip. The fact that he's not here does not automatically mean that he's dead. If he had died, they wouldn't just leave the reception desk unmanned for ever, with his pens and mints and newspaper kept eternally the way he had left them on that last fateful morning, as if he'd just walked away to go to the Gents. A lovely tribute to a sweet and helpful man, but absolutely fucking stupid.

Unless he died some time earlier today. They wouldn't have had time to put someone else out on reception by now, would they? I try to imagine Rupert de Witter watching horror-struck with Ron's distraught colleagues as paramedics frantically massage his chest on the floor, then leaning towards Carol from Accounts and quietly asking her to cover the reception desk.

No, no, Rupert de Witter is definitely not that unfeeling, I'm sure of it.

I creep nearer to the desk like Bruce Willis in a *Die Hard* film, dreading what I might find on the other side. Is Ron's cold, lifeless body lying face down in a pool of blood behind there, cut down where he stood, proudly defending the company he had grown to love?

No.

In fact, a quick sweep of the lobby proves that there are no dead bodies anywhere – on the floor, under the table, behind the huge Christmas tree twinkling silently near the lifts, not even standing up with their eyes open in the stationery cupboard, ready to fall out the minute I open the door. I head over to the lifts, jittery from the quiet.

The managers' offices are on the seventh and eighth floors, so I get out at the sixth. Maybe I'll be able to snag one of them on the stairs. I remember that some of those halfwits used to run down the seven flights on their way home instead of using the lift, to get the circulation going after sitting for eight hours at their desks eating croissants. Might have been worth more if they had run up the stairs every morning, but that would be far too time consuming. Oh, and hard.

Coming round the corner from the lifts on the sixth floor, I feel uneasy tingles raising the hair on the back of my neck. There's no one around here either. The carpet is thick and makes no sound, but I am tiptoeing anyway. I slink towards the lush kitchen area that I have only ever seen once, when I 'got lost' and came up here 'by mistake', and press myself flat against the wall next to the door. As a safety precaution, I slide my mobile out of my handbag and dial three nines, then rest my finger on the Connect button, ready to press at the first sign of international terrorists. 'I've got a mobile phone and I *will* make a call if you come any closer.' I take a deep breath, hesitate for a second, then fling myself round the door jamb into the kitchen.

I see immediately three dirty cups and a plate covered in crumbs by the sink, but no masked gunmen hiding behind the Klix machine. My finger on Connect is so tense it almost goes off by accident, so I ease it gently off the button and put the phone into my other hand for a few seconds so I can flex the cramped muscles.

153

Coming back out into the corridor, I can hear, or rather feel, the pulse of loud music, but it's not on this floor. It's coming up through my feet, so it must be somewhere below.

I go back into the lift and press '5'. When the doors open again, I am met with the same sinister, deserted silence. The same thing happens on floor 4, although the pulsing vibrations are more discernible here. I go down again.

This time, when the lift doors slide back, there is an almost deafening, unhindered cacophony of thumping music and shouting voices that means Party. Hanging from the ceiling is a rather tired-looking tinsel decoration, with the remnants of another one, now absent, stuck to each end with Blu-Tack. Of course! It's not a vicious gang of crazed, sadistic terrorists bent on revenge; it's the office Christmas party. Letting out my tightly held breath with relief, I delete the nines from my phone, lock the keypad and holster it safely back in my bag.

This is great. I can mingle undetected, chatting to people about their work without arousing any suspicion. They will just think I'm one of the typists or receptionists that never gets seen by anyone.

I come out of the lift and turn right, towards the conference rooms. The first one is more of an auditorium really, for those huge corporate functions, and sure enough the party is in here. I slide in unnoticed and head to the bar.

The bar is made of a long conference room table with lots and lots of bottles on it and behind it, but it does the job. A white tablecloth might have made it look a bit less like a working men's club, but I'm guessing the staff preferred to spend the budget on actual alcohol rather than niceties. I get a white wine – there isn't much choice – and turn to face the room. Who shall I speak to first?

Perched on a stool to my right is a girl in a tight basque and shiny sateen skirt, with short brown hair. I smile at her and raise my eyebrows in a 'Fancy a chat?' kind of way, but she does a 'What the fuck are you looking at?' head jerk. OK, maybe not her. On the other side of her is a girl in a too-tight black skirt and boots, sweating into her plastic cup. She looks too uncomfortable even to stand next to.

Someone on the dance floor, then. I eye them all from my seat. There's one guy who's seductively undoing his shirt buttons, shimmying the sleeves down his arms while the woman he's dancing in front of looks nervously around. Suddenly he throws his head back and flings the shirt off to reveal a white, hairless midriff that is starting to pile up at his waistband. He swings the shirt around his head and hurls it across the room, as if to a horde of screaming fans. I'm betting someone at home will not be pleased about that.

I'm not sure any of the dancers are in a fit state to chat about what it's like to work for Rupert de Witter. The girl in the short skirt next to me is being led away by a very young, very beautiful boy, so that rules her out. And him. Her friend is left desperately trying to look like she's really glad that she's been left at the bar on her own because she's been dying for a chance to get her breath back. I turn towards her to strike up a conversation, but my eyes land on a head ten feet behind her and I freeze.

It's Rupert de Witter. He's here, at the party, standing

near enough to me to see me, if he turns round. I recognize him instantly thanks to his very blond highlights and rugged, designer stubble. My throat goes dry and all the organs in my abdomen start to rearrange themselves. I can't take my eyes off his broad shoulders. Well, I can, but only to look at other bits of him. He's talking and nodding vigorously, obviously deep in conversation with someone, so I'm not going to introduce myself. Well, now is not the time anyway, not while I'm trespassing, and have stolen a glass of warm Liebfraumilch. I can hardly ask to set up a more formal meeting while his security team are ejecting me from the building.

'I have a window on Monday, at ten?'

'And stay out!'

So I sink down a little further onto my seat, and turn slightly away from him so that I can stare at him uninterrupted without looking like I am staring at him.

I take a sip, then choke down on the coughing spasm that threatens as the sickly sweetness clings to my throat. Don't want to draw attention to myself and cause them to look over at me. It seems the conversation is drawing to a close as Rupert is now shaking hands with the other man, who is holding Rupert's hand in both of his. Hmm. Probably would be interesting to have a chat with this guy, once Rupert has cleared off. I turn again so that I am almost back-to-back with them, then discreetly glance up over my shoulder as they part and the other man's face comes clearly into view at last. I freeze again.

It's Brad.

Not Brad Pitt. Not an imaginary, made-up Brad from

a dream. I mean real, flesh-and-blood, three-minutes Fast Love Brad, who has not got back to me and whose call or email I have been longing for for days. Oh my God. As I stare open-mouthed at him, I can feel a change coming again, and this time it's definitely a good thing. This time, the change is tall and handsome and charming and funny, and involuntarily my mouth starts to smile and I get up off the stool to go and speak to him.

Hang on. I sit back down again. The bastard isn't in a full body cast. He's not on crutches, or even wearing a sling. In fact, I can't see as much as a Band-Aid. Which definitely means he hasn't called me in the past five days because he chose not to, not because he couldn't press the phone keys with broken fingers.

Bloody hell, good job I didn't go over there and embarrass myself. Not that I would have leapt on him and started licking his face, but I might have looked pleased to see him and that would have been mortifying.

I glance casually over again. He's smiling at Rupert now and without me meaning it to my belly gives a little flip. He is so incredibly sexy. In fact, standing there next to Rupert with his highlights and his golden skin and fluorescent teeth, Brad looks big and solid and manly all on his own, without needing a single chemical anywhere. He is the most attractive change I have ever seen.

Right. That's it. I am going to go and talk to him. I mean, who am I to judge, after all? I think, in the interests of natural justice, I should give the man a fair chance to explain himself because there is bound to be some really simple explanation for the lack of contact and, let's face it, I would be fucking stupid not to.

But what am I going to say? Hi, Brad, remember me? Why haven't you called me? That sounds a bit lame. Actually it sounds a bit like Glenn Close, back in her *Fatal Attraction* days. Or possibly Cruella De Vil. Either way, it's more likely to send him speeding away from me towards the exit than leading me towards a bedroom.

God, come on, Beth, get a grip. There aren't any bedrooms here.

There are board rooms, though.

Jesus. OK. I am just going to walk up to him with a nonchalant little smile and say, 'Well, hello again, fancy seeing you here.' And then he will reply with, 'Wow, Libby, so great to see you again, I tried to call but my dog chewed the wires.' No, no, he'll say, 'I'm sorry I haven't contacted you, I was called away the next day to an urgent meeting. In Pretoria.' No, not Pretoria. I'm not an expert on geography but I think they probably have phones there. It'll be an urgent meeting in . . . God, where don't they have phones these days?

Doesn't matter, doesn't matter. I am going over to talk to him. It's a party so no pressure, just chatting and flirting, and then, when everything is all cleared up and explained, we can arrange a date for a future meeting. And the real beauty of it is that I can chat to him quite genuinely about his job here and what he thinks of Rupert, and the training, and it will look like I'm just interested in him, which I am, but I'm also collecting data for my research and future proposal. It couldn't be better!

No. Wait.

I freeze again, one buttock off the stool. If I go over there now, after I've just seen him talking to

Rupert, and start chatting to him about his work and everything, and then he finds out later that I'm researching Horizon for my training bid, he will think that I only wanted to talk to him to find out about Rupert. We will have been together, blissfully happy, for three or four months, and he's thinking about taking it to the next stage, and suddenly he hears that Love Learning are now providing all the training for Horizon Holidays. What a coincidence, he will think, as he fingers the red velvet box containing a gorgeous diamond solitaire ring, my Libby works at Love Learning. Oh, no, hold on, he will be thinking, My Beth works at Love Learning, because by then we will have been totally honest with each other and I'll have come clean about the name. Although he might choose to carry on calling me Libby – it will become his pet name for me.

Anyway, there will probably be a bit of blurb about LL, and me, and how I came to be the one who persuaded Rupert de Witter to change his ways, after years of doing it wrong. And at that moment, standing in the dining room, waiting for me to arrive, with a beautiful salmon roasting in the oven and champagne in the fridge, candlelight glinting off the crystal glasses and gold cutlery, he will realize suddenly that he has been used. He will go cold all over and he will drop the red velvet box and me, in that order, right there where he's standing, grab his jacket and walk out of my life. Even though, technically, I am innocent. But I won't have a chance to explain myself to him because the next day he'll move to Hong Kong.

Oh my God. That is so typical of my life. My long-awaited happiness to be snatched away like that, just because of a silly misunderstanding. I absolutely cannot let that happen. I sit back down fully on my stool and turn completely away from where he is standing. He only saw me for three minutes, he couldn't possibly recognize me from my back, could he? I hunch over to disguise my back, just in case.

A minute later, I glance quickly behind me and find that he and Rupert de Witter have both gone. Phew. I think perhaps I won't bother chatting to anyone now, and will just get going. Covert infiltration is so bloody exhausting. I take one last look at the couples on the dance floor, arms looped around each other's necks, hips clamped together like flower presses, gyrating to 'Lonely This Christmas', and I am struck that maybe the Christmas party isn't the best setting for in-depth interviews about job satisfaction.

Further along the darkened corridor, outside the door to one of the smaller conference rooms, Rupert de Witter is frowning. He squints down into the darkened corridor, as if slightly narrowing his eyes will enable him to see more effectively. He shakes his head.

'You must have imagined it,' his associate says.

'I don't think I did, Harris. Although I suppose I could have been mistaken. I've only seen her once before.'

'What's going on?' says a third man, coming out.

Harris turns to him. 'Rupert thinks he saw a mystery woman.'

'Really? Who?'

'Well, if I knew that, Hector,' Rupert snaps, 'she wouldn't be a mystery woman, would she? She'd be Carol, from accounts, or Val, from telesales.'

'What do you mean, a mystery woman, then? I mean, you recognized her from somewhere – does she work here?'

Rupert shakes his head slowly, still peering into the dark corridor. 'I don't know. She might. I feel I might have seen her here before. It's certainly possible.'

'Well then. Mystery solved. You've seen her working here but never spoken to her.'

'No, no. I know for sure that I've met her before, and it wasn't here. We spoke. Not much, admittedly, but I did meet her.' He smiles. 'I really liked her. I just didn't know at the time that she worked for me. If she does.' He frowns. 'But if she works here, how come I haven't spoken to her, or seen her around more? And if she doesn't work here, what on earth is she doing here now?'

'Why don't you go and ask her?'

Rupert turns to look sharply at Hector. 'Don't think so.'

'Why not?'

'Because.' He turns back towards the open door. 'Now come on, let's get this finished.'

'Don't be such an arse. Just go and talk to her.'

'No.'

'Go on,' says Harris, pushing lightly on Rupert's back. 'There's nothing to it. You just say, "Hi, I'm Rupert de Witter, fabulously wealthy, charming and devastatingly handsome, can I get you a drink?" And then she says, "Oh, hi, Rupert, I'm Crown Princess Incognita of Denmark, I would love a drink, thank you." And then you get a drink, and you ask her if she wants to sit down, so you sit down and then you start chatting. Easy.'

Rupert clears his throat, thinking. 'OK. Hang on a minute.' He jogs a few steps forward, then stops. 'What am I doing? She's already gone.' He turns and walks back to where the other two are standing.

'You can catch her if you're quick,' Harris urges. 'Go on! She will like you. She'd be a fool otherwise.'

'Well, maybe. But she looked like she was in a hurry to get out of here. Probably on her way home, or on to another party. I'd just end up making her late.'

Hector rolls his eyes. 'Jesus, Rupert, why not just try it and find out? I mean, what's the worst that can happen? She tells you to get lost. And that's that.'

Rupert nods. 'I know, you're right.' He turns to stare down the empty corridor. 'I just didn't really want to be running down a corridor after her, grabbing her by the arm. Looks a bit desperate, doesn't it?'

'So what are you going to do?'

Rupert shakes his head slowly. 'Dunno, mate. I really liked her, but I've got no way of getting in touch with her. And I don't even know if she liked me back. If I knew that for sure, I would be sprinting down there right now. She's so great, Hec. Enchanting, radiant, and I'm just—'

'Rupert de Witter, millionaire.'

'Yeah, well, that doesn't mean anything, does it? We both know from experience that it doesn't mean that girls will like you. Or at least, not the girls that you want to like you.'

'So at the risk of the girl that you like not liking you, you are actually going to do nothing? Which means you will definitely end up with no girl, rather than maybe ending up with no girl.'

'Yep.'

'Really? Even though there's a more than fifty per cent chance that she will like you back?'

'Yes. When we meet again, I'm not going to be out of breath, panicky and wearing a shirt I've been in all day. I want to make a good impression.'

'You're an idiot.'

'Thanks. You're absolutely right.' He pauses. 'No you're not. You're completely wrong. I've just thought of a way I may be able to meet her again.'

'What do you mean?'

'Not going to tell you, mate. Don't want to jinx it. It's a plan. Just think of Clark Kent and you might get an idea.'

'You're going to dress in blue tights and prance around the place with your underpants on show, rescuing people from burning buildings and stopping dams from collapsing?'

'No, that's Superman, you idiot. Come on, man, get a grip.'

Eleven

A Range of Options

**Short-term Goal: Wow. Richard, Sean and Rupert.
And maybe Brad. Three men and a maybe. I need
to make one of them a definite.
Obstacles: I think I might be a teeny bit unhinged.
Long-term Goal: Probably start wearing a tin-foil hat
to protect me from alien rays.
Obstacles: Foil outerwear looks utterly ridiculous.**

'Christ, men really are like buses, aren't they?' Vini says the next morning.

'You mean, none for ages and then three at once?'

'No, I mean late, unreliable, covered in piss and always going down the same fucking route.'

She's pissed off because her Ant and Dec turned up wasted for the Christmas lights being turned on in the precinct last night. Dec could hardly stand up, apparently. Not a great night for Fake Face.

I'm sitting here at the kitchen table eyeing Vini suspiciously. I am almost seventy-five per cent positive I saw her last night, in the Patch and Parrot, with a man. I caught a brief glimpse of pink highlights when

I first got there, and there was the suggestion that she was standing next to someone very tall, but then they were gone, and my attention was drawn elsewhere. I'm waiting for her to tell me about it, but as time is going on, I'm becoming more and more sure that she isn't going to. Which is not in the rules. I told her I had a date with Sean last night, in line with rule number 3 (I can't remember the actual wording, but it's something about keeping each other informed), and she is clearly in breach. I am not happy about that.

I haven't told her about the events of yesterday afternoon. I can't quite believe that I thought sneaking into Horizon was a good idea. Or that I would be able to do it. I had to sneak *away* in the end, as I thought I saw Brad on the pavement when I came out. I also thought I saw Elvis Presley chatting to ET, so I could have been wrong. By the time I got home I was ready for a nice healthy evening meal – poached salmon fillet, steamed broccoli spears and salad followed by fat-free lemon sorbet, washed down with sparkling mineral water. Or half a bottle of Pinot Grigio and a box of Milk Tray – followed by a candle-scented bath and an early night with Dan Brown. But of course I still had the dream date on my schedule, so it was a quick shower, change and bowl of chicken soup. Then off to the Patch and Parrot.

After not quite seeing Vini in there, I spotted Sean, who, thankfully, was there waiting when I arrived. Walking into a pub on my own is bad enough, but having to sit down alone and wait for someone is tantamount to flashing your boobs at a busload of drunk football fans and shouting, 'Free to a good home!'

Anyway, I didn't have to do that because he was there. He bought me a drink and we started talking about films, I think, but I just couldn't get my mind off Rupert de Witter and Brad. I mean, the fact that they know each other is almost unfathomable. It's like, I don't know, as if there's some kind of huge plan made up by someone, and we're all nothing more than little play pieces, unwittingly following a path that we have no control over because everything has already been decided for us millennia ago. Which is completely stupefying! It means that there definitely *is* a god of some kind, no question, and therefore all religions around the world can unite at last, bringing about an end to conflict and misery, and heralding in a new era of peace and joy to all peoples, regardless of creed or colour.

No, wait. It's probably more to do with the fact that Horizon is one of the biggest employers in our town. Hardly surprising that Brad would work there, really. I used to work there. Most people in the town have worked there at some time.

Obviously Brad is quite high up in the company, the way he was so familiar with Rupert de Witter. They seemed to be really getting along, like old friends. A picture popped into my head at that point of Rupert and Brad wrestling in check shirts and heavy boots on some very dry ground, kicking up huge dust clouds as they roll around grunting, while I stand nearby in a gorgeous yellow dress, clasping my hands and looking dead worried.

'Beth? Helloo-o? Are you in there?'

That was the moment Sean realized I wasn't listening to him at all, which was very embarrassing. I had to make something up.

166

'Oh, I'm really sorry, Sean, I was miles away. Just a bit preoccupied with this contract thing.'

He nodded. 'Yeah, me too. How are you getting on?'

'Not as well as I'd hoped, actually. How about you?'

And what he said next held me gripped to the spot, utterly transfixed. 'Well, I've had a bit of a brainwave, as it goes. It suddenly occurred to me that Whytelys have never come to us for any training before, not in all the time that we've been operating, so it's possible their training is in need of an update. I rang them on the off chance, chatted it up, and got an appointment to go and see the regional manager next Tuesday afternoon.'

'Whytelys? Regional manager? Tuesday afternoon?' Notice how I drove straight to the crux of the matter and neatly filtered out all the irrelevancies.

'Yeah. I'm pretty chuffed about it. Could be big enough to do the trick, couldn't it?'

Well, that was that. If Sean had had trouble keeping my attention before, it was a lost cause now. I might as well have not been there. In fact ten minutes later, I wasn't.

'I had a great time,' he said in the car park, moving in slowly.

'Yeah, me too. See you Monday.' And I was out of there.

Oh my God. Whytelys. What an absolutely fuck-off brilliant idea. Why the bloody hell didn't I think of it? Well, because I have been utterly fixated on Horizon, and Rupert de Witter. But Whytelys would definitely be better. My God, it's a national chain, it would probably be enough on its own to keep the company going, even if we lost all our other clients. Next to the Olympic gold of a Whytelys contract, my possible conquest of Horizon suddenly looks like a six-year-old coming second in the sack race.

At the office on Monday Sean comes over to speak to me almost as soon as I've sat down at my desk. I've barely had time to get myself looking nice. My head is still split totally into two parts over his Whytelys thing, which is not a good look, and I'm not sure how to act. Should I be excited and pleased that he's going to solve single-handedly all of Love Learning's money worries, thereby ensuring we all keep our jobs, no one takes a pay cut and everyone is happy and secure? Or should I be thoroughly pissed off about it? You get the idea. In the end I come up with a kind of neutral expression, which I think will cover all options while not giving anything away to the person looking at me.

'You look a bit pissed off,' he says, sitting on Fatima's chair. 'Everything all right?'

'Oh, yes, fine. No, I'm absolutely fine. Not pissed off at all. Why would I be? No, I'm just really pleased you've got this Whytelys thing. I mean, it takes the pressure off the rest of us, doesn't it?'

He flinches a bit when I say 'Whytelys', and does one of those really fake surreptitious glances around that you see all the time in bad British sitcoms. 'Yes, I suppose it does. Look, Beth, that's what I want to talk to you about.' He pulls Fatima's chair nearer to me and pins me with his gaze. 'I told you about the . . . W . . . thing,' and he raises his eyebrows expectantly to make sure I've got it (I nod because I have), 'because I trust you. But you're the only one, OK? Please don't tell anyone else about it. I mean, I know that it's all good news, no matter who gets the deal, but I'm pretty excited about it and really want to follow it up myself. Do you know what I mean?'

I nod again, more vigorously. 'Oh, yes, totally. I know exactly what you mean. Don't worry about it, I won't say anything. I promise.'

He leans in a bit further. 'I knew I could trust you, Beth. Thanks.' Then he stands up, winks at me with a grin and goes off to his own desk.

I know what you're thinking. Why didn't I return the favour and tell him about my Horizon deal last night? Because he sure as hell isn't going to be interested in a poxy little roundabout holiday company, now that he's got Whytelys on the table. No, actually, Horizon isn't poxy, or little, but it is on a roundabout, and it is only one company. Whytelys is nationwide. So why not confide in Sean about it? Why not have a bit of faith and show the same respect for him that he's given to me?

Because I don't bloody well trust him, remember? Have you forgotten his dog, and his fiancée, and the only horse?

Right. I'm logging on to my Hotmail account to see if there's anything from Brad. It is always possible that he was ill for the past week, confined to bed, delirious, touch-and-go even, and didn't feel well enough to get up and go out until Friday. And now he's at work and can finally send me the email that he's been composing in his head ever since the first moment when—

No. He hasn't. But in my work inbox is a message from gorgeous Rupert, which stirs up my insides as I hunch forward to read it.

169

From: Rupert de Witter
To: Beth Sheridan
Subject: OK, not for ever

Dearest Beth,

Well, I'm back from Nepal after a disastrous trip. I didn't realize that the yeti colony was going to be quite so huge. Why didn't you warn me? Our camp was attacked by a family group one night and they made off with all our shampoo and conditioner, so we had to come back early.

Regrettably, I was unable to get any photos of them, as no one in our group would allow me to use the camera once we had lost our conditioner. I did bring you back a gift, though. It's a plaster cast of a footprint. The little touristy gift shops that are everywhere in the Himalayas sell them by the bucketload, together with hand-crafted foot-shaped pottery ashtrays, locally mined gems cut into amusing foot shapes, and some rather lovely leather belts. I hope you can forgive me.

Your friend,

Rupert

He's so funny! I read it again, and then again, grinning broadly the whole time. Well, it's a modified broad grin – a completely unconscious expression of the amusement I'm feeling, toned down slightly so I don't look like a loon. You never know who might be watching. I take a quick glance around: no one is, but you never know when someone might start.

But look at this message! Rupert de Witter is actually flirting with me. It's so obvious, with this silly joky tone about the yetis making off with their conditioner! I stifle a persistent giggle, covering my lips with my fingers.

170

He is flirting, isn't he? God, is he? I mean, as far as he knows I could be a sixty-eight-year-old grandmother of four, with a blue rinse and bandaged legs, so maybe he's just being friendly.

But if he really thought I had bandaged legs, would he have written to me in this way? Wouldn't he just have kept our correspondence businesslike and sensible?

A thought has just occurred to me. What if he's remembered my name from when I worked there? That would mean two very significant, thrilling things: one, he knows that I am not sixty-eight, or a grandmother, and don't have oedema, so therefore he *is* flirting with me; and two, he has fucking remembered me from six years ago, which means I must have made an impression on him when I was there, even though I never actually met him!

No, no, hang on. If I never actually met him, how would he know that I am not sixty-eight and oedema-free?

Because, duh, of the conversation he had with one of his aides when Richard stormed out, and I crept out behind him, to form Love Learning. 'Beth Sheridan has left too?' Rupert said, a bit puzzled. 'Who is she?'

'She's Richard's assistant,' he was probably told. 'She's only twenty-two or so, madly in love with Richard, apparently. Follows him everywhere.'

'Really? She sounds incredibly sexy and interesting, I'll have to remember that name so that I can marry her one day.'

All right, that last bit is ridiculous, but it is certainly possible that he was told my name back then, and has remembered it now. Oh my God, he's worked out my age.

Well, there's only one way to find out. I'm smiling broadly as I click Reply and start typing.

From: Beth Sheridan
To: Rupert de Witter
Subject: Welcome home!

My dear friend Rupert,

Then I stop. Oh, God, is that too forward? I snatch my hands back from the keyboard and put them quickly in my lap, as if they might act without my permission and embarrass me. I read those four words again, and then again, and then I go back over all our previous correspondence, rereading each message in the correct order, finally ending with these four words. No, it seems OK. He has signed his 'Your friend', and he put 'Dearest Beth' at the beginning, so 'My dear friend' is probably exactly the right tone.

My dear friend Rupert,

But what on earth does he mean by hoping I can forgive him? Is he still talking about the other message when I thought he was taking the piss? Or is it a joke about not being able to get any photos of the yetis? Christ, should I acknowledge it as a joke, say it doesn't matter about the yeti photos? Or should I respond seriously, say that I have forgiven him, it doesn't matter, I realized it was just a joke all along blah blah blah?

172

I'll acknowledge it as a joke. He can assume I have forgiven him by the fact that I am writing back.

My dear friend Rupert,

What the bloody hell am I on about? Come on, Beth, get a grip. I am in contact with Rupert de Witter for one reason and one reason only: to get a contract out of him. I absolutely must stay focused on that. I glance quickly at Fatima for motivational purposes. Today, she's wearing a top that says, in large pink letters,

Mastermind Champion 2005

I blink and read it again. She's obviously been given it by a cruel relative having a joke at her expense. Probably a cousin. And then I spot the much smaller letters underneath:

Lives next door to my mum

'Ha!' bursts out of me suddenly, making Fatima flick her head round in my direction.

'You all right, Beth?' she says, all concerned. Then she notices I'm grinning and her mouth relaxes and curves up too. 'What?'

'I just noticed your top. It's brilliant.'

She smiles with pure pleasure and looks down, as if to remind herself of what she's wearing. 'Thanks. I really loved it the second I saw it and I thought it would be perfect for me, you know, coz there's no way anyone would ever think I was a Mastermind, would they?'

Mike is sitting with her, going over some paperwork on her desk, and as she says this, he raises his head and shakes it gently. 'You've got lots of wonderful qualities, you know,' he says, somewhat patronizingly, I think. But Fatima flushes a bit and turns towards him, saying, 'Do you really think so?'

'Fancy a tea break?' I blurt out, to stop Fatima making a fool of herself. 'I'll make it. Come on, you've been working really hard.'

'For forty minutes!' Fatima says with a giggle.

'Yeah, but . . .' I hesitate. It is a bit difficult to justify a break after only forty minutes, but I really want to talk to Fatima and remind myself what it is I need from Rupert de Witter. Apart from . . . well, let's leave that there. But I do feel that I have wandered away from the point a bit. Starting out at training contract and ending up at yetis is about as far away from a point as anyone could get. 'Come on, let's have hot chocolate. It's raining, it's winter, what more persuasion do you need?'

It's strangely difficult to lock my computer and walk away from it, knowing that Rupert is at the other end, waiting for my reply. I feel like Ralph Fiennes, leaving Kristin Scott Thomas waiting for him to return to her in a cave in the desert. Well, OK, Rupert isn't going to lie paralysed in agony, scrawling his last desperate thoughts in blood on a scrap of paper, then die slowly of dehydration and exposure and get eaten by rats while he's waiting for me. But he might get a bit fed up.

'So how's your hunt for contracts going?' I ask Fats and Mike as I hand out the steaming mugs. There are eight comfy chairs set out in a U-shape in the kitchen, all empty, and Mike has chosen to sit in the one immediately next to Fatima. Their elbows are almost touching – it looks uncomfortable.

'Oh awful,' Fats says immediately. 'I just can't seem to get anywhere. I don't know what I'm going to do if I can't sort something out.'

Mike turns to her and smiles. 'Don't you worry about it,' he says, shrivellingly condescending. I can feel my top lip start to curl with disgust but manage to force it down. 'Something will turn up, I'm sure of it.' She turns to face him again and dips her chin Princess Diana-like as she looks at him, doing that trying-to-appear-coy thing.

Oh, no, my mistake. She *is* coy.

'That's so nice of you, Mike,' she's saying. I blink at her. Sorry, what's nice exactly? She's thanking him for *saying* she doesn't need to worry? Yeah, great, big deal. How about actually helping her, you supercilious twat? 'And I'm so grateful for all your help.'

Oh. OK.

'It's been my pleasure, Fatima, you know that. We'll get there, never fear.'

'Oh, I do hope so. I'm just so worried about Chas, you know? I mean, sometimes I think, even if I manage to sort out a really, really good contract, with, like, loads of money in it, he's still going to get rid of me, just because he hates me so much.'

'He doesn't . . .' I begin, at the same time as Mike says, 'That's his problem.' I turn to him with wide eyes.

'Mike! You're not agreeing with her, are you?' I'm

175

widening my eyes even more and rolling them a bit, to mean 'Don't confirm Fatima's fears that the boss hates her as it will seriously dent her confidence leaving her incapable of reasoning. And then she might do something totally mad, like mix with seriously hard criminals, out of desperation to save her job,' but he doesn't seem to be catching on. 'I mean,' I say, a bit more blatantly, 'you don't agree that Chas hates her, do you? That would be ridi—'

'Of course I agree,' he says boldly. 'It's plainly obvious to everyone who works here, and to deny it would just be patronizing Fatima.'

Me patronizing her? What a hypocrite! And now he's patronizing me! Fuck's sake, he's obviously declared himself King of Patronizing, and has made it his sworn aim to travel the land from end to end, patronizing and condescending wherever he goes.

'It's all right, Beth,' Fatima says, smiling at me uncertainly. 'I always knew he hated me. And Mike agrees, so I know I'm right.'

'But Fats,' I try, but I know it's no use. She's shaking her head.

'Don't try to make me feel better. It's OK. I just need to try to make him like me. In fact,' she adds in a worryingly upbeat tone, 'I've had an idea. What if I make him a cheerful hat? Do you think he would . . . ? Why are you looking at me like that? What?'

Oh my God. How to tell her? 'Don't make him a hat, Fats,' I start, hoping she won't say—

'Why not?'

'Well, um . . .'

'Because you shouldn't waste one second of your life on someone who doesn't appreciate you,' Mike

176

declares assertively. I turn to look at him. He's pretty good – Fatima doesn't even look upset.

'OK, well, in that case, I'll just have to hope for global warming,' she says enigmatically.

'You what?'

She smiles at me. 'Global warming. You must have heard of it? Everyone around the world suddenly starts to realize that everyone else isn't quite as bad as they at first thought, and pretty soon everyone is friends. If he gets affected by that, he'll start liking everyone, won't he? Even me. I'll just have to hope for that.'

I stare at her, but she just sips her hot chocolate, making 'Mmm' sounds. 'Fats, did your mum tell you about global warming?'

She nods. 'Mmm-hmm. Why?'

'No reason.'

Right. I'm back at my desk after that rather surreal break. I stare at my blank computer screen for a few moments, trying to collect my thoughts.

OK. Fatima. Fatima has got her massive debts and might actually go on the game to pay them off, so I have got to get this contract and save her. I know that Sean stands a good chance of getting Whytelys, but right now, Horizon seems like the most likely, so I have to focus on that. I look back at the last four words on my screen:

My dear friend Rupert,

Suddenly I realize that all the nonsense emails with Rupert have been just that – nonsense. He is definitely the sexiest, most fabulously gorgeous man I have ever

177

not quite met, and, if I'm honest, I wasn't exclusively thinking about the contract when I was emailing him. I was kind of hoping that I might get a chance to suck Southern Comfort out of his belly button too.

But that is just fantasy. It's an unrealistic dream and I need to banish it from my mind and steer this conversation back to the contract.

Oh, but . . .

No. I open my eyes, surprised to find that I had closed them. Come on, Beth. I have got to write a sensible message now about Love Learning, and keep the yetis well out of it. I can quite pleasantly refer back to our previous messages regarding the shoes that need to fit, and try to set up a meeting.

My dear friend Rupert,

But then, if I'm going to get all serious and try to book a meeting with him, I need to address the message in a serious way. I can't go calling him my dear friend, and then ask him to check his schedule for next week. I've got to walk into his office and shake his hand soon, and it will be a bit awkward if I'm calling him 'dear friend'.

Oh my God, walk into his office and shake his hand. The thought of it has turned my insides to jelly. That someone has drizzled Southern Comfort over and set on fire.

So what shall I do? The contract is my objective, my only objective now, but it's a bit awkward to try to bring this conversation back round to shoes. How can I do that, without offending him, or making him think I am cold and businesslike?

But I want him to think I am cold and business-

178

like, don't I? I want him to sign on the dotted line, so I need to impress him with my professionalism. Right. So what the bloody hell have I been doing messing around with yetis? Ditzy girl is very cute but fails to impress shrewd businessmen enough to get contracts.

Dear Mr de Witter,

No, too cold. I can picture him now, blinking at his computer screen as he opens that message. He will jerk back in his chair, as if he's been slapped in the face. Then he will read the rest of the message, which will ramble on about the training policy and what we at Love Learning can offer, and when is he available for a preliminary meeting to discuss a range of options. He will shake his head and sigh and say out loud something like, 'So that was it all along.' No, he won't say that because he knows that I only contacted him because I wanted to sign him up. He saw that straight away. What he will say out loud will be something like, 'And I thought we were friends.' No, he won't say that because we're not friends, he couldn't possibly have thought that. He will sigh and close his eyes and lean back in his chair and say, 'What a fucking bitch.' Yes, that's it.

Which leaves me with no alternative but to keep the banter going. It's true. My hands are tied. I have thought seriously about ending it and it's perfectly clear to me that if I stop the banter now, I jeopardize any possible hope of getting his signature on the contract. And what I am sure of is that keeping it going is definitely not *harming* my chances with him. Of getting a contract, I mean.

179

My dear friend Rupert,

I was so glad to receive your message, although obviously quite distressed to learn of your horrifying encounter with the yetis. It must have been terrible. I'm sure it is some consolation to know that at least now they will look more presentable to the next party.

I was very interested to learn about the foot-shaped knick-knacks that are for sale in all the gift shops in that part of the Himalayas. Did you happen to notice what size the yetis' feet were? I am wondering whether they have the correct size shoes because, as we all know, ill-fitting shoes can make one very grumpy, which could explain their poor behaviour.

Your friend,

Beth

What a stroke of genius! I am inwardly cheering myself – managing to bring the conversation back round to shoes and feet will provide the perfect opener.

Hang on, I'm getting a message. Blimey, that was quick.

From: Rupert de Witter

To: Beth Sheridan

Subject: At last

Hello, Beth, it's me, Rupert. Are you there?

Twelve

Specific Concerns

Short-term Goal: Gotta keep cool. He's just a person, like me. With about a million times more sex appeal and pound coins than anyone else I know.
Obstacles: He's a Sexy Millionaire! Oh dear God, how the hell am I going to keep cool?
Long-term Goal: Regain the power of speech and retire to a nursing home to collect yogurt pots.
Obstacles: Got to get the Horizon deal first.

I'm frozen in my seat, staring at that last message. This is suddenly quite different from writing an email and leaving it somewhere he'll find it. This is now, immediate, a proper conversation. I can see him so clearly in my head, his face and hair, and the rest of his body, poised in front of a computer screen of his own, waiting for my reply. My eyes have probably glazed over, but I'm not even aware of it. Hmm, he must have spilt coffee down himself some time earlier as right now he is sitting there with no shirt on. His chest and arms are bronzed and firm, smooth and beautifully formed. I can hardly take my eyes off them. He is

181

smiling with anticipation, but you can also see a hint of anxiety, as he waits for the message, which suddenly pings onto his screen.

Yes, I'm here.

How the hell did that get there? I swear to God I didn't type anything.

My computer pings again and my hand trembles slightly as I open the message. My hand isn't the only part that's trembling.

Well, hello. It's so great to talk to you properly at last instead of just leaving notes for each other. Which were mainly nonsense, I might add. Where on earth did the yetis come from? I nearly choked on my bagel when I read that!

Don't think about the millionaire part, just focus on the sex. Oh, God, no, that's a mistake. Don't think about the sex, just focus on the millionaire. Still no good, the sex is right there, on my desk. I picked up a brochure from Horizon when I was there on Friday and I've opened it at the back page, where Rupert's photo is. Truthfully, it's been permanently open at the back page since I got it. I've always thought he was fuck-off gorgeous in that picture, but now I look at it and I can see how kind he is, how thoughtful, how sensitive.

OK, come on. Gotta compose a reply. Keep him interested.

Bagels are famous for that. Impossibly dry. Did you know there are as many as four bagel-related deaths every year, worldwide? If people would only stick to croissants, lives would be saved.

182

My computer pings again forty-six seconds later.

> I am staggered, and will certainly try to be more careful in future.
> Thanks for the warning.
>   On another, non-bagel-related matter, I would really like to
> speak to you properly. What's your phone number there?

Oh my God. He wants to talk to me on the phone. I can't talk to him on the phone! It will be a disaster. His sex appeal and millions will keep distracting me and I will be about as witty and clever as a baboon's arse. Which, as you know, is funny, but not in a good way. Only in a skirt-tucked-in-your-knickers, chocolate-moustache, hair-burnt-off-your-bum kind of way. I will be a totally crazed, babbling buffoon. I might even drool.

The thing about email conversations, of course, is that you get time to think about your answer. Then you can check it through a few times, edit out a word here, replace a word there, until you are sure that you are presenting to the world the most accurate, the most *real* version of yourself that you can – the one that's unfailingly eloquent, witty, clever and, not least, unbelievably sexy. I am sure that if politicians and drugged-up rock stars only ever spoke via email, or text, tabloid newspapers would go out of business. Think how different things would have been if President Clinton had thumbed 'Did nt hav sxl reltns wiv dat wmn' into his mobile, then read it through, thought, Oh, no, wait a minute, what am I thinking of? and deleted the 'nt' before sending. Hmm. Maybe not.

Anyway, I am panicking. Internally, the blood has

drained from my face, I am biting my nails, frowning, looking nervously around and rocking on my seat. But don't worry: of course I do none of that. I am outwardly calm and poised, smiling a little to myself, the picture of serenity; while secretly I am rummaging frantically through every compartment of my brain, trying to come up with either a) a plausible reason for not giving him the number; or b) a plausible reason for a five-minute delay during any imminent phone conversation. As far as a) goes, there isn't one. Love Learning's phone number is in the Yellow Pages, so he could get it from there if he really wanted to speak to me. Hmmm. That makes me wonder why he doesn't. I mean, I know absolutely nothing about him, apart from his passion, or antipathy, for anchovies. It's possible he's actually asking me for my home number, so he can track me down and loiter outside my flat with binoculars and a meat cleaver.

No, no, that's ridiculous, he's clearly after my work number, which is why he said, 'What's your number there?' and not, 'What's your home number, address and postcode, and do you ever get dressed near the window?'

I can't really imagine it, can you? I mean, Rupert de Witter, sexy millionaire (deep breaths, pant through it), hanging around in the bushes outside someone's flat? Now I come to think of it, if I'm this panicky over Rupert having Love Learning's number, I should be more worried about all the spotty psychopaths or sexual deviants that can also get it. Although I can't really see lots of violent blood-obsessed freaks hunched over their desks, frantically Googling learning and development agencies. Slamming the laptop shut when their mums come in.

'What are you up to, Herman?'

'Nothing, Mum.'

'Have you been looking at learning and development sites again?'

'No, Mum, course not.'

'Well, you'd better not be. You know what the judge said.'

Which all means (I think) that there is no plausible reason for not giving him the number, which only leaves me with option b) – finding a plausible reason for lengthy delays during telephone conversations. And the only possible reason I can think of is a satellite delay, which is ridiculous because I would have to be in Borneo or something.

Although maybe I could have gone there on an educational visit, to see what techniques the Borneo-ites use when delivering training, to ensure maximum learning.

Thankfully at this point my computer pings again, succinctly telling me that I need to get a grip, stop being completely off my head and read my new message. Before I open it, I realize that it's been a few minutes since Rupert asked for the phone number, he knows I am sitting right here at my computer, so he must be wondering why I haven't replied. And God knows, so am I. I lean forward, hoping he hasn't got pissed off. Hoping he still wants to talk to me. Hoping he doesn't.

It's from Sean.

From: Sean Cousins
To: Beth Sheridan
Subject: A repeat?

Hi you. Haven't had a chance to speak to you yet today. You look like you're engrossed in something now so I won't come over.
Just wanted to ask if you fancied going out again some time?
S

Wow. A repeat. Now there are two words designed to sweep a girl right off her feet. I am very surprised that he wants to go out with me again as I know I wasn't great company when we went out on Friday. In fact, I spent the entire evening thinking about two other blokes, although he won't have known that. I didn't at any point say, 'Shut up a minute, will you, I'm trying to fantasize.' I think. But it can't have escaped his notice that I was elsewhere all night – particularly when I sped off in my car just as he was moving in for a kiss. And yet he still wants to go out again. How curious. A strange thought occurs to me. Could it possibly be that he isn't interested in me for my sparkling wit and interesting conversation, doesn't give a damn what films I like or what I was doing when I heard Princess Di had died, and just wants to get into my own personal inbox? Could a man possibly be that *shallow*? Oh my God, I think I may be onto something big.

I click Reply and start typing 'Sean, I really don't think—' But then my computer pings again and my hand automatically takes me back to my inbox. The sight of Rupert's name in the 'From' column causes the whole of the rest of the column to white out, like one of those pink dot optical illusions. I double-click to

186

open it and settle back with a smile to read the lengthy message that appears.

From:	Rupert de Witter
To:	Beth Sheridan
Subject:	Satellite delay

My dearest Beth,

My eyes get snagged at this point and I am unable for a few moments to move on from the subject box. I've suddenly got ice-cold fingers playing chopsticks on my vertebrae and my arms are covered in goosebumps. I glance up and around the office, as if I am expecting to spot him crouching in his suit and size-nine lace-ups behind the photocopier with those binoculars, spying on me. Then I shake my head quickly to dismiss the idea. That is probably the most ridiculous thing I have ever thought, and that's saying something. He couldn't possibly be hiding somewhere in this office because it's all open-plan, there's absolutely nowhere he wouldn't be seen. And anyway, peering at me through binoculars would not make him able to see inside my head. Of course it's nothing sinister like that. In fact, there's no doubt a very, very simple explanation. It'll be either incontrovertible proof of the existence of God or coincidence. Just two minds thinking alike.

I read the rest.

My dearest Beth,
I have constructed three theories regarding your lack of immediate response to my last message:
1) You have been called away from your desk – probably to go

and do some urgent mind-mapping or draw a vital flowchart
on some unfeasibly large paper;

2) You are out of the country on an educational trip and are
   emailing me on a work laptop from your hotel room in Nairobi
   and there is a long satellite delay. (Is there a satellite delay
   over the internet actually? I thought the whole point was that it
   is pretty much instantaneous. I could very well, and likely, be
   wrong about that);

3) My third and, frankly, rather unsettling option is that my
   request for your phone number has disturbed you in some
   way and you are wondering what on earth I want with it, and
   whether or not you should give it to me.

In response to number 1), I want you to know that I am waiting by
my computer for the rest of the day, so whenever you're finished
doing what you're doing, I will be here.

If it's number 2), I will expect a response in the next half-hour,
although if you're in Nairobi, you've got far more interesting
things to do than email a bored businessman sitting at a desk in
England.

And if it does happen to be number 3) (unlikely, I know, but
I need to cover all the options) I thought I should let you know
that I have just got the number out of the Yellow Pages, so if I did
want it for some sinister reason, nothing you or anyone else can
do will stop me now. Ahh ha ha ha ha ha, the world will cower
before me, etc.

Rupert

The moment I finish reading, two things happen quite
quickly. First, I hear the phone ring on Ali's desk. And
second, Ali shouts across to me to tell me there's a call
for me.

I grab my Horizon brochure from my desk and focus
on the picture on the back page for a few seconds while

Ali transfers the call. Mm, there he is, in godlike glory. My belly squirms and gurgles as the call arrives and I reach out to pick up the phone that holds the voice to that gorgeous face.

'You all right, Beth?'

Ali's concerned voice comes through the earpiece and I nod dreamily. 'Mm, fine. Just . . .' Just lost the power of speech as I'm about to speak to the sexiest man alive, who's also very witty and belly-floppably charming, I try to say, but having lost the power of speech, I just grunt. Then I cough a bit and bang my chest, using my palm as a kind of do-it-yourself defibrillator. Sure enough, my heart restarts.

'OK, well, here he is.' And he clicks off.

'Beth Sheridan,' I croak after a few seconds of wondering how I should start. 'How may I help you?'

'You know, I was wondering the very same thing.'

Oh wow. What a voice. I sway in my seat a bit as all the blood rushes from my head. It's like the audio equivalent of the first festive sip of Baileys liqueur after not drinking it since last Christmas – warm and rich and in some strange way comfortingly familiar. A slight dizziness sweeps over me. 'Sorry, can I ask who this is please?' I say, attempting to sound as if I'm busy casting a final glance over some notes on a brilliant presentation I'm about to give.

'It's Rupert,' he says meltingly, 'de Witter. From Horizon Holidays.'

'Oh hello,' I say, trying to sound enlightened. 'You got the number, then?'

'I had to, for two very good reasons. And probably more.'

'Oh. Well. What are they?'

189

'OK. Number one: to prove to you that I have no sinister reason for asking for your number, and, in fact, could easily obtain it from the internet, or directory enquiries, or the Yellow Pages. As can anyone, and as, in fact, I did, as you know. Or, well, as my assistant did.'

'Ah.' I'm not being deliberately cool here; I'm simply unable to articulate consonants.

'And number two: I wanted very much to speak to you.'

Vowel sounds have gone now, too. There's a protracted silence as we both wait for me to say something. When I don't, he says, 'To arrange a meeting.'

I nod, glancing around me at the rest of the office. He's not here, of course, hiding under the desk, but I do need to look as if I am in control of the situation for the benefit of anyone watching me. So I make a pensive face, pushing out my lips, and nod again. My face is saying, 'I very much like that idea and can definitely see the mutual benefits,' even if I'm not.

'The thing is,' he goes on, 'before I sign any contracts, I have to meet the person I'm dealing with face to face, particularly when they bring up yetis in their introductory correspondence. It's a formality I insist on in those circumstances.'

I giggle and some of my voice returns. 'Do they come up a lot, then?' I manage to croak out.

'What, yetis? No, not really. It's quite rare, actually. To tell you the truth, you're my first one. Took me a bit by surprise, as you know.'

'Ah yes, the bagel. I hope you are fully recovered now?'

'Well, it was touch and go for a while but it went down eventually. Are you free tomorrow?'

All the air rushes out of me in a gasp, which thankfully I manage to keep silent. Tomorrow. Oh. My. God. I'm meeting him tomorrow. I breathe deeply a few times to prepare my voice for calm, dignified speech. And not squeals of excited delight.

'Miss Sheridan?' he says in my ear. 'Are you still there? Oh, sorry, it is Miss, is it? No, um, I mean . . .' He breaks off suddenly, as if someone has clamped a hand over the mouthpiece at his end. I hear the muted sound of a throat clearing, then the muffled static clears again. 'Sorry about that. So, are you free tomorrow?'

'Tomorrow is fine,' I breathe, sounding extraordinarily calm and sexy, even to my own ears. 'And it is Miss.'

'Excellent,' he says, and I'm not sure if he means about tomorrow, or about the 'Miss'. There's a definite smile in his voice and I close my eyes for a moment. Then open them again as soon as I realize I can't look at his face with them closed.

'Where then? Shall I come to your offices?'

'No, let's do it somewhere neutral. Um, no, I don't mean . . . you know, *do it* . . . That's not what—'

'Somewhere neutral will be fine,' I come in smoothly, feeling cool and seductive. I half close my eyes, but leave just enough gap for light bouncing off Rupert's picture to get in. 'Where would you like to meet?'

I hear nothing but laboured breathing for a few moments. Maybe he's asthmatic. Maybe he's aroused. I find myself shivering suddenly.

'Are you all right?' I ask quietly, partly out of

concern and partly out of longing to hear more from that smooth body-butter voice. It's mostly concern, of course. If he were having an asthma attack, it would certainly explain why he's stumbling over his words like this. But so would arousal.

'Mmm,' he says, then clears his throat. 'Sorry.' I close my eyes briefly at the sound of his voice. It's so gorgeous, I feel like I've been listening to it all my life. Either that or he sounds just like Daniel Craig. 'Just trying to think of somewhere neutral.'

'Switzerland?'

He chuckles loudly. 'Yes, that is a possible. Bit far though, wouldn't you say?'

'Hmm. 'Spose so. I would have to be back by five thirty to lock up the offices.'

'How about Paris then?'

'Oh, yes, of course, much more doable. With the Eurostar connections, I need only be gone a couple of hours. I could meet you in my lunch-break and be back for the afternoon sessions.'

It has occurred to me suddenly that he could be completely serious about Paris and by laughing it off like that, I might just have missed out on a fabulous trip in a private jet, or helicopter, or something. He's bound to have access to that sort of thing. Of course I wouldn't have gone, though. It would have been my duty, as a professional, to turn him down. If it ever got out, there might be a 'Favours for good training rates' scandal in the local *Herald*.

'Oh, I'm not sure about that,' he's saying. 'I think we will probably be gone the whole day. I was planning on taking my hot air balloon.'

Images and sounds swiftly rush into my head, one

after another: silent, gentle rising; the rush of wind and heat; a picnic basket; the clink of two champagne glasses; breathtaking, rolling hillsides; a first kiss in the clouds.

I shake my head like a cartoon dog and the pictures burst. I really must get a grip. I have never even met this man. I think my desperate need to secure this contract is starting to impair my rationality. That must be what it is. Yes, just my anxiety over my job and the strong sense of responsibility I am feeling towards Fatima right now.

Or it's that face.

No, now come on, Beth, focus. Get the contract with Horizon, then you can go back to acting normally.

Yeah, and I'm almost convinced until I catch sight of Rupert's picture again and fierce heat licks up inside my abdomen.

'I expect your wife has got used to you being out late, has she?' I hear myself asking, although I swear I never made my lips move. I grab them and press them together with my fingers, to stop them from acting on their own again.

Oh God, he hasn't answered. Why did I mention his wife? What on earth has that, or she, got to do with my business meeting with him? They are completely irrelevant to each other. And now his long silence means that my question has raised specific concerns that he needs to think about for a moment. Clearly he has just realized that I am that mad customer at table four – the plump middle-aged one who flutters her eyelashes coquettishly at all the horrified seventeen-year-old waiters and asks them what their girlfriends think about them chatting up a lot of desperate

193

housewives – and he is going to say something like, 'I fail to see how that could possibly be—'

'I'm not married.'

'Sorry, what? Oh, you're not? Oh.' And despite myself, a huge sigh of relief comes flooding out of me. Quickly I stop it mid-blissful smile and glue my lips together again.

'No, I'm not.' He pauses. 'I'm still looking.'

'Ah.' Consonants have gone again.

'So no one gets fed up, no matter how late I'm out.'

'Mmm.'

'Even if it's all night.'

'. . .'

'Oh, look, sorry, Beth, that's not what we were talking about. What's the matter with me? You are very distracting, you know.'

'No. Ahem. No, don't try and blame me. We were just talking about your hot air balloon.'

'And you asked me if I was married.'

'No, I asked you if your wife minded you being out late.'

'And whatever answer I gave would tell you the answer to the question that you didn't actually ask. So no, I'm not married.'

God, he's good. He sees straight through me, just like with my opener about shoe sizes. Damn.

'All right, Einstein. At least I didn't stumble over it, like "Oh, it is Miss, is it? No, whoops, sorry, um, fiddlesticks, what am I saying, sorry, didn't mean it that way."'

Now he's laughing. 'All right, you got me too. Let's say we're even.'

194

'And we're both single.' Holy crap. What the flaming hell is going on with my lips today? I think they, like me, are preoccupied with what it would be like pressing up against that beautiful face.

'Hmm, we are, aren't we?' He sounds like he's doing interested nodding. Pleased nodding, even. Or is he doing that horrified nodding you do when you realize the person you're talking to is certifiable?

'So, Beth, where are we going to meet tomorrow? It is probably too cold for the hot air balloon, plus it takes ages to inflate it and I can never remember where I left the foot pump.'

'Can't you blow it up yourself?'

'I could do but it always makes me feel dizzy.'

'Not enough hot air?'

'That's what I've found. So how about lunch somewhere? Madeleine's?'

Madeleine's! I've lived in this town all my life and have to admit to never having been there before. It's very posh and ritzy and I have never been out with anyone posh and ritzy enough. And it is not the sort of place you can go to on your own. 'Madeleine's is perfect,' I say easily, as if I go there all the time. 'Shall we say one o'clock?' I hope to God I can afford it. Perhaps I'll just have the soup. I hope to God there's soup.

'One o'clock it is. I'll book a table, and see you there.'

'Lovely. I'll look forward to it.'

'So will I.'

We both hang up and I stare unseeingly at the space in front of me for a few seconds, keeping my insistent grins down to enigmatic smiles. I have got a date tomorrow with Rupert de Witter! Of Horizon Holidays! The multi-millionaire.

Jesus Christ in a hot air balloon.

In his office, Rupert puts the receiver back in its cradle and rests his hand on it for a moment with a distracted smile.

'Well?' says a voice to his left. He looks up towards Harris who is watching him interestedly from the comfy chair. 'How did it go?'

'Got one, no problem. Tomorrow, one o'clock.'

'At Madeleine's? Bloody hell, how did you manage that this close to Christmas?'

'Piece of cake, Harry. They know me there, remember?'

'But if all the tables are booked, they can't produce another one out of thin air, can they?'

'Actually, they did produce another one, although not out of thin air. They were all booked up, but when they knew it was me, they said they would set up the table in the pavilion.'

'No way! They never open that up in winter. It'll be freezing.'

'That's where you're wrong, old friend. They are filling the place up with heaters around the edge, and lighting it with a hundred candles. It's going to be stunning.'

'Oh, right. I see. Stunning. Hm.' He rubs his chin thoughtfully.

Rupert watches him a moment. 'OK, come on, what're you thinking? No, don't say "Nothing", you've obviously got something you want to say. Out with it.'

'All right, well, I was just wondering whether this is a

196

business lunch or a romantic dinner *à deux*? You know – Madeleine's, the pavilion, a hundred candles, romantic music, good wine, delicious food, moonlight –'

'One o'clock, Harris.'

'– and the two of you.'

'And five electric heaters.'

'Oh yeah, plus the heaters.'

Rupert considers a moment. 'The truth is, I'm not really sure. I started off being impressed by her because she was original and funny, and that could only be good for Horizon – a fresh outlook for our training policy. But then, after we had emailed each other a few times, I started to like her for all sorts of other, non-work-related reasons. She's got this way of writing – charming, intelligent, interesting. Waiting for her emails to come through is like, I don't know, waiting for . . . exam results. Yeah. All that wondering if you did well enough to impress, did you get it right, have you passed.'

'That's not exactly a sexy image, you know.'

Rupert pushes his hands through his hair. 'Really? Maybe I've said it wrong.' He pauses. 'No, no, maybe you're right, actually. It probably isn't sexy. I mean, we're just corresponding at the moment, that's all there is to it. But I'm interested. I'd like it to be more. And that starts with lunch tomorrow.'

'OK, I get it. But my question still stands – is lunch tomorrow pleasure or business?'

Rupert pauses, one hand on the back of his head, then grins and shrugs. 'I don't know. Obviously I have to meet her to sort out the business side of things. And that will allow me to see what she's like in the flesh, and decide where I want to go from there.' He raises his eyebrows. 'Kind of made up my mind about that already, actually.'

Harris stares at him a moment. 'Hang on a minute. Isn't this the girl you saw at the party on Friday? The one you've met before?'

'No. Different girl altogether.'

'For crying out loud, Rupert. What's the matter with you? I thought you really liked that other one?'

'I did. I do. But there's no point thinking about her because I don't really know her name, or where she works, or anything about her. There's no way I will ever be able to find her again, so I may as well move on.'

'Right, OK, so let me get this straight. This one you're meeting tomorrow is . . . who, exactly?'

'She works at Love Learning, that training business Dickie Love set up when he left here.'

'And you've never met?'

Rupert shakes his head. 'Not to my knowledge. Rhonda says she recognizes the name, though.'

'Really? In what context?'

Rupert shrugs. 'She may have worked here at some point. Rhonda's got an amazing memory for names. She's looking into it for me.'

Harris raises his eyebrows. 'Fancy that. But you didn't meet her then?'

'No, as I told you, as far as I know, we've never met.'

'But you've got feelings for her?'

Rupert raises his eyebrows, glances down, then looks back at Harris and nods.

'So she could be fifty-nine, with eight grandchildren and be as wide as she is tall?'

Rupert shakes his head dismissively. 'Could be. Doesn't matter.'

'Really?'

'Nope. Don't look at me like that – I'm absolutely serious. Obviously I'd prefer it if she wasn't years older than me, but even that isn't really important. She makes me laugh and she's good company. That on its own is incredibly attractive to me. Jesus, how many beautiful people have I met who can't speak in full sentences? They bore you rigid talking about their hair or their shoes or their mobile phone. People like that think they don't need to make an effort because their looks will get them through anything. And the trouble is, Harry, most of the time they're right. Everyone is so bloody shallow these days, like being good-looking is the most important thing about anyone. Forget wit, manners or interesting conversation. If you've got good skin and a tiny waist, you'll be a success. It pisses me right off.'

Harris puts his hands up with a grin. 'Hey, mate, I'm only kidding. I happen to agree with you; I was just winding you up. It's irrelevant in this case anyway, isn't it?'

Rupert looks at him. 'What do you mean?'

'Well, don't you remember what Dickie Love is like? Everyone who worked for him had to meet certain specific . . . *criteria* . . .'

There's a pause as Rupert stares at Harris, then stands up and moves over to the window, rubbing his hand over his face. He looks down at the street for a few seconds before turning back. 'So, you're saying that . . . you think . . . she might be . . . beautiful as well?'

Harris nods. 'No question. Unless the sad pervert has changed his habits. But that I seriously doubt.'

Rupert sits down heavily in his chair and stares at a point on his desk. 'Wow.'

Harris leans forward in his seat. 'Rupe, listen, I've just thought of something.'

Rupert looks up. 'What?'

'You say she initiated contact between you? OK. So she emailed you, Rupert de Witter, presumably after getting the email address from the Horizon brochure?'

'I suppose so.'

'I would say therefore that there is a strong likelihood that she has seen the photo in the back. Wouldn't you?'

There's an extended silence, while both men stare expectantly at each other.

'Bugger,' Rupert says finally. 'I'd completely forgotten about that.'

Harris presses his lips together. 'I have been trying to get you to update that photo for years . . .'

'Yes, yes, I know. I should have got round to it, but it's just not important, is it? I mean, everyone here knows about it, what does it matter?'

'Well, nothing. *Then*. It matters slightly more *now*, I think. Don't you?'

Rupert stares at him for a few moments, then says, 'I can't go.' He shakes his head. 'I can't do it.'

'Course you can. Just walk right up to her and introduce yourself.'

'Christ no. What on earth is she going to think, after looking at that picture? No, no, I can't go.' He drops his head in his hands.

'Oh come on,' Harris says gently. 'What about everything you just said about looks not being important? About everyone being so shallow? I'm sure she won't think less of you, and you've got to get out there sooner or later. You've got to show your face . . .'

'Nope. No way. Not doing it. Forget it. Fuck it. Fucking fucking *fuck* it.' He looks up suddenly at Harris, the expression on his face changing gradually from depths of despair to 'milligram of hope'.

'Harris, old pal. You're my accountant. You go and meet her.'

'WHAT?'

'No, no, I don't mean pretend to be me. I just mean have lunch with her, sort out the business, talk about me a bit, you know, tell her what a great guy I am, and then come back here and tell me all about her.'

'No.'

'Harris, please. As a friend?' Harris shakes his head. 'A business associate?' More shaking. 'All right then. I didn't want to have to do this but you leave me no choice: you're fired.'

'Oh that's low, Rupert. Really, that's low.'

'Yes, I know. And I'm sorry. But I really need you to help me out here. I mean, I'm not asking you to walk across hot coals, or have lunch at Eggz N Beanz. This will be a lovely, candlelit lunch for two, in the pavilion at Madeleine's, with a charming and funny young woman, who is also likely to be beautiful. I will pay.'

'Damn right you will.'

'So you'll go then?'

Harris closes his eyes for a moment, then looks wearily back at Rupert. 'All right. But you will owe me, big time.'

'Course, mate, course. And don't forget to tell her what an all-round great bloke I am, all right? Now the meal is tax deductible, isn't it?'

Thirteen

Honouring Commitments

**Short-term Goal: Find something engrossing to do
that will take about twenty-seven hours, so I can
check my watch and realize with a shock that it's
time to leave for my lunch appointment.**

**Obstacles: What on earth can I do that takes that
long?**

**Long-term Goal: A twenty-seven-hour-long sex
session with Rupert de Witter. Nnnhhhhh . . .**

Obstacles: Not sure if that's really possible.

I would love to be able to cut straight to 12.59 and
walk into Madeleine's now, wearing killer shoes with a
glossy brochure under one arm and a Gucci bag under
the other. But several other things have got to happen
first.

Firstly, it's still Monday, so if I walk into Madeleine's
in those shoes at 12.59 today, no one will be expecting
me, and someone will be embarrassed that there's no
table available for me. It will be me.

So I've made lots of other plans to keep me occupied
in the meantime. At 12.59 today, I intend to be in

the kitchen pulling the cellophane off my Healthy Options turkey, stuffing and cranberry sandwich. I will probably also enjoy a virtually fat-free mince pie and a Crunchie bar, and make myself a cup of tea to dip it in. Then there has to be a whole afternoon of work, followed by the evening with Vini, and a night's tossing and turning in bed. Even then, it's only going to be seven o'clock in the morning, with a hideous six hours of nothingness to get through before my meeting at one.

The first hour goes by like a Christmas pantomime. You know that if you just grit your teeth and keep smiling, they'll get on with the story *in a minute*. I glance up at the clock, feeling sure five hours have passed and it must be almost time to go home, but it's only quarter to twelve. Bugger.

The next hour passes like the Mesozoic era. Entire species were begun, evolved beyond their means, and died out. I sip my tea but it's gone cold. Doesn't matter, it passes the time.

My computer pings! Yippee! I practically fling myself head first into my inbox in my eagerness to distract myself from the clock, but it's disappointingly quick and from Sean. Can you believe it takes less than eight seconds to receive and open a new message?

> Hi! You OK? Just wondering if you had a chance to read my earlier message about going out again. What do you think? Please let me know soon and put me out of my misery!
> Sean

Hmm. Odd decision to put an exclamation mark after a word like 'misery'. I mean, it's not like he's written something like 'Surprise!' or 'Wake up!' It feels like he's saying 'put me out of my misery' with an ironic smile on his face. Or, as it's an email, it would be an e-smile. E-irony. Anyway, what's the point of implying that wondering whether or not I'll go out with him again is causing him misery, and then taking all the misery away with the exclamation mark? It doesn't make any sense. I find I am frowning slightly as I try to puzzle it out, so I consciously smooth out my brow. Is he in misery or isn't he? It hardly seems likely. In fact, the only credible explanation is that the man is a complete di—

'Did you see my email, Beth?'

'Shit! You made me jump.' God, I only jumped as much as that because I feel like I've been caught doing something I shouldn't. He's standing right behind me, resting his hands on the back of my chair, but it's not like he can see what I was just thinking. I close my eyes and lay my hand on my chest, partly to show him that I really was startled, and partly to disguise my guilty expression. His face creases a bit around the eyes and he crouches down by my side.

'God, sorry, sweetheart, didn't mean to scare you. You all right?'

'Yes yes, I'm fine.' But call me sweetheart again and I will rip your tonsils out with my fingernails and re-place them with your testicles. 'How are you?'

He does that very masculine thing where he nods by jerking his chin up once, and grins. 'Couldn't be better. D'you see my email, then?'

'Oh, yes I did, thanks. Erm, haven't had a chance to reply yet, sorry. Been really busy.'

His eyes widen like Macaulay Culkin seeing Santa

Claus, and he gets a hungry, urgent look on his face. He leans in close and says, 'Busy? What with?'

'Oh, you know, working. Prepping, researching, same old thing.'

'Contract hunting?' He breathes it as if he hardly dares believe it.

'Well, yeah, a bit of that. Why?'

'You getting anywhere?'

I open my mouth to tell him that I've set up a meeting for tomorrow lunchtime, but then I realize that he will expect me to tell him who it's with, given that he's told me all about his Whytelys appointment. So I close it again. Then open it and say, 'No, not really. Can't seem to get beyond the receptionists so far.'

'Where've you tried?'

I hesitate before answering. I'm actually frantically making something up in my head, but he obviously misinterprets this and speaks again before I have a chance to.

'Oh, no, look, let's not talk about this here. I only came over to see if you wanted to go out for a drink tomorrow night? We can talk properly then, yeah?'

Well, it's a no, obviously. I mean, can you imagine how I will be feeling after having lunch with Rupert? I am fully expecting to be unable to vocalize, or walk, so will not want to be spending the evening with anyone other than him, even if it's just the memory of him. And secret parts of me are urging me to keep the evening free, just in case lunch goes really, *really* well.

'Actually, Sean, tomorrow isn't—'

'Please, Beth.' He's put his hand on my arm and I look down at it. I can feel the heat of it through my blouse. He's practically on fire. 'I really don't want to be sitting at home on my own tomorrow night. I won't be able to stand it.' And incredibly, his eyes start to look a bit misty.

'Oh. Are you all right? What is it?'

He shakes his head, all strong and silent, and rubs his eyes with his thumb and forefinger. 'Nothing. Sorry. Look, please have a drink with me tomorrow night. You'll be helping me out of a real spot. Please?'

A man in tears. Is there anything more alluring? Well, yes, there is actually, just one – a man standing on his own yacht. The Horizon brochure is still lying open on my desk at the back page, and the picture there is practically radiating light and magnetism. I can feel my eyes being drawn to it involuntarily. Oh God, I really wanted to keep the evening free.

'All right then. One drink, to help you out.'

'That's terrific.' He grins and stands up abruptly, all hint of those tears gone. 'Shall we meet in the Patch and Parrot again? Eight o'clock? I'll look forward to it.' And with one final, somewhat creepy, slow wink, he returns to his desk.

Buggeration. Well, there is one upside. Vini always says you shouldn't be too available to start with, so having something booked for tomorrow evening is pretty cool. I just hope to God Rupert does ask me out to dinner so that I can say, 'I'm sorry, I'm busy tonight.' Otherwise my evening with Sean will be pointless. Of course, I could say I'm busy anyway, even if I wasn't going out with Sean, but, truthfully, I probably wouldn't. Plus, this will give it authenticity. You need a bit of authenticity when you're being aloof and hard to get, especially when actually you want to suck liqueur from his navel.

The afternoon inches past. It's lucky that I haven't got much work to do today, because I have been far too busy passing the time. I've written my Christmas list on an Excel spreadsheet. I've made a comprehensive to-do list, including 'Make a Christmas List', so I can cross something off straight away. That's very satisfying. I've cleaned out my handbag and made a shopping list of all the things I need to buy to replace the things I've thrown away. I've had three cups of tea and gone to the toilet four times; and frankly I am running out of options. Finally, at three thirty, something interesting happens. I've decided to log into my personal email account, just in case there happens to anything from Brad, and just as I am rooting around in my bag for my nail file, which I can't find because of all the lists, my computer pings.

I drop my bag instantly – the nail file falls out onto the floor – and zoom in to the inbox. Please please please let it not be about penis enlargement.

It's not. I peer closer at the strange name.

From: VPickford@FastLove.co.uk
To: esp79@hotmail.co.uk
Subject: Contact details

Dear Elizabeth,
Following your attendance at a Fast Love meeting last week, one of my other clients is anxious to make contact with you, but unfortunately the contact number we have for you seems to be innacurate. The client in question was selected by you on your sheet also. He does not have access to a computer and is therefore unable to contact you by email, therefore would you please send me at your earliest convience a phone number that

I can forward to him and a speedy resolution may be gained to everyone's satisfaction.

Yours

Val Pickford

My jaw practically hits the floor as I read this message. Can this really be true? Has Brad been trying to contact me all this time? Has he been frantically trying to honour the commitment he made when he ticked my box, and I accidentally wrote my mobile number down wrong? Fucking arses and bums, what a dunce! I could almost laugh, it's so stupid and wonderful.

It's odd that she says he hasn't got access to a computer. I mean, I know he works at Horizon, I've seen him there. And I know for sure that there are lots and lots of computers there. Is it a lie? Is he lying to Val Pickford or to me?

Oh my God, it doesn't matter! I can ask him when I see him. Which should be today or tomorrow, if I sort this out now. I email Val back my mobile phone number immediately, and then dial Vini's mobile number. She'll be stunned.

Hang on a minute. Quickly I press the 'End' key and put the phone back in my bag. Vini doesn't officially know about Brad – she only guessed that I'd met someone, I never confirmed it. And she still hasn't told me about her uncharacteristic use of pink lipgloss the other day, or what she was doing in the Patch and Parrot the other night, so I'm certainly not going to give her the satisfaction of hearing about this. Yeah, and I just know she will try to tell me that I wrote my mobile number down wrongly on purpose, to sabotage any chance I might have of meeting someone new because

I am still in love with Richard.

Richard. Hmm. Haven't thought about him for a while.

Anyway, she's completely wrong. I mean, what would be the point of writing my number down wrongly? All I had to do to avoid the possibility of falling in love with someone new and being happy for ever was not tick any of the boxes. Simple. Absolutely no need for any silly messing around with fake names and numbers.

Except, as Vini will remind me, I did use a fake name.

So what? And anyway that doesn't count. It is part of my name. My parents still call me Libby, or Elizabeth, or Beth. But that's not the point. The point is I didn't have to give a false name or number because unless you both tick the box, no one gets numbers or addresses anyway. I pick up the phone again.

Yes, but Vini will say I did it subconsciously. I slam the phone down again. She will say that I didn't even know I was doing it, but it speaks more clearly than anything I might try to say to her about how much I am over Richard and ready to move on. I did it on purpose to thwart my own desire for happiness, even though I didn't know about it at the time.

God, she's got a bloody answer for everything.

Which brings me back to the fact that I can't tell her about the phone number. I will just have to tell her later that Brad took a week to get in touch because . . . because . . . oh, because he was in a car accident on the way home from the Fast Love meeting! Fantastic.

My mobile phone beeps in my bag and I freeze. Fuck, that was quick. I stare for a few seconds at the bag, as if it might magically transform into a handsome prince, then seize it from the floor, yank it open and rummage frantically for my phone.

It's showing one unread message, and is asking me, very politely like a member of household staff, 'Read now?' No, I think I'll wait until tomorrow. Of course I want to bloody read it now, and I stab the 'Y' key.

> Hi u gorges creture! Hav bin tryng 2 get u 4 days but no joy. V v
> exited to meet agen as soon as u want. Giv me a call or txt luv
> Nigel no. 15 xxxy

What? *What?* Who the fuck is Nigel? I stare at the message, frowning hard, not even worrying about the lines on my forehead. What the hell is going on? I don't know who this guy is but I can tell from his spelling that I didn't tick him. Not in sixty-five million years, if the human race depended on it. The world can do without these genes. I know – I KNOW – I only ticked one person, and that was Brad, and he was number fifteen. So how has this freak got my mobile number?

I find myself looking up and around the room, as if I expect to find the answer on the Investors in People poster, but of course there are never any answers there. I turn back to the phone and read the message again. This is clearly not from lovely Brad after all. I sag in my seat for a few moments, disappointment and misery pulling me down like gravity. And then I am invigorated by fury. Vini is the only person who knows I went speed dating last week. Which means that either Nigel is real and actually has got my mobile number somehow, which is impossible because I know I didn't tick anyone like this, or Vini is playing a trick on me.

Oh my God. The bitch. No doubt she remembers me asking her what she thought of number fifteen and is now using it against me.

Quickly I press Reply and key in a message.

How luvly 2 hear from u. Meet me 2moro nite, Patch and Parrot, 8.30. L

Perfect. Now she will feel really guilty for winding me up and will have to come clean before tomorrow night to stop me from going down there. No, wait, I am going out with Sean tomorrow night and am bound to let slip about that. She'd know it was a fake answer. Quickly I change it to Wednesday night, and press Send.

Finally the day ends and I go home to sit and wait for tomorrow to come. Vini is in the kitchen picking freeze-dried cranberries out of a bowl of cereal.

'Hiya,' she says, looking up. 'Good day?'

I narrow my eyes. She wants me to mention the message from Nigel so she can do some kind of infantile 'Gotcha!' but I'm not giving her the satisfaction. 'Yes thanks. Got a lunch meeting tomorrow with Rupert de Witter.'

'Fuck, no way!'

'Well, yeah. Why not?'

She scoops the dried fruit into her hand and pours it into the bin. 'You are talking about Rupert de Witter of Horizon Holidays, the richest man in the whole of this God-forsaken little town? The man who is therefore completely impossible to see anywhere, ever?'

'Um, yeah, I suppose so.'

'Jesus, Beth, how lucky are you? This bloke's bound to have a completely full schedule, booked right up to

May no doubt, and you just happened to be able to set up a meeting with him *tomorrow*? It's incredible.'

'Vin . . .' I start, and then I pause. She's got a good point. Businessmen like Rupert have got such incredibly busy lives their diaries have to be managed by someone else. Sometimes two people. So how come he could arrange a lunch with me for tomorrow, just like that? Just happened to have an opening in his calendar for lunch tomorrow? Unlikely. Cancelled something to make room for me? A hot plunging sensation fills me from my chest right down to my thighs. Could that be possible? No, no, it's just as unlikely as him happening to be free tomorrow. Unless . . .

No, I'm not considering that. It's a business lunch, that's all. It's no more important to him than countless other business lunches he's had, and will be having today, tomorrow and the whole week, no doubt. He must have had a last-minute cancellation, like the hairdresser. People are always getting unlikely appointments because of last-minute cancellations. Other people, that is. It never happens to me.

'Anyway, I'm off out in a minute.' She's scoffing the cereal standing up by the sink.

'Where are you going?'

She shrugs dismissively. A bit too dismissively, actually. 'Oh, nowhere, nothing, just a business dinner. Seeya.' And she dumps the empty bowl in the sink and goes to her room.

I stare after her. I know Vini. She's eating cereal before going out for dinner so that she's not starving when she gets to the restaurant and can pick daintily at her food. That's no business meeting she's off to.

To get my revenge, I rummage through her Fake

Face wardrobe after she's gone. These are some of the costumes and outfits she keeps at home for her clients to wear when ordinary clothes won't do. Indiana Jones is in there, as is Jack Sparrow, and Neo from *The Matrix*. I am expressly forbidden from touching the stuff in here, and even more forbidden from taking anything out and, heaven help me, wearing it. Yeah, well, I have never had need to wear anything from in here before (although I have tried everything on, of course, even Forrest Gump – it's the principle), but now I want something jaw-droppingly sexy to wear to lunch tomorrow. My clothes aren't bad but I think I might look more businesslike if I wear a shorter skirt, and higher shoes. And maybe painted my nails.

I linger for a moment over the *Charlie's Angels* jump-suit. God, that would be fantastic, wouldn't it? I could stride in and be all commanding and forceful, as if I know how to handle a gun. Maybe I could even turn up in a crash helmet and then shake my hair out after taking it off. God, it's a seductive image – Rupert agog as he spots me in the doorway. I know I do look pretty good in this, and now, with the blond hair too . . . No, come on, Beth, you're selling training, not riding a motorcycle fast after a drug dealer. Eventually I find something that looks like it might have been worn by Michelle Pfeiffer – above-the-knee skirt, silky cream blouse, killer shoes – and hide it in my room for to-morrow.

I spend the rest of the evening getting ready. I won't go into details; suffice to say there's wax. Actually, it's been a while since I did any of this stuff, so by the time I walk into the office the next morning, I am smoother than I have been for quite a few months and the silky

Michelle Pfeiffer clothes are sliding sensuously over my skin.

Sean wolf-whistles at me once I've taken my coat off and suddenly I feel a bit self-conscious.

'Wow, you got it going on today, blondie,' he says in a low voice. 'That sexy secretary look really suits you. I am so looking forward to tonight.' And he does that creepy slow wink again before going off to his own desk.

What the hell does that mean? Surely he doesn't think I have dressed up like this for him? Oh God. Must make sure I put on something frumpy and un-attractive before I go to meet him tonight, just so he knows. Vini'll have something.

Right, the lunch is at one so I have got just over three hours to kill, allowing thirty minutes to drive into town and find somewhere to park. I slide the Horizon brochure out of my desk drawer and let my eyes linger on the photo at the back. Oh my God. Quickly I put it back in my drawer, grab my bag and coat and head into town.

Parking was surprisingly easy, seeing as it's still relatively early, so at quarter past ten I find myself aimlessly wandering round the town, trying to look like I've got loads to do. Actually I have got loads to do – still got to get something for my little cousin Charlotte and her parents – but I can't do any of it until after I've had lunch with Rupert. I can't look poised and seductive arriving at Madeleine's with a pair of bunny slippers, an electric screwdriver and a foot spa under my arm.

Actually it's more to do with *feeling* poised and seductive when I arrive. I could leave the bunnies in

214

the car, but I would still know they were there.

So how do I kill the time until twelve thirty (allowing half an hour to walk back to the car, drive out to Madeleine's and park again)? I'm wandering up the pedestrianized precinct, hands in pockets, looking all around me and suddenly my gaze falls on Whytelys. Well, it's this fuck-off enormous five-storey building in the centre of the town, with a series of pumpkin-sized gold baubles and multicoloured lights flashing and blinking in every window display. I couldn't fail to see it. But at this point, a thought occurs to me.

Sean has got his meeting with the regional manager this afternoon, probably around the same time that I am meeting Rupert. What if I wander around the shop now and see if I can find out some stuff for him? Then I can call him at the office, tell him what I've learned, and he will be able to use it in his pitch this afternoon.

This is fantastic! Not only will it give me something purposeful to do so I can stop looking like I've been stood up, it also means that if Love Learning is saved by the Whytelys contract, I will be able to say that I had a hand in it.

That sounds terrible and I don't mean it like that. I only mean that I won't have to be one hundred per cent grateful to Sean. No one will.

So I stroll in and mingle discreetly amongst all the embroidered cardigans and navy slacks, who are looking at the Royal Jelly sets. My Michelle Pfeiffer outfit does stand out a bit here so I think the best thing to do is look like I'm here officially. Quickly I pop outside and go up to WH Smiths, where I buy a ring binder and some paper to put in it, deciding right at the last minute to get some subject dividers too. I clip the paper into the binder, shove the dividers in, and hold it against my chest. Then I go back into Whytelys and stride purposefully over to the Customer Services desk and ask to speak to the manager.

It turns out she knows nothing about the training policy. 'I manage the shop, love,' she tells me. 'Blouses I know. Ties I can handle. Bath salts, scented pillows, padded coat hangers, I'm your woman. Policy – wouldn't have a clue. That's all managed by the bods at head office. People who sit around all day deciding what to do next! Like they would know anything about running a shop floor this size, eh?'

'Right.' I open my ring binder pointedly and hold my pen poised on the first page. 'But you must know what training the staff are given when they first join the group? I mean, do they get an induction? Is there a mandatory health and safety . . . ?'

'Like I said, love, if the flowery nighties need straightening, I'll know what to do. If suede slippers are required, come to me. If you want to talk about training, you need to speak to head office. You follow?'

'I follow,' I say. 'Don't suppose you've got a number for them, have you?'

'Can do, love. Just a mo. NERYS!' she shrieks, and over by the Christmas puddings a tubby woman with tinsel in her hair starts, then comes running over.

'Yes?'

'Head office number for this lady, please, Nerys.'

'Oh, right. OK.'

We both watch Nerys's tubby little body bounce away and exit through the 'Staff Only' door at the back, then the manager turns back to me.

216

'Anything else I can help you with?'

'No, that's fine, thank you so much.'

'Free mince pie if you buy a gingerbread latte in the café?'

I shake my head. 'No, really, I'm fine, thanks.'

'Right you are. Nice meeting you, then.' And she flings her hands behind her back and stalks away, straightening a cardy here, a camisole there.

When Nerys returns, I consider asking her what training she received when she started working here, but after handing me the slip of paper with the phone number on it, she skitters away before I have a chance to say anything. Damn.

Well, that was a complete waste of time. Excellent – objective achieved then. Although there's still an hour to go before I can start my journey to Madeleine's. What shall I do now?

'Stood you up, love?' someone says, walking past.

'No!' I shout indignantly. Why is it that you can't even stand still in one place without someone feeling the need to comment? For fuck's sake.

'I'll take you out!' the man calls back over his shoulder, and at this point I notice that he's got some lovely broad shoulders.

'Forget it!' I call back with a smile, and accidentally let my coat fall open.

He almost stops so I quickly look down at myself just to make sure I haven't accidentally come out stark naked. No, it's all right, the clothes are there. I look back up at the man, who stumbles a bit, shakes his head with a grin then waves and walks off.

'Wait!' I almost shout. I don't though. My brain is already sending an electrical impulse to my arm to raise and wave at him, but I manage to interrupt it. Thank God. This imminent meeting with the delicious Rupert has got me so heated up I am becoming a menace to society. Perhaps I should go and lock myself in the car for the next hour, before I get arrested. I start walking back.

As I'm passing the pet shop, I decide on impulse to go in and see if I can find a Christmas present for my mum's cat. I know, it's ridiculous. I bet it's not even religious. But Mum lives on her own so Sybil is her only companion. And Christmas isn't about religion for a lot of people anyway.

Wandering through the aisles of cat treats and doggy stocking fillers, I suddenly hear something going on over by the till. It's a conversation and one word in particular clangs a gong in my head. Someone says, 'Training.'

'Do you think they'll want to do it?' another voice asks.

'Doesn't matter if they want to or not. I'm sending them on it, and they'll bloody well learn something from it.'

This is great. I turn towards the voices and walk a bit more quickly, already forming an opener. And I'm dressed for the part, complete with ring binder and pen! Fantastic.

But just as I'm about to approach, I hesitate. Actually, I stop completely and stand motionless for a few seconds. Then I walk back to the door and out onto the pavement, pulling my mobile phone out of my bag. I can't quite believe I'm doing this, and my head shakes a little as I dial the office number.

'Hi, Ali, can I speak to Fatima please?'

When Fatima comes to the phone, all panicky and out of breath, I tell her that she might do well to give Animal Instinct a call, as I was just in there and heard them talking about Customer Care.

'You . . . wh—' she says, by way of a thank you.

'That's all right, Fats,' I reassure her. 'Good luck.' Then I read off the shop's phone number from the sign above it, and ring off.

Wow. That was weird. I just gave that one away. That is the first time I have ever done that, in all the years I have been working at LL. Amazing. It must be because I am so confident about the Horizon thing. Plus, I am a bit incoherent with excitement at the moment. Which reminds me, what time is it? As I look at my watch, I notice that I am still holding my phone in one hand, and the slip of paper Nerys gave me in the other. It's fate again. No point fighting against it. Some higher being somewhere is convincing me to ring that number, and has engineered this moment, to make it happen. I am not in control, I can't help it. And anyway, what harm can it do? I will simply say I am Sean Cousins' assistant, doing some research prior to his meeting this afternoon. Which is kind of true, in a don't-look-too-closely kind of way.

'Whytelys,' a young female voice says in my ear suddenly, taking me by surprise. I thought I was still having an internal debate, but it turns out I've made up my mind and dialled already.

'Yes, hello, I am calling from Love Learning. Would it be possible to speak to someone about the store's training policy please?'

She puts me through and I listen to 'Santa Claus is Coming to Town' on the pan pipes for a few seconds.

Eventually I speak to someone called Annette, but she doesn't know anything about Sean's meeting this afternoon.

'Are you sure? It's with the regional manager.'

'Do you know which manager?'

'Um, well no, I don't. It was booked with the regional manager, so I thought that—'

'Well, there are four regional managers, and I'm afraid I can't see Love Learning written down in any of the diaries, so unless you can tell me the name of the person you were coming to see . . . ?'

'Oh, no, no, it doesn't matter. Never mind.'

'Would you like me to make you another appointment?'

Look, I didn't ask her to say that, did I? I mean, I am not trying to steal Sean's contract, it's just happening. No, no it isn't just happening because I won't let it happen. I will simply tell Annette thank you very much, but there's really no—

'Yes, thank you, that would be very helpful.'

Oh fuck. My lips have taken over again.

By the end of the conversation I have an appointment with one of the regional managers at three o'clock next Tuesday, the nineteenth, in their offices. Which I can easily cancel, once I've spoken to Sean about it tonight. I mean, it's really just in case there's been some mix-up and his appointment this afternoon has been overlooked. I swear I will let him go along to the appointment next week, if his appointment today has been messed up. Lips, you can shut up.

220

Fourteen

Gathering Information

Short-term Goal: Eat lunch without dribbling.
Obstacles: Rupert's face.
Long-term Goal: Rupert's face.
Obstacles: Eating lunch without dribbling.

I march quickly back to the car and drive what turns out to be the eight-minute journey out to Madeleine's, where I pull in under a giant Christmas tree. So now I have about twenty minutes to kill before I can go in. For fuck's sake. Who would have thought such an exclusive place would be so near the dual carriageway? Never mind, I'll just wait in the car until about four minutes past one so I can look like I haven't been checking my watch every two minutes since I got up this morning. Whatever happens, I absolutely must not arrive first.

Precisely six minutes later I am nervously being led through the restaurant by the maître d'. Waiting in the car was a cretinous idea, it turns out, for some very subtle and obscure reasons that I couldn't have been expected to think about in my current state of mind.

I mean, who could have predicted it would be so cold out there? Anyway, Rupert might have spotted some pale, pinched-face hag sitting freezing in the car park, and rolled his eyes at her mad behaviour, and then later discovered she was me.

So here I am, being led past all the people sitting in those hideous embroidered cardigans I was looking at in Whytelys earlier today, to a table right at the back. No, not a table right at the back. Christ, where are we going? We've walked past every table and are now going through the doors out onto the decking. Yes, this is lovely but it's bloody freezing. I came in from the car to be warm, for crying out loud. He's taking me to some kind of structure on the end of the decking. Jesus, am I going in there? I feel an irrational moment of panic when I suddenly wonder whether this man is simply posing as the maître d' in order to lure innocent young women into a remote, unidentifiable outbuilding where he keeps them for weeks chained to a radiator pipe with nothing but a rusty old handsaw for company, and then he opens the glass door and I step inside and my breath leaves my body.

It looks like Santa's Grotto. Minus the actual Santa. There is room for about five tables in here, but only one of them is made up. I catch a brief glimpse of the beautiful table setting, with gleaming gold cutlery, sparkling crystal glasses, flowers, Christmas crackers, candles, all shining cream or gold, then I realize that everything is sparkling and shimmering like that because the room is covered with candles. It's almost ablaze with candlelight. There are only two on our table, but around the room every wall has at least twenty sconces, or thirty even, and every one has a beautiful gold candle flickering away in it. I'm not sure if there are heaters in here or not, but the room is very warm. Deliciously warm. And alive with movement. I step over the threshold, still gazing around in wonder while the maître d' stands just outside.

I turn to him. 'Did you . . . ? I mean, is this . . . ? Is it usually . . . ?'

He smiles knowingly. 'Ah, Mr de Witter asked for this arrangement specifically, madam.'

I'm gaping. I know I am but I can't stop. There's probably a bead of moisture on my bottom lip, but I don't care. He asked for this arrangement specifically. Rupert did. Rupert de Witter, the man I'm meeting. He did this, specially. For me. He did it for me.

'I'm sure Mr de Witter won't be long, madam,' the maître d' says, smiling at me.

I can barely keep myself on my feet at this point. The thoughts going through my head are searingly carnal, my inner heat from the prospect of meeting Rupert suddenly erupting in a fierce blaze into all the other parts of me, as if someone left a paraffin trail from my belly outwards. I turn to thank him and notice that my first impression of him as a little moustachioed man of about forty-five was incorrect, and I can see now that he is actually very attractive in a Latino kind of way, and he has a very sexy voice. I can practically feel my pupils dilate as I look at him. I wet my lips.

'Thank you so much,' I say breathily. 'This is . . . in-credible.'

He bows slightly. 'Our pleasure, madam. I hope you will let Mr de Witter know how pleased you are . . . ?'

My sultry eyes fly fully open. *What?* What is he suggesting? That I have sex with Rupert right here in this room, to say thanks for lunch? Just because of a few candles? That's absolutely outra—

My eyes begin to close as my head falls back and my knees start to sink.

No. Christ, what am I thinking of? It's a ridiculous idea. How *dare* he? Whatever he may think standing there gawping at me like a Dolmio advert, I am not some cheap slut who would—

Oh, wait a minute. No. He probably means that he would like me to tell Rupert how pleased I was so that they all get a good tip. And plenty more of Rupert's custom in future.

Jesus, I should sit down and chain myself to the chair, for the safety of all mankind.

So I've only got about fifteen minutes to kill. I order a drink and when it comes I drink it casually, like I really don't care whether I'm here or not. Then I order another one. Still nine minutes to go. I feel incredibly sexy sitting here, with candlelight dancing all over me, the warmth from the flames bringing a slight flush to my cheeks (or it could be two glasses of Sauvignon on an empty stomach), and my Michelle Pfeiffer skirt up round my thighs (it's meant to do that when you sit down). I imagine for a moment that I am Rupert de Witter arriving, and try to see myself through his eyes. OK, I look good. Although it's a bit difficult to see as the wine has gone straight to my head. My hair is good – in candlelight the blond colour has turned golden. My eyes look a bit droopy so I widen them, then droop them again. Don't want him to think I've just spotted something terrifying behind him. Smile looks a bit gormless, so I tone that down. Yes, that's good – seductive eyes, silky thighs and sweet, secret smile. House.

The door bangs open suddenly and I jump in my seat and turn to look as a voice starts speaking. 'Oh, Miss Sheridan, Beth, I'm so sorry you've been waiting.'

My heart is hammering, my eyes are wide, my breath is short, but I look calm and languid as I raise my eyebrows at the man standing in the doorway. Who is not Rupert de Witter.

'Who are you? Where's Rupert?'

That's out before I can stop it. It sounds dreadful, I know, like some idiot blonde sidekick who's just about to be dumped by the hero's accountant.

'I'm Rupert's accountant.'

Shit.

'My name is Harris O'Neill. Rupert was called away at the last minute, I'm afraid, and he asked me to come and apologize.'

'Oh.'

He comes a bit further into the room. 'May I?' he says, indicating the other chair at our table, then politely waits for my permission. I try to say 'Yes of course, please do,' very graciously, but what starts to come out is 'WHY AREN'T YOU RUPERT?' so I just nod.

'I do hope you are going to stay for lunch anyway?' he says, pulling his chair in. He's quite nice, in a grey-suit-and-tie, accountanty way. 'The food here is lovely.' He leans forward across the table towards me so that I can smell his aftershave, and lowers his voice. 'Rupert is paying, so we may as well push the boat out. And the whole meal is tax deductible, as long as we do the business during it.'

WHAT? What is he suggesting? Have I now got to have sex with Rupert's accountant as well, right here on the floor, in this gorgeous room, with candlelight flickering on our naked, twisting bodies, a whole restaurant full of people just yards away, able to see us if they stood up and walked to the door, and the waiter about to come in and catch us at any moment, just so he can write the whole thing off as a business expense? I can feel my breathing getting heavier and my heart pounding. There is something distinctly Matt Damon-y about this man . . .

No, no, what am I thinking of? Christ, what is the matter with me? I really do need to strap myself down to something. And not Rupert de Witter's accountant.

Focus, Beth, come on. Why are you here? Why are you so desperate to meet Rupert de Witter? Here's a clue: it's not to have sex with anyone on this decking.

'Well, that's why we're here, isn't it?' I say finally, discreetly sweating and shifting uncomfortably in my seat, while giving the impression that I am neither crushingly disappointed by Rupert's non-appearance nor sexually frustrated to the point of deviancy.

'Great. Hopefully the business part will only take a few minutes and then we can enjoy ourselves. God, I am starving. The salmon fishcakes are bloody gorgeous, by the way.' He grabs a menu. 'Have you eaten here before?'

I hesitate before answering. My instincts are telling me to lie and pretend that I come here all the time, so that it will get back to Rupert that I wasn't completely overwhelmed by the whole experience, but I know from *Mrs Doubtfire* that if you pretend to be something you're not, the only result will be disaster.

'Actually no, I haven't.'

'Well, I've only been here a couple of times, and I

had the fishcakes both times, so I think I'm going to have something different today.' He peers at the menu. 'Hmm. Venison, maybe.' He looks up at me and grins broadly. 'Which will make this the last time Rupert ever pays for a lunch for me!'

'Well, you are covering for him, aren't you?'

He lowers the menu and peers at me. 'You know, you're right, I am. And he bloody well owes me for it, too.' He continues to look at me, then smiles and adds, 'Although I have to say that I am very glad he asked me to do it.'

Ah. What do I say now? I can't agree with him and say that I am glad too because I'm not. As nice as his eyes are, I would much rather be looking into Rupert's. In the end I go for an ambiguous smile and meaningless nod, which he seems happy with.

After we've ordered our food and a bottle of wine, Harris picks up his glass and raises it towards me. 'Here's to you and Rupert,' he says cheerfully, and I am instantly transported to our wedding day. I look fabulous in an off-white silk and wild pearl . . . Oh, forget what I'm wearing, just take a look at Rupert! He's got a high wing collar on with a deep red cravat, waistcoat and dark grey morning suit. He's standing next to me in the marquee, gazing down at me in awe, his eyes sweeping over every inch of me, hungrily devouring what he sees, as if he can't get enough of the sight.

'. . . business partnership,' Harris finishes, and swigs his wine. I blink. Oh, right. Shit, what did I miss?

'Absolutely,' I say, sipping my wine.

'Rupert is a bloody good person to work for, actually,' Harris goes on. 'I've been working for him for almost nine years and we've never argued. Of course, he's a total nightmare with his receipts and records, never writing down expenses accurately, missing deadlines, turning up late for meetings all the time, not doing his paperwork properly and expecting me to read his mind, but apart from all that, he's a great bloke.'

As he's speaking, I'm coming round to the idea that this lunch without Rupert might not be such a dead loss after all. I mean, clearly this bloke Harris knows Rupert very well, so it's a perfect chance for me to gather some information about Horizon, and its boss. Mentally, I open a notebook and lick the end of my pencil.

I'm not sure about what I've heard so far though. He sounds a bit irresponsible. I mean, he's the owner of this fuck-off enormous holiday company, and he can't even be bothered to turn up to meetings? Doesn't he know what running a business is all about? Does he know how many people are completely dependent on him? Will he pay his invoices on time?

Harris is searching my face, which must be looking disapproving because he starts to look a bit panicky, and puts his hands up. 'Oh, God, no, look, I didn't mean . . . In fact, he's actually an all-round good . . . What I mean is, that's just what he's like with me. I'm only his accountant, remember. I only deal with his money, which doesn't interest him. He drives me absolutely mad with his careless attitude to money because he ends up paying more tax than is necessary. I see it year after year when the bill arrives, but he just doesn't care. I feel like I'm not doing my job properly, you know, not doing the best for him, but he keeps on hiring me to do it for him.' He smiles and although he's smiling, he looks a bit sad. 'He even gives me a bonus every Christmas. Even though I have completely failed to save him anything like the amount I could. I just think money is very low down on his list of priorities.'

Oh God. Could he have said anything more sexy? A millionaire who isn't interested in money? Is that even possible? I suppose with that amount of money, no matter how thoughtless you are, you're never likely to end up in debt, are you?

My thoughts jump to Fatima. The opposite of Rupert. Not a millionaire, does care about money, hideously in debt. Something occurs to me suddenly. Oh my God. I am having lunch with an accountant – maybe this guy can give me some tips to give her?

'Um, so, Harris, you're an accountant?'

He grins. 'Yep. Why?'

'Well, a friend of mine at work, Fatima, has got some money problems. Well, no, it's the opposite of money problems, actually. More absence-of-money problems. She's in a terrible state, incredibly anxious and upset, crying in the office, worrying about losing her job. She's gone a bit mad, actually, behaving totally out of character, mixing with some dodgy types, getting arrested . . .' I tail off. God, Fatima's situation sounds really terrible, now that I say it out loud, all at once. How can it have got so bad? And what if Chas really does get rid of her? She is genuinely likely to end up, I don't know, planning a bank heist or something, to try to pay it off.

'Beth, don't look so worried. Honestly. Your friend – Fatima, was it? – she'll be fine. There's always a way out, as long as she's sensible.'

'Do you think so?'

'Yes, of course. What did she spend on? Got any assets?'

I nod. God, this is great! He's going to come up with something only accountants know about because of all their years of specialized training, and once Fatima does whatever it is he suggests, her problems will all be over. I can feel the relief starting to soak into me already.

'Yes, she's got a Mini. Cost her nine thousand. What should she do?' I stare at him, eyes wide, breath held, waiting for him to drop diamonds from his lips and sort everything out.

'She needs to sell it, pay off the debt and buy herself a cheaper car.'

I stare at him across the table without moving. My face is still doing an expectant, give-me-the-answers expression, eyebrows raised, lips slightly parted, but Harris is slugging wine again and doesn't notice. Buggeration, is that what all those years of arduous and complicated training has led him to? *Sell the Mini and buy something cheaper?* Well, thank God I thought to ask him, what a huge relief that is, now that I can pass on some fantastic advice from an actual accountant.

'Yes, after a lot of careful thought and weighing up all her options, Fatima and I had kind of already decided that that would be her best move. She's having trouble selling it though. No one wants to pay nine thousand for a third-hand Mini.'

'Oh I see. That's a shame.' He raises his wine to his lips again, takes a drink then puts the glass down. But he doesn't say anything else, and then our food arrives, and he grins at me as he picks up his cutlery and digs in and I realize that that's it, he's not going to solve anything, he's got nothing.

The fishcakes are gorgeous, though. They're the only good thing about this whole fiasco. Now that Harris is well and truly pissed, it seems pretty unlikely that he's going to be a fount of information about Rupert. As I eat I am starting to feel the teensiest bit resentful towards Rupert for not being here. I mean, Harris is very nice but he's clearly not the world's greatest accountant. And my date – I mean, my appointment – was with Rupert himself, not his accountant. Why send his accountant, for heaven's sake? Why not just postpone and rearrange? Vini was right, he is totally impossible to see ever, anywhere.

'You all right?' Harris says suddenly, looking across at me. I can feel my face – it's doing 'pissed off', which is not good. I force myself to smile and Harris visibly relaxes.

'Yes, fine, sorry. Just thinking about work. I'm going to have to get back quite soon, actually. Shall we sort out the business now?'

'Oh, yes, of course. How thoughtless of me.' He folds his napkin and drops it onto the empty plate. 'Look, Beth, Rupert did want to be here today, you know. I only spoke to him yesterday – he was looking forward to it.'

'Oh, no, look, it doesn't matter at all. I can explain Love Learning to you just as well as I could to him, so please, you know, it's not a . . . It's completely . . . Don't worry about it.'

'The thing is,' he goes on, as if I haven't even spoken, 'he's a very hands-on manager. You know? He likes to get involved in absolutely everything if he can. That place takes up all of his time.'

'Well, yes, that's exactly what I would—'

'Trouble is,' he goes on, 'he leaves himself no time for a private life, really. He rarely spends an evening away from his office, so any chance of a social life is virtually non-existent.'

What? What is he trying to tell me? Is he warning me off? I shrug and try to look as if that's not really any concern of mine. 'Oh, really? That's a shame, isn't it? So, what sort of—'

'Yes, yes, it is a shame,' he says urgently, leaning across the table again. 'He puts his work before everything and everyone and it's not good for him. He will end up alone and full of regret and I don't want that for him.' He takes another shaky slug of wine and nearly doesn't stand the glass up properly when he puts it down.

'No, well, of course not, you're his friend, you only want—'

'What he needs, Beth, is a reason to work less. Because at the moment he has nothing else, which makes him work more, which means he has nothing else. Do you understand me?'

He is staring intensely at me and eventually I have to look away. 'Um, well, I'm not really sure . . .'

'It's a vicious circle, Beth, and it needs to be broken. He needs something meaningful in his life because at the moment all he's working for is money and he doesn't care about money.'

'Ohhh kaaay . . .'

At this point the waiter arrives to clear the table, and Harris asks him to put the bill on Rupert's account.

'Was everything to your satisfaction, Mr O'Neill?' the waiter says, and I have a sneaking suspicion Harris may have been here more than just twice before.

'Oh, yes, thank you, Dan. Lovely. Don't worry, I'll tell him.'

'Thank you, sir,' Dan says, and practically backs away.

Harris turns back to me. 'Come on then, Beth, pull this cracker with me. And then let's talk about what lovely Love Learning can do for hunky Horizon Holidays.'

Fifteen

Minor Revelations

Short-term Goal: Get another date with Rupert. He owes me a face to face.
Obstacles: The words 'face to face' keep conjuring up a very distracting image, which prevents me from doing anything. Even breathing.
Long-term Goal: Get my face onto Rupert's face. Then we can have interface.
Obstacles: Actually meeting him would be a good start.

I get back to my desk at about twenty past three and find a huge bouquet of flowers on it. An enormous daft grin breaks out on my face and I don't even try to stop it. Smiling in delight at receiving flowers from an implausibly sexy millionaire is number one on my list of things I want to be doing when Richard comes looking for me. I picture Rupert phoning the florist and dictating what he wants on the card, thinking about me as he does it, deciding what words to use, what flowers to choose, and my heart swells a bit as it pounds and pushes into my lungs, making my breath come faster. I sit down delightedly and start rummaging through them for the card.

Looking through the blooms for the card gives me the opportunity to notice what types of flowers he's chosen for me. There are lots of pretty little pink petals, in a cloud of greenery, and then lots more different pink petals. They're very pretty. Really nice. Not terribly original, but that doesn't matter. I am so thrilled to be getting flowers for something nice for a change. This is only my third bouquet and the last two did not bring good news.

Although sending flowers generally is a bit *old*, really, isn't it? And if I'm honest with myself, I just know that it won't have been Rupert himself phoning the florist. His assistant probably did it, while he was busy doing whatever it was that was so important he couldn't make it to the meeting that he himself suggested and set up. So he lets me down and then thinks everything will be fine because someone called Lucy or Howard phoned Interflora and made up some words based on what Rupert said happened today. I can feel my lip curling now, and I do make that stop. Sneering over the flowers some millionaire has sent me as a lame apology for standing me up is not at the top of the list of things I want to be doing when Richard comes back. Not even in the top ten.

Maybe I should just give up on Rupert. We've never met, and as soon as we tried to he failed to show up and is now sending bouquets of cliché to make up for it. Maybe I got the wrong impression of him from his emails.

'You like them?' Sean says, coming over to me. I don't want him to know who they're from, or why, or

235

that I'm a bit fed up with them, or why, so I beam up at him broadly.

'Oh, yes, I love them. Aren't they beautiful? All my favourite colours. And the fragrance . . .' I shove my face into them and take a deep long sniff, but don't smell a thing apart from a plasticky aroma of cellophane. 'Totally gorgeous,' I say, resurfacing.

'Great. I thought you would like all the pinks, so that's what I went for. Just a little token, you know. Looking forward to tonight. I'm off to my – *meeting* – now.' And he does that slow wink again. Urrrrhhhhh.

I stare after him as he walks away and realize suddenly that the meeting he's off to is with Whytelys' regional manager. So it's still on, then. Well, that's good – that means I can cancel the meeting I have inadvertently set up with them. I'll do that tomorrow, to give Sean a chance tonight to tell me how it went.

At least Rupert not turning up means that going out with Sean tonight isn't going to get in the way of any other invitation I might have received. Although I was going to say I was busy anyway, wasn't I? Which means going out with Sean tonight is pointless. But I think I owe it to him, after I might have accidentally gone behind his back at Whytelys. I look down at the flowers and realize how perfectly Sean and this plastic pink bouquet go together. How could I have thought a little pink bunch like this would have come from someone like Rupert de Witter? He probably doesn't send flowers at all. He sends diamond bracelets or rare first editions. And if he does send flowers it would be orchids or something else really exotic. Not little pink begonias, or whatever they are. While I was smelling them, I realized that in fact they're not from Interflora, they're from the black plastic bucket that sits next to the tiny, bald Christmas trees at the petrol station just round the corner from the office. That's why there's no card. I am almost, but not quite, overwhelmed.

OK, back to work. I have got a Motivation workshop coming up next week and I really need to do some preparation for it but I can't be bothered. I log on to my emails and while I wait for it to load an image comes into my head of Harris, now going into Rupert's office, Rupert hurrying him in, all impatient and anxious, sitting him down, perching on the desk in front of him and saying, 'Well?'

But Harris has got a bit of a headache. He's had too much wine. He waves Rupert away and stands up. 'Give me a minute, Rupe. Need some water.'

'I'll get it,' Rupert says, moving quickly over to his desk and pouring a glass out of the jug that's standing there. He slops some of it over the side onto the desk but he doesn't care. He strides back to Harris's side and places the cup in his friend's hand. Harris closes his eyes and drinks deeply while Rupert stares at him, arms folded.

'You weren't supposed to get drunk,' he says, disapprovingly. 'I wanted you alert, taking mental notes.'

Harris shakes his head. Carefully. 'I'm not drunk. I'm just enjoying the Christmas spirit.'

'Yeah, OK then, Harry. Whatever. Just tell me what she is like, please, and then you can go home to bed.'

'What do you want to know?'

Rupert shrugs and raises his hands. 'I don't know. Was she funny?'

Harris nods. Carefully. 'A bit.'

Rupert is nodding too. 'OK. Right. Well. Kind of knew that already. Did you manage to talk about me?'

Harris stares at him. 'Don't you even want to know what she looks like?'

Rupert stares back, his face frozen. 'I don't know. I haven't thought about it.'

'You haven't? You sure?'

'All right, yes, I've thought about it. But now it comes down to it, I don't know if I want to know. Do I want to know? No, don't answer that. Let me think a minute.'

Harris waits in silence while Rupert paces for a few moments. Then he says, 'OK, look. How about I tell you now how the meeting went, and if you decide you want to know how she looks later, you can call me?'

Rupert stops pacing and turns. 'I don't know. Would that . . . ? OK. Yes, all right. No. Yes. Yes. That's a good idea. How was it?'

I'm hoping that Harris's standards are a lot lower than Rupert's and he's telling him right now that I am somewhere between Victoria Wood and Halle Berry. I mean, the wit of one, the body of the other. And let's not forget that he was pissed. That helps.

OK, I need to try to concentrate on what I'm doing. I've logged into my emails although I'm not expecting anything interesting. Rupert won't have sent a message as he has been in some kind of urgent meeting all day. Although what kind of situation could possibly arise in a holiday company that's urgent enough to call someone away from a lunch appointment, I can't imagine. Freak accident on the inflatable banana? Cheap foreign beer in headache and nausea shocker? Cruise liner run out of Pimm's? I turn to my inbox and amazingly there *is* a message from him. I am very conscious of the fact that he heartlessly stood me up today, but am struggling not to burst out in beaming smiles anyway. Then I read the message.

From: Rupert de Witter
To: Beth Sheridan
Subject: Lunch today

Dear Beth,

Can you forgive me? Please say that you can. I feel terrible for letting you down today and can only imagine how much you must hate me now. I want you to know that nothing except the gravest, most serious holidaying emergency could have kept me away from you today. And it was.

It seems that the more I look forward to something, the more likely it is to be disrupted, so our lunch being ruined today was practically inevitable. If we do manage to rearrange, I will try my hardest not to look forward to it quite so much. Then we might have a chance. Although I'm not sure I will be able to help myself.

Anyway, I did the next best thing to actually turning up and sent my accountant as a spy. It's a well-known holiday company technique. This way, I get to find out all about you from Harris later, so that when we do meet in the future I will be better prepared.

Please write back and let me know that I am forgiven.

Yours,

Rupert

Forgiven? There's nothing to forgive. Obviously he couldn't help it that something really serious came up. What was I thinking about? Pimm's, for goodness' sake. I expect he's been going frantic all day trying to sort out some kind of hideous holiday disaster, making difficult phone calls and press statements, and I'm talking about a giant inflatable banana.

As I'm reading the message for the fourth time, I realize exactly what he means in the second paragraph. To be fair to me, he could have written 'My donkey has run out of peanuts, Yours, Rupert', and I wouldn't have worried about the meaning. I am just grinning soppily, completely delighted he has sent me a message at all after being embroiled in catastrophe all day. But when the meaning does finally soak through, I get that sudden, hot plunging sensation in my belly again. He says that the more he looks forward to something, the more likely it is to get disrupted. And then he says that means our meeting being disrupted was inevitable. That must mean that he was looking forward to meeting me. He was *really* looking forward to meeting me. So much so that he actually caused it not to happen. Indirectly, I mean.

Sounds a bit unlikely, actually. I mean, he must have been excited when he was setting up Horizon. He must have looked forward to buying things. I know for a fact he has at least once stood on the deck of a very expensive-looking yacht, with the sun shining and a deep blue sky behind him. He must have been looking forward to that, and there is photographic evidence to prove that it still went ahead. I click on Reply straight away.

So you're telling me that you've never looked forward to a holiday, or a night out at the opera, or buying a car? Simply because if you looked forward to it, it wouldn't happen?

240

I've clicked Send before I've thought about it. God, I hope that doesn't sound like I'm being argumentative, or sarcastic or cynical. Because there are few things less attractive than—

Oh crikey, here's the reply.

> Hi! You're there! How was lunch? No, don't answer that. At least not yet.
>
> I don't actually like the opera – I'm not Richard Gere! (sadly) – so I was looking forward to cutting my toenails this morning more than I would look forward to that. And when you've already bought every car you've ever wanted, that loses its appeal too. Usually when I need a new car, I get someone to go out and get me one.
>
> I'm only kidding. I don't have every car I've ever wanted, of course. And I do get pleasure out of buying one. I'm not that spoilt. But I don't like opera, and I was really looking forward to meeting you. I didn't much enjoy cutting my toenails, though.
> Your Rupert
> PS Do you think it's a mistake to mention toenails?

OK, it's all right, calm down, I'm not reading anything into that, it's not a declaration of undying love and devotion, with an unspoken promise that he belongs heart and soul to me and always will. It's a typo. He clearly meant to write 'Yours, Rupert' and simply left off the 's'. And the comma. By accident.

Quickly I log on to the internet and put 'Freud' into a search engine. Then I close it down again. Jesus Christ on a couch, Beth, get a *grip*.

I pick up the Horizon brochure and flick to the back page. Oh come on, who am I kidding? – it was already open at the back page, folded back on itself with

Rupert's picture uppermost. My belly is going all hot and squirmy again as I look at that picture and think about 'Your Rupert'. It's nonsense, I know. He's so beautiful and so rich, there's no way in hell he would be interested in a boring little person like me. He probably can't move round his way without bumping into a page-three girl. In fact, he probably had some gorgeous babe on that fabulous yacht with him when this picture was taken. I lean forward and squint at the picture, my nose almost touching the paper. Is that a curvaceous yet strangely shallow and self-obsessed shadow I can make out on the deck behind him?

'Research is it?' a slow voice drawls behind me and I sit up suddenly. Sean is standing there, coat on, car keys in hand. 'Don't work too hard.'

'Oh, no, nothing like that.' I slam the brochure shut and drop it casually on the desk, where it immediately opens again at the back page. 'Just thinking about a holiday.'

He raises his eyebrows. 'Really? Thought you might receive information telepathically from the photograph of the boss then?' He jerks his chin towards the grinning photo of a sun-kissed Rupert.

'What? Oh, you mean . . . that? No, no, that's just . . . It's . . . Well, it's . . . It's my old boss. Remember? I used to work at Horizon, so it's strange to see the photo again, after all these years. You know.'

'Oh, right. Well, don't get so carried away you forget to come to the Patch and Parrot later, will you?' And he winks and leaves the office. Thank God, because while he was talking I realized that the last email from Rupert is right there, in plain view on my computer screen, and I've gone into full paranoid panic mode. Did Sean see it? Did he have time to read it? What would he have thought of it, if he did? Would he think I am having a relationship with Rupert de Witter? Would he work out that I'm going for the Horizon contract? I have no choice but to assume the answer is 'No' to all of them.

Sean leaving has drawn my attention to the fact that not only is he back from the Whytelys meeting, but it's after five and virtually everyone else has left. Ali and Skye are deep in conversation at the other end of the room, and no doubt Chas is still in his office, but other than them, I am alone. Right. I'll write one more message to Rupert, and then I'm leaving. I've got dream date number two to prepare for tonight. The Motivation prep can wait until tomorrow.

From: Beth Sheridan
To: Rupert de Witter
Subject: Body parts

Dear Rupert,
I am all for full and frank discussion of body parts at the earliest opportunity. That way, no one has anything to fear from it coming up in later conversations. I can tell you now, quite openly, that I am leaving work shortly and heading for the gym to work on my inner thighs, which are sadly lacking when compared to my outer thighs. You in turn could then mention your biceps, and I would reply with details about my abdomen. We could swap information like this quite freely, knowing that we will be saved any embarrassment later on.

However, I would draw the line at toenails. Nasal hair, also, has my veto.
Yours,
Beth

Yes, I know. Very naughty. I am definitely moving our flirtation up another level. I almost don't send it. My cursor hovers over the Send key for more than ten seconds before finally clicking on it apparently out of sheer frustration.

More frustrating than that is that I don't have time to wait for a response, which I am desperate for, as I have to go and get ready for this date with Sean. I am planning to prepare very carefully to make sure I get it just right. Make-up will need to be practised a bit before I do it for real. Hair is going to be tricky to get perfect. Then there's the outfit. I will need to choose it very carefully, to make sure I get something that accentuates all the bits I want to accentuate and hides everything else. It's not going to be easy but when I walk in I want him to turn and see me looking drop-dead disgusting.

Sixteen

Major Revelations

Short-term Goal: Make myself utterly repellent to look at.

Obstacles: My self-respect, sense of personal pride, ingrained decency and gorgeous hair.

Long-term Goal: Get ~~Rupert~~ the Horizon contract.

Obstacles: Date with Sean. I have no time.

It turns out that going out of the house looking like Waynetta Slob is not as easy as it sounds. I couldn't do it. I really don't know how all those women in white velour jogging trousers and vest tops manage to cross their thresholds. Hats off to them, as Chas would say. Next time I see one, or a group of them hanging around outside the post office, I will nod in silent recognition of someone who's got real balls. I mean, I'm not actually going to say anything to them. Or, you know, make eye contact. But I can – I won't say *admire* – I can glance at them furtively then look away quickly with new eyes.

But it goes against every instinct and belief in me to make myself look as hideous as possible before going out in public. Apart from my self-respect, there is always the possibility that I might get *seen*, as you know, which would be disastrous if I looked like I might have recently given birth. To a child called Destiny.

I tried, I really did. I scrubbed my face until it was red and shiny, scraped my hair away from my face into a tiny little ponytail, and even rubbed a dot of grey eyeshadow under each eye. Then after dressing in Vini's joggers and the lumpy grey fleece she always wears when she's not feeling well, I gleefully looked in the mirror to get the overall impression, and burst into tears.

So I cleansed and toned, GHD'd, and reapplied my make-up so I didn't look like I had eaten nothing but chips for eight years, then changed into jeans and a long brown cardigan. After an hour and forty minutes getting ready, I have achieved the appearance of someone who got ready quickly and with little effort because they're not interested in getting off with their date. Perfect.

God I hate the Patch and Parrot. It's a desert island setting, with fake palm trees and exotic plastic birds and bananas everywhere. All the staff have to wear pirate costumes, and when I walk in the person at the door says, in a lifeless monotone, 'Welcome to the Patch and Parrot, my hearty, arrr, where dead men tell no tales.' I glance at her and notice she's got her eye-patch up on top of her head. She's clearly got either fed up with her lack of depth perception or really sweaty. Completely incongruous in this Caribbean scene is an uncomfortable-looking Christmas tree trying to fit in by the fireplace, and plastic snowflakes hanging from the ceiling. I make my way over to where Sean is sitting.

'Hi, sorry I'm late,' I say, sitting down opposite him quickly before he has a chance to lean towards me for any reason. 'Is this for me?' There's a glass of white wine on the table in front of me. 'Thanks.' I take a gulp. The evening is looking up.

'Yeah. So. How are you? Haven't really had much chance to chat at work. Get much done today?'

'Oh, yes, loads. Very productive.' I nod meaningfully, then clamp my lips round the rim of the glass again to stop that conversation right there.

'Really?' Clearly Sean isn't taking the hint. 'What, contract hunting? Does "productive" mean that you got one?'

I put my glass down and look at him. He's leaning towards me, both arms stretched out on the table, eyebrows up and drawn together, mouth sagging. Either he's intensely interested in my contract hunt for some reason or he's just suffered a small stroke. And then I remember.

'Forget me, what about you? How did your meeting at Whytelys go?' But he's shaking his head even before I've finished asking the question.

'Fucking awful.' He drags his arms across the table towards him and leans back with a sigh. 'They weren't remotely interested. Didn't even want to hear what I had to say. Apparently, they had heard something crappy about us from Eastern Star Bank, but I don't know what that was. Far as I know, Eastern were happy with what we gave them. Do you remember anything? No, nor do I. I don't know. Anyway, they practically laughed me out of the building. It was so humiliating.'

'You're kidding? Shit, Sean, that sounds awful.'

'Well, yeah.'

247

'I don't get it. What on earth did they agree to see you for, if that was their opinion?'

He shrugs bitterly. 'Get a good laugh, probably.'

'Oh, no, I really doubt that. They wouldn't waste their time on—' I stop. Something has occurred to me. 'They? Who did you see? More than one person?'

'Hmm?'

'You said "they". I wondered if you had seen more than one person?'

'Oh, no, no, only one person. I was meaning, you know, Whytelys collectively.'

'Oh, right. So who did you see?'

'The regional manager. I told you.'

'Well yes, but . . . I think . . . I might have read somewhere . . .' I shrug oh-so-casually. 'Isn't there more than one regional manager? Like, maybe, I don't know, four of them?'

He stares at me. 'Well, fuck, Bethy, maybe there are, but the bloke I saw didn't bother to inform me, as he was shoving me out of his office, that there are three others like him who would no doubt all find me equally entertaining.' He does one of those 'for crying out loud' eye rolls, and swigs his lager.

Which puts me right off telling him about the appointment I've made. I mean, the man is obviously shamed and broken after his disastrous meeting today – how can I possibly tell him I made a back-up appointment? It makes it look like I didn't expect it to go well in the first place, that I expected him to fail, because he's such an arrogant, condescending, lazy, inarticulate, sexist piece of—

'Christ, I really needed that contract,' he says suddenly, rubbing his eyebrows.

'Yeah, I know what you mean.'

He looks up and his eyes meet mine and I can see that suddenly they're fierce and intense and I am pinned by them. 'No, Beth, you don't. You don't have a fucking clue, tripping through your little life where nothing ever goes wrong and the only thing you have to worry about is what to wear to work each day. And when the company closes down and we're all out of a job, spare a thought for those of us out there in the real world, will you, as you pack up your pink fluffy slippers and go back to Mummy and Daddy.'

Incredibly, infuriatingly, my eyes start to feel hot and tears spring into them. For God's sake, Beth, it's bastard Sean, what did you expect? I try to blink them away, calming myself down with the soothing thought that he's obviously prone to violent mood swings and murderous tendencies due to a serious drug habit. That makes me feel better. Obviously he's now worrying over how he is going to fund it. Well, tough luck, I think to myself. Should have thought of that before you became dependent on an illegal substance.

That makes me feel a *lot* better and I sniff and start to get up. 'Well, it's been lovely—'

His hand shoots out and grabs my arm. 'No, Beth,' he says, low and urgent. 'Please don't go.'

I look down at him. 'Why not?'

His eyes don't leave mine but after a second or two his hand moves off my arm and reaches behind him into his jeans pocket. He pulls out his wallet. Christ, if he thinks I'm going to stay for another drink . . . But it's not money he's pulling out. It's too thick and rigid. It's a small, white rectangle, and I slowly sit back down as he hands it to me.

'That's my boy,' he says simply and I look down at the photo into the eyes of a child of about seven or eight. He looks like he's trying to smile because that is what he is expected to do when someone takes his photo, but it's not a natural grin. He's outside, it looks like a park somewhere, with swings in the background, and he's holding an ice-cream cone. The ice cream has melted onto his hand, trickled along his wrist and run all the way down his forearm in thick, creamy rivulets to his elbow. He's wearing a T-shirt with SpongeBob Squarepants on it and little orange shorts that show dimpled knees.

Sean is a dad. He has a little boy. I can hardly take it in. All this time I thought he was a secretive, untrustworthy, shallow, womanizing gambler, and it turns out to be parenthood. How could I have mistaken one for the other? How could I have been so wrong about him? I raise my eyes to look at him anew after this major revelation, and am astonished at what I find. Sean the dad is much more attractive than Sean the low life. Suddenly I can see how warm his eyes would be when gazing down lovingly upon his precious child, and it makes me feel warm too. Well, hot really. I feel like Kirsten Dunst, realizing that when she looks at her bespectacled geek-boyfriend, she is actually looking at the huge, hunky superhero Spider-Man. I'm looking at Sean with new eyes and suddenly all the secretive, sneaky looks, all the untrustworthy actions and suspicious deeds have a reason behind them, an explanation, and it's this, right here in my hand, this beautiful little blond-haired boy, squinting and trying to please whoever is holding the camera.

But now I think about it, what has Sean ever done

to make me mistrustful or suspicious of him? Little more than speak slowly, smile in a certain way, and never talk about what he does at weekends. Which is why I chose to believe that his weekend activities were illegal, distasteful or shameful. I can't actually think of a single concrete thing he's ever done to me to make me so wary of him. In fact, he's been very open and honest with me, telling me all about his Whytelys idea, keeping me up to date with the details of when the appointment was, confessing how badly it went, even though it must kill him to admit that. And now, as I look at him, I am blasted by skin-shrivelling shame at the way I have behaved in response to his trust and respect. I have stabbed him in the back, wiggled the blade around and then broken the end off so he can't pull it out and save himself. I am utter scum. I am worse than what I thought Sean was and turned out not to be.

'That was taken about three years ago,' Sean says suddenly, reaching out and taking the photo from my hand. 'It's his birthday today. He's nine.' He gazes down at the picture and seems to forget for a moment that I'm there. 'Happy birthday, Alfie mate. Hope you like the monkey.' He looks up at me then, anxious again. 'I got him a giant cuddly monkey – do you think it's a bit too young for him? I mean, he's only nine, he's still just a baby . . .'

I reach over and put my hand on his. 'I'm sure he's going to love it. It's from his dad, isn't it?'

He nods. 'Yes, you're right. God, I hope you're right. I just don't know what a kid his age is into. He lives with his mum and stepdad, so I only see him once a week. They're getting him a PSP.'

'What's that?'

'Little hand-held games console. Really smart. Pretty expensive, too. Wish I could have bought it for him but there's no way I could afford it. And if . . .' He doesn't finish but I know what he's saying. If Love Learning goes under, what will he be able to do for his little boy then? I stare at him and understand completely his anxiety over the contract hunt, his repeated enquiries about whether or not I had had any success, the stress he must be under, the worry of wanting to do more for his son and the possibility that he might have to start doing less. It's exactly like *The Full Monty*.

'Look, Beth, I'm so sorry I snapped at you earlier. It's just . . . I want to do so much for him. I want to take him away on holiday, just us two, and give him a fantastic experience somewhere. I want to give him exactly the thing he wants for his birthday. I want him to adore me, to look up to me and want to be like me. I want to be his hero.' He rubs his eyes with his finger and thumb and I look away towards a vinyl treasure chest on the bar that's spilling out plastic gold coins and jewellery. There's a small cotton wool snowman next to it.

'Anyway,' Sean goes on, and I look back at him. He's smiling sadly now. 'Thanks so much for agreeing to come out with me tonight. I hate being at home on my own on Alfie's birthdays. And today, with the Whytelys fiasco . . . I'm really glad of the company. I mean it. Let me get you another drink. Let's face it, it might be the last drink I can afford to buy you!'

As he stands up I put my hand on his arm, as he did mine only a few minutes ago. 'Hold on a minute, Sean.'

He looks down at my hand, then lowers himself onto his seat again.

'What?'

He's staring interestedly at me, his frank blue eyes meeting mine, not wavering, not darting away, just steadily, calmly holding my gaze. 'Sean, you don't need to worry about Love Learning going under.'

His eyebrows go up another millimetre. 'Why do you say that?'

I swallow. 'Because I have found out that a major company in our town is going to be looking for training very soon, and I am the only one who knows it.'

He jerks a bit and sits forward on his seat. 'You're serious? How do you know? That you're the only one, I mean?'

I smile. This feels good. 'Because they haven't published their intentions yet. I found out by chance and contacted the CEO. He confirmed it.'

He is staring at me, open-mouthed. 'Really? So the company won't go under? I won't lose my job? Fucking hell, Beth! That's fantastic! Who's it with?'

'Horizon Holidays.'

'Horizon? Is that that place on the roundabout in the town centre? They're looking for training, are they? God, that place is enormous, it would probably be enough to save the company, wouldn't it? Are you sure you're the only one in the running? I mean, have you met up with someone? Got a signature?'

'Well no, not exactly. Not yet. But I'm very confident.'

He looks so earnest, so troubled, I have a fierce desire suddenly to offer him comfort and make him feel better, protect him. Cradle his head on my bosom. Although that last one may be coming from somewhere else. 'Really?' he says again, trying to accept it. 'You're the only one who knows? Fucking hell, this is brilliant!' His anxiety gives way at last to a broad grin as he finally allows himself to believe me. 'This day started off pretty crappy, got worse, then became a fucking disaster; and now it's one of the best days of my life, all thanks to you. Come on, let's have another drink to celebrate.'

He's like a different person, isn't he? And not just different from what he was like before I told him about Horizon. I mean completely different from the Sean that I have worked with for the past couple of years. He's enthusiastic, excited, practically bouncing in his seat. And like Kirsten Dunst, I can suddenly picture him swinging through the streets of our town, fifty feet up, rescuing people from blazing buildings and car wrecks. In very tight lycra.

'You didn't tell him?' Vini demands incredulously later on.

'Well, there wasn't any reason . . .' I start saying, but she's shaking her head.

'Isn't this the man who would shoot and eat his own dog?'

'I'm not sure that he would actually eat—'

'The man who would sell his own girlfriend to escape?'

'You know, that's not really the sort of—'

'The man who would burn down the whole building to hide his embezzlement, even if his wife, best friend and dad were inside?'

'I may have exaggerated—'

'You *may* have stepped out of your head,' she finishes calmly. This from a woman wearing orange mascara.

At work the next day he's already at his desk when I get there, and that's probably the first time that has ever happened. He looks up as I walk in and flashes me a huge grin. No more slow creepy winks. Although what was it about that that I found so creepy anyway? I smile back without showing my teeth – this new phase in our relationship doesn't mean I can afford to start looking like a loon – and walk slowly to my desk. I can feel his eyes on me so I try to make my side look sexy as I move. Then I raise my arm above my head and push my fingers through my hair slowly, then sit down and tuck one foot under me, maintaining a tiny smile the whole time, to keep an air of—

'Extension four five seven please,' Sean says loudly from his desk, and I look over to see he's got his back to me, hunched over his mobile phone. Right. Well, never mind. I turn to my computer screen and log on.

A sudden hot thrill of anticipation jolts through me as I remember that I sent a very saucy email to Rupert yesterday, and then left without receiving a reply. Oh my God, why did I *do* that? I must have been completely shit-faced and out of control on the two glasses of wine I had had at Madeleine's three hours before.

The question is, has he replied? I can almost not bear to look. There's probably going to be some very formal, curt rejection, like: 'Dear Beth, Thank you for your email. I found it very informative, although I feel perhaps not quite in line with the current Horizon Holidays policies. I wish you well in your future endeavours. Yours etc., R. de Witter.'

What a fucking hypocrite, after he was the one that

made Harris get me pissed in the first place! Probably just so he could see if I was going to be indiscreet and shag someone on that sexy wooden decking. What kind of slut does he think I am, to entertain thoughts like that? Well, if he's going to go all cold and self-righteous, I'm not sure if I even want to work with him, let alone spend the rest of my life with him bringing up our three children. If he contacts me again after a message like that, begging me to sign a contract, or a register, whatever, I think I will have to say, 'This ship has sailed, baby.'

My eye falls on the picture in the Horizon brochure. Maybe that would be a bit hasty, actually. I mean, I have put a lot of work into this contract, it would be nonsensical to chuck it all away now, over something so silly and trivial. I think I can find it in myself to forgive him. Then we can make up properly.

But there's no message. I scanned my inbox so quickly, not allowing my eyes to rest on the names there for any longer than half a second, that it is possible I missed it, so I look again. Then again. Then I turn the inbox over and look on the back; stick my hand in and rummage around at the bottom, and eventually turn it upside down and give it a good shake. But it's no use: he hasn't replied.

And, hell, that is so much worse.

It doesn't matter, it doesn't matter. I have got to get this Motivation prep done – or at least started – today, otherwise the whole thing will be a fuck-up. Today is Wednesday the thirteenth and the workshop is on Monday, so I have got three work days left now to get it done. Plenty of time, as long as there are no distractions. Emails from Rupert would be a serious distraction, so it's actually better that he hasn't replied. I'm glad.

Trouble is, not getting a message from him is almost as distracting as getting one. I spend the rest of the day busily staring off into space, gazing around the room, drumming my fingernails ineffectively on the keyboard and sorting out my desk drawer, but still no message comes through. I look over at Sean and hear him on the phone – 'Mm-hmm. That sounds ideal. How many does it seat?' – obviously sorting out something to do with the next presentation he's got, which I think is tomorrow, some Interview Technique thing somewhere. Fatima is talking quietly to Mike about something – 'Guinea pigs,' she's saying in an amazed tone, *really*?' – and even sloth-like Cath Parson, who moves more slowly than internal mail, seems almost animated. She's typing something up and I think she must be packing in about ten words a minute. So it's only me, then, who hasn't got anything to present to Chas the next time he enters our orbit. Terrific.

'Beth! Phone!' Ali shouts suddenly, and I jump. So do Fatima and Mike.

'Oh my God, Ali, you really made me jump, shouting out like that, for goodness' sake. You nearly stopped my hair from growing,' she says.

'What?' Ali says, then when Fatima starts to say, 'Well, my mum told me . . .' he says, 'Oh, right, sorry, I'll get her.' Then he cups his hand over the mouthpiece and shouts, 'Sorry, not Beth, Fatima. Fatima, call for you.'

How odd. Why would he have thought that the caller wanted me, when actually they wanted Fatima?

I mean, no matter how you say it, Beth and Fatima sound nothing alike. Be-ah-atima-eth. Fe-eth-atima. Christ, I have got to get on with this Motivation stuff.

'Guess what?' Fatima says breathlessly, appearing at my side five minutes later. Today her T-shirt says,

i know the answer, i've just forgotten it

'What?'

She sits down and rolls the seat right up to me. 'Someone is coming to look at the Mini. Tonight! Can you believe it? I'm so excited! I'll be able to pay off all that money I owe at last, and it won't even matter if I don't keep my job here. Well, no, of course it will matter, I don't want to lose my job, I love my job here, it's brilliant, but at least I won't be going to prison, which is the best news ever.'

She is actually clasping her hands together in heartfelt joy at the wondrous God-given change that's about to happen. I have to warn her. 'Look, Fats,' I say kindly, but then Ali shouts that there's a phone call for me, and it really is for me this time, and Fatima rolls away.

'Beth Sheridan speaking,' I say, knowing that I will have to spend most of tomorrow consoling Fatima about the fact that the one and only person who has phoned her up about the car didn't buy it immediately, instantly solving all her problems and bringing an end to world poverty at the same time, and then I hear the voice on the other end.

'Beth? It's Rupert.'

Seventeen

Providing Support

Short-term Goal: Get through the next few minutes without mentioning my fingers going through his hair.
Obstacles: That's pretty much all I can think about.
Long-term Goal: Is something happening after this?
Obstacles:

I really hate being unprepared. This phone call is so out of the blue, after getting no email from him today, I feel as if the breath has been knocked out of me a bit. I try to take a couple of deep but silent breaths to calm myself.

'Beth? Are you there?'

'Yeh, yes, I'm here. Hi. How are you? I was just about to go home.'

'Well, I'm glad I caught you. How's your day been?'

'Superlatively unremarkable. How about yours?'

'Much the same. Intense meetings, budget decisions, staffing issues, approvals, rejections, acceptances. You know.'

'Yes, that's exactly what I've been doing too.' Oh

my God, this is terrible. It's so obvious that we are both avoiding talking about the very flirty and highly inappropriate email I sent yesterday. It makes this officially one of the most uncomfortable moments of my life, second only to the time when my drama teacher wrote 'Thank you Elizabeth' next to a profession of undying love for him that I had written alongside my homework and then forgotten to erase.

Hopefully, Rupert will be far too embarrassed – mortified even – to mention what I said yesterday, and we'll just continue on in this way, pretending it didn't happen, until we both eventually forget about it. Or die of old age, whichever happens first.

'What a coincidence,' he says. 'How was the gym?'

OK, maybe not. 'The – er – the what?'

'The gym. You said yesterday that you were on your way there to tone up your thighs. Your *inner* thighs, I seem to remember.'

Oh God. Oh God, oh God, oh God. Why didn't I prepare something in advance for this moment? Everyone knows that when you send suggestive and inappropriately flirtatious emails to the insanely sexy millionaire businessman you're trying to set up a contract with, you should always prepare some witty answer to his enquiries about it later.

'No, no, you're mistaken,' I say, suddenly inspired. 'I said I was going to see my cousin Jim. You clearly weren't paying attention.'

There's a bemused silence. I picture him jerking his head to the side, as if what I've just said has physically struck him. But he's smiling. 'Oh, sorry. My mistake.'

'I have only been to the gym once in my life, and I vowed the minute my face hit the floor that I would never go again. So I can't have said that yesterday.' I have the satisfaction of hearing a snort of laughter, which makes me smile too.

'I don't blame you. So how is Jim these days?'

'Oh, he's much better now. He sends his regards. Says thanks for the muffin basket.'

'The mu—' And he breaks off into chuckles. 'You are a very unusual person, Beth Sheridan.'

'Thanks for noticing. Commonplace is so uninteresting, isn't it?'

He laughs again but quietly, bemusedly, and I kind of wish I had answered him a bit more seriously that time. Why didn't I just say, 'Why thank you, Rupert,' in a soft, sexy voice full of promise, conjuring up a lot of interesting images in his head?

'I have actually called you for a reason,' he says eventually.

'I hoped you might have.'

'Well, you were right. I have. I called you to arrange another meeting. To sort out the Love Learning stuff. And I promise, promise, promise that I will turn up this time. When are you free?'

How about the rest of my life? No, no, I'm not going to say that. Apart from being sad and embarrassing, it's also very cheesy.

Oh, and not appropriate.

'Well, I will have to check my diary. I know I am pretty much booked between now and next Monday but I should be able to get away after then. And for the rest of . . . um . . . the . . . er . . . the . . . week.' Holy crap, I swear to God I nearly said 'the rest of my life'. 'I don't mean I could get away for the rest of the week. I mean I could, you know, get away from the office for

261

a meeting at some point during the rest of the week.' What is the matter with me? I'm sure he wasn't even thinking that I meant an actual trip away for the rest of the week.

'That's a shame. I was just about to text the manager of La Belle Etoile hotel in Paris.'

I am saying nothing.

'But anyway, the meeting. How about next Tuesday, lunch, then? The nineteenth? Madeleine's? Or do you fancy somewhere else?'

Now, I know I have officially got an appointment with the Whytelys regional manager on the nineteenth, but I am probably going to cancel that. Or else let Sean go. Which makes me free.

'Yes, the nineteenth is fine. And I have no objections to having lunch at Madeleine's again. I really liked it there.'

Oops. That sounds suspiciously like I had never been there before yesterday. Hopefully he won't notice.

'Had you eaten there before?'

Bugger. I open my mouth to say, Oh yes, of course, you can't keep me out of the place, but then I remember that thing about how disaster is the only possible outcome when you tell lies. I think about the terrible repercussions that have ensued as a result of lies: so many needless wars started; countless innocent lives lost; dictators risen and kings fallen. And of course there's *Mrs Doubtfire*.

'No actually,' I say quickly. 'Yesterday was my first time. Thank you so much for it – it was lovely.'

'That's great.' I can hear in his voice that he's grinning. 'So you're a Madeleine's connoisseur now. Brilliant. Shall I send a car to pick you up, or shall we meet there?'

I hesitate. It's very tempting to have a chance to look at Grace's face as I am swept away in an expensive limousine, to a lunch appointment with a sexy millionaire. But if the lunch goes *exceptionally* well, my car will be unprotected in Love Learning's car park all night. 'Let's meet there.'

'I'll book the table then.' He pauses a moment. 'Did you like the . . . arrangement?'

'You mean the candles? Oh, yes. It was breathtaking. Magical. I've never seen anything like that before. Do they always do that in there?'

'Not always.' His voice is low. 'I could ask for that room again.'

I feel a tremor, as if he's talking about a hotel room. 'That would be lovely.'

'OK then. I'll sort it all out. We're less likely to be disturbed in there, too.'

'Mm.' I can't seem to clear the hotel room image from my head. Now I'm seeing a 'Do not disturb' sign hanging on a doorknob. And it's rocking gently with whatever motion is going on inside.

'Are you all right?' the voice in my ear says suddenly, and I realize that I have been silent for some moments.

'Oh, er, yes, fine. Sorry.' He's emerging from our en suite bathroom, damp from the shower, approaching me where I am reclining on the bed. 'I was just thinking about towels.'

'*Towels?*'

Shit! 'No, no, not towels. *Owls.* I was just remembering that I thought I saw one when I was at Madeleine's yesterday.'

There's a bemused silence, and I imagine him

263

smiling and frowning at the same time. 'Did you? How odd.'

'I know. That's what I thought. I might have been wrong, though.' God, could I sound any more insane?

'Listen, I've got to go,' he says after a few moments.

'Oh, yes, me too. I was about to . . .'

'Go home,' he finishes for me, and goosebumps raise suddenly on the back of my neck.

'Yes. That's right. I was.'

'I know. I'll see you next week, Beth. One o'clock, Tuesday. Madeleine's.'

'It's a date.' Shit. 'No, I mean, it's an appointment. I didn't mean . . .'

'See you then.' And he's gone.

Which means I have somehow got to get through almost an entire week before I get to meet him. What the hell am I going to do with myself until next Tuesday? Getting from last Wednesday until yesterday was easy enough; why is it suddenly so hard this week?

I glance hopefully at Sean's desk, but it's empty. He's out all day today and tomorrow, doing his Interview Technique thing. He's been so busy sorting that out, he's hardly spoken to me since our drink together. Anyway, he may be a very sexy dad, but he's not a sexy millionaire, and that is who I am having lunch with next week.

Oh, don't get me wrong; I don't fancy Rupert because of his money. I would have fancied him anyway. It just makes him even more attractive. I mean, it's part of who he is, isn't it? If it wasn't for his personality and character being what they are, he would never have made a fortune in the first place, so without the money

264

he would be a totally different person. Love Rupert, love his money.

I wonder if I could get some plastic surgery before next Tuesday.

'Uh-uh,' Vini says wisely in the evening, shaking her head. 'Four to ten days you'll still be puffy and blue. It's not until fourteen to thirty days later, depending on the procedure, that you can go out without a dressing.'

'Vin—'

'Oh God no. Not me. It was Joan Collins. Had her eyelids lowered a couple of years ago. You know her – she works in the post office. She did your car tax last year.'

So on Thursday night, out of desperation, I agree to go out with Vini. I'm providing support, that's all. 'I saw this in the paper today and thought it would be really great,' she tells me as I'm straightening my hair. 'Didn't suggest it though cos I thought you would say you didn't wanna come. And then barbecue the soles of my feet.'

'Why would I do that?' She hasn't actually admitted to sending that prank email and text from 'Nigel' yet. Maybe she's about to.

'Because of the disaster of the last time. You know. No matches.'

I'm getting a prickling feeling in my brain. She's obviously not going to cough up. Well, I'm not going to make her apologize. As far as she knows, I spent last night waiting in the Patch and Parrot for someone called Nigel.

'Doesn't matter about that. We'll call that a trial run.'

She looks at me intently in the mirror. 'You're not getting your hopes up about this Rupert guy, are you? Because it'll be just like Richard all over again, you know.'

I stare right back at her. 'God, I hope so.'

I've got my fingers crossed.

An hour later and we're turning up at the Oast House Hotel. 'It's not speed dating,' Vini says to me in the car park.

'Oh, thank God.'

'No, it's completely different. It's Pick 'n' Mix. Or Mix 'n' Match. Or something like that.'

Fuck. 'And that is different to speed dating how exactly?'

She turns to look at me with a peeved expression on her face. 'In every way that matters, Beth. There are no rules this time. We're just in a room, with a lot of other single people. It's an ordinary social event, except this time everyone who's there knows that everyone who's there is a) single; and b) fed up with it. If you want more than three minutes, you can have more. If you want less, ditto. If you want to sneak off into an un-used conference room and get down and dirty behind the projector, go right ahead. You look fantastic, by the way.'

'Thanks.' I glance down at myself. Under my coat it's only black jeans and a pink T-shirt – nothing special.

'It's not the clothes, dope. It's the hair. Nothing fantastic about jeans and a T-shirt.'

'Thanks. Again.'

'Don't be like that. I'm paying you a compliment. You look like someone.'

I get a little surge of pleasure from that. I know she

doesn't mean I look like I'm important, a force to be reckoned with, someone with influence. She means I look like a celebrity. She's always on the lookout for people who look like other people and won't hesitate to approach total strangers and give them her card. I've often thought how glad I was that she didn't ever do it to me because I want to look like me, not someone else. I have told myself that over and over again since she's had Fake Face.

When we walk into the Mix 'n' Match room, I notice immediately with a sinking feeling that there are hopeful little sprigs of mistletoe dotted randomly around the ceiling again. Obviously the people who organize these things have never been partnerless at Christmas, and think that enforced smooching is going to make us feel loved.

There are only two other people there, and they're both women. We smile at each other, but it's not a 'Hi, how are you, isn't this embarrassing, wish we didn't have to do it' sisterhood kind of smile. It's more of an 'Are you younger/slimmer/prettier than me?' type. We don't take one step nearer to them than we have to to establish that they are older – by quite a bit – than us. I don't know whether to be glad about that or seriously depressed. I get some drinks and we go and stand against the wall.

'Why aren't there any chairs? Or tables?'

'Because this way it's more like a party, and people will mingle better. We're not out for a drink together, remember. We're here to meet someone.'

'Does this mean that I'm definitely giving up on the guy I met at the speed dating, then?' I ask, looking sidelong at her.

She turns to me, her lips round a bottle of watermelon-flavoured alcohol. 'Well, if you haven't heard from him . . .' she says, innocently.

'No, not a word,' I say, then raise my eyebrows expectantly. This is it, surely. This is the perfect opportunity for her to admit, in a flood of regret, the awful prank she played on me the other day. How she realized, almost as soon as she had sent the messages, just how cruel it was and wished she could take it back. And how she couldn't bring herself to admit to me that she had done something so unfeeling because she couldn't bear the idea that I might think less of her as a person. Plus, she didn't want to admit to herself, or me, that she could be responsible for causing anyone pain, least of all her own flatmate and best friend.

'Oh, that's a shame,' she says, then swigs from her bottle again.

God, she's good.

Or. She didn't actually send that text. Which means that last night, someone with bad spelling called Nigel spent the evening sitting . . .

An idea occurs to me suddenly. 'Do you still have the number of the organizer?'

'Of the speed dating? Yes, why?'

I pull my mobile out of my bag. Vini doesn't even try to hide her look of dismay. 'Don't look like that. I just want to know, for sure. Just in case there have been some crossed wires, or something.'

'Christ, this is fucking Richard all over again as well.'

'It most definitely is not. What I had with Richard was so much more than three minutes at a table.'

'OK, whatever. Here's the number.'

When the woman finally answers her phone, it's obvious from the noise in the background that she's at another speed dating event. I wonder why there are so many speed dating events. Surely if it worked, there would be no need for them any more?

'Well, I've checked my records, love,' she says, coming back to the phone after a minute away. 'According to my list, there were no matches on your sheet.'

'Well, that's not right. I know for sure that we both ticked the box.'

'I know it seems harsh, my darling. But sometimes people who seem really nice, just aren't.'

'But he said he—'

'Look, I'll be honest with you, babe. He was probably just trying to go home with you that night.'

I open my eyes wider and Vini does a 'What?' at me. I shake my head. 'Is that possible?' I whisper.

'Oh, love, it happens all the time. These blokes make a great big deal of ticking your box, and then they don't even bother to hand their forms in at the end. All they have to do is engineer a chance meeting in the car park afterwards or something, and Bob's your uncle. You take him home because you saw him tick your sheet, so you know it won't be a one-off. But you don't get his contact details, because he didn't hand his form in.'

My jaw falls open. I even let it. 'Bastard.'

'I know, hon. But boys will be boys. I'm sorry it didn't work out for you. But we are having another event in two weeks, if you're interested?'

Is she kidding?

While I'm recounting to Vini what the woman said, the other Mix 'n' Match people start to arrive. Vini is looking at them keenly, almost as if she's searching for someone, but I've got a cold feeling of dread squatting in my belly – this crowd reminds me of nothing more than a puppeteers' convention. Without puppets. So even less fanciable, if that's possible.

'Here we go,' murmurs Vini, and launches herself cheerfully into the crowd. I stand where I am for a few moments, trying to get up some courage.

'All right, darling?' a voice says at my left. I look round and immediately wish I had plunged in with Vini. Obviously standing still is a mistake – it leaves you vulnerable, your defences open. 'I'm Eric.'

'Hi, Eric,' I reply. He's wearing a red felt Santa hat, pulled over to one side into what he probably thinks is a jaunty angle. I deliberately don't make much eye contact, or smile, or give him my name, or look remotely interested. Don't want to send out the wrong signals.

'You done this before, then, love?' he asks me, showering me with a fine mist. 'Nah, doubt you 'ave, fit bird like you.'

I blink a few times. 'Not really.' I have broken eye contact altogether now and am looking interestedly around the room.

'What's your name then?' he says, apparently not picking up my fuck-off-I'm-not-interested signal.

'Er, Paula.'

'All right, Paula? Nice to meet you.' He holds out his hand even though I'm not looking at him. I turn my face almost completely away from him, but still in my periphery I can just make out his grinning red face, with outstretched hand, waiting expectantly for me to shake it.

'Sorry, um, er . . .'

'Eric. Remember?'

'Eric. Sorry, need the loo.'

'Okey dokey. I'll get you a drink while you're gone. What's your poison?'

But I don't answer. I am sprinting in my spike heels across the packed room, darting through and around the awkward conversations in a zig-zag pattern because I got an email once that said that that is the best way to escape an assailant. I can feel the heat of Eric's inflamed blood vessels boring into my back, but I'm not going to look round, not even if I'm sure he can't see me because knowing my luck he'll still be watching me and as soon as I make eye contact he will—

'Oomph!'

My left shoulder smashes hard into someone else. I was concentrating so hard on not looking behind me I forgot to look in front of me. 'Oh, God, I'm so sorry, are you all right?' I stop speaking as I'm turning and my eyes finally find and lock on to the tall, broad-shouldered body, then the sexy, stubbly face, and finally, with a jolt, the gorgeous, warm brown eyes of Brad.

Eighteen

Effective Communication

Short-term Goal: Not kill or shag Brad. Yet.
**Obstacles: He is probably the sexiest man I have ever
    wanted to kill.**
Long-term Goal: Kill or shag Brad.
Obstacles: If I kill him, I can't shag him.

Elusive Brad of the speed dating, Brad of the intense
connection, the huge crush and then the days of no
communication. I am doing a kind of gulping with my
eyes. Visual gluttony. It's awful but I can't stop myself,
staring and staring, eyes wide, lips slightly parted, a
smile forcing its way onto them; and then I realize that
he is doing the same as he stares back at me.

'Are you . . . ? Is it . . . *Libby*? That is you, isn't it?
Christ, you *are* here! I was so hoping you might be.
How are you? What happened to you? Where have you
been?'

My lips twitch with wanting to smile and my arms
jerk a millimetre towards him as I narrowly avoid
throwing myself into his embrace with a daft grin. But
just in time I remember exactly what happened last

time we met, and exactly what the organizer of the event has just told me, and exactly what this luscious, lip-lickingly lovely man was trying to achieve. The smile freezes on my lips, then drops with an almost audible clang. He's out to get into someone else's knickers tonight. Obviously he uses these meeting events as opportunities to . . . well, meet people. How terribly sad and pathetic.

'I have been exactly where I always am,' I say, trying really hard to be aloof and contemptuous, while being intensely, almost irresistibly attracted to him. I'm not sure I'm pulling it off though, particularly as he looks incredibly pleased to see me. And – although this is totally irrelevant as the man is a cold, heartless predator – throat-achingly sexy. I fold my arms and turn my head slightly to the side, as much to disguise the fact that my pupils are dilating all on their own as to appear indifferent.

'But where *is* that?' He takes a step nearer to me, effectively closing out the rest of the room. 'I've been searching for you for eight days – didn't find so much as a DNA trace.'

My feet are trying to move me nearer, so I force them to take a step back. Then my body tries to lean towards him without my feet. I nearly fall over. 'At home, in the car, sometimes in the supermarket. At work. You know. Or at least, you would have known, if you had any intention of actually finding anything out about me.'

He flinches a bit and his eyebrows flicker in bewilderment. Yeah, good act. 'What do you mean? Of course I wanted to find out about you! That's the only reason I'm here now, because I couldn't think of any other way to find you. And you saw me tick your number. Number six. I still remember. It was the only number I ticked.'

'Oh well, in that case, let's go somewhere quiet and get to know each other better,' I almost say. My lips are forming the words and I have to wiggle my jaw a bit to stop them coming out. Which must look a bit like one of those old women you see on the bus who permanently chew on absolutely nothing. Sexy.

'Really?' I say eventually, to give my lips something to do. 'But you only did that to convince me you wanted to know me, so that I would be more inclined to go with you later in the car park when you . . .'

Actually, he didn't accidentally bump into me in the car park afterwards, did he? In fact, I didn't see him at all afterwards.

'When I . . . ?' He's got a tiny smile on those incredible full lips, which have a slight sheen on them, and a hint of stubble underneath. As I stare, the smile broadens. Shit, I'm staring at his mouth. I drag my eyes away.

'When you, you know, do something underhand and sinister, which I fall for because I saw you tick my number, but of course you didn't even hand your form in at the end, so the whole thing was . . .' I've been gradually slowing down as I speak, and now I seize up altogether.

His eyes are wide now, eyebrows up, broad smile. 'So the whole thing was an elaborate plot to get you to sleep with me without giving you my phone number, or address, or any other information? Is that it? Is that really what you thought?'

'Well, I didn't until about ten minutes ago. Then I did for a while. Then after that, I began not to again.'

'I could have gone to a nightclub to pick someone up for meaningless sex, you know.' And at this moment there is one of those inexplicable lulls in the conversation and ambient noise in the room, which always seem to happen when someone is either talking loudly about meaningless sex or insulting the person standing behind them. Brad's words hang in the air in great big bold capital letters.

'You complete tosser,' a woman spits as she passes. We both flinch and follow her with our eyes for several seconds, but she doesn't stop or even look back. Eventually we turn back to each other.

'Who was that?'

He shrugs nonchalantly. 'My mum.' I laugh daintily. At least I hope I do: at this point, I could be guffawing away with all my fillings showing, and I wouldn't be able to stop it. 'Anyway, look, why would I need to go through this whole elaborate deception when, as I said,' he lowers his voice and glances surreptitiously around him, 'there are other options?'

'Oh, God, there you are,' Vini says, rushing up to me, '*Libby.*' I primed her in the car to use this name. I didn't think she would remember.

'Oh, hi, Vini.' I flash her a grateful smile. She must have spotted me when her eyes were drawn to Brad along with everyone else's during the sudden silence just now. 'What's up?'

'I've met someone,' she says excitedly. 'Remember that guy, from the puppet conference?'

'Which one? God, not the one on the fake ostrich?'

'No, no, not him.'

'The one with the goatherd and all the little goats?'

'No, not him. Listen—'

'The one with the horse on the end of his arm?'

'No. Fuck, will you stop interrupting? It was the guy who was coming out of the Fast Love room just as we were going in. Remember him? Adam.'

'Oh, yes, I do remember. He didn't have a puppet, did he? But he was looking for them, which is not a good sign. You can't go out with someone who has puppet zeal, Vin.'

Brad splutters down a stifled laugh. Vini shoots him a look, then comes back to me. 'I've been out with some wankers in my time, *Lib*, so I don't think I'll write him off just for that. Not yet.'

'OK, but he's not bringing puppets round to the flat. I mean it, Vin. I'm not waking up to find Lord Charles face down on the bathroom floor, or bumping into a pantomime horse on the landing. I don't care how sexy it is.'

'Oh shut up,' she says, getting stroppy. Brad is giggling openly now and covers his mouth with his hand, trying to convert it into a cough. 'Yeah, yeah, ha ha, very funny. Glad I have been able to entertain you. I just came over here to tell you that I'm leaving, OK? Adam and I are going somewhere else. I feel like a walking target in this place, so we're gonna go somewhere quiet.'

'There's a lovely little stripey tent on the beach,' I suggest helpfully, trying to keep a straight face. 'Really cosy.' Brad is choking loudly behind his hand and actually turns away, shoulders shaking.

'Yeah, great, thanks. See you later.' And she marches away.

'Who *was* that?' he splutters, still forcing down laughter.

'My flatmate, Lavinia. Vini. She was number five last week, remember?'

He sobers up instantly. 'No, I'm afraid I don't. Once I'd got to number six, all the others went out of my head.'

He's smiling at me softly and I can feel parts of me melting. Lots of me. 'And all I can remember is number . . .' I pause. 'Hang on a minute. What number were you exactly? Because I know I ticked fifteen, but then I got a strange message from someone who said he was . . . What?' He's shaking his head.

'I wasn't fifteen. I was sixteen.'

'No, you weren't, you were definitely fifteen.'

'Sixteen.'

'No, I remember, because you flashed your hand at me three times – five and five and five. Last time I looked, three fives were fifteen. Don't tell me they've changed it?'

'No, they haven't, you're right about three fives. And I did flash you three fives, but then I added a one. Five, then five, then five. Then one. Grand total – sixteen.'

I'm staring at him, eyes wide. 'Oh no. I didn't, did I? But how can I have missed . . . ?' And then I remember. My sheet had fallen on the floor and I was panicking about picking it up and getting his number before the next person arrived, and I must have missed his final 'one' when I was frantically looking around . . .

Now I put my hand over my mouth. 'Oh . . . shit. It's all my fault. Oh my God. All this time and it was . . . Jesus, I'm so sorry. What a complete idiot. I must have flaming dumplings for brains.'

'It's a powerful image, but don't be too hard on yourself. It's all worked out well in the end, hasn't it?' He takes a teeny step nearer to me. This time I don't move backwards.

'I don't know. Ask me again in an hour.'

He smiles and gazes at me. 'I will.' He pauses, then his arm shoots out and grabs mine. 'Are you all right?'

Oops. My legs just wobbled a bit. Was kind of hoping he didn't notice. 'Oh, yes, I'm fine. Just a bit . . .' What am I a bit? Tired, I was going to say, but that makes me sound . . . I don't know, pathetic. I could say I'm a bit drunk but that's probably a no-no when you're just getting to know someone. So what can I say made me wobble?

'Do you want to sit down?' he says gently, his face all concerned, rescuing me from my dilemma. He's bending his head down to be on my eye level.

I nod. 'Yes, I think I do.' Before my out-of-control lust pushes me over onto my back, naked.

He leads me to a table flanked by two sofas in the corner, then goes off to get us both a drink. When he comes back, I project a powerful tractor beam from my body, dragging him down onto the sofa next to me where our thighs can touch. It doesn't work though. He hesitates a second, then moves round the table to sit on the opposite side. I stare at his face in desperation – no, not desperation, disappointment – and notice that he's looking a bit confused. Or maybe troubled. I'm not sure I like that. Maybe my body language is coming over as a bit keen (sprawling backwards on the cushions, top three buttons undone, knees slightly apart, eyes half closed, lips moist and parted) so I sit up like a librarian and mentally tuck my hair behind my ears (I don't really do this – I'm not stupid).

'I think I saw you,' he says, smiling suddenly.

'Did you? When?' And why didn't you come over and say hello, will you marry me? I stop myself from saying.

'Um, let me see.' He presses his lips together and looks up, trying to remember when it was. I mean, come on, obviously it wasn't that long ago, we've only known each other nine days. 'Last Friday. The eighth. Seventeen minutes past one.'

I blink. 'Oh, really? Well, you said you hadn't even found DNA, and yet here you are now telling me you saw me. Why didn't you say hello?'

'Well, I would have done but you were in your car.'

Oh my God. It's bound to have been one of those times I was driving home thinking about Rupert and not focusing on my face. I probably looked like a complete loon. 'What was my face like?' I just manage to stop myself from blurting out. Instead I say, 'So it *was* you who served me at the burger drive-in that time. Spot of moonlighting?'

He smiles. 'You caught me. I volunteer there, twice a week.'

I'm nodding, all serious. 'Admirable. Really giving something back.'

'That's why I do it. So how is that girl you were with? The one in the car with you? When I saw you, she looked very upset. That's really why I didn't come over and speak to you.'

Oh thank God! I wasn't driving.

'I wanted to, though.'

More occurs to me. The first thing is the softness of his voice as he said those last words. The second thing is the fact that he wanted to come and speak to me

279

when he saw me. And the third, very late and most important thing, is that not only was I not driving looking sour when he spotted me, but was caught in the act of consoling Fatima on the way back from the police station last week. I have actually been spotted helping a friend! And I didn't even realize that I was being watched, which means that everything I did was absolutely natural, and it still looked appealing.

I'm suddenly aware that he's still waiting for an answer about Fatima.

'Um, she's fine, really. Well, no, not entirely fine. She's got a few problems. That's why she was crying. I'm really worried about her.'

'I could tell.' He gazes into my eyes for a second with a warm smile. 'I wish I could have spoken to you that day.'

'So do I.' We sip our drinks in silence for a moment. He looks at me, then looks away, then at me again. I know this because I can't take my eyes off him. Eventually he clears his throat.

'So we both know why I'm here tonight,' he says with a grin, 'but what about you?'

I shake my head. 'No, no, hold on a minute. We don't both know why you're here at all. *You* know, but as far as I am concerned you're just here for meaningless sex.' I've lowered my voice a bit at that last bit, just in case. 'All right, you've convinced me that's not the case, so you must be here in a serious capacity. Which is a bit . . . well, shallow, given that you ticked my box last week and made noises and gestures suggesting to me that you wouldn't need to keep looking. And yet here you are – looking. Why?'

He stares at me earnestly for a few moments and I

feel heat fill my face. And neck. And other parts. Then he says: 'You.'

'Hmm?'

'Libby, I am here because I wanted to find you. I thought you realized that?'

'Um . . . you . . . you're . . . ?'

He smiles and tilts his head forwards a little. 'Unlike you, when I didn't get your contact details from the Fast Love people, I didn't assume that you were some man-mad nympho who was only after one thing.'

'I didn't think you were that either.'

He laughs out a puff of air. 'Well, whatever you thought I was up to, I didn't think you were doing the same. I simply assumed there had been a mix-up with the forms, or something, and that all I had to do was find you. At that point, the only thing I knew about you was that you once went to a singles event, so that was the only thing I could try. Hence,' he holds out his hands, palms upwards, 'here I am.'

'Oh.' You know, now that I think about it, it does seem ridiculous that I thought he was some kind of lothario like that. I mean, he would have to have been a seriously good actor to pull that off.

'To be honest, I didn't really expect you to be here. Or at any other singles event. You seemed so out of place at the last one. Plus, I now know you thought it was a complete disaster, peopled only with deceitful sex-fiends.' He grins mischievously. 'Which leaves me wondering just exactly why you are here?'

'Vini,' I say simply, and he nods with understanding.

'Of course. What's her real name?'

'That is her real name.'

'No, really.'

'I'm serious. Her parents called her Lavinia because it's an unusual name, and her surname is so ordinary.'

'What's her surname?'

'Jones.'

'Jones? You are kidding? Vini Jones? No way.'

'Absolutely. Actually, I think shortening Lavinia to Vini is a stroke of genius on her part, don't you?'

'Well, yeah. And totally does away with the need to use a fake name at these type of events.'

I start a bit. Crap, has he guessed? I study his face but he's not looking at me expectantly, as if he's waiting for a confession of some kind. I'll just bumble on, then. 'You're right. No one would ever believe that was her real name, would they?'

'No, exactly. Although I can't understand anyone who thinks they should use a fake name anyway. I mean, it's a huge part of who you are; you can't expect to meet people sincerely if you hold back your identity.'

'Oh God, I totally agree. I would never, ever use a fake name. It's despicable.'

'Ah, Paula, there you are,' says red-faced Eric, arriving suddenly with two tall, green drinks and a grin. I glance at Brad, who mouths *'Paula?'* at me silently. 'You never said what you wanted,' Eric is going on, 'so I got you a crème de menthe and lemonade. Can't go wrong with that. Here you go.'

He presses the glass into my hand and then stands there waiting for me to drink it. I can see in my peripheral vision to the left that Brad is staring at me not smiling, although I'm sure the corners of his mouth are twitching, and I feel in the air between us the threat of hysteria. Or maybe that's just me.

'Go on, Paula,' he says eventually, a slight tremor in his voice, 'take a swig.'

'Oh, yes, do, Paula,' Eric urges. 'It's bloody gorgeous.' He swigs his own drink. 'Mm, yum yum.'

'Oh, Eric, look, thank you so much but I'm afraid my dad,' I gesture towards Brad, 'is here to pick me up now, so I'm going to have to go.' I'm rewarded by the sight of Brad flinching in his seat and his smile faltering. I hold out the glass to Eric, who seizes it and pulls it tight to his chest almost before I've let go.

'Your dad?' he says, looking from me to Brad, then back. 'How old are you?'

'I'm fifteen. It's so unfair. How did you know where I was, Dad?'

I can see that Brad is struggling with the fact that Eric has simply accepted this scenario. 'Er, er, well, I, er . . .'

'Oh, crap, you didn't read my diary again, did you? For fuck's sake, why do I keep meticulously writing down everything I'm doing in great detail, and then leaving the bloody thing lying around?'

'Now watch your language, young lady,' Brad says, leaning forward towards me. 'That's fifty pee off your pocket money.'

'Bye then,' I call out as Eric turns away quickly and walks back across the room. As he retreats into the crowd, we hear, 'All right, gorgeous. Eric here. You look like the sort to appreciate the subtle flavours of crème de menthe and lemonade . . .'

Two hours later and we're standing by my car in the car park. Brad has got my mobile phone number and my home number, as well as my Hotmail address. All he doesn't have is my actual name.

'I'm so glad you were here tonight,' he says softly. He's looking straight into my eyes but again I can detect in his face a flash of . . . regret? Yes, I think that's it.

'Is there something wrong?' I hear myself asking. Bugger, my lips are off again. For God's sake, they don't even know the right questions to ask. Everyone knows that no one ever answers the 'Is there something wrong?' question honestly.

'Well, kind of,' Brad says after a moment's hesitation. 'Not wrong, exactly. More right than anything. Too right. It's difficult to explain.'

I put my hand on his arm to reassure him, but also because I so desperately want to touch some part of him. I squeeze a bit, grabbing the chance to feel the muscles there. It feels damn good. Reassuring him, I mean. 'No, look, sorry, I'm not trying to pry. You don't have to explain anything.'

He's so close to me now, his eyes on my face, then my hair, then my eyes, my lips, my hair again; while I am gazing with ferocious intensity at his lips. I can't help it – they're at eye level. Also, I am trying to pull them towards me with the power of my mind, but telekinesis as a form of communication has never been all that effective for me.

'No, I know I don't,' he says, 'and I don't think I could anyway. It's just that . . .' He closes his eyes and rubs the back of his neck. 'It's just that, since I met you last week, I've kind of . . . I mean, there's been a . . .' He looks at my lips again and his face takes on a kind of hunted expression. 'I really want to . . .' he says slowly, then closes his eyes again and slumps his shoulders a bit. 'No, I can't. Not until . . . Never mind. It's my problem, I'll sort it out. It doesn't matter.'

I'm not convinced. He's quite clearly either got married or murdered someone since last Tuesday, and now regrets it because he's met me again. I take my hand off his arm. 'Oh Christ, you're not married, are you?' I ask, because obviously I can't let on that I know about the murder. That would put me next on his list.

'No! For God's sake, of course not! Why would I be speed dating if I were already married?'

I look at him as if he's the most naive person ever to stand in a dark car park. 'It's been known.'

'Well, I'm not. I swear. And even if I were, she wouldn't understand me.'

I laugh a little. 'Of course she wouldn't.'

He smiles back. 'But you do. Which is why I'm leaving her. The marriage has been over for months anyway.'

I'm actually starting to worry now that in fact he is married, but he's treating it like a joke so that I'll think it's a joke, and dismiss it. And then when I find out about the wife for real in six months' time, he'll be able to say, with total honesty, 'But, baby, I told you I was married – don't you remember? In the car park at the Oast House Hotel. I assumed that you were fine with it because you never mentioned her again and then slept with me all those times.'

Maybe I could just do that.

'I'd better go,' I say instead, and he nods. Bum. 'I'll see you soon.'

'You certainly will,' he says, and leans in suddenly and grazes my cheek with his lips. As he does this my knees wobble again and my eyes actually roll back in my head as they close. I'm glad he can't see my face at this point. Actually, I'm glad no one can.

'Goodnight, Libby,' he whispers into my hair.

I get into the car and start the engine, then roll down the window. 'Night.' And as I reverse out of the space and drive back onto the road, I can see in my rear-view mirror that he is staring after my car the whole time.

Nineteen

Active Listening

Short-term Goal: Choose between Brad and Rupert.
Or maybe just sleep with both of them.
Obstacles: I have my morals. No, really, I do.
Long-term Goal: All that will be left to do is pick out
my dress.
Obstacles: There are so many to choose from, with
only six months until June.

Rupert is in his car, driving probably too fast. He's grinning and singing along to the radio, which is apparently having an '80s day. 'All the hits, all of the '80s, all day,' the DJ keeps saying.

Rupert taps his fingers on the steering wheel and jerks his head energetically in time to the music. It's Friday morning and he knows he should be at work, but there's someone he needs to speak to. Someone who has helped him talk through problems in the past. Rupert is hoping this person will be able to help him again.

He's so involved in Roxy Music he almost misses the turning when it comes. He slams on the brakes and

the car screeches around the corner. He follows the
road two or three miles before turning through a high
hedge onto a wide gravelled driveway, which leads up
to a large three-storey house. He parks in front of the
house, jumps out of the car and bounds in through the
front door.

'Hello-o? Mum? Dad? Matt? Where are you all? It's
me! Hello?'

'Sitting room!' comes a voice, apparently from a long
way away.

Rupert turns into a hallway on the right and follows
it down to the end where it opens out into a large,
bright room with one wall made entirely of glass,
looking out over a misty field. At one end of this room
a man and woman, both about sixty, are watching
television: kneeling on the floor is a young man of
about twenty-five, completely occupied with copying
a map of Sweden from an atlas onto a large piece of
paper. The drawing is larger than the original, but it's
exactly to scale.

'Hi all!' Rupert calls, jogging into the room.

'Rupert! Hello, love.' Caroline de Witter gets up and
hugs her son. 'This is lovely.' She gazes at her son as he
embraces his father and greets his brother.

'Hi, Matt.'

'Hello,' the young man answers quietly, without
looking up. 'I'm enlarging this map of Sweden,' he
says, his nose almost touching the paper. 'I'm making
it one-eighth bigger than the one in this book. This
one is too small so I am drawing it bigger. There are
lots of difficult bits around the edge, very fiddly, but
I'm doing it right.' He is not hurried in his task, not
trying to complete it as quickly as he can. In fact, he

is engrossed in it, placing his index finger on the map, studying it for a few seconds, then drawing an exact replica on the paper.

'That's incredible,' Rupert says, partly to his brother, partly to his parents and partly to himself. 'How are things today?'

'Quiet today. Quite good,' Caroline answers. 'We've got no plans, nowhere we need to be, so he's happy.'

'Great. Can I take him then?'

She nods. 'Of course. Just half an hour, though. Make sure you tell him.'

'I know, Mum. I won't forget. Have I ever?'

She smiles. 'Well, only that one time . . .'

'Yes, I know, I remember. And I have never forgotten since then, have I?'

'No, I don't think you have. But I'm always going to remind you anyway. Just in case.' She turns to her other son. 'Matthew, your brother is here and he wants to take you out for a walk for half an hour. Can you close the atlas and put it with your map up on the table now please?'

Matt looks up but not at his mother and obediently picks up the atlas and the paper and puts them on the table. He does not touch the coloured pencils, which are spread out messily on the rug.

'And now pick up the pencils,' Caroline says. 'I forgot about them,' she adds to Rupert. 'Now go and get a jacket from the hall cupboard and put it on please. Then stay with Rupert.'

'Half-an-hour walk,' Matt says quietly. 'Half an hour.'

'Yes, mate, just half an hour,' Rupert answers, following his brother out to the hallway.

'Oh, you are coming for the whole weekend, aren't you, Rupe?' Caroline says as the two brothers move towards the front door.

'Of course I am. Not going to miss my little brother's birthday celebrations, am I? I'll come first thing tomorrow morning and go back Sunday evening.'

She smiles at him fondly. 'Thanks, Rupe. That will be a great help.'

Outside Rupert decides to walk around the house and gardens, but before setting off he spends five minutes explaining to Matt exactly the route they will follow. Matt doesn't look at him but Rupert knows his brother is drawing a map in his head. Rupert checks his watch and says quietly, 'In at quarter to twelve.' Matt looks at his own watch but says nothing.

'So, how have you been, little brother?' Rupert starts talking as they walk. 'Everything all right? Still drawing your maps then? That's amazing, what you've done of Sweden. You're such a clever lad. I'm really sorry I haven't been to see you for a couple of weeks. I've been meaning to but I've been sorting out this crèche at work, and then something else happened which has been amazing.' He turns to look at Matt, longing for a reaction, for his brother to look up at him with a grin and say, 'What, Rupe? What's so amazing?' But it doesn't happen. It never happens. Matt walks on, doggedly staring straight ahead, following the route in his head.

'I need to ask your advice, Matt. Do you mind?' Rupert turns away again and looks ahead too. 'The thing is, I've met someone. A lovely, funny, gorgeous girl called Libby. I can't stop thinking about her. She likes me too, and this time it's different because she doesn't know who I am. She thinks my name is Brad.'

'You're Rupert.'

'Yes, mate, that's right, I am. Of course I am. But she doesn't know that. You're not going to understand this, Matt, but if she knew who I was, it would change everything. She would be different, I would be different. Girls usually just like me because of the money – or at least I think they do – so I get really nervous and can't act normally. And they have preconceived ideas about what being with me will be like. But when I'm Brad, I am different.' He turns and looks at his brother animatedly, his eyes bright. 'I mean, I'm me except I don't feel scared because I know she doesn't have any expectations of me. I can relax and be completely myself. And she likes me, Matt. For myself. I didn't get her phone number so I went to a couple more of those singles meetings, hoping to see her again. And last night I did.'

'Half past eleven,' Matt says without making eye contact.

Rupert checks his watch. 'I know, mate. Fifteen minutes left. Through the vegetable garden now.' They turn at the end of the lawn and pass through a gap in the tall hedge. 'So all that sounds really fantastic, doesn't it? Especially after last night, because now I've got all her phone numbers and email addresses. And she was so—' He breaks off and smiles down at the ground for a moment. 'She's funny. And she's so easy to be with. I want to be with her all the time.' He shakes his head a little and rubs his face with his hand. 'It should be so simple, so wonderful. And it is. But . . . God, I wish you could understand this, Matt.

It's so ironic. After so long of not finding anyone I could see myself with, two come along at once. Can you believe that?' He looks at his brother who is still facing forward, unmoved. 'No, of course you can't. It's too ridiculous. Two at once! No one would believe it. But that's what's happened. I mean, I haven't actually met the second one – Beth – but she has got me seriously hooked. She is so funny, and clever, and imaginative, and lively. And someone I know has met her and told me that she's pretty too, if you can believe that. I am dying to meet her, not just because she is so fantastic but also because I feel like I can't really make up my mind about her until I've seen her in the flesh. Spoken to her, face to face.' He breaks off and puts his hands in his pockets, walking on thoughtfully for a few minutes. 'The difference is that she knows that I am Rupert de Witter—'

'You are Rupert.'

'Yes, mate, I am. And Beth knows that, which maybe isn't a bad thing. But she thinks I look . . . different. She thinks I've got all this gorgeous blond hair, and these perfect teeth . . . God, I am such an idiot. I don't know what to do about that. I don't know anything. Which one should I go for? Beth knows who I am but thinks I look like a model. And Libby knows what I look like but thinks I am someone else. I think they both like me, and I like both of them. A hell of a lot. I have got to decide, which means I will have to say goodbye to one of them, which I don't want to do. And if I see both of them for a while, I will feel like I'm betraying both of them. God, this is so hard. So what do you think? Libby or Beth? Beth or Libby? Any ideas?' He glances at his brother again, but Matt is still looking ahead. He does not offer any words of advice or support. Rupert runs his hands through his hair.

'Well,' he says, 'perhaps you're right. Perhaps I don't have to choose just yet. I mean, I'm not proposing marriage, am I? I'm just getting to know them both a bit better. People do see more than one person these days, don't they? It's all right while it's just friendship, isn't it?' He's nodding, but frowning too. 'And then once I've met Beth next week, and we've chatted, and maybe gone out together once or twice, then I will decide.'

'Twenty to twelve. Five minutes.'

'Yes, I know. Look, we're nearly back at the conservatory now. Does that sound all right to you, then? See them both, at least for the time being, just to see what happens? I mean, there's nothing wrong with seeing more than one friend, is there? I will just have to make sure that it doesn't go any further until I've made up my mind. I think I can do that. I hope I can.' He pauses and rubs his head. 'I am really worried about what Libby will think when I tell her who I am, though. I mean, I have deceived her into believing I was someone else. But she is an intelligent, sensitive woman, she will understand why.' He turns to look at Matt again and smiles fondly at his brother's tousled hair and impassive face. 'Talking things over with you really does help me, you know, Matty, even though you're not actually listening. I love you, mate. Any chance of a hug?'

'Eleven forty-five. In now.'

Rupert sighs. 'Yes, mate, in now.'

*   *   *

On Friday morning, I am at work, sitting in front of my computer, staring at a lightning-bolt-shaped groove that's been scratched onto the desk. I'm hard at work on my research and preparation for the Motivation workshop on Monday, but I keep finding myself strangely distracted. My mind keeps filling up with alternate images of Rupert and Brad flying in and out of sight on broomsticks. It's very weird. First Rupert, with his thick blond hair and his white smile; then Brad, taller, broader, darker. Each time they arrive, they seem to come very close to me, then pause, frozen, smiling in mid-air, to give me a chance to ogle them close up. Rupert's chiselled chin, movie-star eyes and beautiful hair; then Brad's warm eyes, stubbly chin and boy-next-door looks. Each time Rupert replaces Brad, I am glad to see him. And each time Brad in turn replaces Rupert, I am glad about that too.

This dilemma of mine is so common, so basic and so ancient. The classic triangle – two men, one woman. It's a dilemma that has plagued the human race since the beginning of civilization. On one side, fantastically sexy and beautiful millionaire businessman who possibly may not have been sincere, has only communicated through email and telephone and who is, let's face it, probably completely out of my league. On the other side, friendly, funny, dead fanciable chap-next-door with boyish good looks and slightly dishevelled appearance, who has met me in person, kissed my cheek so softly, and definitely fancies me. Our history books and classic literature are littered with stories exactly like that.

Right. Come on, Beth, get a grip. I must must must get on with this Motivation stuff. I've only got today and the weekend to get it ready and I've barely even started. Motivation is about fixing your mind on an achievable goal, committing yourself to it, and then setting some milestones designed to celebrate . . .

Christ, look at that, Rupert's flying robes have blown open in the wind, revealing smooth, bronzed skin and rippling pectorals. I can see the muscles stretch and shift as he maintains perfect balance on the speeding broom. He's so close, I could almost reach out my hand, stroke my fingers across that flesh and push the material away from—

'Do you know where Sean is?' Chas says, suddenly standing right behind me.

My eyes snap round to face him and I quickly rub the droplet off my bottom lip. 'No, I don't, Chas.' And why is he asking me anyway?

'Big plans, Beth?' he says, rubbing his hands together. 'Irons in the fire? Fingers in pies?'

'Um, yes, definitely.'

'Great, great. Only a week left, you know, before we close for Christmas. Don't want to be dithering about booking holidays.' He raises his eyebrows at the Horizon brochure, which has inexplicably appeared on my desk. 'Remember the early bird, eh? He who hesitates, you know? Or she, of course. No time to lose, Beth. *Carpe diem*, you know. Chop chop.'

Fuck off and die, you pathetic little wanker. I don't say this out loud – I'm not mad. I send it to him telepathically, while I smile and nod. He jerks his head once downwards and wanders away.

I glance over at Sean's desk. Interesting that he hasn't featured in my freaky little broomstick fantasy. Just as well he's out of the office again today – he might start to complicate things.

I turn back to my computer and type listlessly for a few minutes. 'Primary motivation is to find food and shelter. Once these two essentials have been achieved, the next most important need is sex. Probably outdoors, on a blanket somewhere. The sun would be warm on bare skin, shadows flickering across the twisting bodies like a light show. Or on a yacht maybe, the rhythmic rolling of the waves and creaking of the ropes a sensual addition to the passion of the moment . . .'

Shit. I'll make a cup of tea to clear my head. I stand up but at this moment Chas comes back and claps his hands.

'People, people,' he calls out, interrupting everyone in their work, 'I hope you don't need me to remind you how hard you should all be working?' He glares ferociously round the room, daring people not to be working when he looks at them. No one is, of course – we've all turned away from our desks to look at him. He goes on. 'Today is Friday, which means you have a week left, people. One week. Just seven little days. Next Friday will be the twenty-second and on that day we will close for Christmas. That day is an important day, people. On that day big decisions will be made. On that day, our fates will be decided. Well, yours will. On that day, I want a contract from each and every one of you, signatures on lines, deposits in the bank. This is critically important. Love Learning cannot survive without new money, so it is up to each of you to make sure we get it. Otherwise your jobs will be no more. I don't want that to happen, but my hands are tied.' He holds his hands up in front of him, joined at the wrists, in case we didn't understand what 'my hands are tied' meant. He glowers around the room, then softens and smiles. 'I didn't want to have to tell you that. It is in my nature to be a caring person, and a kind person, so I have tried to spare you from the real situation. But now you know.' And abruptly he turns and goes back into his office.

'What a twit,' Mike says immediately. Fatima giggles.

'Twat more like,' Grace says behind me. 'God, that man is an arsehole.' I turn to face her, then watch her push her hair away from her face with open fingers, then pull it all forward again. I grit my teeth.

'Well,' I say, fiddling with a lock of my own hair, 'he's got a good point. And you've got to admit it was decent of him not to let on how serious the situation is.' Defending Chas feels like mud in my mouth, especially since I know I am talking a load of bollocks.

'Oh, Beth,' Grace says and looks at me pityingly, 'you're so incredibly naive, aren't you? He says he kept it to himself and you blindly go along with it, regardless of what your own mind is telling you. Don't you remember, little Bethy, that he told us this last week? Hmm?' She's tilted her head on one side as she looks at me, the way that she would probably look at a dead squirrel in the road. 'Maybe you didn't understand what he was talking about last week?'

I clench and unclench my fists and all the muscles in my body and legs tighten, ready to spring. I've gone into Rip-Her-Hair-Off-Her-Head or Flight mode. 'Oh goodness, Grace, of course I realize that,' I say with eyebrows raised in surprise. 'Maybe you just didn't notice the difference between what he said last week and what he's just said today.'

'Well, I'm sure I would have done, if there had been a difference.'

'Oh yes, of course you would, silly me. It's a bit scary, isn't it, that last week he said four of us would go, and today he said we all would? Looks like we'll all be on the dole come New Year.' I tilt my own head slightly and look at her with a teensy, lips-closed smile, the way that I might look at a small child who's just peed in his pants. Then, as I sadly rotate my chair to face my own computer, I'm rewarded with the brief sight of her smug expression being replaced by a sudden, fierce panic. Then she drifts out of my eyeline.

But that news has rattled me. I always thought that my job, at the very least, would be safe, seeing as I'm the one who has been responsible for about eighty per cent of all the contracts we've had. Suddenly it seems we're all in the firing line. God, this is disastrous – for me, for Fatima and for Sean. I look around the room at my colleagues, all looking a bit shocked and pale. No doubt they all have their own reasons for needing to keep this job too, reasons that I can only guess at. None of us has ever been particularly open with the others, I realize now, in spite of working together for years. I don't even know if Derek is gay.

I stare at Chas's office door with disguised loathing – I don't quite let my lip curl – and a sudden thought occurs to me. Maybe someone amongst us will snare the most massive contract that Love Learning has ever had, and will take Chas's job. Maybe someone among us will snare *two* massive contracts. Maybe Chas's job would be a certainty for that person. Wow, I had just about given up on achieving management status here, as the only way I have ever thought it would happen was through my relationship with Richard. But now, maybe I could get that status anyway, even with him out of the country. I glance over at Sean's desk. Well, he's probably given up on the Whytelys contract anyway, and is no doubt right now working hard on something else almost as good. Which means that it won't hurt him one single bit if I do go along to that meeting next week. If they wonder why I'm there when they've already kicked Sean out of the building, I'll just tell them it's a follow-up visit, out of courtesy. Or I'll say I'm just checking they haven't changed their mind, after a cooling-off period. And then I'll get them to sign with me, and I'll give Sean all the credit when he finds out. He'll be fine with it, I'm absolutely sure of it. Anyway, I could be the manager by then.

I spend the rest of the day working on the Motivation material, finally galvanized into action by wanting to eviscerate Chas. Which proves that having a clear goal does help you to focus on what you've got to do. I write that down in my notes.

In the car on the way home, my mobile rings. I pull the car over to the side of the road and start the frantic search through my bag for the phone. Rupert's gorgeous face keeps coming into my head, all expectant and excited as the phone rings, even though I don't think he's got my mobile number. Aha, there's the phone. It's showing a number I don't know. 'Hello?' God, what if it is him and he wants to meet up right now for a little informal cocktail somewhere . . . ?

'Hi, Libby, it's Brad.'

My heart swoops and I bounce a bit in my seat. I stop this before I speak, and do my best to engage my sexiest voice, which is quite hard to do before you've actually said anything. 'Hi there. How are you?' Yep, that's OK.

'You know what? It sounds corny but I feel much better now. And that's the truth.'

'Oh, really? Why, you sitting by your own private indoor pool with a cold beer in your hand?'

Sitting by his own private pool holding a bottle of Beck's, Rupert gets goosebumps and jerks his head a little. 'Wow, you're good,' he says.

'Thanks. How was your day?'

'Astonishingly unremarkable. How was yours?'

I'm flummoxed for a moment here. He's said something that sounds really familiar but I can't quite put my finger on what it is, or why it seems like I've heard it before. 'It . . . um . . .'

'Libby? You still there?'

'Oh, yeah, fine, sorry. Just went under a bridge.'

There's a slight pause. 'You're not driving, are you?'

'No, God, of course not. What kind of person do you think I am? Maurice is at the wheel.'

'Maurice?' he says, a smile in his voice. 'Who's Maurice then? Aged uncle? Doddery next door neighbour? Fat old second cousin?'

'No, nothing like that. Maurice is my French chauffeur. He's twenty-four and is training to be an Olympic decathlete. Say hi, Maurice. Oh, no, sorry, Brad, you won't hear him, the partition is up.'

He's laughing. 'What a shame. I do hope Maurice doesn't suffer a strangulated hernia, or a groin injury.'

I smile. Who says jealousy is a sin? I think it's

incredibly pleasing. 'Oh, no, don't worry, he's very strong in that area, so I think he'll be all right.'

'Terrific. I'm glad for him. You never said how your day was.'

'Oh, didn't I? Well, it started strangely, became a bit fuddled as it went on, turned confusing later and ended up baffling with some weird patches.'

'And what's the outlook for tomorrow?'

I think for a few moments. Actually, I'm not thinking, I'm just pausing so he doesn't think I had this answer planned. 'Clearer.' I say it very softly, with my lips very close to the mouthpiece.

There's no sound from either of us for several seconds. Then he sighs, long and deep. Not sure I like the sound of that.

'What?' Me, trying not to sound too anxious.

'What?'

'You sighed. What's the matter?' Sounding too anxious.

'No, nothing's the matter. I wasn't sighing.'

'Weren't you? Oh shit, that means you were yawning then, which is so much worse.'

'No it isn't. It just means I'm tired, not sad. Surely that's better?'

'Fuck no. It suggests a complete lack of involvement. A sigh could mean happy, sad, depressed, resigned, pissed off, contented, loads of things. The thing is, they're all emotional. A yawn is one of two things – tired or bored. Either way it is a purely physical reaction, a reflex that the body does automatically without the brain even being involved. That is definitely worse than a sigh, speaking from this end of the line.'

'Jesus, you've done a lot of research on this, haven't you?'

'Uh-huh. Had to. If you can get these things resolved at the beginning, there is less likelihood of confusion later.'

At his end of the phone, Rupert jolts and frowns quizzically. Something he heard then sounds familiar, but he can't work out what it was, or why it sounded familiar.

'All right, I can't lie to you, Libby. I was sighing, but it's not that anything's the matter. It's just . . . I think I may finally have got my head clear, for the first time in . . . well, I don't know how long.'

'Really?'

'Really. I mean, so many times in the past, things haven't worked out the way I'd hoped they would. Because of . . . my job, people have certain expectations . . .' He stops, leaving me dangling on the other end, in a darkened lay-by on the bypass, pressing my phone painfully into my head.

'Your job?'

There's a pause. Then he says, 'Do you mind if I don't tell you about it right now? I mean, I will tell you, of course I will. I'd just rather leave it for now. Maybe until we know each other a bit better.'

Oh Christ. Oh crapping bugger and arse. He's an assassin. I'm going out with an international paid assassin. This is going to have disastrous consequences for me and almost certainly isn't going to end in a beautiful white wedding, a three-bedroomed semi and a cat. I'm picturing a smashed hotel window, furniture upended and broken all over the floor and my naked body, face down on the bed, riddled with bullet holes.

302

'It's nothing illegal,' he says suddenly, and I take my hand off my mouth. 'Libby? Are you still there? I've frightened you, haven't I?'

Now I don't know what to believe. 'No.'

'I have, I can hear it in your voice. Look, please believe me, it's nothing dangerous or illegal. Bugger it. Libby? Are you still there?'

'Mm-hmm.'

'Good. Look, my job is just a bit high profile, that's all. I promise. That's all.'

To be fair, if he was an international assassin, he probably wouldn't have raised this at all. He'd have just said he was a plumber or something.

'Do you believe me, Libby?'

I pause. 'High profile, you say?'

'Yes, yes, that's all.'

'So you're like, I don't know, the next person in line to manage the England football team?'

There's a surprised silence. Then he says, 'Oh my God, I can't believe it got out. Right, well, you'll just have to promise that you won't tell anyone. Gary Lineker doesn't even know yet.'

'Who's he?'

He snorts out a closed-lip laugh. 'Doesn't matter. The point is, if it gets to the papers, I'm going to have to kill you.'

I am instantly silenced. Which makes me think of silencers. On long-barrelled guns fired through pillows. Feathers bursting out in a cloud.

'I'm kidding,' he says, laughing. 'I won't really kill you.'

'Thank God for that.'

'But I promise this will all become clear in time.'

'I'm very intrigued.' And a teensy bit terrified. 'How long do I have to wait until the big revelation?'

'I don't know. There are so many variables, it would be impossible to guess. You're just going to have to be patient.'

'Well. All right then.'

'Thank you. Now, I did ring for a reason and it's this: I would like us to go out on a prearranged date. For more than three minutes. As soon as possible. Tomorrow.' He pauses and kind of clears his throat a bit. 'It's my brother's birthday tomorrow. There's a small party – just a few close . . . Ahem. Anyway, I would love it if you . . . I mean, I'd be so pleased . . . Will you come?'

I bounce up and down in the seat for a while, then stop before some passing motorist thinks there are two of us here, parked in this layby, bouncing away in the dark. 'Brad, thank you so much for inviting me. I'd love to.' *I am free tonight, as well.* I don't say this, I send it to him telepathically. He doesn't get it, though. Or if he does, he's too polite to say so.

'I will pick you up at eleven thirty,' he says. 'What's your address?'

Twenty

Poor Performance

Short-term Goal: Get through the sixteen hours and fourteen minutes that separate me from Brad picking me up.

Obstacles: Sixteen hours and fourteen minutes. Obviously.

Long-term Goal: God, it's so hard. I have got to choose between Brad and Rupert. Each one is so perfect, how can I ever decide?

Obstacles: Brad and Rupert. Obviously.

'Christ, you didn't give him our address, did you?' a horrified Vini says ten minutes later. She's wearing a sleek white jumpsuit, gold belt, white cloak and boots and has two Chelsea buns made of hair stuck to the side of her head.

'Carrie Fisher?'

'Natalie Portman, for goodness' sake. Keep up. Anyway, you've only met him that one time . . .'

'Twice. No, three times actually.'

'All right then, if you can count the first time. He could be a serial killer and you wouldn't know.'

'It's perfectly possible. I mean, we did meet at speed dating, which makes it so much more likely than the blokes you meet in pubs and bring home here.'

She pouts. 'I'm a good judge of character. Anyway, I'm not doing that any more, I told you.'

'OK, OK, I know. Anyway, you needn't worry, I've agreed to meet him at The Blooding.'

'What, that gross fountain? Bit of a passion killer, isn't it? A pack of grotesque slavering dogs ripping a fox into pieces, water dribbling out of their mouths like fresh blood. Hardly moonlight over the Seine, is it?'

She's pretty much summed up in that sentence what the statue looks like. In fact, it's a very popular tourist attraction in our business park – tens of thousands of visitors every year, if the council is to be believed – although not because of its aesthetic beauty. It's more because it makes people who see it feel better about their own towns. 'We're not going to spend the day there, Vini. We're just meeting there. What's that?'

She's holding up a suit carrier and smiling meaning-fully. 'You did say you were going out with him tomorrow, didn't you?'

'I don't know. Tell me what that is first.'

'So you're free tonight then. It's an outfit. A surprise. Put it on, and I'll do your hair.'

The surprise is the black PVC zip-up jumpsuit from *Charlie's Angels*, a push-up bra and some killer black boots. She crimps my hair so it falls to my shoulders in tiny zig-zags, then pins the sides back loosely and finishes me off with make-up that she won't let me see until it's finished.

'Ta-da!' she says eventually, showing me the mirror. 'Fucking Barrymore!'

I start in horror but then look at my reflection and realize she means Drew, not Michael. Fuck me, she's right. I stare at my face, turning my head from side to side. The thought enters my head that she dyed my hair explicitly to suit this purpose but I banish it. Doesn't matter – the magic hair dye got me Brad. 'So the surprise that you've lined up for me turns out to be me making an appearance at the opening of a new Morrisons as Drew Barrymore? And there I was thinking that you were giving me a pair of tickets to see Kylie.'

'Don't be like that. This is going to be quite a special appearance, as it goes. There's a Cameron Diaz and a Lucy Liu, so you can be the Angels. You'll spend the entire night fending off lust-crazed men, just you wait and see.'

Vini thinks an evening doing that is time well spent.

'Rupert de Witter will probably be there,' she adds as she walks towards the door. She didn't need to; I had decided to go already, actually.

The venue is a hotel called Wickham Lodge, which makes it sound like a charming little ivy-covered cottage, with chickens and dogs in the yard and several filthy kids squatting in permanent wellies and anoraks, where they do bed and full English breakfast during the season. It isn't. It's an enormous eight-storey structure of concrete and glass with about three hundred rooms, a cash machine and as much character as Britney Spears. Actually, I think she stayed here once. Not out of choice. I mean obviously she was on her way to somewhere better.

Vini leads me through a forest of Christmas trees,

307

past a festoon of banners that say 'Merry Christmas' and along a corridor that is eerily quiet given that there is evidently a party going on somewhere. This place really is gargantuan.

'Vin, are you sure people will want Drew Barrymore and Carrie Fisher—'

'Natalie Portman.'

'OK, Natalie Portman then. Are you sure they really want us here? At a Christmas party? It's not exactly traditional, is it?' As we advance along the corridor, the sound of music is getting nearer, and louder.

'Chill,' she says, stopping at a set of double doors labelled 'Bingley Suite'. Behind them is the music's source, and I am starting to have a terrible feeling about that. 'We're definitely booked. I promise you.'

She pushes open the doors and the first thing I see in the mêlée is Elvis, in white and diamanté trouser suit, open to the waist. My bad feeling about the music is proving correct, because Elvis is singing 'Can't Get You Out of My Head' enthusiastically, if perhaps a little flat, into a mic that is attached to an enormous slab of technology, bracketed by two free-standing speakers. I blink. Standing nearby is Sylvester Stallone, complete with headband, bloodstains, filthy vest and huge gun, chatting pleasantly with Audrey Hepburn, who is, inevitably, holding a long cigarette holder. As we walk past them, I hear Rambo saying, '. . . keep the seedlings inside until then because if there's one hard frost . . .'

'Over here,' Vin is saying, pulling me across the room. I pass Clark Gable, Keira Knightley, Robbie Williams and Trevor McDonald, but I have noticed that there are others amongst them who aren't recognizable. Ordinary partygoers.

'What is this, Vin?' I shout to her as we finally come to a halt at the back of the room. There is a bar here, thronged with mostly ordinary people and as I watch, I notice that, for the most part, they are buying two drinks and then walking swiftly back across the room to where Princess Diana or Will Smith or Bob Geldof is waiting. 'Is this really someone's party, or is it some kind of look-alikes' convention?'

She shakes her head. 'No, it is a party. The guy who hired me wanted as many look-alikes as I had. Everyone. Hence . . .' She performs a sweeping motion with her arm to indicate the room.

'What, everyone on your books? They're all here?'

'No, not everyone. Shirley Bassey is in Fuengirola, and John Travolta's dog has just had surgery. Shame really.' She juts her chin towards Olivia Newton-John who is standing on her own, gently swaying to the music, her head tipped on one side, cardigan across her shoulders.

'So how many are here, then?'

'Thirty-one, including you and me,' she says grinning. 'He said he would give me a three-hundred-quid bonus if I managed more than thirty and I did it! And before you say anything, I would have done it even without you, and you can have your share of the fee.'

I turn back to her fiercely. 'Vini, you know I didn't . . . I wasn't . . . How much is it, incidentally?'

'Hundred and fifty.'

My jaw drops. 'A hundred and fifty quid? Per person? And there are thirty-one here? That's . . .'

'Four thousand, six hundred and fifty pounds,' Vini says gleefully, eyeing the room. 'One of those hundred and fifties is mine, and one is yours, and then I get

309

fifteen per cent of the rest, which is six hundred and fifty-two. Add on my bonus, plus my hundred and fifty, and that makes a grand total of eleven hundred and two pounds. For one night's work. Fan-fucking-tastic.'

I nod, wide-eyed. 'Yeah, it is.'

'And you can keep the outfit. Happy Christmas. I'm working on getting him to ask us all to come back next year. Maybe even every year.'

'So who is it, then? Who's the moneybags?' I ask her, squinting into the room.

'Well, you've heard about the plans to tear down some of those old buildings on the industrial estate, and build a new gym or something? Well, this Mr Finn is the . . .'

She carries on talking but suddenly her voice stops registering in my ears. The din around me, even the singing, fades away, and all the people around me recede into the darkness at the edge of the room. All except one. Standing not fifteen feet away from me, talking animatedly to Madonna, who is shamelessly wearing her bra on the outside, is Rupert de Witter.

Oh my God. I am rooted to the spot, my eyes fixed on his handsome, chiselled face; that beautiful hair; those white, white teeth. I take him all in – the perfect suit, the broad, strong shoulders, the smooth, square jaw, the deep, golden tan. Suddenly, Madonna flounces off – she's such an attention seeker – and Rupert is left alone. My eyes are so wide as I stare at him that I am almost not surprised when he eventually feels the heat of them boring into his body, and slowly turns towards where I am standing. His eyes meet mine, and they are so clear, so blue, so piercing, it is like being jolted by electricity. My belly is liquefying where I am standing, and I may even have drool on my bottom lip. I lick them both quickly. He smiles at me, a broad, white, welcoming smile, and my knees almost buckle. I am suddenly, fiercely, furiously grateful to Vini for dressing me up in this slutty outfit. Why am I wearing this? Thank God I am wearing it. He starts moving towards me, and it's as if he's pushing a magnetic field before him, as the nearer he gets to me, the more I sway. He is six feet away when I suddenly hear, '. . . thirty-eight quid for a year's membership. Jesus, Beth, what are you gawping at? Oh.' Vini spots the advancing deity, notices that our eyes are locked, and melts away.

He reaches my side, then comes a little tiny bit further, so he's inside my personal space. I can feel his body heat pulsing through the air between us, and I wonder if he can feel mine. He's still smiling, although it's not such a broad grin as before; this is more gentle and seductive, as his eyes flick over my face and neck. I think he likes what he sees as his eyebrows move up and down and he doesn't move away.

'Hi,' he says.

'Hi,' I croak, trying to sound like I am approached by devastatingly handsome millionaires all the time. I put my hand out. 'I'm—'

'I know exactly who you are,' he says, taking my hand gently in his own and not letting go. He sounds so different in real life – much higher. I didn't realize how much travelling through telephone wires can distort your voice.

'Do you?' My blood is pounding so hard in my ears, I can't be sure that I made any sound at all.

311

'Oh yes, Miss Barrymore. Let's leave it at that for the moment, shall we?'

'Oh.' Bit disappointed here – thought he had worked out that I am Beth of the emails, but never mind. 'All right then. I know who you are, though.'

He looks pleased, but tries to disguise it as surprise. It's so sweet. 'Do you really? Well, that's a shock. I don't usually get recognized.'

'Really? I would have thought—'

'Especially since I've had these new highlights. Most people know me with my old ones. I used to have Golden Sunrise and Mountain Spring, but these are Barley Gold and Silver Fountain. Most of my friends think it looks great, but I'm not sure. What do you think?'

'Um.' I pause before answering and use the time to run a critical eye over his hair. Not because I'm really considering his highlights, but because I need thinking time to produce a similarly ironic and witty response. Plus, I'm trying not to laugh. I know what Rupert is like, but I can't let on that I know. I want to play along for a while without the complication of the contract getting in the way.

Yes, I know what you're thinking: the contract should be top of my list of reasons for wanting to talk to Rupert de Witter, not second. Or, let's face it, third. But tonight I am not Beth Sheridan, I am Drew Barrymore. Or at least some unidentified woman pretending to be Drew Barrymore, pretending to be one of Charlie's Angels. If I let on that I'm actually Beth Sheridan of the Love Learning emails, I will lose some of my mystique. And he will lose his. I want to observe him, see what he's really like, when he hasn't got his professional guard up.

312

'Well,' I say at last, trying to look serious and thoughtful, 'in my opinion the colours you've got now give you the appearance of someone formidable, someone to be reckoned with, someone who drives an amazing car and dresses stylishly, hangs out in all the best places and regularly mixes with the rich and famous.'

He stares at me for a few seconds, his lips slightly parted. 'Wow. You got all that from just these two colours?'

'Oh yes.'

'That's incredible.' He shakes his head once and looks thoughtfully over my left shoulder. 'I wonder what you would have made of the Burnt Amber, if I'd had that in too.'

I frown. 'Oh, good God no, not Burnt Amber. Only people who have no idea of fashion and can't get in anywhere use that colour. Everyone knows that.'

'Wow. Do they? Wow. I didn't know. Jesus. Thank God I didn't have that, then. Thanks, Drew.'

I'm grinning. He's so convincing! 'It's my pleasure.'

'Great!' He's smiling at me again, and even this close up his teeth look fantastic. Although as I drink in the sight of him, something not quite right catches my attention. I lean in for a closer look. Is that . . . ? 'Your hair is stunning,' he says in a low voice. 'I just love blondes.'

That is a bit flirty, isn't it? I'm not happy about that at all. I mean, what about Beth, you git? As far as he knows, she could be sitting by her computer even now, waiting for another email, a joke, a little banter, a marriage proposal. 'Oh, you do? That's . . . good.'

'Oh yes, too right I do. Much hotter than brunettes.

313

So-oo much more sexy, baby.' And he nods apprecia-
tively, although not at my hair.

'Um, thanks.' Suddenly the zip on my jumpsuit
seems far too low. God, Vini, what were you thinking
of, pulling it down like this?

Eventually he manages to drag his eyes back to my
face. 'Can I get you a drink, Miss B?'

'Something soft, please. Can't drink alcohol on an
empty stomach.'

'Really?' He arches his eyebrows again. 'That's odd.'
And he moves up to the bar.

As I watch him move away I frown a little. He is
undeniably sexy, from the back too, but so far the
conversation hasn't gone how I imagined it would.
I know from his emails that he is charming, funny
and charismatic, but I'm not getting that tonight. As
I watch him, he flicks his hair back with his fingers,
then fiddles with it a bit, looking off into the middle
distance, and I realize that he has caught sight of
himself in a mirror behind the bar. He gazes at his
reflection for a good fifteen seconds, turning his head
to the left and right, touching his hair, fiddling with
his collar. I could be flattered that he is taking so much
time over his appearance, but something about the
way he's pouting over there makes me think that he's
not doing it for me. I can't stop my mouth from sagging
a bit and my eyes narrow as I watch him. Oh God, I'm
so stupid. I'd forgotten all about the Pecs Factor.

To be fair, I haven't had much experience with the
Pecs Factor in my life. Most people living in little
nondescript towns like mine and going to routine
office jobs like mine in four-door saloons and jackets
from Top Shop like mine don't. It's most commonly

encountered in the fabulous, insubstantial world of the glitterati – breathtakingly beautiful models, devastatingly handsome actors and shining, dazzling popstars, where beauty is commonplace and everyone drifts about smiling in a haze of shimmering perfection, worshipped like gods, adored the world over.

The Pecs Factor is all about bodies. The better yours is, the more of the Pecs Factor you've got. These people are so heart-stoppingly gorgeous and sexy to look at, and have been since childhood, they've realized it's their most powerful tool, it's what people notice about them, and they come to rely on it. The more attractive they are, the less effort they feel they need to put in to actual human relationships. People just fancy them, even if they're vain, shallow and obnoxious, so they never work on their people skills. This is why celebrity marriages always fail, and the couple in the paper celebrating their sixtieth wedding anniversary look like they could be products of an alliance between Skeletor and She-Man.

Unless it's just a case of ugly people clinging desperately to each other for comfort.

No, no, it's definitely the Pecs Factor. There's loads of evidence. I mean, if you were a bloke, and you somehow managed to marry Jennifer Aniston, you'd probably sit back and think you were the luckiest bloke on the planet, wouldn't you? You wouldn't think, Hmm, Jen's lovely but I think I could get Angelina Jolie.

Or maybe you would. You bastard.

Anyway, Rupert has obviously got the Pecs Factor in gym-bagloads, and I can't believe I didn't think about this before. In this moment, watching him winking at Uma Thurman as he leans against the bar, my mind is made up for definite, and I choose Brad. There is no way I could ever entertain a relationship with a twat like Rupert.

Oh but . . .

No. Come on, Beth, get a grip. He is beautiful, rich, funny and charming in writing, but that is all superficial. Everything that counts is wanting, and everything else is not enough to fill in the gaps. I gaze at his faintingly fabulous physique as he walks back towards me, and feel a wave of melancholy break over me; suddenly I feel heavier, more attached to the earth. My shoulders slump and my head bows. This silly romantic dream is over.

But I still want to get a contract with Horizon, so I will force myself to talk to him and maybe do some impromptu research ready for our lunch next week, which has now lost almost all of its allure. He could be lunching with a cardboard cut-out and wouldn't even notice.

'Strawberry and kiwi,' Rupert says arriving at my side. He holds out a tall glass with dark pink liquid in it. 'Hope that's OK.'

'Mmm, looks lovely. So how's your work these days?'

He's drinking something golden from a shot glass, and swallows with gusto before answering. 'My work? You know that I'm . . . ?'

I nod. 'Yes, I know what your work is. I told you, I know who you are.'

He smiles, almost shyly. How fake. 'Oh yes, you did, didn't you?' He looks wistfully over my left shoulder again, his eyes focused on something very far away, and raises his right hand to his head, running the fingers through his gorgeous hair. Like this, he reminds me so much of the photo in the back of the Horizon brochure. 'Well, it could be better, to be honest.'

'Oh?'

'Yeah. Well, things have never been particularly easy in this country. People here just want you to fail, you know? And everyone is so demanding all the time. I mean, I think I can be forgiven for not pandering to everyone's whim. I've got my own standards, you know? It's all do this, stand there, hurry up, get it right. They're all pushing me around and trying to get me to do it their way, when I think I should know what will be best for me, you know?'

'Mm.'

'I've definitely got something, I know it. I am going to be huge one day. You know, much bigger than now. But all I ever get are little people bringing me their little problems. Why should I care about their problems? They've got their jobs and I've got mine, you know? I am good at what I do, but how can I help it if everyone else keeps screwing things up?'

I shake my head sympathetically. 'You're so right.'

'Anyway, I've got big plans. I'm not going to stick around in this artistic wilderness much longer. I need room to grow, room to breathe, and I can't find the space here. England is just so provincial, you know?'

'Oh, well, erm . . .'

'So I'm going stateside. Big ol' US of A Soon as I can. I know they'll love me over there. It's their culture. I will really suit the culture, you see. My image, what I represent, it's perfect for their market. Everything I've done here is small potatoes compared to what I'll achieve over there.'

Oh my God. Is he selling Horizon? 'So you're . . . ?'

He looks down at me suddenly, as if he's just re-membered I'm there. 'I'm moving, baby. In six months' time, a year tops. Just got to get a few things sorted, then I am outta here. Wanna come with? You,' and he puts his hand on my neck, 'will be a big hit out there. They will love you. What do you say, sexy?'

Get a few things sorted? That must mean he's selling. Which panics me for a moment. Will any contract I get with him hold after he sells? It must do, surely. And if it doesn't maybe I can still get a six-month contract, before he goes. That's still going to be worth having. I look back up at his face and he's staring straight at my cleavage again. What a poor performance. I grab the hand that's touching me and remove it coldly, dropping it like a dirty sock. He pulls a hurt, I-don't-understand-your-problem face. What an arsehole. 'No thanks. I prefer something a bit more substantial.' And I don't even care if he's angry with me when we meet officially on Tuesday.

He raises his eyebrows and tilts his head down to-wards me. 'The United States is enormous, you know. Much bigger and more substantial than England.' He nods, knowingly, as if he's just imparted some valuable nugget of wisdom. He obviously doesn't even realize that I've just insulted him.

'OK.' I smile, and start to step away.

'Oh, hey, where you going? You're not leaving, are you? We were just starting to get to know each other.'

'Precisely.'

I sneak out and get a taxi home. Vini was busy chatting to Richard Gere in full officer's uniform, so I didn't bother her. She got her bonus, so I am free to go.

Back at the flat I wander around for a few minutes, opening and closing doors, looking into cupboards, slamming them shut again, flicking lights on and off. I throw myself onto the sofa and grab the TV guide, but nothing takes my interest so I'm up again and heading for the kitchen. There's nothing in the fridge worth having so I wander back into the lounge and then on into my bedroom. I strip Drew off and tuck myself up in bed, hoping to sleep; knowing I won't.

How could I have been so bloody stupid about Rupert? Now that I've met him and have learned exactly what he is like, all the emails that he sent me, all the jokes and the charm, seem so phony. It was clearly just a homage to his own vanity, flirting with me simply because he could. Or simply because he realized, very early on, that I was attracted to him. Of course I was: everyone is. That's what the Pecs Factor does for you.

I screw my eyes shut and roll over. I won't think about him any more. I am spending the day with Brad tomorrow and he is completely and utterly wonderful.

Twenty-one

Further Development

Short-term Goal: At last this is easy. Get the Horizon contract and single-handedly save Love Learning.
Obstacles: Sean may also be single-handedly saving Love Learning. Although, actually, that's not an obstacle. Of course not.
Long-term Goal: Easy too. Keep Brad. For ever.
Obstacles: Now that my feelings for Rupert have completely evaporated, there are no obstacles.

At ten o'clock the next morning, Rupert is pulling up in his car outside his parents' house. He looks up at the house as he walks towards the front door, apprehension prickling his skin. Please let it be all right, he thinks, as he takes in the apparently peaceful scene. Please let it be a good day.

He uses his key to let himself in, but doesn't call out as he enters this time. Instead he stands perfectly still for a few moments in the hallway, head tilted back, eyes fixed on the upstairs banister, listening intently. No sound comes down the stairs, so he starts to go up them.

At the top all seems quiet. A small bud of hope starts to open in his chest, but as he walks quietly along the landing towards the bedroom at the end, he begins to hear a muted wailing sound that raises the hairs on the back of his neck and covers his body in gooseflesh.

'Oh God,' he mutters softly as he reaches the door. The sound is clearer here but still not loud and it is the sound he has been dreading since he got up this morning.

He knocks once on the door then goes in. The room is large and light, and white on all six sides – walls, floor and ceiling. Very few adornments break up the monotony of the space: a few maps of Europe on the walls; a bed, desk, chair and wardrobe on the floor. The faint keening sound is coming from the bed where a figure is curled tightly in the foetal position, rocking back and forth.

Caroline de Witter is standing in the middle of the room, her whole body focused on the figure, the yearning to go forward, embrace, comfort almost palpable in the room. Her arms are wrapped around herself instead, a more willing recipient of the comfort of human touch, and silent tears are sliding down her face. When the door opens she turns towards Rupert and her face crumples as she reaches for him and puts her arms around his neck.

'Oh Rupe, I'm so glad you're here. I just don't know what to do. We've been trying to get him downstairs for nearly two hours but he just won't budge. Now Dad's gone down to the shed for a break, and I can't manage on my own.' She sobs openly for a few moments while Rupert holds her and gently rubs her back.

321

"S'all right, Mum. It doesn't matter, does it? If he doesn't want a birthday party, he doesn't have to have one, does he?'

'No, I know, I was . . . I just thought . . . maybe . . .'

'Mum, you know he won't enjoy it. You know that.'

She sniffs and disengages from the embrace. 'But . . . I was just thinking that maybe this time . . .'

Rupert shakes his head. 'He's not going to change, Mum, is he? He is never going to change. He is never going to want a birthday party.' Caroline's lip trembles as he says this and he puts his hands on her upper arms. 'Oh Mum, please don't get upset. It doesn't matter. Really, it doesn't. It's only a bit of cake and some presents – it's not important.'

She takes a deep shaky breath as she moves a step away from Rupert and turns back to the rocking figure. 'I don't care about the party,' she says, so softly Rupert almost doesn't hear. 'I don't care that he won't eat the cake. I don't care that he won't unwrap the presents. I don't care that we can't sing "Happy Birthday" and watch him blow out his candles.' She stares a moment longer then turns back to face Rupert, her face wet with tears. 'It's just . . . I just . . . I can't bear to see him upset like this. I can't stand it. He's hurting and I'm his mum, I want to make it better, but I can't, can I? I want to hold him, cuddle him tight and tell him it's all right, tell him that I'm here, that I'm going to take care of him and that I love him. I love him so mu—' She breaks off and covers her face with her hands for a moment, her shoulders shaking as she weeps. Rupert is staring at her, his own eyes brimming, and he feels a too-familiar ache in his throat. He wants these things too. 'I want to tell him I love him, Rupert. And I want

322

to hear him say it back. I just want to hear him say it back to me.'

Rupert takes two steps forward and wraps his mother in his arms, holding her and rocking her the way that she so longs to do for her youngest son, telling her it's all right, making it better. After a few moments, they move together towards the door, go through it onto the landing and close it softly behind them.

Downstairs in the kitchen, Rupert is making a pot of tea while Caroline sits snuffling by the fire in the other room. As the kettle heats up, he places his palms on the side and hangs his head, his eyes closed. Now, where his mother can't see him, where he is unobserved, he allows a single tear to escape between his pressed eyelids, and he leaves it to move slowly but unhindered down his face.

The kettle boils so he rubs his face then makes the tea and carries it through to his mother. She smiles wetly up at him as he approaches her.

'I'm sorry, Rupe,' she says, taking the cup.

'Sorry? What are you sorry for? You've got nothing to be sorry for.'

She shakes her head. 'No, no, I have. I've been pathetic, I know it. You don't need to be dealing with all this when you come. As if you haven't got enough to deal with.'

'Don't be so silly, Mum. I'm not "dealing" with anything. I've come to see my brother on his birthday, and my parents. It's not a chore.'

She smiles gratefully. 'It's so stupid, though, isn't it? I mean, I know what he's like, I know it's always going to be like this, but I still . . . hope. You know? I still think, Maybe today, maybe this time. I just want . . .'

He touches her hand gently. 'I know. I want it too. It's because it's his birthday – we always feel it more on his birthdays.'

'Well, that's probably only because they always upset him so much.'

'Yeah, well, show me the person who doesn't feel like that on their birthday.'

She laughs sadly. 'Ah, Rupert. What would I do without you? You are such a good boy.'

'Mum, I'm thirty-four, for heaven's sake.'

'I know, I was there when you were born.'

He grins. 'Look, I'll go and get Dad from the shed and then I'll start making lunch for you both. OK?' She nods and he rubs the back of her hand. 'Back in a mo.'

Out in the garden, the grass is white and brittle with hard frost. His father's footprints towards the shed are clearly visible but Rupert doesn't head straight after them. He pulls the collar on his jacket up and instead walks through the hedge towards the vegetable garden. He stands by the empty rows of soil and pulls out his mobile phone.

'Hi, it's Brad,' he says quietly.

In the flat, I have already started getting ready for my date with Brad, even though I've still got to wait two hours before I can leave. I don't want to risk being late, though. You never know what the traffic will be like at eleven o'clock on a Saturday morning. My hair is done and now I'm choosing my clothes. The phone interrupts me as I'm deciding between smart casual or casual smart. Or slutty.

'Hi, how are you?' I sit down on the bed with a huge smile. He's calling me up and I'm seeing him in two hours – he must be keen! Then my smile falters. I am seeing him in two hours – why is he calling me? The only reason I can think of to be calling me two hours before we're due to meet is to cancel.

'I'm fine,' he says softly. 'How are you?'

I don't like the sound of this. Why doesn't he get to the point? 'I'm fine too.'

'That's great. Listen, Libby, it's about today.'

I knew it. I don't say anything though, because a cold silence says so much more than a whiny, pissed-off voice.

'I wanted you to come to the party today because I really want you to meet . . . I mean, it wasn't a big deal, just my mum and dad, and my brother, of course, and one or two other family members. And apart from, and as well as, all that, there's something I wanted to tell you. I need to tell you.' He pauses and I can hear him breathing as he walks around. 'I had it all planned, the moment I would do it, the exact words I would use. And I was kind of thinking that, if you saw the real . . . me . . . my family, you know, then the reason for . . . Then maybe you wouldn't . . . be . . . you wouldn't think . . . badly of me. I'm not making sense. I'm sorry.'

I'm silent again but I'm trying to make it a warm, soothing silence this time. Something sounds terribly wrong here and I feel so bad for the coldness earlier. 'What is it, Brad?' I manage eventually.

'I'm sorry, Libby. There isn't going to be a party after all. It was always a possibility that it wouldn't happen. Look, I don't want to talk about it on the phone. Can we still meet up? I can pick you up in half an hour – will that be enough time?'

Three huge jolts of information slam into me in

quick succession. Bang – he's not cancelling! Bang – and he's bringing our date forward by two hours! Bang – how fantastic that I started getting ready an hour ago! I am trying not to bounce around grinning with pure jubilation because obviously something has gone wrong and he's feeling down, so after jumping up and down silently for a few seconds, I sit down and compose myself before answering in my softest, most sympathetic voice. 'Of course, don't worry, that's fine. Shall we still meet at The Blooding?'

Half an hour later and I'm parking in the business park where The Blooding is. From here I can see that Brad is already there, sitting on the rim, checking his watch, looking around him, left, then right, then left again, then checking his watch once more. It's cruel but I actually sit in the car for two minutes, watching him anxiously waiting for me. He looks absolutely gorgeous. The strain in his face and tension in his body are incredibly alluring. I'm staring at him, this tall, sexy, worried man, feeling quite breathless that he is there, and that it's me he's waiting for. Little me, Beth Sheridan. Er, I mean, Libby. Must sort that out.

Eventually I can't resist any more and I get out of the car and start walking towards him. When he sees me he stands up and a wide smile breaks out on his face. And on mine. It's a bit of a struggle to keep moving, since my treacherous knees keep wanting to lie down. Other parts of me agree with them.

'Hello, you,' he says as I reach him.

'Hi.' He steps forward instantly, right up close, and I know he is going to kiss me, he is near enough to kiss me, and my insides are in turmoil. He raises his hand to the level of my face and I half close my eyes,

326

waiting for the touch of that hand on my neck and his lips on mine; but then he hesitates, and lowers it again. He drops his eyes to the ground, then looks about a bit and shuffles his feet. I am still quivering with hot anticipation and feel like I will explode if he doesn't grab me right now and . . . *do something*. But he doesn't.

'Will you come for a walk with me?' he says. 'There are a few things I need to explain.' I nod – I've got some explaining of my own to do – and we set off.

As we walk he doesn't take my hand or put his arm round me, although I am sending him a message to do so telepathically. Our hands are hanging loosely at our sides and once or twice they strike against each other, causing hot sparks to ignite in mine, but he seems oblivious to it. Pretty soon he is engrossed in telling me about his brother, Matt, whose birthday it is today, and the autism that dominates him. His mum, he says, has had such a hard time accepting Matt's inability to express, or feel, emotions. As he talks he doesn't look at me, only stares straight ahead, but I can hear in his voice that it's not just his mum who craves Matty's love and recognition.

'The thing is, he's so incredibly bright,' he says as we head out of the town. 'You know, he knows who I am. I went to see him yesterday, to talk something over.' He glances at me sidelong. 'I know he doesn't understand but it kind of helps me to talk things through with him, even though he never says anything. But he recognizes me, that's the point. Even though I don't live there any more and he doesn't see me every day, so I'm not part of his routine, but he still said my name, when I was talking. He said, "You're R—" He breaks off

327

suddenly and I turn to look at him. He's watching me but breaks eye contact as soon as I make it. 'He said, "You're Brad." So I know he knows me.'

I don't know what to say. I can't offer any advice – this is unknown territory for me. Although I'm pretty sure that platitudes like 'I'm sure he loves you in his own way' won't be terribly helpful. Eventually I settle for, 'It must be so hard on you all', and he nods.

'It is. Well, for Mum it is. Dad tends to shut himself off from it when it gets bad, which seems cruel but they've accepted that that is how he deals with it. I think Dad understands much more about it than Mum does. When Matty gets upset, she always tries to comfort him, which actually makes it worse. Dad knows that the best thing to do is retreat and let Matty calm down on his own.'

We walk in silence for a while, our breath billowing out of us like souls. I am starving but I can't say that – our relationship is not at the stage of admitting to bodily functions yet.

'Are you hungry?' he says, stopping suddenly and turning to face me. I nod sweetly and he smiles. 'Good. Me too. Let's eat.' And at this point I realize that we have stopped outside the Patch and Parrot. 'Have you been here before?'

'Um, once or twice. It's quite funny. I've never eaten here, though. I wonder what's on the menu.'

It turns out to be Starfish Cakes, Dead Man's Breast of Chicken and Crow's Nest Soup. We smile together at the menu and I order the soup. Don't want to eat like a whale (mouth wide open absorbing any edible material that comes into range). Brad is having the Bluebeard Burger, with potato medallions.

'So what about you? Have you got brothers or sisters?' he asks me as we eat.

I shake my head. 'Nearest thing I've got is Vini – you met her.'

'Ah yes, the incomparable Miss Jones. How is she?'

'Bloody irritating,' I answer, thinking about the party she dragged me to last night. 'She's got this look-alike agency – Fake Face.'

'Great name.'

'It is, isn't it? Anyway, she was asked to bring as many look-alikes as she could to this party last night, so she made me go, dressed as . . .' Suddenly the idea of me in that sexy jumpsuit and those boots, with the hair and the make-up and the cleavage, seems completely ridiculous. I can't say it.

'Dressed as who? Come on, Libby, you've got to tell me who you went as. You can't offer that little titbit and then renege on the pay-off. I need to know, so I can picture it.'

I shake my head, laughing. 'No, it's too embarrassing. Suffice to say that that git Rupert de Witter was drooling all over me.'

He flinches when I say the name and I remember suddenly that they know each other and were shaking hands at the Horizon Christmas party. Shit, they're probably friends.

'What do you mean?' he says urgently.

'Oh, look, Brad, I'm sorry, do you know him?'

He stares at me for a few inexplicable moments, as if I've just asked him to find the square root of 693. Then he says, 'Um, well, yes, I do know him. A bit. Why, do you?'

'No, not really. Not in any real sense. I used to work

at Horizon, years ago, and just lately, I've been . . .'
Whoops, can't tell him about the Love Learning thing
– he might ring me at work and find out that I'm not
actually Libby. Which is not in itself a bad thing but I
want to be the one to tell him that myself. It's such a
turn-off when you find out from a third party that the
woman you've just opened up to about your autistic
brother has been using a fake name. 'Well, he isn't the
man I thought he was, let's leave it at that.'

'Why? What did he do?' He still sounds urgent, anxious. They must be close friends.

'Oh, no, nothing. Honestly. It's just . . . Well, he
couldn't take his eyes off my . . . you know,' I flick my
eyes downwards, 'and when we were chatting, it turns
out he's incredibly shallow, self-obsessed and vain.
Which, you know, I should have suspected, really,
shouldn't I? I mean, with his money how could he
possibly be anything else? No doubt he surrounds
himself every moment with sycophantic arseholes
whose only desire is to do everything he asks. Ugh. I
despise that. Why is it that people like him who have
got a lot of money are always convinced the whole
world is there for their amusement?'

He says nothing for a few moments and I sit there
in agony, imagining that I have just seriously insulted
his closest friend. Then he says, quietly, distractedly, 'I
didn't realize he was as bad as that.' Which makes me
feel even worse as I am convinced I have just destroyed
a twenty-five-year friendship.

'Oh, no, don't say that, I'm sure he isn't. Maybe he
was just having an off day, you know? Maybe he had
just been dumped by his girlfriend and wanted to get
revenge on the entire female population. Maybe he

was pissed. Maybe he stubbed his toe. Maybe he was just coming down with a cold and was feeling really grumpy because of the—'

'No. No, Lib, there's no excuse for bad behaviour. Other people get colds or get dumped or stub their toes, and don't behave badly.' He shakes his head. 'I will have to do something about this. I was kind of thinking about it anyway, and it's certainly been long enough. The whole thing is ridiculous.' This last he says more to himself than to me and I've got icy octopus tentacles creeping up and down my spine. He's making it sound like there's some kind of illicit relationship between him and Rupert and it's very creepy. Could they possibly be sharing some dreadful secret, from years and years ago, that they'd both like to bury but can't because each one keeps threatening that he will expose the other, and each one knows he has too much to lose to risk it? Oh my God, what if they were both involved in something . . . criminal? You hear these stories all the time – two successful men, happy, well respected, comfortably off. Dropped a breeze block on the campus caretaker fifteen years ago.

Or maybe they're secret lovers.

'You – you're not . . . ? You and Rupert, are you . . . ? You're . . . not . . . ?'

'What? What are you looking so worried about?' He raises his hand again only this time he doesn't stop, doesn't back out at the last moment but reaches over and touches my cheek with his fingertips. It's the lightest touch, the merest brush, but I am electrified by it. 'What's going on in there?'

I can't speak. The part of my face that he touched has just burst into flames.

331

'Look, whatever you are imagining about the situation between me and Rupert de Witter, I can guarantee you that it's not the actual situation. I will explain it to you, very soon, but . . .'

'But what? Why don't you just tell me now?'

He stares down at my face, his eyes on mine. Then does a teensy, almost imperceptible shake of the head. 'I can't now. Not now that I know how you feel about . . . him. I will need to do it when . . . Another time. When I can explain everything properly and there's less chance of spoiling . . . this.'

That's not good. It's obviously something seriously bad. 'Spoiling it? Do you think telling me this . . . thing . . . whatever it is, will spoil it?'

He shakes his head. 'I don't know. I really don't. I hope not.' He sighs again and looks down at my hands. 'This is not sounding good but I swear to you it is nothing to worry about.'

'Really? If it was something to worry about, would you tell me anyway? Like, if you killed your caretaker with a breeze block when you were twenty, would you tell me?'

He bursts out laughing at this, but I really don't think it's a laughing matter. 'Oh, no, no, no, Libby, it's nothing like that. I promise you. There are absolutely no skeletons in my closet, not even small ones. Not even mouse skeletons.'

I stare at his face and I so want to believe him. Could a secret killer have such lovely eyes? 'None?'

'None. I promise you. I have never been to prison, I have never hurt anyone, I have never – to my know-ledge – broken the law.'

'And you don't have an identical twin brother?'

332

He shakes his head with a smile. 'No, no, definitely not.'

'So you are definitely Brad . . . Brad what? What's your second name?'

'Witt.'

'Witt? Brad Witt? You're kidding. Really?'

'Absolutely.'

'Jesus. OK. Well then, are you definitely Brad Witt?'

He hesitates only a moment, blinks a few times and breaks eye contact. 'Um, well, no. My name isn't really Brad. I used a fake name because actually my real identity is incredibly well known and powerful and I didn't want you to know that until you liked me for who I am.'

I smile. 'Yeah, sure, OK. I used a fake name too.' And I reach up and kiss his cheek.

Twenty-two

Favourable Returns

Short-term Goal: Make eight people intensely motivated and committed by standing in front of them talking and showing them some pictures of graphs.
Obstacles: Can't really be arsed.
Long-term Goal: Get a lifelong, loving commitment from Brad. Or at least a lunch date again. (Oh, and the Horizon contract.)
Obstacles: Waiting to hear from him. (And dealing with R d W – arsehole.)

Monday morning finds me at my desk by 7 a.m., going through the Motivation stuff. My mobile phone is sitting on my desk by my hand, in case Brad calls me on it. He said on Saturday that he would call me today, so I have been waiting for him pretty much since today started, seven hours ago.

When I kissed him on Saturday, he was a bit surprised, but pleased, and didn't really stop smiling. I did catch him once or twice looking a bit anxious but as soon as he saw me looking he smiled again. He didn't kiss me back though, and there was no more physical contact between us, in spite of my tractor beam latching onto him and dragging his whole body towards me. It didn't work – again. Nor did all my telepathic messages. Well, it's refreshing, after lecherous Rupert, to meet a man who wants to go slowly. Brad is definitely worth it – I can be patient. I expect.

Everything for the Motivation workshop is ready and I've still got over an hour before I need to start, so I log on to my work emails. There are three new ones – one from Fatima, one from Sean and one from Rupert. I open Fatima's first. It's called 'My Car!'

> Hey Beth guess what? I sold my car at the weekend! That man that rang up about it came round to see it yesterday evening and gave me ten grand in cash, just like that! I had to leave my personalized number plate on it, but I don't care about that. He's picking it up in a few days. Cripes, what a relief. No more worries for me. I am going to pay off the loan today at lunchtime, which will only leave £3,896.47 to pay and I am selling some other stuff too so soon it will be only two or three grand left, which I can do easily, especially as I'm probably not going to lose my job since I got that contract at the pet shop. And it's all thanks to you. You are such a good friend. See you at tea-break. Fats xxx

I know what you're thinking: Get to the message from Rupert, quick. I know, I want to read it too. But I'm taking my time. I want to savour the moment when he tries sucking up to me again and I can say, 'This ship has sailed, tosspot.' He doesn't know that I'm on to him, remember, so any email from him today is likely to be all chirpy and fakely friendly. I can feel my lip curl at the thought, so I focus on Fatima's good news and sure enough a smile starts. I turn towards her, sitting at her desk next to me, and she looks up at me. She's got a flush on her cheek and a sparkle in her eye. She grins delightedly and I smile back. Then I notice that Mike is sitting on her other side, talking intently to her and she turns back to him, their heads almost touching. He's obviously helping her with the pet shop contract. How dull. Why doesn't he just leave her alone to be excited and happy for a few moments?

So. The next message is from Sean. He's sitting right there, at his desk, so why he didn't come over and talk to me I don't know. Although I'm glad he didn't. I'm not relishing the idea of having to break it to him that I'm involved with Brad. Poor man, so worried about his little boy, and all the money worries that parenthood brings, and now the girl of his dreams has found someone else. When is he ever going to have some good luck? I open the message.

Hey Sexy. Haven't spoken in a while. Everything OK with you? Sorry I've been neglecting you a bit, been v v busy. Got something pretty much sorted now, so can make it up to you soon as you like. S x

It's just not my idea of a romantic proposition – he can make it up to me? As soon as I like? He doesn't get it, does he? I feel even more sorry for him now. Not only has he lost me and his son and can't compete with the new stepdad, he's also got absolutely no skill in the charm department. What kind of chance does he stand finding someone else?

Well, pity is all very well but you can't base a relationship on it, whatever Vini may have said last year when she was seeing fake Dean Gaffney. I click Reply and type very quickly.

Sean,
Thanks for the lovely offer, but in the days since we've spoken, I've started seeing someone. It's pretty serious. I'm sorry to let you down.
Beth

I put a kiss after my name, then go back and delete it. It's not fair to torture him with false hope. He has to know there is no chance of anything ever happening between us. I hesitate for almost a minute before I click on Send, knowing that the light will go out of the day for him when he reads it, and everything will seem just a little bit more . . . difficult. But it has to be done. He has to start to mend himself so he can move on. I owe him that. I hover my mouse over the Send button and then, with one final glance over my shoulder at his back, hunched over his desk, I click.

As soon as I've sent it, I press my fingers to my mouth and wish that I hadn't. How could I have been so thoughtless? He should not have to learn about this disappointment by email, it's so cold. The least I could have done was break it to him in person. Maybe rub his arm and soften the blow a bit with an 'It's not you, it's me' speech. Oh God, I am such a callous bitch. I wish I could reach into the wires and pull the message back, or reverse time. I can't, though, so I just hunch over a bit and focus my ears on Sean's reaction behind me, waiting for the gasp, the stifled sob, the head clutched in hands.

337

I hear his computer ping, hear the mouse as he clicks open the message, a short pause as he reads, and then . . . Then nothing. I dare a quick peek over my shoulder to see what he's doing, and watch as, with one rough click, he deletes it! I actually flinch as he does it, as if he's slapped me, and turn back to my own desk, my mouth and eyes still wide. How could he do that? Why isn't he devastated? I sneak another look, but now he's on the internet, surfing through holiday pages! It's almost as if he doesn't care that I've finished with him.

And now I come to Rupert's message. The subject says 'Please read me', but I don't for a while. I am steeling myself against an onslaught of images of that beautiful face. The Horizon brochure is on my desk, open at the back page as usual, and I peer down at the picture, superimposing onto it the image of Rupert that I met at the party. I thought I noticed something amiss there and as I stare hard at the picture, I can convince myself that it's there in the photo too: an orange line around his jaw where the fake tan ends. Well, it was either fake tan or foundation I saw, but either way it's not attractive. I lean over the photo, staring hard. Yes, there it is, a definite line around his jaw. Or is that just the perfect manly squareness of his chin?

No, come on, Beth, get a grip. I know what he was like on Friday – vain and shallow. He probably forgot about me the moment I walked away, and nothing about me would have remained in his memory. Or, no, maybe one thing. Two things. 'Nice tits,' he would probably say, if he was asked to describe me later.

OK. I'm ready. I open the email and start reading.

My dearest Beth,

Is everything all right with you? I know that we have arranged to
meet for lunch tomorrow but I was hoping to exchange an email
or two with you in the meantime. I really enjoy chatting to you.
The fact that I haven't heard from you is making me worried. I
am sensing that something has occurred to make you think twice
about continuing with our friendship. Am I right? Beth, I will find
it very hard to accept our friendship and correspondence are
over, if you have decided to end it. I want to tell you that I like you
very much, and was starting to think that we might become more
than business associates. I'm not embarrassed to say it; the
cold, impersonal medium of electronic mail gives me the courage
I need to be intimate. But I think you probably guessed how I
felt from our communication anyway. The point is that I think
something has happened to change your opinion of me, and
you're backing off. Am I right?

God, he's so perceptive and sensitive. Apparently. I
shake my head, as if clearing it of dust. If he wasn't
such an ignorant wanker, I would find this intensely
attractive. He is though, and I don't. Not a bit. I click
Reply.

What you don't know is that it was me you were talking to at the
party on Friday night. You made it very clear then what your
intentions are.

I stop myself from writing more. I don't want him to
know how crushed I am, how I was hoping that we
would be more than friends. It sounds so pathetic,
now that I know what he's really like. The reply comes
quickly.

339

We met? Really? At a party? Oh my God, Beth, what on earth
did I say to you? It sounds terrible but I'm so sorry to say that I
don't remember it. Not everyone that speaks to me tells me their
name, and I'm ashamed to admit that, even if they do, I meet so
many people every day that I often forget their names instantly.
Did I offend you in some way? Because I want you to know that
anything I said to you, in person, at that party or anywhere else,
was not real. It wasn't me. I mean, not the real me. The real me
is this one, the one who writes to you, the one who admires,
respects and likes you. Very much. I will explain everything to
you in time, but right now I just want to know that you don't hate
me. I can't sleep, I'm grumpy and it's affecting my work so now
please put my life back in order, Beth. Tell me you don't hate me
because of something I said to you at that party.
Yours affectionately,
Rupert x

Oh bum. I am still incredibly attracted to him. My
brain is pointing out that he's just a lying prick, only
wanting to get himself back in my good books for his
own vanity's sake, but all the other bits are shouting
in unison that the brain should shut up, and isn't that
the most amazing, romantic email I've ever had? He
is so unlike what he was like at that party – he seems
like a completely different person. The Rupert that
spoke to me at that party would never have been
able to articulate like this. The Pecs Factor ruled out
any conversational ability he might once have had.
This Rupert is the complete opposite of that. I feel
some activity low down in my belly, like the guys
down there are starting to make a few preparations in
case a visitor calls. For God's sake, what is the matter
with me? I love Brad, so any visits to that area will

340

be made by him, and him alone. When I'm good and ready.

Hang on. What if someone else is writing Rupert's emails for him, like Steve Martin in *Roxanne*, writing to Daryl Hannah? I am deeply attracted to this person calling himself Rupert who has been emailing me, but all the evidence points to the real Rupert de Witter being an airhead. Beautiful and desirable to look at, but self-centred and ignorant. And I couldn't be attracted to someone who is so deeply in love with someone else – namely, himself.

I click Reply.

Who are you really?

It's short, but it does the job. It lets him know that I am prepared to speak to him, but only tentatively, and it also lets him know that I am on to him and I know that he is not the real Rupert de Witter.

I am Rupert de Witter. You know that. The man you met last week was—

At this point my phone blares out the *Superman* theme, alerting me to the fact that I have got a text. I drag my eyes away from the screen, knowing that this will be from Brad, but then I open the message and find that it's not from Brad at all, but from someone called Nigel.

Nigel here. Wher were u lst wk? Waitd 2 hrs for u in Ptch n Prrt, no show. U all rite? Meet agen soon? Luv ur admirer Nigel xxxxxx

What? Who the fuck is Nigel? I don't know anyone called Nigel. It takes me a moment, but then I suddenly remember the mysterious text I got last week from a Nigel, purporting to be someone I had ticked at speed dating. I thought it was Vini messing around because I knew I had only ticked one person and that one person was Brad, so I replied . . . Oh shit. Oh bloody hell. I suggested we meet up in the Patch and Parrot, then I forgot all about it. And now I know that I accidentally ticked the wrong number, and this poor Nigel character must have ticked me to get my contact details, which means he really did think I had ticked him and really did text me and really did think we had a date in the Patch and Parrot last week. What the hell shall I do about him?

Well, Nigel is going to have to wait as it's time to go and do the Motivation workshop.

My mind is in turmoil, with Brad and Rupert swishing in and out of focus, each one's appearance causing major pubic plate tectonics, so I feel as if I spend the whole day alternating between feverish lust and quivering anxiety. I don't know how I get through it, but at the end of the day the eight delegates burst into a round of spontaneous applause, and one of them cheers. As they all leave, they shake my hand and thank me profusely, telling me how determined they are now to finish that application, get that promotion, run that marathon. Their faces are enthused and bright, they are alive with opportunities, anything is possible, they can do it, they have the motivation to stick with it and see it through. I couldn't give a fuck.

This is quite surprising for me actually. Usually I take

great pride in my work. But these last couple of weeks, I have been so distracted by Rupert I have not been focusing as intensely as usual on anything else. Even my unconscious actions have not had my attention, let alone my conscious ones. I am determined to get back to normal once I have secured the Horizon contract, but right now I am walking with single-minded intensity towards my desk, where I quickly sit and open my work emails.

It's four thirty and I haven't sent a message to Rupert since this morning. He is no doubt assuming that nothing he says can make up for whatever was going on last week when we met, and that I am ending our relationship for ever. I need to read the rest of his message and send him an answer.

My brain is demanding to know why I am doing it as I am already crazy about Brad, which is not fair on him, Rupert or me; but the rest, and much larger part, of me is loudly advising me not to put all my eggs in one basket. At least, not until there is clear evidence that one of the baskets is superior, and is definitely the best equipped to offer the greatest comfort for all eggs, until death parts them.

I go straight to my inbox and click open Rupert's second message again. As it's opening, I notice that there isn't another newer one from him, and my heart sinks. He must have given up.

I am Rupert de Witter. You know that. The man you met last week was just an idiot, pretending to be something he wasn't, as a joke. If I'd known that was you, I would never have let it happen. The evening would have ended completely differently, believe me.

343

So, that's the truth. If you still feel angry with me, please please write back and tell me. Then I won't spend more hours of my life waiting fruitlessly by the computer. If I don't hear from you, I will assume you are deep in thought. Or unconscious on a trolley in Casualty.

R x

Well, I didn't reply so does that mean that he thinks everything is OK again? I hope so. I reply quickly.

Had you taken drugs, then? Or were you drunk? Or simply entertaining yourself? Because another girl might have been taken in by it. It seems a bit cruel, that's all.

Sitting in his office, Rupert has his elbows on his desk and his head in his hands. He is running his hands through his hair. He frowns at the screen, then stands up, walks for the fifteenth time to the window, rubs his head again, then comes back to the seat. He sits down and picks up his mobile phone, then scrolls through the phonebook to 'Libby'. As he is selecting 'Connect' from the menu, the computer pings and he jumps. He drops the mobile carelessly on the desk with a clatter and seizes the mouse, directs it to the new email and sees who it is from. A relieved smile spreads across his face as he reads quickly, then composes a reply.

From: Rupert de Witter
To: Beth Sheridan
Subject: So relieved you're not on that trolley

I know. You're right. It was thoughtless and childish and potentially wounding. Well, it did wound you, so it was definitely

344

wounding. But I wasn't on drugs, Beth. I'm not into that. There is
the slightest possibility that I may have been a teensy bit tipsy,
but it doesn't excuse what happened. All I can say is, please
forget it. It wasn't the real me, this is. This is me, Rupert de
Witter, of Horizon Holidays, talking to you, Beth Sheridan of Love
Learning, hoping, hoping that you'll talk back.

R x

Wow. My insides are in a frenzy of activity now. They're
obviously speeding up their preparations, having been
triggered by my feelings as I'm reading, but the fact of
Rupert not being physically next to me right now, and
actually in a different building, in a different part of the
town, making any physical contact an impossibility,
has obviously passed them by.

'You're wasting your time, guys,' I whisper, but they
don't calm down. Actually, I'm not sure I want them
to. I write:

Are you honestly telling me the truth now? I mean all of it? Is
there anything else I should know?

I don't know what I'm expecting him to say, but some
more of that passion would be very welcome. The
reply comes quickly. I read it through and feel a smile
coming spontaneously onto my face.

I'm absolutely certain that there is plenty more you should know,
Beth. I know for sure there is more I want to tell you, and more
of you I want to know. I hope very much that you feel the same.
But as far as the party goes, the person that you met was most
definitely not worth knowing at all. Can we forget about him?

R x

345

Almost all of me is completely sure that he's talking about getting to know each other better, maybe in a social setting somewhere, so that we can see if anything is going to develop. Which is fantastic. The small but very vocal rest of me has somehow managed to start thinking that he's talking about *knowing* me, in the biblical sense. I slide down in my seat a little as I write my reply.

> I certainly would forget about him, if I could. Unfortunately I have a slight problem there. You see, I have got a bit of a crush on him. Have had for a while now. So even though he behaved very strangely on Friday, which I can forget about, I very much doubt that I can forget about him.

I stare at it for ages before I click Send. It feels like a betrayal of Brad, who I do actually feel quite committed to. But I can easily remind myself that we don't have a commitment at all, we are both free to see whomever we like and send emails to whatever sexy millionaires should come our way.

Plus, of course, it's very forward. There's no innuendo or double meaning about this one. It's right out there, no disguise and no mistake. I click. That's it.

I spend about ninety-five seconds staring at the computer screen, willing a new message from Rupert to arrive there, and for the first time ever, this method actually works. I move closer to the screen, heart pounding fiercely, and open the message.

> I can't tell you what it felt like for me to read that, Beth. I'm sure you know, since I am rubbish at playing hard to get, that I am totally attracted to you too. God, it's great to see that you feel

the same. But I'm a bit worried that you're attracted to the man you met at the party, the buffoon who looks great but acted and spoke all wrong and upset you. Is it him, Beth, the image of him, that attracts you?

The guys down below have got the place ready and they're now all cheering in unison, 'Go, go, go, go!' I close my eyes briefly, succumbing to it, then open them again and reread that message. It's so weird, the way he speaks about himself in the third person like that. He's obviously completely detached himself from his behaviour that evening, which makes me think it really wasn't natural for him. Maybe it was just a joke, or a dare or something. Whatever it was, his detachment makes it obvious that he's regretting it. I write back.

I don't really understand. You're the same person, the one who responded to my joke, who wrote all those funny emails and made me laugh. You're the one who set the candles up in Madeleine's and joked about your hot air balloon on the phone (that *was* a joke, wasn't it?). That's what I'm attracted to, Rupert. Not the person at the party. Sorry, but you need to know. I couldn't call myself your friend if I didn't tell you when you're behaving like an arse.

In his office, Rupert reads this message and inhales a deep breath, which he lets out slowly and calmly. A smile turns up the corners of his mouth and he opens a new message.

Is that what we are then? Friends?

347

At my end, I read this and feel myself frowning slightly. I'm not entirely sure whether this is good or not. Does he want to be friends? Is he glad we're friends? Or is he slightly regretful that we're friends because he wants to be so much more? Only one way to know.

> I certainly hope so. It'll be awkward when you sign up Love Learning if we don't get on.

Yes, yes, I know, it's a cop-out. But I only wrote that in the hope that it might provoke a reaction, maybe some kind of declaration that what he wants has got nothing to do with Love Learning.

The computer pings.

> You're back to that again, are you, you minx? Ever the professional. I am impressed. And quite turned on, actually. The truth is, I haven't stopped thinking about you all weekend. Whenever I think about our meeting tomorrow, I can't concentrate on what I'm doing. What are you doing right now?

Suddenly I become aware of the rest of the office around me. Sean is still sitting at his desk behind me, and Fatima is round at Mike's, diagonally opposite. Next to Mike, Derek's desk is empty – he's away in Brighton doing three days of Management Skills, thankfully. He wouldn't be able to see the messages on my screen, but he would definitely see my face redden, and my pupils dilate. And my breathing becoming laboured. And me sliding down further in my seat. Must try and look a bit less aroused, for the sake of decorum. My next message is more a symptom of how I'm feeling than anything else.

348

> Well, you know very well what I am doing now, Rupert. I am
> pressed up against my computer screen, breathing hard,
> running my fingers up and down the keyboard, teasing out a new
> message.

It's quite accurate, actually. Self-consciously, I move
back from the screen and make myself sit down
properly in my chair. Then I leap forward again as the
next message arrives.

> No work to be done, then, Miss Professional? Time to waste?
> Idle hands?

Oh God, is he criticizing me? Have I made myself look
stupid with my last answer? Is he losing all respect for
me? I write:

> No, I've done all my work already. That's how good I am. And I
> certainly wouldn't call this wasting time.

I click Send, then drum my fingers impatiently on the
desk, waiting for his reply. When it comes, my heart
actually stills in my chest for a second, before plunging
on.

> I can be at The Blooding in ten minutes. Meet me there?

Omigod. The guys down below are all jumping up and
down and waving their arms now, and their cheering is
louder and more demanding. I think they are starting
to realize, as am I, that their frantic preparations have
possibly not been in vain after all. I send a quick 'OK'
and am putting on my coat and shutting down my

349

computer before I've even had a chance to think about it. I am actually going to meet Rupert properly, me knowing who he is and him knowing who I am. It's definitely not a business meeting and it feels like we've just done the foreplay. Or maybe that's just me. Oh God, what if it's just me? Well, I can see what happens when we meet. If he grabs me and starts kissing me passionately, I'll know it's not.

Christ, knees, come on, the rest of us are relying on you two to get me there.

'Seeya,' I call out carelessly as I hurry towards the door, not looking round, not caring if anyone hears me or notices me leaving. I yank the door towards me, shrugging my coat on with the other hand, hurl myself out into the corridor and look up just in time as I bump straight into Richard.

Twenty-three

Unfavourable Returns

Short-term Goal: Uhhh . . .
Obstacles:
Long-term Goal:
Obstacles:

'Whoa there, steady on, darling,' he says, putting his arm out and around my waist. I look up into his face and he stops mid stride. 'Holy fucking Christ. Is that you, Beth? Well, roll me over and tie me down backwards, you look fucking gorgeous. Come here.' My breath has stalled in my chest, my legs are wood, my whole body has suddenly become immovable as I stare in open-mouthed shock at this giant vision before me. In less than one second my eyes have scanned his entire body, taking in his new, tanned skin; his hair, slightly longer, slightly blonder, falling forward now over one eye; his open-necked shirt and rolled-up sleeves; his eyes gazing down admiringly at me; his arms out towards me for an embrace. Suddenly the blood that was so recently busily employed elsewhere surges back up to my head, my breath returns in a

351

rushing gasp, the world spins, I stagger a bit, hit the wall, twist my ankle and fling my arms out with a yell as I lose my balance completely.

'Oh, yikes,' I hear as I crumple into Richard's outstretched arms. 'Someone?'

This is not on my list of things I want to be doing when Richard returns. Not even in the top one hundred. I'm supposed to be charmingly engrossed in something worthy, with slightly dishevelled hair and a sweet smile, happily getting on with my life, not bothered by the fact that he has been gone for three months and completely oblivious to the fact that he has returned and is observing me passionately from the shadows. Falling headlong into his arms does not feature at all.

I'm only down for about fifteen seconds, which is a bit embarrassing really. I mean, if you're going to injure yourself in front of your heart's desire, at least give him a chance to feel sick with worry, punch 999 frantically into his phone, cradle your head lovingly in his arms and run along by the side of your trolley at the hospital. I'm ready to get up again before Richard even has a chance to bite his lip.

As I look up, there is a sense of hurried activity going on, people rushing around, just begun panic, concerned faces appearing. I hear Richard saying, '. . . just fell over, don't know why . . .' and Fatima saying, 'Who is it? What happened? Oh my God, Richard!' Then everything kind of stops, two pairs of eyes meet mine and Richard says, 'Oh, no, it's all right, she's fine. Everyone back to work.'

Fatima goes back through the door to the office and I hear her voice saying, 'Guess what, everyone? Richard is back! Beth fell over!' and other voices saying, 'Richard's back? When?' and then the disappointing sounds of people going back to their desks. I want to shout out, 'I might not be all right, you know!' but Richard is even now crouching down beside me, looking into my eyes. And he does look a bit worried.

'Hello there,' he says softly, his hands on his knees.

'You're back.'

'Yeah, well, Portugal isn't all it's cracked up to be, you know.'

'Really?'

'Nah. Complete nightmare, from beginning to end. I'll tell you all about it later.' He picks up my hand and rubs his thumb over the back. My hand dies and goes promptly to heaven. 'Do you think you can stand up now?'

I nod. My voice is temporarily unavailable. No doubt frantically spritzing itself up somewhere. I leave my hand where it is to make it easier for him to pull me tenderly up into his arms.

'Great.' He drops my hand, puts his own hands back on his knees and stands up. 'Can you come into the office, please? I'm just about to make an announcement.' And he goes back through the door, leaving me lying on the floor like fallen tinsel.

The first thing I do is rush to the Ladies and put on some lipstick. I know Richard asked me to come in for an announcement, but he won't mind if I'm not there. He can fill me in later. Oh God. My eyes roll back and my knees almost give way again as I think about being filled in later by Richard. Come on, Beth, get a grip.

My reflection looks OK, actually. A bit pale,

maybe, but I'm hoping it just makes me look fragile and interesting. I dab on some lipgloss and fluff my hair out a bit. Then smooth it back down again. This occasion calls for cool and chic, not mad professor.

Back in the office, Richard is just finishing off. I limp towards the front of the small crowd that has gathered in front of him. 'I hope I am making myself clear,' he is saying, beaming around the room at everyone. I'm clutching my hands together like Keira Knightley looking at puppies, trying to stop myself from bouncing on the spot, but no one else looks quite as pleased to see him as I am. Fatima is biting her lip and frowning; Mike is shaking his head a little; even Cath looks slightly perturbed. She's scratching her nose with her index finger. 'Just get out there, get on the phone, get into meetings, lie, cheat, sneak, tell them anything, I don't care, just as long as you get them to sign on the line. OK? *Comprendez*? Get them to commit to anything you can, doesn't matter what it is. This is serious, guys. Dirty tactics required, no questions asked. We need full payment in advance, or minimum fifty per cent deposits, OK? This Friday I want details and cash from everyone. That's four more days. Four. More. Days. OK, good. Get to it then.' And he turns and walks into his office.

'Oh my God,' Fatima starts, 'did you hear that, Beth? Can you believe it?' But I say nothing as I am heading as fast as I can towards Richard's office door, pulling it open, going in.

He's just in the act of sitting in the huge black leather swivel chair that Chas bought a month or so ago. He grasps the armrests, running his hands up and down them, nodding. 'This is a bit of all right, isn't it?' He leans back and the chair tilts, allowing him to recline and put his feet up on the desk. 'Ah yes, fantastic.' He puts his hands behind his head. 'It's great to be back.'

'That chair cost over fifteen hundred pounds.'

He looks over at me, eyebrows up. 'Did it really? Fuck. What's it made of, human skin? Ha ha ha.'

'It has a CD player, built-in speakers, massage function, a chill unit . . .'

'Wow! Massage. Where's the button? Under the arm usually . . . Ah, yep, got it.' The chair starts to hum and vibrate. 'Oh my God, this is incredible, Beth. You've got to try it. Come over here, come on.'

I start to go, then stop myself. 'Richard, you should know that Chas has been totally irresponsible while you've been away. The money he spent on that could have been used to pay someone's wages for another month. He's told us we're in dire straits, but he spends that huge amount of money, for nothing.'

'Well, if you're in Dire Straits, Money for Nothing is about right, wouldn't you say? Ha ha ha ha!'

I start to smile, then force myself to look serious. 'Richard, I'm serious.'

He stops mid air-riff and sits up. 'No, sorry, Bethy, you're absolutely right. It was irresponsible of him and I will return it to the shop. I decided to as soon as I saw it, actually. I mean, LL can't afford this kind of expense, especially not now.' He leans forward and pouts, making a lost-puppy expression. 'I just wanted to have a ickle pway wiv it, before de big nasty man takes it away.'

I laugh. I just love Richard's playful nature. 'I don't

mean to be a party pooper, I just want you to know what's been going on.'

'I know what's been going on, Beth,' he says, serious now. 'Come and sit down, will you? Thanks. Right. Now, from what I can make out, the only person who has been pulling in any decent money the last few months is you. Am I right?'

'Well . . .'

'Don't feel any misguided loyalty to your colleagues, Beth. There is no place for loyalty like that in business.'

'I'm not, I just don't know if—'

'OK, well, it's up to you. Doesn't matter anyway. The thing is, I need you now, more than ever, to work your magic and get us some big deals. What do you think? Can you do it?'

'What, by sneaking, lying and cheating?'

He smiles and frowns at the same time. 'If that's what it takes, then yes. But I doubt you'll need to. From what I know of my Bethy, you'll snag that massive contract without the need for any kind of underhand tactics, won't you?'

I can't help smiling at this. It's great to have your skills noticed, especially by the one person you want to notice you. I mean them.

'I hope I don't let you down.'

'You won't,' he says carelessly. He pushes off from the ground hard with his feet and spins a full 360 degrees. Then does it again. I watch him for a few moments and begin to feel dizzy myself. It must be love.

'So, are you back for good, then?' I hear myself asking, which sounds lame, even to my own ears. *Have you left Sabrina?* I just stop myself from asking.

'Yep,' he says, skidding to a halt with a grin. 'You know what, I've really missed this place. I've missed everyone here. You too, Beth.'

He's staring at me, intently focused on me and telling me that he's missed me. My heart does a little leap of joy. 'Really?'

'Yeah, really. I mean, it was great, wasn't it, working together all those years? The excitement of getting new contracts, the hard work writing the stuff, the pleasure in delivering it. I missed it.'

'So did I.'

'Yeah, but it hasn't been the same for you, has it? You've been able to carry on with it, getting the deals, researching, planning, delivering. All those things that you're so good at. I couldn't do any of that out there. My God, the knack you've got for spotting someone who might want training, before they even know themselves. You're a bit of a legend round here, you know.'

'Am I?' I'm blushing with pleasure. This is exactly how I imagined Richard's return would be. Well, except for twisting my ankle and yelling in his face. And him not marching in demanding to know where I am. Or observing me secretly from the shadows. But how important are those things anyway? He's talking to me, we're alone, he's told me that he missed me and now he says I'm a legend.

'Oh yeah. I mean, all those contracts!' He is smiling at me, and his eyes, flecked with gold, are so familiar, so beloved, I feel safe just looking at them. 'The management training, the online training, the insurance company. It was fantastic. Everyone said so.'

'What do you mean, everyone? I thought only you knew about all that. Everyone else thought we did it between us, didn't they? We agreed that we would both take the credit, so that no one became dependent on either one of us.'

He looks down, to the side, the other side, then at my knees, my hands, then the floor again. 'Um. Well, I got so excited each time, I did kind of tell one or two people.'

'Who?'

He grins and takes both my hands, then stands up, pulling me up too. 'Let's not talk about this any more. Not right now. Let me take you out for dinner? You must be starving. I know I am. Come on.'

He takes me to Pizza Hut. I knew he would – it's his favourite place. We've been here together so many times before, it's like 'our place'. We even have 'our table', which is the one in the corner by the window, because we've sat there more than at any of the other tables. Richard doesn't actually know it's our table, though, so he doesn't ask for it.

When we've ordered, he goes up to the salad bar and I watch him from the table. He makes the sides of the bowl taller with strategic lettuce leaves and puts the tomatoes in his pockets, all so he can fit more in. When he comes back to the table, he's got his fingers cradling the top of the salad mountain, to prevent a sweetcorn and bacon-bit avalanche.

'Why do you do that?' I ask him, as the peak wobbles.

'What?'

'That thing with the salad. There's no need.'

He stares at me as if I've got salad leaves growing out of the top of my head. 'I'm a businessman, Bethy. I wouldn't be successful if I didn't always take as much as I could get, would I?'

'But it's not . . . I mean, it makes you look . . .' He's still staring at me incredulously, so I drop it. 'Doesn't matter.'

'Too right it doesn't, love. You've got to be ruthless in business, you know. No room for wimps. Ex*cuse* me,' he shouts as a harried girl in a black apron rushes past, 'is there any chance of getting our drinks *today*? I mean, I have got things to do all day tomorrow so I can't come back for them.'

'Oh, sorry, I'll bring them out,' she says with a nervous smile, then rushes off.

'Christ, the service in here,' Richard is saying round a mouthful of tomatoey pasta. 'They might as well employ fucking chimpanzees!' He raises his voice on the final word and the people at the next table look over. 'So when did you do . . . this?' He wafts his fork up and down roughly in my direction. 'Looks fantastic. Should have done it years ago, you know.'

'Um, thanks. Thought I needed a change, you know.'

'Well you fucking did, girl. It really, I mean *really*, suits you. Know what I mean?' He's peering at me over his food and there's something different in his expression. He's never looked at me like that before.

'Thanks. So where's Sabrina then? She come back with you?' Finally I've managed to squeeze this in. I just hope it didn't sound too clumsy.

He does a mirthless 'Ha', then shovels in another forkful. I wait patiently while he chews and swallows.

'Don't know where she is, and don't fucking care either.'

'Really?'

'Yeah. Stupid bitch. Turned into a right moaner once we were out there. Never bloody stopped. This is untidy, there's no food, there isn't enough money, why aren't you working yet. Nothing but complaints, all the time. Started to feel like I was in prison, so I dug an escape tunnel and got myself the hell out. Now I'm a free agent again. No ties, no responsibilities. Just me to please.'

'Oh.' In all the years we have known each other, he has never, ever sent me a signal like that. He has never told me that I look fantastic. He has never tried to look down my top before, which he is definitely doing now. It's as though he's just realized I have breasts.

'So, tell me who you talked to about those contracts,' I say, trying to get onto safer ground. Except it isn't, it turns out.

'Oh, well, um, not everyone, of course. Chas knows.'

'Right.' I expected that. 'Why exactly did you ask him to look after LL while you were away? He's awful.'

Richard snorts. 'You're probably right. But he's my sister's husband, and she asked me. He's got management experience, apparently.'

'Yeah, but that probably just means he *manages* to put on his bicycle clips in the morning.'

He laughs out loud and a speck of food flies across the table. 'Good one, Bethy! I'll have to remember that. Excellent.'

'So did you tell anyone else?'

'Mm. Let me think. Um. Oh, yes, I think I told Grace. And Skye.'

Grace. Oh my God. He told Grace. Why would he tell her? She was one of the main reasons for us not letting on it was just me.

'My God, Bethy, you are brilliant at this!' Richard had said when I pulled in yet more lucrative work, grinning excitedly. 'You could do it all on your own and everyone else could just relax!' Until I pointed out that if we told the others that I could get enough contracts single-handedly to sustain the business, they really would just relax.

'Grace, in particular,' I'd said, nodding wisely. 'You really think someone like her will carry on working hard and being industrious, once she knows that I've got it covered? You're joking. She'll just sit at her desk flicking her hair around, taking your money for doing nothing.'

And now my mind is racing back to that day three weeks ago when Chas first announced the need to get new contracts. She asked me if I was going to snag a huge contract and save the company, then pretended that she was joking. But she didn't go out that night and hunt, did she? She had more important things to do. Like have fun, enjoy herself and not worry, while I came up with the killer contract.

'Fuck, Beth, you look like you might faint. You're not preggers, are you?'

'Why Grace?'

He breaks eye contact and looks at his glass. 'Well, you know, in the context we were in at the time, we were conversing, chatting, about LL and all the people in it, and I was kind of singing your praises, you know.

If it hadn't been for Bethy, blah blah blah. That kind of thing.'

I shake my head. This doesn't make any sense. 'But where? I don't understand. When would you two have had a conversation like that? Was it a lunch-break or something?'

'Er, no, it wasn't actually in the office.'

'Where then? The car park? But even so, why would you be—'

'No, Beth, not the car park. We were . . . We were in bed. All right?'

'In . . . ?' I feel this one physically, like a punch in the gut. The wind is knocked out of me and I can't speak. Grace and Richard, in bed together. The image of them, in that situation, flashes into my head in vivid Technicolor – him leaning over her, her rising up to meet him. I have dreamed about, pictured, imagined that scenario so many times over the years – a bedroom scene, the lovers entwined, damp skin, breathless whispers – but every time I have seen it, it has always been me in that bed. My hands on Richard's back. My hair on the pillow. My name on his lips. Oh God. I feel sick.

And then, as I sit there in Pizza Hut with a rushing tornado of images and information spinning and whooshing around in my head, the other thing he said finally makes its way into my brain.

'Skye?'

He nods cheerfully, taking a huge mouthful of pizza. 'Yeah, she knows. Although I kind of regret that one. She turned out to be a bit of a kook, if you know what I mean. Into all sorts of stuff that really doesn't do it for me.'

362

He's overlooking the fact that she's about eighteen and he's thirty-seven. And her boss.

I'm not eating any more. My stomach is boiling now and putting hot food into all that acid would only end in disaster. But it's not finished. 'Richard, can you tell me something? I need to know – did you sleep with Fatima too?'

'Ha. Well, no, as it happens. We kissed a few times – or at least, I tried – but I'm pretty sure she's gay. Raving lesbo. Must be. She always pushed me away, so . . .' He shrugs and shoves in more pizza, leaving a greasy sheen on his lips. I stare at them. I have been dreaming about those lips for eight years, and never had so much as a peck. I wanted those lips to brush mine, to press onto them, push down, crush them with desire. I told myself there was something between us, we were so close, always together, partners at work and in life, but we never let it get further because of his loyalty to his girlfriend. She was the only reason it didn't happen and I respected him for that. Loved him for it. Now it seems he tried it on with every female in the office except me. Heat is stinging my eyes, but I'm not going to cry here. He is still cheerfully tucking into his food. He hasn't even noticed that I'm not eating.

'Great nosh, eh, Beth?' he mumbles, his mouth full. 'Ooh, ha ha, maybe later, eh?! Ha ha ha!'

My life is flashing before my eyes: Richard at Horizon, swearing at Rupert de Witter, calling him a dickhead; throwing things around in his office, the temper tantrums, the shouting. The closed office door while he had 'meetings' with other assistants and other members of staff from every part of the building. Why was the girl from Cruise Design visiting him when she had nothing to do with training? Now it all makes sense.

And then I recall something I thought I had forgotten: a phone conversation between Richard and Rupert de Witter. More swearing, more shouting, Richard red in the face, screaming down the phone at Rupert, shouting that Rupert couldn't do it because he, Richard, would walk before he allowed it to happen. I thought Richard walked out on principle. Now I can see clearly that Rupert was going to sack him.

More pictures flash in my head, from the early days at Love Learning, right up to three months ago when he left. 'Beth will do that,' he's saying to Grace or Derek or Sean. 'She's really good at it. You don't mind, do you, Beth?' And I didn't mind, I was happy to do it, whatever it was, because it strengthened the bond between us, brought us closer. It was evidence that he needed me, wanted me.

I look up into his face, that so familiar, so beloved face, and feel myself breaking off and drifting away. He is transforming, shrivelling, metamorphosing into something new, right there by the ice-cream factory. There is no discernible change to his features; his face is the same. But now, instead of bright, sparkling, fun-filled eyes, there are two dark hollows, liquid with cynicism. Instead of a boyish grin, there's a lascivious smirk. Instead of a man with pride, integrity and honour, I see a cheap, grubby little user. I was ready to fall into his arms when I saw him this afternoon – well, I practically managed it – but now I feel a film of revulsion coating me, like the grease from the cheese coating his lips.

He's still grinning, presumably at his 'nosh' joke, and I feel more strongly than ever that I need to be away from him. Again. I pull my coat off the back of my chair and he raises his eyebrows knowingly. 'Anxious to get going, are you, Bethy?' he says suggestively, wiping pizza sauce off his smirk.

I nod. 'Right now, please.'

Twenty-four

Promoting Equal Opportunity

Short-term Goal: Who cares? My life is great already!
Obstacles:
Long-term Goal:
Obstacles:

Back at the flat, I am quite surprised to find that I am alone. The Richard-coming-back-to-find-me scenario I have played out in my head for the past three months has always culminated in Richard coming home with me and gazing earnestly into my eyes over the rim of his champagne flute while we discuss literature, listen to some favourite music, slow-dance round the room to something heartbreakingly soulful, then fall on each other in a frantic lust-fuelled frenzy. But here I am, standing in the cold hallway, lit only by the random twinkling of the Christmas tree lights, my coat still on, my bag on my shoulder, the door closed and Richard on the other side of it. Well, actually he's probably gone by now. I'm sure he can take a hint. But just in case he can't, I told him he wasn't coming in even if every man except him had been wiped out by a freak testosterone-based virus.

Vini is out, too, which is a relief. I so can't face her being right about something *again*. She's left a note on the kitchen table saying she is having dinner with Kylie and Jason, so I've got the flat to myself.

I'm standing. In the hallway. Apparently unable to move. I'm thinking, thinking, thinking, and my brain is so preoccupied with that, it can't do anything else. Even the electrical thing that makes the muscles move.

Eventually, though, I feel some muscles moving spontaneously. My mind is a spotlight, pointing directly at Richard – coming back, sleeping with Grace and Skye, being an arse – and now, finally, my face is reacting to this news. I'm expecting tears: gulping, gasping sobs; hysterical, loud bawling from wide-open mouth; painful, gut-wrenching, silent weeping face down into a pillow. But none of that comes. In fact, it's quite the opposite. As finally I move towards my room, I catch sight of my face in the mirror above the fireplace, and am delighted to see that it's smiling.

I fall asleep instantly and dream of running along a platform in black and white as the train I want pulls away with shouts and whistles and billows of steam; then wake up with a lurch and a start at two o'clock in the morning with the horrible realization that I have left Rupert waiting for me at The Blooding. Jesus Christ on a train.

I leap out of bed, irrationally deciding to throw on some clothes and rush down there, but realize as I'm tugging on my jeans that I'm being completely ridiculous. I mean, it's just stupid to be getting ready

367

to drive down there in the freezing cold at two o'clock in the morning when it would obviously be a complete and utter waste of time. He would be far too cold after waiting nearly ten hours in the icy conditions to be able to do anything.

I'm kidding. Of course I didn't think he would still be there. Not even for about eight seconds.

So I have to go back to bed and fret for five more hours before I can get up and go back to work and send him an email. I lie there for most of that time flat on my back, arms at my sides, eyes screwed shut, desperately focusing on sending him something telepathically; and once I even fancy I get something back from him. Eyes open now, I press my hand to my mouth as the indistinct figure of a man gradually thickens and coalesces out of the shadows at the end of the bed, and it's a painful sight – he's depressed, hunched over, slumped, all energy and animation gone from him. As I stare at him, I know with mounting anxiety that I am to blame for this man's sadness, it is my fault that he is miserable, his wretchedness is down to me. It's so clear that he had hopes about our meeting, had thought that something was developing between us, and that by leaving him there waiting for hours all those hopes have been dashed and he is now more miserable than if he had never heard of Beth Sheridan.

Oh God, that is so fantastic.

No, I don't mean that I'm glad he's miserable. Of course not. I love him, why would I be glad he's miserable?

But what girl wouldn't be secretly a bit thrilled that the droolingly sexy millionaire she had flirted with by email for a couple of weeks, arranged to meet, then didn't, then did meet when he didn't know who she was, flirted with some more, and then finally was prevented from meeting at an arranged place and time by the sudden return of her old boss is a sad, broken man because she didn't turn up? None, that's who. If he didn't care about me, if he wasn't so desperate to meet me, hold me, love me, spend fifty years adoring me, then he wouldn't have been so wretched when I didn't show, would he? I watch rapt as the dark, shadowy figure turns and trudges slowly and sadly away; my heart pounding, pupils dilated, lips slightly parted. Despicable though it is, I am aroused by his wretchedness.

My pupils dilate so much I finally see that it's just my dressing gown hanging on the back of the door.

After about twenty-five years, it's morning again and I haul myself groggily out of bed, pull on some clothes and drive blearily to the office. Actually, today is Tuesday, 19 December, which means I have a meeting with Rupert at one and the Whytelys regional manager at three, so just before I leave I have a long shower using some of the expensive Lauren Oliver shower gel that Vini gave me for Christmas. I rub matching Lauren Oliver body lotion all over me, dig out my sexiest bra and knickers set, spend an hour on my hair and make-up and borrow a Susan Sarandon outfit from Vini. Then I drive blearily to the office.

The truth is I'm not really bleary, in spite of having had no sleep. I know that Richard is in his office behind the wood-panelled door, and I glance at it as I pass, but for the first time in years I don't feel tense or anxious about that. I am invigorated, energized by my detachment from him and I sit down at my desk with high spirits, not even thinking about my posture. Now that Richard is back, I don't need to worry about that any more. But even if he weren't back, arranging myself in all those unnatural, uncomfortable poses all the time seems faintly ridiculous now. Well, not faintly.

I log straight on to my work emails to see what Rupert has sent me, if anything. Right in the back of my mind is a teeny little voice reminding me that I am in love with Brad – actually, it's not really right at the back, and it's not teeny or little – but I am shutting it out for the moment, in spite of it shrieking like a banshee, jumping up and down angrily and pointing accusing fingers at me. Today has to be about Rupert, and I'm telling myself, and the shrieking banshee, that it's because of the Horizon contract. If I don't sort things out with him before our meeting at one o'clock, he's never going to sign on the dotted line. Not if he thinks one of the Love Learning staff is so inconsiderate, disorganized and downright rude as to leave him waiting fruitlessly by a foul fountain in the middle of winter for fifteen hours.

I wonder how long he did wait, before giving up? There's probably CCTV footage somewhere. How would I get access to that? Perhaps I could go to the police and say I was concerned about my—

No, it's immaterial how long he waited. At least with regards to the contract it is. I can ask him about it after we're married.

Oh my God, get a *grip*! I am not going to marry Rupert, I am going to marry Brad. Right now I need to make amends with Rupert, for the sake of Love Learning, the contract and my job.

OK. Well, a quick scan of my inbox tells me that he hasn't emailed me, which means I will have to start. Which is how it should be, of course. I am the one at fault, I need to make the first move. I was kind of hoping for some recrimination or anger – something nasty and sarcastic would have been good – as a starting point for me to start smoothing things over, but there's nothing, not even some good old hurt. Right, well, fine. I will start.

Dear Rupert,

Shit. What if he hasn't emailed me because he wants nothing more to do with me after I treated him so badly yesterday?

Doesn't matter. I've got to make the first move and find out what the situation is. I've got nothing to lose.

Dear Rupert,

Fuck. What if the whole thing yesterday was just a joke? What if he never intended for me to take it seriously, and didn't even go to The Blooding to meet me because he only said it for laughs? Our emails have tended to be a bit silly and we were joking around a bit at the time, so it could have been his idea of fun. And if I write now and try to make it all better, I will look like a sad, pathetic idiot.

No, I won't because he will assume that I knew it was a joke and therefore that my message apologizing for not turning up is also a joke. OK.

371

Dear Rupert,

The worst part is imagining his face when he receives this stupid message apologizing for not turning up yesterday. I mean, I am hoping for a sudden delighted expression to come over him as he sits forward eagerly in his chair and clicks Reply straight away, then composes a beautiful e-love letter, telling me how waiting for two hours in the freezing darkness yesterday crystallized his feelings for me (along with his eyebrows) because he would not have done that for anyone else, and now he knows for sure that what he wants is so much more than a business relationship. But another possibility is a quizzical frown as he wonders what the hell it's all about, then quickly deletes it and gets on with his day. The third, and probably worst, scenario is the one where he calls all his mates and colleagues over to read the message, and they all have a good laugh at my expense.

But it doesn't matter because after today's lunch meeting, I need have nothing more to do with him. Unless he wants to. And I won't know whether he wants to or not until I email him. So why don't I just get on with it.

Dear Rupert,

Now that I have decided to get on with it, I find I can't. I haven't a clue what to say. A simple 'Sorry for standing you up yesterday' isn't nearly profound enough. Plus, I need to make it sound like I'm joking, just in case he was. Bugger.

At this moment, my mobile phone rings in my bag,

giving me the perfect opportunity to not think about this damn message for a while. Thank God. I rummage in my bag and just manage to press the answer key seconds before it stops.

'Hello?'

'Um,' says a female voice, 'is that Beth Sheridan?'

I blink. I don't recognize this voice at all. I take a quick glance at the number display, but it's a number I don't recognize either. I'm immediately uneasy and start to frown. 'Yes, it is. Who is this?'

'My name is Maggie Farrell, I'm the duty ward manager at the Edward Hospital Accident and Emergency. We've had someone admitted this morning who has your name and number in her diary . . .'

My breath stalls in my chest and I drag in a gasp to give myself just enough breath to croak 'Vini?'

'Um, it's a Miss Lavinia Jones. She's been admitted following a trauma to—'

'I'm coming.'

Twelve minutes later, I rush into the hospital through the sliding double doors and practically shout Vini's name out to the teenager sitting behind the bulletproof window at reception. It turns out Vini suffered a blow to the head this morning. She was found sitting on the pavement in the town, and the person who found her was so concerned about her, he phoned an ambulance. 'We're not sure how it happened,' the nurse says to me as she leads me towards a closed cubicle.

'What do you mean? What does Vini say happened?'

'Well, she doesn't know.'

'How can she not know?'

373

The nurse pauses, her hand on the curtain, and lowers her voice. 'The head trauma has given her quite a severe concussion, which has affected her memory,' she whispers. 'She's lost her short-term memory.'

'Oh. Right.' Amnesia. I've heard of that. 'So she doesn't remember what happened this morning – that's quite common, isn't it, when there's a head injury?'

'Not very. And I'm not sure you're completely understanding. She doesn't remember what happened to her this morning, or anything since then.'

'Yes . . .'

'I mean, anything. She doesn't even remember that she's had an accident. She doesn't remember anything she's told for more than three or four minutes. She's unable to make any new memories, at least for the time being.' And with that dramatic announcement, she pulls back the curtain.

Vini is lying on the bed, fully clothed, looking around her anxiously. She's clearly just been crying and there's a huge red and blue bump in the middle of her forehead. She seems so much smaller, lying there. Her shoes are off and there's a big rip in the knee of her pink and purple stripey tights. Red flesh is visible underneath. Her orange vinyl jacket is hanging over a chair.

'Hi,' I say, sitting down on the edge of the bed. She turns her head and looks at me, but there's a strange absence in her eyes. It's unsettling; I can't keep eye contact for long.

'I thought I was having a dream I was out shopping with Adam,' she says. 'I don't know what's happened.' She sniffs and a tear runs down her cheek.

374

'It's all right,' I say, taking her hand. 'You've had a bump on the head . . .'

'Have I?'

'Yes. But you're all right. You're in hospital now and they're looking after you. Don't worry.'

'Oh. In hospital? What happened?'

'You can't remember. But it doesn't matter, the point is that you're all right now.'

'Really?' she says, as if she can't quite allow herself to believe it. 'Where am I?'

'You're in the A and E department, at the Edward. You've had an X-ray already and now they're waiting for the results.'

'Really? I don't remember that at all.'

'Don't you? Well, that's probably because of the bump on your head.'

She turns her eyes to me again. 'What?'

'I said, it's probably because of the bump on your head.'

'What do you mean? What bump? I was just having a dream I was Christmas shopping with Adam. I don't even know what's happened.'

'You've had a bump on the head . . .'

'Have I?'

Our conversation goes on like this for the next half an hour while we wait for the X-ray results. When they arrive they're fine, but the doctor wants Vini to have a CT scan now, so we start to wait for that. Or at least I do. Vini thinks she's only just woken up. While I'm talking to the doctor she stares at us with a confused expression on her face, like a child watching her parents talk about the mortgage. Then when he's gone she says, 'I don't even know what's going on.

375

I was just having a dream I was out shopping with Adam.'

'No, you've had a bump on your head.'

'Have I?'

After another thirty minutes of this, I am starting to get an almost overwhelming desire to hear some different words, like the need for salt and vinegar crisps you get immediately after a chocolate binge. I'm actually considering striking up a conversation with an elderly woman I can hear groaning somewhere, when suddenly the curtain is pulled back and a tall, dark-haired man with a goatee walks in. He glances at me with an almost inaudible 'All right?' then goes over to the bed and leans over Vini. She looks up at him and says, 'I thought I was having a dream we were out shopping.'

Aha. So this is Adam then.

'Yes, Livvy, we were,' he says, sitting down. 'You fell down some steps—'

'Steps?' I can't help butting in. 'What steps? Where?'

He turns to me for a moment and says, 'Near the library,' then looks back at Vini. 'You don't remember it?' She shakes her head.

I've realized straight away that I've asked the wrong question, so I try again. 'What happened?'

He turns back to me. 'She tripped and fell down some steps.'

No shit, I want to say, but don't. 'Yes, but how did she hit her head? Were you there? Did you call the ambulance?' *And who the fuck are you?* I don't say that last bit either.

'Where am I?' Vini interjects at this point.

'You're in hospital,' Adam starts, but I don't want to wait.

'Tell me what happened this morning. I mean, please?'

'Hospital? Why?'

'You've had a bump on the head, Liv.'

'Have I?'

'Yes. But you're OK.' He turns to me. 'We were heading towards Boots and Liv was chatting away about what she wanted to get, and I think she tripped on something. I don't know what,' he says quickly, as I open my mouth. 'One minute she was holding my hand, next minute it was wrenched away and she went flying.'

'Christ, she left the ground *completely*?'

'I thought I was having a dream I was shopping.'

'You were shopping, Liv. You're in hospital now. No, not completely off the ground. It's just an expression.'

'Right.' Christ, course it is. I am such an idiot.

'I don't even know what's happened.'

'You do know, Liv, you just keep forgetting. Anyway, she kind of tumbles down these three steps like a really bad stuntman, so I'm laughing, thinking she's going to feel really silly in a minute, as soon as she stops rolling.'

'Have I had a bump on the head?'

'Yes you have! That's right, you remembered!'

'And then?' I wish he'd stop answering her – there's really no point.

'And then at the bottom she lands on her knees but the momentum keeps her going and she topples forward and hits her head on the wall at the end.' He looks down fondly at Vini's tear-stained face. 'Thwack.'

'God.'

'Fuck,' says Vini. Then bursts into tears.

'Oh, don't cry, my Livvy,' Adam says, stroking her hair away from her face. 'What you crying for?'

'Don't know.'

'Something hurting?' Nod. 'Where's it hurting?'

'Don't know.'

Well, there are a hell of a lot of unanswered questions here, if you ask me. Like what did she trip on? What happened next? Why was she holding his hand and who the fuck *is* he?

'Look,' I say, and they both do. 'What I want to know is, how do you know all this? How do you know Vini? Why were you out shopping together? Are you one of her clients?'

He smiles. 'No, I'm not one of her clients. Jesus, who would I be, Barry Chuckle?'

I shake my head. 'No, she hasn't got him on her books. You can get the real one for the same money. Actually both of them.'

'Is that right? Anyway, no, I'm not a client, I'm Adam – Livvy's boyfriend.'

'*Boyfriend?*'

'Yes, it's like a husband, only not so much.'

'Ha ha. How did you get together then?'

'Speed dating, about three weeks ago.'

I stare at him. 'No way.'

'Yes way. Ask Liv.'

I glare at him for a few moments, but we both know he's got me there. Leaving aside the fact that she probably won't remember which part of her body her hairbrush is for at the moment, there's also the fact that she hasn't even told me she has a boyfriend.

There's no way she's going to explain how they met.

'So how do you explain the fact that I was at that speed dating event and didn't see you there?'

'I know you were there. I saw you. If you remember, Beth, I bumped into Livvy outside the door. I'd gone into the wrong room by mistake and was actually there to cover the puppet convention. When I saw her there, I couldn't believe it. I mean, I have been trying to contact her for years . . .'

'Whoa, wait a minute. How do you know my name? What do you mean, trying to contact her for . . . ?' But in this moment I experience a sudden, inexplicable flash of clarity and realize that I know him, I've known him for years, and now I recognize him so easily I can't imagine how I didn't spot it earlier. 'Oh my God – Adam Beresford! For fuck's sake! From St Leo's?'

'Well, duh. Nice of you to remember me so quickly, Beth, considering I spent two years sitting behind you in French. Nice hair, by the way.'

'Oh my God, I can't believe it's you! This is incredible! How are you? What are you doing now? Do you still live round here? You in touch with any of the old gang? Malcolm Riley? Tessa "Mind-My-Hair" Harris? Rob the builder? I can't believe it!'

He's nodding enthusiastically and grinning as broadly as I am. It's so strange, seeing a man's body underneath a face that will always remain in my memory as sixteen. 'Yeah, Rob's married now, two kids, works in the bank.'

'Fuck off.'

He laughs. 'No, it's true. Malc is living with someone called Ian. They've got dogs.'

'Yeah, no surprises there.'

379

'Really? Christ, you could have blown me over like cards when I heard that. Totally stunned.'

'No way! Old Malc the Talc, with his peach swimming towel?'

'God, yes, I'd forgotten that. Yes, you know, now I think about it—'

'I was having a lovely dream I was out shopping,' says a small voice from the bed.

Adam Beresford had a massive crush on Vini at school, but she was too black-eyeliner-and-bovver-boots to notice his pressed-black-trousers-and-grey-jumper. But he didn't forget about her. He's a photographer on the local paper now and took snaps of Vini when he saw her out with Captain Jack Sparrow that time. Not because, it turns out, he thought Johnny Depp had heard about this nondescript little town in Hollywood and had popped round to see it. Adam spotted it was Vini straight away, had his camera with him, so he snapped her. And all this time, she thought she had been 'papped'.

'Can you imagine how pissed off I was to get assigned to the puppeteers' convention?' he's telling me. We're sitting on opposite sides of Vini's bed. She's dropped off to sleep, so we're talking quietly. 'I mean, puppets? Meeting each other? Christ, that's not news, is it?'

'Absolutely not.'

'But it all turned out for the best,' he goes on, turning to gaze lovingly on Vin's sleeping face. Her mouth has fallen open and a low growl can just be heard on every exhalation. 'If I hadn't gone to that hotel that night, I wouldn't be here now.'

Obviously Vini can't give her version of events at the moment, but it turns out that Adam was the man Vini bumped into outside the speed dating room. He's been trying to get in touch with her for years – Friends Reunited, apparently – and after she saw him that night, and recognized him instantly, I might add, she finally emailed him back. She must have liked what she'd seen. They went out secretly a few times, which explains the pink lipgloss, then arranged to meet up at the Mix 'n' Match thing.

'She only went to that thing to give you a chance to meet someone too,' he says now, and I am acutely embarrassed. God, it looks like I need help in the love department. *Actually, I have got a very sexy millionaire in the offing, thank you very much*, I want to say, but don't. I look at Vini lying there snoring softly and try very hard to be furious with her, but my face keeps on smoothing itself out and smiling all on its own. God, she is so lucky. I mean, the lanky nerd with no eyelashes who has cherished feelings for her for over a decade has metamorphosed into a solid, sexy bloke, with thick arms and dark lashes. Ah, the wonders of testosterone. I bet she regrets ignoring all his emails for ten years now. If only she had realized back then that he wouldn't be a sixteen-year-old skinny for ever.

Twenty-five

Establishing Positive Relationships

Short-term Goal: Get to Madeleine's by one o'clock.
Obstacles: It's already one forty-five.
Long-term Goal: Persuade Rupert to forgive me for
  standing him up twice in a row. And later, turn lead
  into gold.
Obstacles: Haven't got any lead.

The doctor decides to admit Vini for observation, and they even manage to find a bed for her. Adam has to go off to work for a few hours, so I stay with her as she is wheeled along white antiseptic corridors, her eyes darting around in anxious confusion. She still insists she has just woken from a dream, but some things are starting to sink in now.

'I assume I've had some kind of accident,' she says once in a small, frightened voice.

After another hour or so she is taken for the CT scan, and then after a few more, the results come through as clear. I am so relieved I almost start crying, but manage to stop myself because Vini is, and me crying seems incredibly pathetic compared to what she is going through.

'Just going to the loo,' I say quickly and rush out into the corridor. I didn't even realize I was so worried about her.

Eventually Adam returns so I leave her there with him, the blue lump on her forehead like an extra occupant in the bed. And finally, now that I know she is going to be all right, now that I am no longer needed, now that I can start to think about what I was supposed to be doing with my day today, I allow myself to think about Rupert. I have avoided looking at my watch, or any of the eight hundred million clocks that seem to be fighting for every square inch of wall space in this damn place, but in spite of that, I have a dreadful, heavy feeling about my lunch meeting with him. I am sure I am too late, and when I finally check, my watch – and stomach – tell me it's ten to two. Bugger bum arse bottom and balls.

In the car, I pull out my mobile and get the number for Madeleine's, then call the restaurant and ask them to let Rupert know that I'm not coming. I can't leave him sitting there waiting a second time.

'Of course I'll let him know,' the maître d' says. 'Is there any message?'

Yes, can you tell him that I am desperately in love with him and want him to drive straight over here to the hospital car park and make passionate love to me under the 'X-ray' sign, please? I don't say that. I say, 'Can you just tell him that I'm very sorry, please?'

'Of course.'

So at least he's not being stood up again. Well, he

is, but at least he doesn't have to wait for two hours to find out. And I can't even go there now – late, but there – because I've got another appointment this afternoon at Whytelys.

Briefly I consider standing up the Whytelys manager and rushing to Rupert's side, but I can acknowledge to myself that it's a bad idea. Of the two contracts, the Whytelys one would be far more lucrative, and I must stay focused on what I am trying to achieve here. I know that sacrifices have to be made and work has to be done in order to achieve anything, but it makes me feel heavy and low to accept it.

I drive back to the office, my head filled with images of Rupert's wretchedness in the vision I had last night. OK, I know it was just my dressing gown, but I'm thinking about him in that way all the same. It makes me feel better, and worse, to think about his wretchedness.

When I'm back at my desk, I open my work email account and check my inbox. Nothing from Rupert – of course, he's still sitting eating those delicious fishcakes (but very wretchedly) – but there is one from Richard, and one from someone called Anthony Davies. He's apparently the personal assistant to the Whytelys regional manager, just reminding me of our appointment later today, and directions of how to get to their offices. I stare at it for a few moments, wondering why on earth I didn't cancel this ridiculous appointment, or at least tell Sean about it so that he could go. I glance over at his desk but he's not there again. After his last disastrous meeting with them, he probably wouldn't want to put himself through the humiliation of turning up a second time anyway. So why am I going? He's already been rebuked, why am I setting myself up for the same thing?

Because the truth is I think I've got a better chance of impressing them and securing the contract than Sean. That's what I have been avoiding acknowledging to myself until this moment, but now I can be honest with myself. It's happening more and more lately.

Well, so what? Sean failed with Whytelys, but that doesn't mean I am not allowed to have a go. If I succeed, everyone will benefit, including Sean and his little boy. I check the directions and work out that I need to leave around half past two – that's in half an hour. Good. That leaves me plenty of time to write to Rupert.

Before I start to compose the important and difficult email to Rupert, I have a quick glance at Richard's email. It says he had a fantastic time last night, hopes I did too, and is inviting me round to his house after work tonight for 'a meal and whatever follows'. I know he doesn't mean profiteroles and coffee. I click Reply.

> Richard,
> Thank you for the kind offer, but shove it up your backside with a torch.
> Beth.

Then I delete that and write:

> This ship has sailed, baby.

I stare at those words for a long time before eventually deleting them without sending them. And then I delete his message.

385

So. Time to write to Rupert. I can't delay it any more.
I open a new message and start writing.

Dear Rupert,

I know that nothing short of being knocked over by a taxi in the
shadow of the Empire State Building and being paralysed from
the waist down would be a good enough reason for not meeting
you yesterday, but I do have a reason, even if it's not a very good
one.

Just as I was rushing out of the office yesterday afternoon on
my way to The Blooding, a huge shadow fell over the building
and car park, and I looked up to see an enormous silver disc
hovering a hundred feet above the ground. I glanced at it, then
continued hurrying to my car. Unfortunately, the beings inside
saw me, because everyone else was still inside the building, so
they beamed me aboard, and kept me their prisoner for twenty-
four years. Eventually, they decided they had had enough of
me and returned me to the earth, strangely enough at the exact
moment in space and time where they had snatched me. Imagine
my delight when I found I was back in good old 2006, on the very
day, at the very minute, that I was hurrying to meet you.

I started to run to my car, hoping you would still be waiting,
but at that moment I slipped on some ice and sprained my
ankle. It's my left ankle though, and it wasn't too painful, so
I continued towards the car. Suddenly, the strap on my shoe
broke and my shoe came flying off. I retrieved it and carried on
towards my car. When I got into the car, I realized that I had left
the sidelights on all day, and the battery was completely flat.
Luckily, a man was just getting into his car in the space next to
me, so I asked him if he could jump-start me. He did, and I got
the car going. Just as I was reversing the car out of the space,
a woman walked behind the car and I knocked her over. She
got up straight away, apologized, and walked off. Just at this

moment, my mobile phone rang. I put the car back into neutral to answer it and found it was my mum, telling me that she had had the dog put down. She then told me she was going on a last-minute short break in Lisbon and was just about to get on the plane. I said goodbye to her and hung up the phone. I put the car into first gear and started to pull away, when suddenly I noticed that the car wasn't handling properly. It was obvious I had a flat tyre. I got out, quickly changed the tyre, then got back in. Now I was finally ready to drive to The Blooding and meet you, but at that moment one of my colleagues ran out into the car park to tell me that our manager, Richard Love, had returned from four months away in Portugal, and I was required back inside for a meeting. I turned off the ignition and limped slowly back inside. Then I limped back to the car, turned off the sidelights, and limped back inside again.

So you see, I did everything I could to make our rendezvous, but even with all the fates on my side, helping me to get there, I couldn't make it.

My reason for not making our lunch meeting today is much more mundane. My flatmate has had some kind of accident and suffered a concussion, causing her to lose her short-term memory. I have had to spend most of today at the hospital with her while she's had a series of tests, none of which she can remember. I am so sorry to let you down twice in a row. It seems as though I am trying to avoid meeting you but I want you to know that is not the case at all. I really do want to meet you, if you still want to. Any time is good, although this afternoon is out as I am having my tyre repaired.

Please let me know whether you're still interested in meeting me, in a social context. I am waiting by my computer for your answer.

Love, Beth x

PS I am fifty-two now, by the way.

I read it through before I send it. Then I read it again. Then I get up, go to the kitchen, make a cup of tea, have a wee, then come back and read it again. I think it's OK. It's jokey enough that it won't matter if the whole meeting at The Blooding was just a joke in the first place; it's long enough to give him the idea, if the meeting wasn't a joke, that I am truly sorry I didn't make it and am prepared to do some almighty grovelling to make it up to him; and it's funny enough to make him smile and decide that he will give me another chance. Oh God, I hope. I click Send, then shut down the computer and drive out to Whytelys.

The offices of their management team are actually very easy to find. They're in a retail estate in the next town, above a Whytelys outlet. I'm a bit early so I have a quick browse amongst the embroidery and elastane trousers. Even twenty-five per cent off doesn't make this stuff desirable.

At three o'clock I am shown into a small, stifling office where the man behind the desk introduces himself as Gregory Matheson, the regional manager for our area.

'Did you say you were from Love Learning?' he asks me as we both sit. I open my mouth ready to explain hurriedly why I'm there, seeing as they have already met and rejected one of our other members of staff, but he keeps talking. 'I've heard of them, but I don't know much about them, I'm afraid. We've never booked external training before, so if you can persuade me, and I am ready to be persuaded, this will be a departure for Whytelys.' He smiles at me and puts his hand out. 'Go on then. Persuade me.'

I've stalled. That is not the speech of someone who

met someone from Love Learning recently and kicked him out of the building amidst cackles of laughter. There is an enormous lump of confusion stuck in my throat, making speech impossible. I clear my throat and swallow a couple of times while I pretend to refer to some notes in my hand. It's actually just the printed-out directions they emailed me, but he doesn't know that. I put my index finger on the text and frown.

'Ahem, I'm sorry, Mr Matheson—'

'Greg.'

'Oh, thanks. Well, I'm sorry, Greg, but I was led to believe you have already had a meeting with a representative from Love Learning? Have I been mis-informed?'

He nods. 'I think you have, Miss Sheridan.'

'Beth.'

'Thank you, Beth. Yes, as I already told you, Whytelys have never considered external training providers before.'

'Ah.' I look down at the sheet of paper again. 'Oh, no, wait, sorry. My mistake. I was misreading it. Stupid. My information actually says that you received a preliminary telephone call from a Love Learning representative about two weeks ago. Is that correct?' I know I am on dangerous ground here, but suddenly I'm feeling a deep chill and I need to know the answer to this one.

He shakes his head with a little laugh. 'I don't know where you're getting your information from, Beth, but I'm afraid you're wrong again. The only Love Learning rep I have spoken to is you.'

I nod and smile and look down at my sheet of paper, but my breath has got stuck again. There's a roaring in my head and a pounding in my throat and I cough a little. Sean never came here. He never even contacted them. Which makes me wonder why he told me that he had? Did he just say all that to impress me? To make me want to go out with him? It seems incredible.

'Is there something wrong?' Greg asks, leaning forward in his seat, a concerned expression on his face.

I shake my head and pat my chest with my hand, clearing my throat. 'Bit of a sore throat,' I croak. 'Sorry. Could I trouble you for a glass of water, please?'

'Of course. It's no trouble.' He presses a button on his desk and speaks into an intercom. 'Anthony, could you bring Miss Sheridan a drink of water please?' He was right – it was no trouble.

Anthony is incredibly efficient and turns up less than a minute later carrying a plastic cup of freezing water. I drink half of it, then put it down on the floor. My mind is racing, electrical currents fizzing along synapses, millions of new connections burning pathways into my brain. All that activity has shown me a possibility, but do I dare go for it? Do I want to?

'I'm so sorry,' I say. He waves his hand dismissively with a broad smile, but then I catch him glancing at his watch. I need to work fast. 'Well, as you say, apparently I have been misinformed about your intentions with Love Learning. Which is something of a relief, I must say. It would have made things quite difficult.'

'Oh? So you're not from Love Learning?'

Richard flashes into my head, and the wasted loyalty I have shown him for so many years. I think about Grace, sleeping with him while I did her work. Supercilious Derek; airhead Skye; ineffective Cath.

And Sean, lying about this contract for some reason. What do I owe them right now? Is Love Learning really where my future lies, or am I in need of a major change? I lay the clipboard down on my lap and look directly at Greg with a broad smile.

'No, I'm not. I *was* with Love Learning, so I do have experience there, but now I'm here to represent a new company that has just been set up. It's called Keep the Change.'

'Oh, I see. Well, what sort of training does Keep the Change offer to large retail companies like ours, then?'

I can't believe I just did that. I'm in the car driving back and every so often I let out a little scream. It's not fear making me scream. It's an almost uncontainable excitement. Apparently I am setting myself up in business, and Greg Matheson knew about that almost before I did. I bounce in my seat and squeal a bit more. I feel like someone is blowing a balloon up inside me.

Right. This is for real now. I managed to pitch all the training available at Keep the Change pretty coherently, I think, and I promised I would put some brochures in the post to Greg within five days. If I can get Whytelys, and Horizon, I will be set, although it will be so much work I will have to take on another person straight away. Oh God, that means interviewing. But before I do that I've got to get premises. I wonder where is available at the moment. But before I get premises, I will have to get some guaranteed work. And that means I have now got to make some brochures. Which means a night on the computer. Thankfully, the ridiculous and woefully outdated Horizon training policy insisted on putting me through a PowerPoint workshop when I worked there.

At six fifty the next morning, I'm standing at the colour photocopier, surreptitiously printing out forty copies of the mini brochure I spent all last night preparing. It's not easy being surreptitious when you're hauling over two hundred sheets of paper around, but no one is looking at me now, so I think I'm safe. At least, no one I can see is watching me. And you know what? Even if someone is watching me secretly somewhere, I don't even care. Suddenly getting Keep the Change started has become the most important thing in my life – more important than how I might appear to someone secretly observing me, more important than making sure my hair hangs right, my lips aren't smiling too broadly, my eyebrows aren't frowning – and it's only now that I realize that this is what I have been wanting for months. Probably since Richard left.

No, fuck that. I have wanted this for years, even when Richard was around; I just thought I wanted him more. That's why one of my long-term goals was to become manager of the company. Just not this company.

Actually, now I think about it I'd better make sure I'm not smiling too broadly after all. Don't want anyone coming over to see what I'm doing, having seen my very huge and excited grin and thought to themselves, There's nothing exciting about photocopying handouts, so what the hell is Beth beaming about over there by the photocopier?

I'm going to pay for all this paper and ink anyway, that's not an issue. But I don't think Chas or Richard would smile and say, 'Oh, OK, Beth, you go right ahead and use our resources to help you set up a rival company, that's fine,' even if I told them that they will get a cheque in the post to cover it in a few days.

Anyway, only Derek is here at the moment, and he's got his face behind an unfeasibly large newspaper, so I'm pretty sure I'm not being observed. Which, for once, is a good thing. I spent most of the night designing these brochures and then scouring the internet for advice about setting up a small business, so I would be bloody annoyed if someone strides over now and says, 'What the hell do you think you're doing, you traitorous little bitch?'

Setting up a business is surprisingly easy, actually, if you have the right guidance. I've got my own adviser already, helping me write a business plan. I can work out of my living room if I have to. And after Christmas I've got an appointment with the bank about a loan. Amazing what you can do at 3 a.m. on the internet.

OK, forty copies have now printed out so I gather them up and lug the sheets over to my desk to start stapling them together. When I arrived this morning, I thought the office was deserted, which was why I came in so early. The funny thing was, Richard was here already.

'Oh, shit!' he shouted when I came in. 'Jesus, Beth, you really made me jump!' He was holding some papers and the hand holding them dropped abruptly to his side.

'Sorry.'

'No, no, 's fine, no problem at all. So. You're here then. Early. Getting some work done, no doubt. Excellent. Always could rely on my little Bethy to get the job done, couldn't I? Well, looks like you've got your teeth into something pretty major, so I'll just . . .' he was walking away from me backwards, moving towards the wood-panelled door, '. . . leave you to it. Right. OK. See you later then.'

Yes, I know, there was something distinctly odd about that, but I was so terrified that he would work out what I was up to and then so relieved that he didn't, I just heaved a huge sigh of relief and got on with the photocopying. The prototype brochure was in a carrier bag so he couldn't possibly have seen it, but I felt so guilty I wouldn't have been surprised if the word 'Traitor' had suddenly appeared in blood on my forehead.

By the time everyone else arrives and Derek emerges from his paper, the brochures are all finished and safe inside the carrier bag, which is stashed in the boot of my car (yes, I even managed to go out to the car park carrying a large pile of papers without Derek noticing). Today's 20 December, only two days until we stop for Christmas, so there is no training going on for the rest of the week. Most of us have got admin jobs and research to do, but I can't focus on anything right now. Any work I do for Love Learning now would be in direct competition with, well, me, so I would be bloody stupid to do any.

That's my excuse for not doing anything today. God knows what everyone else has come up with. Grace is looking at Turkish holiday resorts on the internet, Derek is doing the crossword and Ali and Skye are absent – presumably in the now empty training room consummating their relationship. Maybe everyone is secretly setting up their own rival companies and justifying not doing any work the same way I am.

394

Anyway, I don't care. My fingers are itching with anxiety to check my emails and see if Rupert has replied. I open my inbox, my stomach churning like a washing machine.

I only have one new message, and it was sent about ten minutes ago. It's from Rupert. My heart leaps and I start grinning. It's all OK. He's got my message and he liked it and forgives me for not meeting him yesterday and Monday, and has emailed me now to arrange another meeting, which means I can still get the Horizon contract and start up my own business, and that we are still good friends and possibly even more. I open it.

Dearest Beth,
As you know, I received a message yesterday informing me that you are no longer my contact at Love Learning, and that all my business with that company will now be handled by an alternative representative. I was very surprised, not to mention saddened, to receive it, but can only assume that you have good reasons. I greatly enjoyed your message yesterday explaining why you did not come to meet me at the fountain on Monday, but I understood from it, and the later message, that the return of Richard Love has brought about some major changes in your life, which now prevent you from maintaining contact with me.

It has been a real pleasure writing to you, Beth. You have single-handedly recommended Love Learning to me sufficiently to make me want to book it. I can only hope that you will be the trainer who visits Horizon to deliver each session, as my faith is only in you, not the company.

I wish you all the best for the future, dear Beth, and the very best of luck in everything you do,
Your friend,
Rupert de Witter

Twenty-six

Hidden Agendas

**Short-term Goal: Get the Whytelys contract, find
   premises, hire staff, sort out a syllabus, get the . . .**
Obstacles: Not enough time.
Long-term Goal: Forget Rupert. Marry Brad.
Obstacles: Forgetting Rupert.

I stare at the words, trying to find the joke, trying to
make out the real meaning, but I just can't see it. That
lump of confusion is back in my throat, only this time
it hurts. It hurts so much the ache is spreading up to my
eyes, making them water. He doesn't want anything to
do with me. If we had ever got together, this would be
him dumping me. It's the email equivalent of a bunch
of flowers – 'You're quite nice, but I don't want you.'

I bite my lip and grip tightly to my self-control. No,
it's all right, I'm not rejected. Brad still likes me. I still
like him. I am not completely undesirable.

This thought consoles me for three seconds, then I
catch sight of the Horizon brochure on my desk, open
as always at the back page, and Brad slips from my
thoughts.

I lock my keyboard and get up, not really knowing where I'm going or what I'm doing. In the end I go where every girl goes when she is rejected by the sexy millionaire she has fallen in love with over the course of a three-week flirty email correspondence and desperately needs some comfort and solace: ladies' loos.

They're empty, thankfully, so I go to the mirror and stare at myself crying. This doesn't actually help at all. My nose is red, eyes running, face crumpled, hurt and let down, so I stand and cry at myself for a few moments.

After a while, I spot something else in there, tucked away, barely visible. What is that? I lean closer to the mirror and try to look beyond the shattered dreams and unrequited love. My face stops crying and the reflection becomes all focused and concentrating, and in that moment I see what it is, and wonder how I didn't see it straight away. It's determination. And frustration. And injustice. And cynicism. And fury. Mostly fury – a white-hot, scalding rage that is burning me up from the inside as it moves through my veins like molten lava. That message wasn't Rupert dumping me; that was Rupert reacting to what he thinks is me dumping *him*, which I would never do. Let's face it, no one would ever do. I watch in horror as my reflection contorts before my eyes, like Dorian Gray, from sweet, hurt girl to twisted, bitter, vengeful harpy in one easy step. I'm practically snarling at myself as the realization crystallizes that I have been stabbed in the back. By one of my colleagues. Someone I work with has lied to Rupert, ousted me and set themselves up as his new contact. Someone is trying to steal the Horizon contract from me.

397

I narrow my eyes at myself, feeling quite impressed with my own fierceness. I am not going to let this happen. I am going back out there and I am going to get Rupert back and find out who is behind this. Because there is no way I am going to go out without a fight.

I stomp violently towards the door, head down, fists clenched, little tongues of flame practically issuing from my nose. Then I stop, turn, come back to the mirror and spend a few moments smoothing out those bitter, angry lines and restoring my cool, sweet smile. This is nothing to do with wanting to look lovely in case Richard, or anyone else, should happen to glance my way. This is to do with wanting to hide my fury and appear to be blissfully unaware of the fuck-off enormous machete that's sticking out of my back, so that if whoever has done this should happen to glance my way, he or she won't realize that I'm on to them. That way, they won't feel the need to hide their tracks, which will give me a much better chance of finding out who is hiding a, well, hidden agenda.

Back in the office and suddenly everything seems suspicious. What only a few moments ago was a fairly quiet and relaxed – if currently unproductive – group of people sitting innocuously at their desks or loafing about ineffectively has become a room charged with sinister undertones and barely concealed menace. Are there hidden cameras in the corners? Bugs in the telephones? Tiny concealed microphones in Fatima's giant felt hat? Now nothing is sure, nowhere seems safe. Like a predator, I am alert, eyes darting about, ears pricked, nose quivering. The tip of my tongue flicks out to taste the air and I narrow my eyes a bit. I didn't taste anything, but it made me feel powerful. I feel as if my back is arching and my hackles rising to make myself look bigger and I am practically tiptoeing across the carpet tiles, arms hanging loosely.

'Sciatica?' Cath says behind me and I whip round.

'What?'

She raises her eyebrows a millimetre. 'I get it a lot,' she says and nods towards me. 'Recognize the signs. You need anti-inflammatories – they're the only thing that'll touch it.'

I stare at her. 'Right, OK, thanks, Cath.' I straighten up a bit and move on, heading towards my desk, watching my colleagues with new eyes. Ali walks past me, holding something behind his back. What's he trying to hide from me? I stop by the filing cabinets and pretend to be hunting through them for a folder as I watch him go over to Skye's desk. There's Skye, looking up at him, smiling, reaching out to take something. It's small, shiny, rectangular – it looks like a mini voice recorder! Is that possible? Oh my God, they've been working together, sneaking around behind my back, planting recording equipment on my desk and listening to everything that I've . . . Oh, no, it's a bottle of perfume. Who knew that they looked so much alike?

God, this is hopeless. I am rubbish at spotting when people are apparently acting normally while all the time working secretly behind my back to steal my ideas and bring about my undoing. What I need is some blatant treachery-type behaviour, but whoever has stabbed me in the back is obviously not going to give themselves away by staring at me openly, rubbing their hands together and cackling.

I glance furtively once round the office.

399

No, I was right, no one is doing that. So how can I work this out? I need to use the power of my intellect. Think it through. See if the synapses in my brain can make some startling connections again. I sit down and put my elbows on my desk, my head in my hands, concentrating. Come on, brain, you're up.

The first thing that needs saying is that Rupert received the message telling him I was no longer his contact within days of Richard coming back.

I'm not saying there's a connection. I mean, he's innocent until proven guilty, right? I need to find some hard evidence before I start going around pointing the finger willy-nilly, he deserves that at least. On the other hand, everyone knows there's no such thing as a coincidence, and he is a lousy piece of shit with no morals. I'm keeping an open mind, but I've got no doubt at all that Richard is responsible. The question is, how did he know about Horizon? How did he know about my contact with Rupert? I only found out about the possibility of Horizon changing their training policy through that teensy article in *Any Port* magazine. I'm as sure as I can be that no one else saw it. Or if they did, that they didn't make the connection with training that I made. At the time, Horizon had not published their intentions, or put out tenders, so it wasn't public knowledge. Which means Richard must have been sneaking around, spying on me, that lowlife rattlesnake.

Hang on. Something occurs to me. Maybe I don't need to be so hasty condemning Richard after all. Maybe Horizon have made an announcement by now that they're on the market for training and Richard sent them an email introducing himself and saying

400

he would be their contact here. I haven't looked at the Horizon website for a while, maybe it's on there. God, maybe I've judged Richard all wrong – again – and he is simply working hard now that he's back to bring some much needed money into the business. Bloody hell, there he is, diligently slogging away to try to save the company and all our jobs and I'm wildly accusing him of industrial espionage.

Quickly I click onto the internet and run a search on Horizon Holidays. I'm scrolling through their entire website, from Aberystwyth to Zanzibar, but I can't find any mention of new training plans anywhere. OK, well, that doesn't necessarily mean anything. Maybe it's on the business news pages . . . no. How about all the most popular learning and development sites? Not there either.

So Richard is a lowlife belly-crawling piece of shit with money for morals. Apart from being wrong about him for eight years, I judged him exactly right.

I am left now frowning and tapping a pencil against my desk. I feel sure if I could work out how he betrayed me, I would know for sure it was him. And if I had proof of it being him, then I would know how.

'Stop that tapping!' someone shouts across the room. I jump and the pencil flies out of my hand, through the air, and lands on the floor behind my desk. For crying out loud, now I've got to roll my seat out, bend down, pick up the pencil . . .

As I raise my head from the floor, pencil between my fingers, my eyes inadvertently land on a smooth, linen-clad back. I freeze in my seat, still bent over in the act of leaning down to pick up the pencil. My brain is doing that fizzing thing and I can almost hear it go as totally independently it puts two and two and two together and adds things up as unerringly and coldly as a computer. Insight follows awareness follows realization, all thought and comprehension mixing and expanding and building, the answer crystallizing at the end, a clear, bright understanding that I know as much as I have ever known anything is the truth.

One other person in this office did know about Horizon's plans, and that person only knew because I told him myself. And I told him because he told me about his.

Sean.

Twenty-seven

Reflection

FUUUUUUCK!

Twenty-eight

Research

Short-term Goal: Not stab anyone.
Obstacles: Really really really want to stab someone.
Long-term Goal: Get the Horizon contract, and
revenge at the same time.
Obstacles: Really really really want to stab someone.

I am still bent over, pencil in my fingers, frozen in my seat. My eyes are locked to that blue linen shirt. Seconds tick by like decades but I can't move. My blood, stalled in my veins, eventually restarts, slowly at first like a steam train, then gradually gathering momentum.

'Anti-inflammatories,' Cath says, moving past me in the distant background. I start to sit up again, my eyes never moving from Sean's back, my brain still buzzing, memories, distant and recent, playing out before my eyes like a film reel. Sean, suddenly noticing me after years of working together the day after I dyed my hair – but it was also two days after Chas announced the threat of job cuts. Sean's narrow-eyed smile, his secretive nature, his mysterious weekend activities.

Oh, well, no, that's all cleared up actually. He was obviously just spending time with his little boy and didn't want everyone to . . .

Shit. I pause again and sit motionless in my seat. His little boy. My brain is relentlessly piecing it all together, and little Alfie never did quite fit. Eyes still locked on Sean's back, I stand up and move towards him. As I get nearer I can see that he is reading a web page about Horizon. I pretend not to notice as he quickly minimizes it, revealing a site about quad bikes.

'Christmas present for little Albie?' I ask innocently as I move past.

'Hmpf, God, I wish,' he says seamlessly. 'He'd love one of these but I'll never afford it. Not without winning the Lottery.'

'Ah, well, maybe one day,' I manage to force out, even though I am snagged and choking on the fact that he didn't correct me when I called his son Albie. I keep moving, somehow putting one foot in front of the other without falling over or crashing into something because I am not looking where I am going. I am focused inwards, on what Sean said about his boy at the pub that night. I am positive he said his name was Alfie – it stuck in my mind because I had a cat called Alfie when I was twelve. But when I referred to his boy as Albie, he didn't even flicker. Which means . . .

I go towards the door at the back of the office because my head is about to explode and I don't want everyone seeing that.

Back in the Ladies I lock myself in a cubicle and sit down. I stare wide-eyed at the back of the door for a moment, then drop my head in my hands. I have been played. Oh my God, he has got me good. It is so clear to me now what has been going on and I can't believe I have let this happen. I always thought of Sean as untrustworthy, a bit sneaky and shallow, someone who might sell his grandmother's home while she was still living in it, but I changed my mind about him. He made me change my mind by producing Alfie.

Images are flooding into my head, one after another: Sean telling me about the Whytelys idea. Sean in the pub, upset and desperate at the prospect of losing his job. Sean producing a son out of nowhere. And then Richard, telling me that everyone knew that I had got all those other contracts on my own. Now I can see, now it is obvious, that 'everyone' included Sean. He knew right from the outset that if he was going to get a decent contract, the first place to start looking was not out in the high street or the industrial estate, but the desk diagonally behind his.

How could I have been so right about him?

After a few moments I get up and go back to my desk where I sit down and stare so hard at his back it doesn't surprise me that eventually he feels two scorch marks on his shirt and turns round. We lock eyes and I know from the way his eyes widen, his lips open a little and he moves involuntarily back in his seat that my face is not showing a sweet little smile. We stare at each other coldly for a few moments and then he says, 'Will you stop that flaming tapping, Beth. It's driving me up the wall.'

I freeze the pencil in the air without taking my eyes off his. He looks back at me for a second longer, then drops his eyes. 'Right, thanks,' he mumbles and goes back to sticking a knife between the ribs of a colleague. I pinch the sharp point of the pencil in my fingers.

Well, at least I needn't feel guilty about stealing the Whytelys thing from him. I mean, technically, I didn't even steal . . .

Oh my God. The Whytelys contract. Yet again I realize how stupid I have been. Suddenly it makes complete sense why they had no idea what I was talking about when I mentioned a call from another Love Learning representative. Sean didn't even call them, let alone go there. He made it all up. He was too bloody idle to do any research or prepare anything, or phone anyone or go to any meetings himself, so he made up a fake contract bid and a fake son and then cried as he pretended to confide in me so that I would trust him with the contract I was working on. Then he would have *my* contract, his job would be guaranteed, and no work necessary. I slide off my seat and stalk silently towards him, freshly sharpened pencil clutched in my fist. I've read that if you stab a pencil hard enough into the ear or eye, you will almost certainly cause death. So if I stab it not quite hard enough, I will definitely cause excruciating agony, and still be out in about eighteen months.

Of course I am not going to do it. That would be totally stupid; getting arrested for aggravated assault would almost certainly lose me the Whytelys contract. What I need to do is fight him for the Horizon contract, find out what he has already arranged and steal it back. Very casually I stroll nonchalantly past his desk towards the kitchen, clearly on my way to make a drink.

'Anyone want a drink?' I call out to the room, pausing by Sean's desk as I do. I try to accidentally let my eyes just fall on what is there, but pretty soon I have to abandon that idea in favour of jotting down all the hot drink orders. Bugger.

I spend the rest of the day finding fake reasons to walk past and hover by Sean's desk, like Chevy Chase trying to cheat off Dan Aykroyd in the brilliant *Spies Like Us*. Sadly, all I have managed to do is irritate the hell out of him, and send him an overt message that I am trying to observe his activities covertly.

'More coffee?' he said ironically at half past two, as I made my third pass.

'Toilet,' I said nonchalantly, looking the other way on purpose so that he didn't think I was trying to see his work.

'Got the trots?' he asked sweetly at ten to three, as I went by again.

'Crisps,' I replied, and then of course couldn't return to my desk without a bag of crisps in my hand. Which meant going all the way to the end of the corridor to use the vending machine. After I had made a quick detour back to my desk to get some money.

'Stretching your legs?' he commented, at three twenty-five, as I stretched and yawned near his desk.

'Stapler,' I replied, leaning over to reach it.

Eventually, he logged off, gathered up all his papers and left the office. I watched him through the window walk to his car, check his watch, get in and drive away. I could have followed him but I doubt he's going to do any more work tonight. Probably going to watch an illegal cockfight, or play poker for high stakes in some smoky basement bar. Instead, I've decided to focus all my energy on getting some killer research on Horizon done. I want to know everything there is to know about that company – their predicted profits, their stock performance, their pension plan, their staff turnover, the perks, the pitfalls, the percentage of job satisfaction. I need to know what cars the senior management team are driving, how many children they've got and where their spouses like to go on holiday. It's the best way to get my revenge on Sean.

I must have been so engrossed in Horizon's business that the next time I look up everyone around me has gone home and I am left here on my own. I glance at the clock: ten past six. Jesus. I have been working on this for over two hours. I stretch my back and reach my arms up over my head. I need something to eat. I stand up and glance around the deserted office. It's creepy with no one here, all still and silent, like a sleeping child's bedroom. I blink and think I almost see the photocopier move slightly with a thump, like all the toys coming alive in *Toy Story*. But it doesn't. As I'm starting to turn away, shaking my head with a smile, I hear the noise again. A muffled thump, coming not from the entirely static and inanimate office machinery, but from behind the wood-panelled door.

Evidently Richard is in there, also working late, although what he could be doing is a mystery. I'm as sure as I can be that he isn't struggling to get a load of research together for a last-minute bid to win the contract and the heart of Rupert de Witter.

Doesn't matter what he's doing. It doesn't concern me. If I manage to get the Horizon and Whytelys contracts for Keep the Change, I will be out of here and nothing Richard does will ever interest me again. Well, apart from the fact that I will be obsessively watching everything he does and everyone he speaks to from now on. Can't let my main competition get ahead of me.

As I look away from the wood-panelled door, it occurs to me that right now, Sean is my main competition, and right now, with no one here, is the perfect chance for me to conduct a little private research: namely, root through his desk and see what I'm up against.

Keeping one eye on the wood-panelled door, I stand up and move towards his desk. It gives me almost no pleasure to be rooting through my colleague's things, believe me, but this is war and he started it. No sound comes from Richard's office so quickly I grab the four files from Sean's desk and look inside.

The heady sense of imminent discovery I had been experiencing moments earlier dissipates instantly and my shoulders slump. They're all genuine training material and research notes. Shit. I put them back carefully, hoping I've got them in the right order, and move to his desk drawers. Of course he wouldn't leave anything incriminating lying about on his desk, it was stupid of me to think he would. People with things to hide always put them in their desk drawers. And lock them, apparently. Of course they fucking do. The bottom one is the same. I try the top one again, just in case I wasn't pulling hard enough, then the bottom one, yanking so hard the desk itself starts rocking. Neither one budges.

I stomp back to my seat and sit down. Well, that effectively brings me to the end of my ideas. I'm reminded suddenly of an advert I saw in the paper when I was seventeen for a recruitment drive at MI6. I tore it out and was excitedly filling in the application, my head full of foreign travel, exotic locations and dangerous assignments when Mum came in and said, 'Military Intelligence, love? Not really you, is it?'

Except . . . My eye lands on the waste-paper bin sitting underneath Sean's desk. There's a very slim chance . . . On impulse I get up and grab it, then put it down on the floor next to my chair. At this moment, the wood-panelled door opens suddenly and Richard appears there, a bundle of papers in his hand.

'Shit!' he shouts, at the same time as I shout, 'Fuck!'

We stare at each other wide-eyed, both apparently horrified at having been caught in the act of doing something we shouldn't have been doing. Except I am sitting quite innocuously at my desk with a waste-paper bin near my feet, and he is emerging from his own office carrying some papers. All outward appearances suggest that we are both completely innocent, but we both act guilty. My heart is thudding so hard my whole body is jumping, and it's got nothing to do with Richard's manly shoulders.

'Oh, you're still here,' he says at last, his free hand still on the handle of the wood-panelled door. He makes no move at all to advance further into the office.

'Uh-huh.'

'Mm. Me too. I was just . . . er . . .' He glances behind him and waves a hand in the general direction of his desk.

'Right.' It's hard to meet his eyes with the hot bin at my feet and the knowledge in the back of my mind of the mutiny that I am even now plotting, but he too is having trouble maintaining eye contact. In fact, he looks decidedly uncomfortable – fidgety, shifting his weight from foot to foot, clearing his throat, fiddling with his tie.

'Well,' he says eventually, lifting the papers in his hand, 'better get these down to the . . .'

I have no idea what he means, but I nod encouragingly. 'Oh, yeah, better had.' The sooner he leaves me alone again, the better.

He pulls the wood-panelled door shut behind him, hesitates a moment, then says, 'Seeya,' and leaves.

Hmm. He is so definitely up to something. Twice in the same day I have startled him and he has acted secretively in response. I stare at the wood-panelled door for a few moments. I should probably go and investigate, just in case. Just in case what? Just in case he's planted a bomb in there? Or maybe he was even doing some late-night photocopying, at the company's expense. Heinous crime. Nah, forget it. Who cares? I've got to find out what Sean is doing.

I kneel down on the floor by the bin and have a look inside. Fortunately for me Chas insists on all organic waste going in the bin in the kitchen. For Cath, this translates into, 'Fuck that, I'm gonna stick it in the waste-paper bin anyway,' because the kitchen is such a long way away from her desk. Not Sean though. His bin is almost empty, just a few sheets of screwed-up paper. I pull them all out and spread them out on the floor. There are a few A4 sheets of old session notes on After Sales Service, with some amendments scribbled in the margin, which means that he actually seems to have been doing some good old honest work today. Although these sheets could have been in here for quite a long time – the bins aren't emptied every day.

OK. Nothing interesting there. I screw them back up as near to their original screwed-upness as I can get them and replace them in the bin. The remaining three sheets look like they have been torn out of a notebook.

This will be more interesting. I spread them out on the floor excitedly, but realize very quickly that they're all blank. For God's sake, has this man even heard of the environment?

On impulse, I take a soft pencil and gently shade over the first page. I've seen this done so many times in films, it must be true. I mean, all those different writers couldn't be wrong, surely?

Actually, I think they were. All I'm getting is a splodge of grey shading with some faint white lines in the middle, which are completely illegible. I screw the sheet up again and hurl it back into the bin. This kind of thing makes me so angry. I mean, the lies we get told routinely in films, just for the sake of a convenient way to move the plot along. Somehow the hero has got to find where the baddie has taken the hostage, and of course every baddie always feels an overwhelming need to write down the name of the hotel and the room number, together with clear, concise directions, on the telephone notepad in biro, pressing hard, then tear it off and take it with him, leaving a clear imprint behind.

Not Sean though. Whatever he wrote on his notepad, he didn't press hard enough with his pen. Sneaky little shit.

I sit back on my chair. Yet again I've reached the end of my admittedly pretty short list of ideas. Bloody hell. I'm staring down at the two remaining sheets, wondering where on earth I should go next. Hmm. It is very odd that he would throw away three sheets of blank paper. It makes no sense. I picture him, sitting right there at his desk, notebook open, tearing out a page, screwing it up and tossing it in the bin. Then he does it again, and again. Then he closes the notebook, puts it in the drawer and locks it. Why would he do that?

Because, Beth, you dimwit, he didn't want anyone to come along and rub a soft pencil over the top page of his notebook and find out what he's up to, that's why. Oh my God. My brain has done it again. I fall onto the two sheets of paper left on the floor and rub my pencil over the first one. A few more verticals and horizontals are visible, but I still can't read it. I chuck it quickly back in the bin and seize the third one, rubbing it like a lottery scratch card. This time I am rewarded with:

LANGHORNE HOTEL, FRIDAY 2 P.M.
WILLOUGHBY SUITE
SET UP THURSDAY FROM 6 P.M.

Bingo! I sit back on my heels as a deep and satisfying thrill of pleasure runs through me. Hah. I outsmarted you, you twisted little sneak. All those weeks I spent watching old episodes of *Moonlighting* and *Jonathan Creek* after John Wilson of the estate agent's dumped me with a bunch of flowers have finally paid off. Who needs Military Intelligence when you've got UK TV Gold? Eat shit, Mum.

I didn't mean that. Sorry, Mum.

OK. Time to act. Quickly I roll the sheets of paper back into balls and put them in his bin, but as I'm returning it to its place under his desk, it occurs to me that he is probably the kind of sly, mistrustful tosser who would arrange the paper in a certain way, or balance something invisible on top of the bin, so that he would know if anyone had been sneaking around rooting through his rubbish. Jesus, what kind of complete wanker doesn't even trust his own colleagues not to go through his rubbish bin when he's not there? Git. I stare at the bin. There is no way in hell I am rummaging around the bottom of that with my fingernails, trying to locate and collect a stray human hair. Forget it.

Half an hour later finds me driving blithely home with a car full of rubbish, leaving all the bins in the office mysteriously empty. Well, not mysteriously I hope. I hope that everyone will assume tomorrow when they come in that the cleaner emptied them all first thing that morning, before anyone else arrived, and therefore any incriminating bits of paper that were among all the rubbish went undetected. Sean will never know that I was there late tonight and discovered his little arrangement before the bins were emptied.

Which now leaves me with one thing to do: call the Langhorne Hotel and confirm that the information on Sean's notebook is what I think it is, namely a sales pitch presentation by him to Horizon Holidays. Then get all my information on Horizon together for an even better, more detailed and more convincing presentation. I'll have to get to the Langhorne in plenty of time on Friday to set up my things, without Sean seeing me or sussing what I'm up to. Then I'll have to work out some way to sabotage his presentation and neatly step in to deliver mine instead, winning the contract myself and thereby gaining enough work for my new training company to get started with, and keep me and two employees safely in work.

OK, that's technically four things, but they are all leading to one, single conclusion: get Horizon.

And maybe get Rupert too.

Twenty-nine

Decisive Action

**Short-term Goal: Ruthlessly stab Sean hard in the
back, twist the blade and break the end off,
pitilessly rip everything from his grasp, shove him
aside and leave him powerless on the floor in a
pool of dribble, wretched and bleeding.**
Obstacles: Um . . . no, nothing.
**Long-term Goal: Finding it hard to see beyond the
short term at the moment.**
Obstacles: As above.

The Willoughby Suite is huge and quiet. Swags of
plastic greenery dotted with red berries and little
white lights are hanging tastefully from the ceiling.
The carpet is deep and muffling, so absolutely anyone
could walk around in here, pick things up, open them,
rummage around inside, switch them for something
else, completely undetected. Someone has arranged
four rows of seats, six in each row, all facing front. Each
seat bears a glossy, navy blue and white Love Learning
brochure and a little goodie bag, containing spa
vouchers, writing paper, eau de cologne samples and

a nice pen. At the front of the room someone has set up a portable overhead projector on a small table, and there is a box file next to it containing eleven slides. At the back of the room is a pair of long tables pushed together, with about twenty cups and saucers on them and a variety of drinks – an urn for hot tea, another with hot spiced wine in it, water, orange juice and coffee. There are also several empty silver platters – the promise of mince pies and biscuits to come – and I'm staring at them in amazement. What the hell is Sean thinking of? He knows full well that Love Learning can't afford such extravagances at the moment. Just as well I am going to pay the bill myself.

Behind these tables, this section of the room has been partitioned off from the rest of it – it would be far too enormous otherwise – by a pair of very thick and heavy red curtains. Behind these curtains is me.

Thankfully, this end of the room is not in use this morning. I'm not sure what I would have done if there had been a meeting or a training session in here. Well, yes I do. I would still be standing here, repeatedly peeping through the curtains, and hoping that my inexplicable, silent presence at the back of this part of the room wasn't too much of a distraction for the delegates.

It's Friday morning, about eight thirty. I have spent the last two days frantically acting as if nothing was going on, whilst staying late, coming in early and studiously avoiding absolutely everyone. I don't think anyone noticed.

Brad has called and we have chatted on the phone, but I just haven't had time to see him. We have got the whole day together tomorrow, though. I think he's got

418

quite a big plan for the day, possibly involving water. I'm thinking lengthy boat trip, to include swanky lunch. Or possibly rowing on the canal, salmony picnic and champagne. He rang on Wednesday, while I was at work, and left a few really lovely messages. The first said:

'Hi, Libby, just me, Brad, your three-minute man, wondering if we are technically a couple, or have I inadvertently become a stalker without realizing? If I have, I'm really very sorry. I'll go and turn myself in directly.'

I smiled to myself at that and went to lift up the phone to call him, but it bleeped again to let me know there was another message. This one had been left about four minutes after the first one:

'Me again,' he said. 'Well, the police didn't want to know. They said that if the person I am *supposedly* stalking – their words – hasn't made a complaint, then technically I'm not even a stalker! That's an interesting loophole, isn't it? Anyway, as you haven't made a complaint, I'll assume that we are still a couple and will continue to phone and harass you until you can't stand it any longer and finally speak to me.'

There was another bleep, and the next message, left fourteen minutes later, started:

'I was just thinking that maybe I hadn't made myself completely clear earlier, which would explain why you haven't got back to me. Well, just in case you are in any doubt, I would love to see you. Straight away, if possible. Well, of course, I can see you right now, but it's not the same through a pair of binoculars. Please ring me, as soon as you can. There's something I really need to . . . float. Bye.'

419

By the time I had taken the contents of everyone's bin from the office out of the car, separated out the Coke tins and manky lunch rubbish (apparently Cath isn't the only one who doesn't bother to stick to the kitchen bin rule), put all the paper into black plastic bags ready to be collected for recycling on Monday, then spent the evening writing my killer Horizon presentation, it was gone half past eleven when I listened to the messages so I didn't call him back. It would be inconsiderate and rude to disturb someone as late as that, and I didn't even know if he shared accommodation with anyone, so potentially it could be disturbing more than one person. Assuming he was at home when I rang him. And if he wasn't, I certainly didn't want to disturb . . . whatever he might be doing at twenty to midnight.

But then, who on earth an independent, single bloke in his early thirties could be sharing with I have no idea. If it's his parents I may have to back off. I've seen exactly where a set-up like that will end. There will be snide remarks, mean comments about my hair or my clothes, food I can't eat, outings I can't take part in. Finally efforts to make me look stupid or uneducated will eventually cause Brad and me to have an almighty row, culminating in a huge confrontation with his mother, who will act saccharin sweet as she denies everything, then embrace him and smile victoriously at me over his shoulder. That I can do without.

I did actually go to bed, but was up again within ten minutes calling him. What was I thinking of? Of course he doesn't live with his parents. And if he does, a midnight phone call would definitely bring it out into the open.

Well, he doesn't. Or at least he said he doesn't, which is good enough. If he does live with them and is lying about it, I've already won. Anyway, we had a lovely chat, which went on for over two hours and ended with him asking me to spend the day with him on Saturday. He really needs to tell me something, apparently.

'Why don't you tell me now?'

There was a lengthy pause before he said, 'No, I can't. I want to see your face when I say this. I need to see your reaction.'

'Look, if you live with your parents, just tell me. You don't have to lie about it.'

He laughed. 'I'm not lying about it! I told you, my parents live with my brother, just outside the town.'

'OK.'

'Why do you say it like that, all suspicious? It's the truth!'

'Sure, fine. No probs. I believe you.'

'Well good.' There was a slight pause, then he took a deep breath and when he spoke again it was like someone had turned the bass up on his voice. It had gone all deep and serious and kind of gravelly – obviously a telling-the-truth kind of deeply emotional voice. 'It's not in my nature to lie about things, Libby. I want you to know that.' A thrill went through me and I felt hot pulsings in my belly. He'd used his emotional voice on me already. I paused before I responded, just so he knew I was serious and emotional too.

'Me neither. I hate it. People who tell lies just think everyone is stupid except them. And don't forget a fairy dies each time, too.'

'Oh, Libby, you are so right.'

OK, well that is technically my name anyway, so it's

421

not a lie. I have been meaning to tell him about that but I can't do it on the phone and I haven't seen him for a few days, so there just hasn't been an opportunity. But after I've got through today, after I've found out whether or not I am leaving Love Learning at the end of the day, then I will do it. We'll have all day tomorrow to get a few things off our chests.

So today will go one of two ways: either it will be fantastic, the best day of my life, where I will secure the Horizon contract, humiliate Sean and walk out of Love Learning, just like Dickhead Love walked out of Horizon all those years ago, but this time I am walking away from him, and Grace, and all the others, with my head high, barely suppressing hysterical and delighted laughter; or . . . it won't. I daren't even put into words in my head what the other scenario might entail. I am operating in ten-minute bursts at the moment. If I can just get through the presentation this afternoon, then I will start to think about the results.

Suddenly, my mobile phone rings in my bag. When I look at it, I see it's Richard trying to get hold of me. I drop the curtain and turn round instinctively, imagining that he will be there, marching towards me, snarling and wondering what the hell I am doing trying to sabotage Sean's efforts to land a major contract, but the room is still empty. I look back down at the phone in my hand, my finger hovering over the 'Answer' key, but I don't press it. I don't want to speak to him now. Or later. Ever, in fact. I will have to go back to the office, though. Can't have Sean working out why I am not at my desk. It looks as though he's not coming back straight away anyway, so now's the time for decisive action.

Quickly I slip between the curtains into Sean's end of the room and spend a few moments replacing all the Love Learning brochures with Keep the Change ones, then swap the box of projector slides with a small bag of my own, placing Sean's box on the floor in the far corner of the curtained-off part of the room. Please God let him not come back and see this before I do. My KTC brochures are cunningly similar in cover design and colour to the LL ones, so someone popping their head into the room to check everything was still OK wouldn't notice anything amiss. Probably. Hopefully. Please God.

Nothing more I can do about that. If I'm not back at my desk in about ten minutes, I will be drawing a lot of unwanted attention to myself.

Back at the office, there is an air of panic and frenzied activity. Everyone seems to be up from their desks and moving around the room quickly, carrying papers, riffling through things, rooting through drawers. Even Cath is standing up. Fatima grabs my arm as I walk in, and says, 'Oh, Beth, thank God you're here, it's so awful,' then hurries off. Mike is kneeling on the floor sifting through a pile of papers spread out around him, and looks up at me with a sad shake of the head. He looks as if he might be about to say something, but I break eye contact to check out Sean's desk. Please let him be at it, please.

He isn't. Oh no, oh crap, that could mean he's driving back to the Langhorne to pace nervously in the presentation room for a few hours before everyone arrives. And if he goes in he will definitely check through his slides and find them gone. Which means he will notice that the brochures don't look quite right and will realize that they're not his LL brochures, but my KTC brochures. And then he will start frowning and wondering what the hell is going on and will find out I am behind it as soon as he takes a closer look at them and sees my name and company logo on the front. Then he will pick up my KTC brochures and fling them around the room, shredding my projector slides and snarling and howling at the strip light, saliva spraying from his lips and landing on the soft velour furnishings. And when he's done that, he will contact Rupert, move the presentation forward and deliver it early without me even knowing or being able to stop it.

Oh no, there he is. Jesus Christ in a suit, I need to sit down.

Maybe he's already phoned and changed the time of the presentation anyway, to throw me off, just in case by some unlikely mistake I happen to be on to him. Oh God, I'll bet that's what he's done. He knows me so he must know there is a chance I will use my massive intellect to work out what's going on. He would be a fool to stick to the original plan.

Well, there's only one way to find out. I take out my address book and find Rupert's secretary's number. I can't face actually speaking to Rupert, not with everything else that's going on. His beautiful voice would throw me right off and I have got to do the presentation of my life this afternoon. Can't do that after – or possibly even during – a lust frenzy. Not a good look.

When I get through to his assistant and tell him who I am, he tells me that he has instructions from Rupert to put anyone from Love Learning straight through to him if they should ring in. I panic and splutter that it's not necessary, I'm only ringing to confirm the time of the presentation this afternoon. 'I'll be seeing him later anyway, so if he needs to speak to me about anything, he can do it then. There's really no need to disturb him.'

'Well . . .' He's wavering. I bite my lip to stop myself from saying any more. Don't want to sound as if I'm desperate not to talk to him. Even though I am. Because I really, really do want to hear that voice again. 'All right,' says the assistant at last, 'but I'd be grateful if you didn't tell him that you called in.'

'Absolutely, as long as you don't. Don't want him thinking I can't remember the start time of my own presentation.'

'Oh, yes, of course. Fantastic.' He lets out a held breath and his voice softens and becomes more relaxed. 'Well, according to his diary, he's attending the Langhorne Hotel today at two p.m.'

I close my eyes and feel relief loosening all my joints. Sean is so arrogant – or underestimating me – that he has assumed I would never work this out. 'Thank God.'

'Pardon?'

'I said, that's odd.' I'm getting an idea.

'Oh? Why?'

'Well, I've got one thirty in my diary, and I know that the facilitator, Mr Cousins, has got one thirty in his diary. But you've got two p.m. – I wonder why that is?'

I hear computer keys clicking, pages turning very fast, and loose sheets of paper being moved around. 'Well, I . . . it's right here . . . I wrote it down . . . I can't—'

'Look, it doesn't . . . What's your name?'

'Jason.'

'Well, Jason, it doesn't really matter, it's only thirty minutes. I'm sure everyone can wait for him to arrive.'

'Oh God, no! No they can't! Mr de Witter hates being late. He would be mortified if he walked into a room to find all those people had been waiting for him for thirty minutes. It looks so unprofessional, he always says. And it insults the host. He would be furious with me.'

'Oh dear. That's a bit difficult, then. See, I can't get hold of the facilitator and tell him that the time is two p.m. He's not here at the moment and I probably won't see him until the presentation actually starts.'

There's a long silence while more papers are moved and pages turned. I've got my eyes closed and both sets of fingers crossed, and I'm biting my lip again. Then finally he says, hesitantly, as if he's just forming an idea, 'We-ell, I *could* tell him the start time is one thirty? I mean, he doesn't remember the times of things most of the time anyway. And it'll be easy enough to let everyone else know of the time change. That's what he pays me for, isn't it?'

'Well yes, I suppose it is. That sounds like a pretty good idea. That way, everyone is there at the same time, which is what everyone wants. Shall I leave it with you, Jason?'

'Yes, yes, no problem, I'm sure it'll be fine. Oh, but don't forget, please don't tell him you rang.'

'I won't if you won't.'

My God. I have become underhand. I am stealing my colleague's presentation and have now arranged for it to start early so he won't even be there! How utterly sneaky and contemptible. I like it.

No, no, I'm not underhand. I have simply managed to wrestle my own presentation back from the under-hand sneak thief who stole it from me in the first place. I am still upright and honourable, but now I am fighting dirty to see justice prevail. Yes, I am still the plucky heroine with right on my side.

'Flipping heck,' Fatima says, rushing past, and an idea occurs to me suddenly.

'Fats,' I say, and she stops abruptly, then whizzes round to face me, her expression one of pure anxiety.

'Yes, Beth?'

'I wondered if you might do me a bit of a favour. Maybe Mike too. But you can't tell anyone, all right?'

Her expression smooths just a fraction. 'Course I will, Beth. Anything.'

'That's brilliant Fats, thanks. Are you free from about one o'clock today?'

Five minutes later I go into the kitchen to find Sean standing by the kettle with his back to the door. Quickly I back out and return to the office. I may have right on my side, but if I speak to him now, I will probably blurt out what I've just done and I will be my own undoing.

As I walk past the wood-panelled door, it opens and Chas appears, looking flustered. He sees me and seizes my arm.

'Christ! I've been looking all over for you.'

'No, no, I'm Beth. I know it's nearly Christmas, but I don't think Christ is putting in an appearance this year.'

'Shut up and get in here.' He drags me into the office and shuts the door.

'What's going on, Chas?'

He shoves his hands into his pockets and stalks over to the window. 'We are in deep shit creek, Beth. That's what's going on. Nice of you to join us, by the way.'

I glance at the clock on the wall. It's still only ten to nine, so technically I am not late. I want to protest at this unfair dig but I rise easily above it. I have right on my side. 'Why are we in trouble?'

'Because your arrogant, lowlife sneak thief boy-friend has pissed us up the wall, that's why.' He rounds on me, his face contorted with fury. 'And don't try and tell me you didn't know about it.'

'Wh-what?' Does he mean Sean? Everyone knew I went out with him a couple of times. 'Well, yes, I did know about th—'

'Of course you fucking knew, you little bitch. You were in on it together, weren't you?'

'*What?*' I take a step towards him as he steps towards me, leaving only about two feet between us. I am towering over him as we glare at each other, and eventually he drops his eyes and turns away.

'Don't pretend, Beth,' he says quietly. 'Everyone knows. You were seen together, he was looking for you this morning, there's no way you can't have known about it. So even if you're not directly involved, if you knew about it and did nothing, you are an accessory. Or something. I've called the police. Just so you know.'

I put my hands up. 'What? Wait. Hang on a minute. Chas, what the flying hell are you talking about? I mean, I really don't think the police are going to be interested in Sean stealing my presentation. Although technically I suppose it is a kind of industrial espionage—'

'What the fuck are *you* talking about? This has nothing to do with Sean, or any pissy presentation.'

'Well, then what . . . ? You know, it's not a pissy presentation, it's very good actually, and it could mean—'

'Your precious boyfriend, Richard Fucking Love, has emptied the business account again and fucked off back to Portugal. Which means we are totally screwed.'

I gape at him. 'He . . . ? To . . . ?' Suddenly the room seems to rock under my feet and I have no choice but to sink down onto the carpet where I stare up at Chas, open-mouthed.

Chas is staring down on me in silence. Eventually, he says, 'You didn't know, did you?' I can't move, or speak. 'I could have sworn . . .' He falls silent then, leaving me in peace to sort through my head. Richard sets up Love Learning, it becomes very successful and lucrative, and that's the moment he picks to leave. Chas runs it for three months, and we struggle the whole time, culminating in a threat to reduce the staff unless we can all find new contracts. I raise my head.

'You said "again"?'

He stares at me for a few seconds, then nods once. 'Why do you think we're in such financial trouble already?'

I close my eyes. I can't keep them open any more, the room is lurching so much. 'How did he . . . ?'

'Oh, he was very clever. Took the money gradually, altered the books, covered his tracks. You know. No one could touch him.'

'And now?'

'Well, that's the thing. This time it's different. This time it's more like a smash and grab, no attempt to hide it. It's so obvious it was him.'

Something in his voice doesn't sound right. He doesn't sound like someone who is going to get his man.

'So, Chas, if it's clear it was him, the police will get him, right? I mean, it's only a matter of time, surely?'

He shakes his head miserably and moves back to the window. 'Sadly, luck was on the git's side. He was in such a hurry for some reason that he didn't even shred anything, it seems. We've found one piece of paper on the floor under the desk here suggesting that he literally just dumped all the evidence in the bin. I mean, it's ridiculous, it would be so easy to get him, and get all the money back, if it was all right there, intact, waiting. But . . .'

'But?'

He sighs deeply and shrugs. 'The cleaner came early and emptied all the bins. Whatever evidence there was has long since been dumped in some landfill site, or shredded, or pulped or all three. It's hopeless.'

My eyes are wide again and my brain is doing that fizzing, electrical thing. I stand up. Well, I kind of leap up. Chas spins round at the window and his eyes widen as they land on me. I feel like I'm hovering a foot off the ground and my hair is standing on end. It isn't though.

'Chas, you aren't going to believe this, but I have got some fucking fantastic news for you.'

430

Thirty

Outcomes

Short-term Goal: Deliver killer presentation to Horizon execs without stumbling, dribbling, passing out, falling over, giggling or leaping on anyone in a lust-fuelled frenzy.
Obstacles: Rupert's face. Oh God.
Long-term Goal: Stay upright for Horizon. Then spend all of tomorrow horizontal . . .
Obstacles: About twenty-two hours.

One fifteen. It's freezing cold but sunny and dry, which is a relief. I'm striding briskly towards the Langhorne main door, head high, briefcase in my hand, dressed very businesslike in long black wool coat, with Nicole Kidman's black skirt and white blouse underneath, hair pinned up, make-up flawless. I am wearing a faint, slightly superior smile, radiating confidence and poise, and I know that I am a successful businesswoman about to make a winning presentation and secure a lucrative deal for my own company. I probably look like Richard Branson. Except for the beard.

I think I might throw up.

Fatima's little red Mini is parked outside – it's unmistakable with the FAT 5 number plate – so she and Mike must be here already. Thank you, God.

I come into the Willoughby Suite through the far doors so that I can peep through the dividing curtains like a child waiting for her first nativity play to start. I can see all the parents – I mean, executives – filling up the seats and flicking through my Keep the Change brochure. Some of them are reading it avidly and chatting to their neighbours about it. Oh, please let them like it.

I'm scanning the crowd all the time, looking for a blond-highlighted head to appear, but it isn't here yet. My stomach is churning and I am more nervous than I have ever been about anything. Time for one more trip to the loo.

In the Ladies, I smooth my hair and touch up my make-up. My hand shakes as I dab on lipgloss. I'm not sure if I'm more nervous about securing this contract; setting up my own business; sticking the knife into Sean, twisting it and breaking the end off so he can't pull it out and save himself; or meeting Rupert. I lean forward to stare at my reflection but I'm shaking so much all I can see is a shimmering blur. Actually, I think that's down to the smears on the glass, but I am shaking. My heart is thudding at twice its normal speed, I'm panting as if I've just run upstairs and I feel like I might be about to have a panic attack. It's ridiculous – I can't remember the last time I felt like this. I know that some of my colleagues still get very nervous before delivering presentations, but I don't so I have no calming tactic. What do they do to help themselves calm down? Fatima is always a wreck for at least an hour before presenting. Nothing she does has any effect on her anxiety, so she's given up trying and just goes in anxious. Some people find that anxiety gives them an edge when they're presenting. I think Fatima finds that it just gives her voice an exotic, tremulous quality.

Sean always strolls in at the last possible moment, shrugs off his coat and walks straight into the training room, leaving himself no time, I suppose, to worry about it. Well, that won't work for me – I've been worrying about this since I set it up on Wednesday.

Derek just clears his throat a lot and pats his neck, as if he's just about to go and sing 'Nessun Dorma' somewhere. Mike spends twenty minutes counting and organizing his slides. And Cath always goes outside and ingests lots of toxins and carcinogens to make herself feel better.

Well, none of those is any good for me. The slide-checking is covered, and I'm not taking up smoking now – I've heard that you need at least a month to get good at it, before it does anything except make you puke. Instead, I go back to the empty curtained-off part of the Willoughby Suite and have another sip of water.

After I spoke to him, Chas went back out into the office and stopped all the frantic searching for evidence. He then went through the contracts that everyone had managed to get since this crisis started and worked out if Love Learning can afford to keep going. Mike had managed to secure a three-month deal with the Italian restaurant in the pedestrianized precinct; and Cath had at some point in the past three weeks lifted the telephone receiver and connected herself to the office supplies supermarket on the industrial estate, and then managed to talk them into some customer care, after sales, management and accounting training. With those two big ones and the four small ones that the others had managed to book, it looks like they can keep going for now. With one or two minor adjustments.

'It looks like Richard will be going to prison,' Chas said, to a stunned silence. 'This means that his assets will be frozen for the foreseeable future. So. I will take over Love Learning permanently, we will start from zero, and we will have to lose at least two members of staff. I'm very sorry.'

Which suits me just fine. Inside the Willoughby Suite the seats are starting to fill up. Fatima is circling in white blouse and black skirt, offering tea, coffee or orange juice to the executives; and Mike, in white shirt and black trousers, is checking through my slides one more time, making sure they're in order, making sure they're all there. I make my way over to Fatima.

'Oh cripes, Beth, thank goodness you're here, I was panicking. I thought I was going to have to do it, didn't I, Mike? I did. I was in such a state.'

I notice that she's wearing little reindeer earrings. 'Well, don't worry, you won't. I'm here.'

'Oh, yes, phew. I was going to, though. I would have, even though I would have made a terrible mess of it, I know I would. But I would have tried, anyway.'

'I know you would. Thanks. Listen, Fats, I don't think you can leave your car there – it's on a zigzag line.'

She frowns at me. 'What are you talking about, Beth? You got nerves too? I sold my car. You were the one

434

who told me to do it. You haven't forgotten that, have you?'

'Well, that's odd. I've just seen a red Mini with your number plate – FAT 5 – parked outside. That's yours, isn't it?'

'No, Beth, silly. I told you, I sold it.'

'Right. Of course. I am silly. Never mind. You don't remember who you sold it to, do you?'

'Nope.'

'Well, what did he look like? Can you remember that?'

'Not really.'

'Well, his hair. Can you remember what colour it was? Like, you know, was it, oh, I don't know, blond for example? Really thick and lustrous? Make you want to run your fingers through it?'

She looks at me blankly. 'No. Definitely not blond. Brown, I think. Very smart.'

'Oh. Right.' Of course. There are more than fifteen execs from Horizon here, it could have been any of them. Why did I immediately think . . . ? Doesn't matter. Must concentrate. Fatima is looking a bit confused so I give her a broad smile and she visibly relaxes. She may not be the most together person I've ever met but she is fantastic with people. I watch her now as she moves off among the waiting crowd, chatting with the executives, making them smile, helping them to feel relaxed and comfortable. And Mike may be a little dull and predictable, but he is ace at organizing things and checking and double-checking that everything is in order. As the other two members of the Keep the Change workforce, they will be invaluable in organizing me and looking after my clients.

435

My mobile phone rings again so I rush back out into the corridor.

'Beth Sheridan, Love . . . I mean, Keep the Change, may I help you?'

'Ah, hello, Miss Sheridan, this is Anthony Davies, Greg Matheson's assistant?'

Shit. This is it. This is the call I have been waiting for. It's the Whytelys account. Fuck. It's terrible timing. As if I'm not a completely inarticulate, tongue-tied, jibbering wreck of jelly already.

'Oh, good afternoon, Anthony, how nice to hear from you. What can I do for you?' Not bad for jelly.

'Well, Mr Matheson has asked me to contact you to arrange a meeting with his legal team, with a view to discussing terms of a possible contract with Keep the Change. When are you free?'

It takes a couple of seconds for me to be able to speak again. 'That's great news, Anthony. Can I pass you over to my assistant, Fatima, who will book the appointment? Thank you so much.' I press the mute button, fling my arms in the air and jump up and down with my mouth wide open and scream silently for at least fifteen seconds, then straighten my blouse and go back into the room and signal to Fatima to come over. I hand her the phone.

'Go outside and talk to Anthony,' I say breathlessly.

'Who is he?'

'Whytelys. They want to book a meeting with me. To discuss a contract.' Fatima's eyes widen and she starts to grin and clench her fists in preparation for fifteen seconds of jumping up and down. 'Not yet,' I say, and she nods and takes a deep breath to calm herself. 'OK. Right, I am free . . . Well, every day. But don't tell him that. Book it for, I dunno, the twenty-eighth or something. Make it the afternoon. Make it sound like you are checking my schedule. Keep him waiting while you flick some paper, you know?'

She nods seriously and takes the phone from my hands, carrying it before her like a precious artefact. I watch her go, then slip back between the curtains and make my way unseen to the exit. I need a breath of fresh air.

Right. I'm outside on the pavement, freezing my arse off. It's one twenty-two and still no sign of Rupert. Eight minutes to go. Plenty of time for him to arrive. He'll probably be here in the next minute or two. Nothing to worry about, I'll just go back inside and wait there. But what shall I do if he doesn't turn up? I should probably wait for him to get here. There are lots of Horizon execs here who won't mind waiting for their leader. But his assistant Jason said he hates being late for anything. What if I make everyone wait and then he feels stupid when he arrives late? But I can't start without him, that's even worse. Or is it? Maybe it would be easier for me if he's not here, sitting there looking all handsome and seductive, putting me off, making me dribble. Perhaps I could just call Jason, to make sure he got the change of time right. If I don't start on time, Sean will be turning up and then he'll catch me and everything will be ruined.

Get a grip, Beth, for crying out loud. This is ridiculous. I am a professional and as such I will start at precisely the time that I—

Oh fucking hell. Here comes Sean.

It's his car, just turning into the road. I rush back inside and head straight to the front of the room where I assume the position: laser pointer in my right hand, overhead projector to my left, first slide at the ready. I look at Mike, sitting next to the projector trying to look inconspicuous, and he nods solemnly, the second and third slides ready to go when I need them. My watch says 1.27. Can I start yet? I glance at the clock on the wall, then at the door. Sean is out there, parking his car. 1.28. The scary pink and grey blur in front of me that can only be the execs are looking up at me expectantly and a hush is spreading around the room. Still 1.28. Fuck. At the side of the room Fatima is staring at me in horror and I realize suddenly that I have been hunched and frowning in front of everyone for at least a minute. The fact that I am repeatedly glancing over my shoulder is adding to the psychotic-convict-on-the-run image that I've read isn't the most appropriate look when you're about to launch a sales pitch.

I force my face into a relaxed smile and incline my head towards the light switch. Fatima frowns and mouths, *What?* Sean must be at reception now, nodding to the woman who is standing there, *All right if I go straight through?* She smiles and he keeps going, through the double glass doors, across the foul beige patterned carpet. I widen my eyes at Fatima and flick them towards the light switch, then at the lights, then at the switch again. *Oh!* She nods. 1.29. Sean reaches the main door to the suite, puts his hand out towards the handle. Fatima moves towards the switch, puts out her hand, presses it, and the room falls into darkness just as the door swings open and Sean is there, frozen in the doorway, staring at me, gawping around the room, his mouth open, realization and horror dawning on his face, as I smile and say to the room, 'Good afternoon, everyone. My name is Beth Sheridan and I am going to talk to you about how my learning and development company, Keep the Change, can benefit Horizon.'

Thirty-one

Conclusion

Short-term Goal: Get to the nearest alcohol dispenser and drink myself calm (i.e. unconscious).
Obstacles: The Horizon execs, who are so impressed they all want to talk to me about contracts.
Bugger.
Long-term Goal: Marry Brad, preferably tomorrow.
Obstacles: He probably hasn't had his morning suit pressed. (God, I need to get a grip.)

Forty-five minutes later. The presentation is over and I am filled with a warm glowing light that is spilling over onto my face in a serene smile as I glide smoothly around the room. The execs loved my material, particularly as I was able to mention my time at Horizon and talk with some credibility about the woeful training set-up there.

'Hang on,' one of them said quite early on, 'wasn't this supposed to be done by a company called Love Learning?'

'Yes.' I nod and smile, as if in admiration of him managing to spot something not blatantly obvious.

'I worked for Love Learning until today, but they were unable to make the presentation due to some unforeseen circumstances.' I leave the rest unsaid, knowing that they will hear about Richard's despicable desertion first thing tomorrow on the local news stations. Having a flatmate with a boyfriend on the local paper is already proving useful. He's putting a piece in about Keep the Change too; Vini suggested it, once she started remembering things again. 'So I thought that, instead of going away with nothing, you might find that Keep the Change will serve you just as well, if not better, than Love Learning.' Plus the boss isn't likely to abscond with all the cash. I don't say that, though. Let them reach that conclusion on their own, tomorrow.

One or two have shaken my hand and told me that it's about time the system was reviewed, and when am I free for a consultation? Fatima and Mike are handling my schedule now, so I point them all in their direction. A queue of three has formed near Fatima, while the others are helping themselves to mulled wine and mince pies at the back of the room. The air is filled with the warm smell of cinnamon, and the low murmur of comfortable conversations. Suddenly hot breath fills my ear as four little words are whispered into it.

'You fucking little *bitch*.'

I swivel, smile still fixed in place, and find Sean standing there, snarling. I tilt my head to him. 'Oh, hi, Sean. How are you?'

'Don't you "how are you" me, you bitch. What the fuck do you think you're doing?'

I frown quizzically. 'Why, Sean, don't you know? I've just delivered a very successful – and brilliantly written, I might add – presentation to all these lovely executives from Horizon. I have convinced them that their training strategy is all wrong and that what they need to do if they want Horizon to continue to prosper and move forward into the twenty-first century with a workforce that feels valued and is superbly equipped with all the up-to-the-minute knowledge, skills and attitude that they need not only to do their job well but to excel in the industry is to ditch all their current training material and practices and book Keep the Change for all their present and future learning and development requirements. Does that help?'

He rams his face nearer to me so that we are almost nose to nose. It's funny to think that last time we stood like this, we almost kissed. He wasn't showing quite so many teeth then, of course. 'Oh yes, you're fucking hilarious,' he spits. 'Except that this is *my* presentation, in *my* room, with *my* execs, leading to *my* contract. That makes you a dirty little thief in my book.'

'Your book? Would that be the one called *Stealing from Your Colleagues and How to Get Away With It*?'

He opens his mouth to retort, then stops and frowns. 'What the flaming fuck are you talking about?'

'The Horizon contract is rightfully mine, we both know that. You stole the idea from me when I was too . . . whatever to notice what you were doing.' I fold my arms. 'I've just got it back from you. That's all.'

He jabs his index finger at me. 'No, that is not all. Love Learning has paid for all this. That makes you a thief in law too.'

'A thief in law? Is that like, your husband's brother's thief? Or your wife's mother's? Brother's wife's?'

'Oh, for fuck's . . .'

442

'Sister's husband's?'

'. . . sake. You can joke about this as much as you like, but this cost me nearly two grand, which I am sure the police are going to be very interested in when I tell them that you—'

'Oh yes, Sean, you're absolutely right, they will be.' I've lowered my voice so that the execs don't overhear this, and it comes out all raspy and menacing. It takes us both a bit by surprise. 'Because I have paid the bill in full myself already, and it was £795, including VAT. So if you are trying to claim back nearly two grand from a company that is already staggering from huge financial losses through embezzlement and consequently about to have its books thoroughly scrutinized, maybe you should think again. Wouldn't you say?'

He puts his top teeth onto his bottom lip, apparently about to say something starting with the letter 'F', then stops, narrows his eyes, closes his mouth and stalks back towards the door. I watch as he turns, threatens me with another vicious 'F', then walks out.

Fuck me.

I turn back to the room, a bit shaky but feeling like I could slay dragons. I move around a bit, smiling at the execs, chatting about the presentation, nodding at reminiscences of my time at Horizon and who was there then – 'Remember Fat Pat from Printing? White hair with a horrid yellow bit at the front from all the fag smoke? She got *married*!' – but what I'm really doing is looking for Rupert. The presentation has gone far better than I could have hoped, and my new business is officially launched, so I should be gliding around in my own happiness bubble like the queen of training, but I'm not. I'm delighted about this, of course I am, but a small part of me – well, quite a large part, actually; every part, if I'm honest, and not just the obvious ones – is hugely disappointed at the non-appearance of Rupert. I mean, it was in his diary, he was down to attend, so I know he didn't have anything else on.

Quick mental image of Rupert with nothing else on. I sway a bit and grab the edge of the table by the mince pies. Fatima's head snaps round worriedly as I wobble so I smile my reassuring smile at her. I think that mulled wine has gone to my head.

Anyway, it's not as if Rupert decided not to come in order to avoid me because he didn't even know that it would be me presenting today. As far as he is concerned, he's just avoided his new contact, Mr S. Cousins. That maggot. If only I'd swallowed my pride and emailed Rupert back, or phoned him, and asked him who was claiming to be his new contact.

Well, it doesn't matter now. I've saved the presentation from Sean anyway, without anyone's help, and judging by Fatima and Mike's slightly harried expressions, the bookings are pouring in. It's probably just as well that Rupert wasn't in the audience watching me with those eyes while I talked. I might have fainted, which would probably have been quite difficult to come back from.

Besides, I did have a very difficult choice to make, and Rupert not being here has kind of made up my mind for me. Any relationship I thought I might have had with Rupert is irrelevant because I am completely in love with . . .

'Brad!' It bursts out of me at the sight of him, before I have a chance to be cool and professional. A few of the execs look round but I am rapt, gazing at Brad, who has magically appeared in front of me, all brown smiling eyes and messy hair. I'm grinning broadly as I gawp up at him, my whole body twitching with the desire to grab him and wrap myself round that sexy torso. My body inadvertently moves towards him all on its own, as if I'm on a conveyor belt. 'God, it's so good to see you. But why are you here? Oh, blimey, you work at Horizon as well, don't you? I'd forgotten all about that. Thank God I didn't notice you earlier, it would have put me right off . . .' He's got his head tilted over on one side and is frowning a little as he looks at me. 'What? What's the matter?'

He shrugs. 'I'm not quite sure. It all depends on you, really.'

'Me?' I'm starting to get worried.

'Well yes. Because I'm a little confused, Beth. Or is it Libby? I'm sorry, just who exactly am I dealing with here? Is this the wonderful, sincere girl who despises liars of all kinds? Or . . . not?'

I slap my hand over my mouth. Oh shit. Oh shit, shit shitting shitty shit. How come I never thought of this? How come this never even crossed my mind? 'Oh, Brad, crap, look, it's not really a lie, I mean my name is Elizabeth so technically I am both Libby and Beth. I mean obviously I am Libby and Beth, you know that now, what I mean is that my name, er, names, are, or at least could be, both diminutives which means it doesn't count as fake when you—'

'Miss Sheridan, I am going to have to ask you to stop for a moment, please,' he says. 'Thank you. Now. Let's go over the facts, can we? OK.' He holds up a hand, one finger extended. 'One: you flagrantly introduced yourself to me as Libby, when you knew very well that your more common name was Beth; two, you didn't explain the diminutives rule—'

'Excuse me, sir, I'm sorry to . . .' One of the execs has appeared. Brad turns to him impatiently.

'Er, could you speak to me later, please? I'm in the middle of something.'

'Yes, sir, but there's a bit of a problem.'

'Well, we can sort it out at the office. I'll be back there in a few minutes, OK?' I feel a sharp pang of disappointment. I've only got a few minutes before he's going. Oh, but the whole day tomorrow. The disappointment dissolves and instantly in its place is bouncy, grinning excitement. My face muscles are starting to get tired with all this up, down, up, down. I imagine my exhausted emotions inside me grabbing a quick sit-down before they all have to start rushing around and changing places again.

'No, sir, I'm afraid not. It's a problem with your car.'

'What?'

A suited woman with all her hair scraped back from her face sidles up. 'Rupert, you have blocked the entrance to the hotel, you twit.'

Rupert? Did she say Rupert? I jerk my head up and start scanning the room, trying to see who she was talking to. Oh God, where is he?

'OK, look, can I just have a minute—'

'Fraid not, Rupe. They need it moving now.'

It's the same woman. I snap my head back round and find her standing right next to Brad. Looking at Brad. Addressing herself to Brad. Calling him Rupert. And he is answering her. My eyes are going from him to her and back to him while my brain is off again and my emotions have leapt to their feet and started rushing around shrieking with their arms in the air. What the hell . . . ?

Brad – or Rupert – is watching me closely, his expression concerned. 'Here are the keys,' he says quickly, tossing them to the man. He doesn't take his eyes from my face. 'Please take my car back to the office. I will see you there in an hour.'

'S-sorry, sir, which . . . ?'

'Red Mini, chequered roof, parked right outside.' His eyes don't leave mine. 'Now, will you please sort it out, Jason?'

Jason and the woman melt away out of my line of sight. They were never in my line of sight. All I can see is . . . Rupert.

'Buh . . . ?' I ask.

'I knew you were going to ask me that. Come with me.' He takes my hand and leads me towards the curtains at the back of the room. We slip through them into the empty end, then he stops, turns and moves in close, his hands on my arms.

'Yuh . . .' I say.

'You're absolutely right,' he says, stroking my hair away from my face. 'It was a really stupid thing to do. But there is a very valid reason, I promise you, Beth.'

'Wh . . . ?'

'OK then. It's this: being Rupert de Witter all the time has so many advantages. It's so easy to get good service, last-minute restaurant table, candles everywhere . . .'

My hand goes to my mouth again. The candles at Madeleine's. All laid on for me by Rupert – who is

Brad. Brad did that for me. But he's Rupert. Until thirty seconds ago, I didn't even know Brad knew I had gone to Madeleine's that day, let alone that he was the one behind it. I think I might actually be going to faint. No, no, it's all right. I'm not. Rupert frowns. 'Oh God, are you all right? You've gone very pale.' He touches my face with his hand, leading me over to the window with his other, his eyes on mine the whole time.

I nod. 'Uh-huh . . .'

'Well, I'm not taking any chances. Stay there.' And after a last lingering gaze into my face, he slips out between the curtains.

Holy fuck. Rupert and Brad are one.

'Here, come and sit down.' He's back immediately, carrying one of the chairs from the presentation. 'Please. I'm worried about you.'

Obediently I go over and sit on the proffered seat. Rupert watches me closely for a moment, like a parent tucking in a child. 'All right?' I nod. 'Sure? Shall I get you a drink? Some water? Brandy? Tea? What about a glass of . . . ?' I shake my head. He stops. Looks at me frankly. Then rubs his hand over his face and walks to the window. 'All right, Miss Whatever-your-name-is. I will explain. Promise you won't faint? OK.

'I'm going to be completely honest with you about why I did what I did. It was unforgivable and there are no excuses, but it's all my friend Hector's fault. No, seriously. It was his idea to go around using a secret identity.'

'He does it *too*? My God, what the hell are you—'

'No, no.' He walks back towards me urgently, shaking his head. 'God, no I didn't mean that. What I meant was . . . I meant it was an idea that I got from

448

him. It wasn't exactly what I would call his idea per se. He didn't, you know, suggest it to me.'

I nod. 'Not his idea or his suggestion, but definitely his fault.'

He turns away and rubs his head. 'You're right, that does sound terrible. But I'm honestly not trying to blame Hector. It was just . . . He met this girl, you see, and when they first met, she didn't know who he was . . .'

'Who is he?'

'He's Hector McCarthy – owns McCarthy Systems. Anyway . . .'

'My God.' McCarthy Systems is this fuck-off massive computer installation company out on the industrial estate. If anything, it's even bigger than Horizon. My eyes are wide. 'I didn't know millionaires exhibited flocking behaviour. Is it like some kind of innate sixth sense that causes you to form groups without realizing it?'

He laughs, shaking his head. 'No, no, of course not.'

'So when you met, did you find out that loads of things about your lives were parallel? You know, driving the same car, living in the same street, that kind of thing?'

He smiles at me. 'We do both drive a Bentley.'

I raise and drop my hands. 'There we are then – conclusive proof. You're all a load of freaks.'

He's still smiling but it's not reaching his eyes now. 'Actually, we are perfectly ordinary, but everyone always thinks . . .' He stops and shakes his head. 'I'm getting a bit ahead of myself here. Where was I? Oh yeah, Hector and Rachel. He was telling me about her, and she sounded so lovely – sweet, charming, funny

– I was just so incredibly envious. I wanted that, too.' He turns back to face me, then frowns. 'God, are you all right? You've gone a bit green.'

Well of course I have. What girl wouldn't when the sexy millionaire she's madly in love with is talking so eloquently about this fantastic other girl? I bet she's a complete whore. No one can be that perfect. I smile sweetly. 'I'm fine. Carry on.'

He bends over slightly. 'Sure? OK. So Hec is all loved up with this amazing, gorgeous girl . . .'

'Yeah, yeah, I got that bit. What happened next?'

He frowns quizzically as he looks at me, then grins broadly. 'OK, I'll move on. This girl didn't know who he was when they met. Which meant that she had got to know him and like him just for himself, not because of his status.' He stops and stares at the ground for a while. 'Since I've had Horizon, which is most of my adult life, it's been very clear to me that people aren't always . . . genuine. It's a real eye-opener, Lib, believe me. People that I knew vaguely at school fifteen years ago, people I meet once at a party, passing acquaintances, they phone me up all the time trying to get together. There's a reunion, there's a dinner party, there's a barbecue. It's a constant onslaught and I'm under no illusions that they all think I'll make a fantastic, entertaining guest.' He puts on a silly, nasal voice. '"My ideal dinner companions? Oh well, that's easy. I would have Jesus Christ, Oscar Wilde, Stephen Fry and the guy that owns Horizon Holidays." I don't think so.'

He falls silent for a moment, his eyes now fixed on the heavy curtains still separating us from his employees. Then he turns and meets my eyes again. 'I was in love once,' he says candidly, 'or thought I was. We even got married. I was twenty-seven, and she was eleven years older. She enjoyed the lifestyle I gave her, but that was the only thing she wanted from me.'

'Oh . . .'

He nods. 'So. There you are. That's why I pretended to be someone called Brad at that speed dating thing. And of course there was always the chance that you might have been an axe murderer.'

I laugh. 'Oh, for heaven's sake, Br— *Rupert*, that's just ridiculous. Axe murderers don't go speed dating.'

'Oh, they don't?'

'Course not. Just because they're psychopathic, bloodthirsty killers, doesn't mean they're social rejects.'

He blinks. 'Social rejects? Is that how you see your average speed dater, then?'

'Oh absolutely.'

He raises his eyebrows and turns his head sideways a little. 'Me, too?'

He's looking at me so earnestly, so intensely, and his voice is so soft and tentative, I can sense genuine anxiety there, even though he's smiling, making it seem like a joke. As I look at him, I'm reminded of the wretched shape of my dressing gown on Monday night and a lust-induced shudder courses through me.

'No, no, of course not you too. You're nothing like a social reject. You're just a fraud.'

He's still gazing at me, his eyes not wavering from mine. Then he looks down. 'I shouldn't have lied to you, Li— *Beth*. As soon as I met you I regretted it. It's like you said once, using a fake name is like not really meeting someone because you're holding back your identity.'

451

'Actually, I think it was you who said that.'

'Well, yes, but you agreed with me.'

'True.'

'The thing is, once it was out, it was very difficult to take it back. I mean, I wanted to, I intended to, but . . .'

'But you were having far too much fun conducting a very flirtatious email correspondence in your real identity with someone else.'

'Ah. Yes. That is true.'

I fold my arms in mock anger. 'It's totally despicable. I mean, how could you be so flirty with me, while you were carrying on with, well, me? I know we both turned out to be the same person, but we might not have. And then you would have been leading us both on.'

'I know. But I was attracted to both of you, so it was impossible to . . .' He stops pacing and turns to face me full on. 'Hey, look, hold on a minute. Let's not forget, Little Miss Incognita, that you were doing the exact same thing – flirting with me while you were going out with . . . you know, *me*.'

'Well, at least I was intending to end it with you as soon as I realized that I was serious about you. Which is more than you can say.'

'But I was torn every time we met. God, Libby, I so wanted to put my arms round you and kiss you, but I just felt I couldn't do it because of my feelings for Beth. For you.' He pauses. 'Anyway, you didn't end it with me, did you? I ended it with you.'

'You did not.'

'Did too.'

'You didn't. You just got a message saying that

someone else would be your contact from then on, and that I would no longer be corresponding with you.'

'Yes I know, and that meant that you had to stop flirting with me because Richard Love was back, and you were involved with him.'

'I was not!'

'Really?'

'Yes! I have never been involved with him. The man is an arse.'

'Oh. Right. So why did you walk out of Horizon with him six years ago, then?'

I stare at him. 'You *remember*?'

'Absolutely. Him walking, and his assistant walking with him? How could I forget that?'

'I mean, did you remember it was me?'

There's a lengthy pause. Then he says, 'Truthfully, no. I didn't remember your name. But I remembered you. I don't mean what you looked like or anything – I don't think we ever met, did we?'

I shake my head. 'Of course not – otherwise I would have realized that you were Rupert.'

'Oh, yes, of course. So I didn't know your face, or remember your name, but I did remember Dick's assistant going with him and thought at the time that it was a strange thing to do. I mean, she – *you* – took a huge gamble that day, throwing everything away to follow him. I just assumed that you were madly in love with him. That was the only possible explanation.'

He meets my eyes and we stare at each other for a few moments. The guys down below are starting to make their preparations again and this time he's not only in the same part of town as me, he's in the same room, in the same building. And it's a *hotel*. You go, guys.

'Wow,' I croak. 'So for years I have been lusting after a photo that turns out not to be you . . .'

'Lusting?'

'. . . while all this time you thought I was in love with Richard.' It would serve no purpose to let him know how close he was to the truth.

'Yes. And then when we start writing, and Rhonda says she thinks the name is familiar—'

'Hang on a minute. How does Rhonda know we are writing?'

He flicks his eyebrows up once. 'I may have mentioned it to one or two people.'

'Oh God. You're kidding?'

He grins. 'No, I did. They thought your emails were absolutely hilarious. All that stuff about shoes and yetis. It was brilliant.'

'Hmm.'

'Oh, look, don't worry. As soon as it started getting more . . . intimate, I stopped showing them.'

'OK. Good. So, Rhonda recognized my name . . . ?'

'Yes. She said she remembered it from somewhere, so I looked you up on the database and found that you had ended your contract without giving notice, on the exact same date that Dick walked out. And you were his training assistant. I very cleverly worked out from those scant details that you were the girl who followed him.'

'Oh, well done. You didn't have much to go on.'

'Thanks. So after that, once I knew who you were, I was very conscious that I was competing with Dickie for your affections. For all I knew, you'd married him in the meantime. I should have been more careful, but I was encouraged by the fact that you weren't signing

454

"Beth Love" at the bottom of your emails. And I was simply drawn in. Before long, I was smitten.'

I feel faint again. Probably lack of oxygen. 'You were?' I manage, my voice a whisper. Must start breathing again soon.

He pauses, smiles, and softens his voice. 'Completely.' It comes out slowly. 'I thought about you all the time. Every moment was spent waiting for the next message. I so wanted to do something for you, something that would make a difference to your life. So I bought your friend's car.'

'So it was you! Oh my God. Why?'

'Well, my friend Harris, the accountant, told me all about your lunch at Madeleine's. God, I wanted to be there. It sounded so perfect, just as I had imagined.'

'Why weren't you there, then? Were you really called away?'

He glances at me, then looks down at the floor. 'No, I wasn't. I couldn't get up the nerve to meet you in the end because of that bloody photo. You would have been expecting to meet a golden-haired Adonis, and then I would turn up and that would be that.'

'But that's rid—'

'No, it isn't. I told you, I'm not very good at . . . that kind of thing.'

'What kind of thing?'

'Talking. Plus, I had the added handicap of being incredibly attracted to you. I was so nervous, and then when I remembered you would be expecting that tanned demigod, I just couldn't face you.'

'So you sent your accountant.'

'So I sent my accountant. Actually, he's more of a friend who does my accounts than an accountant. And he told me all about it. He was quite smitten with you himself, actually. Went on and on about how lovely you were, how sweet, how concerned for your friend's financial predicament. So I phoned up Love Learning, asked to speak to the woman who was selling the Mini, arranged to go and look at it, and bought it in cash right then.'

I'm stunned. It's like Darcy, hunting down Wickham and Lydia and making them get married, all for love of Elizabeth. Except that Lydia is Fatima and Wickham is . . . well, he's a red Mini with a chequered roof, but the details aren't important. I stare at this beautiful man and think of Fatima behind that curtain and my heart swells a little.

'I can't believe you did that,' I breathe, gazing up at him. He's standing right by my chair now.

'It was all for you,' he says, exactly like Darcy. 'Because of how I felt about you. Because I wanted to do something for you, and your friend's car problem was pretty much all I knew about you at that point.'

I'm breathless. I stare at his face, so close to mine, gazing at me anxiously, waiting for my reaction. But I can't give one because I have no breath to speak with. Eventually I manage to croak out, 'She was so thrilled . . .'

'Good. I'm glad I was able to make someone happy.'

'You did. Me, too.'

'And that is why I did it.'

'Thank you.'

There's an awkward moment where we are both frantically wondering, hoping, or at least I am, if he is going to kiss me. He leans nearer, I hold my breath, then he draws back again, clears his throat and looks away. He stands up and walks away from me a couple of steps.

'Beth,' he says, his back to me, his voice suddenly an octave deeper than before, 'I know that I'm not what you were expecting, or hoping for. I am not the man at the back of the Horizon brochure. Far from it. But that man, the one in the photo, is not deserving of you anyway. He may be good-looking and glamorous, but that's all he is.'

He still has his back to me so I stand up and walk over to him. 'Who is he, then?' He turns round, anxiety plain on his face. My stomach flips.

'His name is Saul Ruggiero. Or at least, that's his stage name.'

'Stage name?'

'Mm. His real name is Jeff Staines. He's a distant cousin of mine trying to break into modelling. He's had some very minor work in this country, but nothing noticeable. For some reason, he says he's thinking about—'

'Moving to America,' I finish for him.

He nods. 'Yes, that's right. I'll be glad to see the back of him, quite frankly. Every time he goes out somewhere, he winds up offending someone, and I'm the one who has to smooth things over afterwards.' He gazes down at me. 'It never really mattered before now.'

'So it wasn't you I met looking for anchovies in the supermarket?'

'That would be Jeff.'

'And it was Jeff I was talking to at the party last week?'

He nods.

'But why is his photo in the brochure, pretending to be you? I don't get it.'

He sighs. 'Because when the brochures were first printed twelve years ago, the people I had got in for marketing thought that . . . Well, they thought that my own picture wasn't . . . sexy enough.'

I stare up at him, with his broad shoulders, gorgeous brown eyes, ruffled hair. 'They didn't?'

He nods, resignedly. 'Yes, I'm afraid they did. I was very young at the time and anxious for the business to be a success, so I went along with whatever they suggested.'

'I can't believe they said that.'

He does that Richard Gere thing of laughing out a small puff of air and smiling down to the side in relief. 'You disagree?' He raises his eyes to mine again and I manage a small nod. He moves nearer, cupping my jaw either side with his hands. Our bodies are in contact all the way down to our thighs. 'You think they were wrong?'

'Mmm-hmm.'

I'm sending wave upon wave of powerful, lustful mind messages, and suddenly, finally, they seem to be working. He moves nearer still, his lips millimetres from mine, his fingertips moving up the back of my neck. 'So if I were to kiss you now, you wouldn't object?'

'Uh-uh.'

'That's the best news I have had all day.' And as he bends his head down and presses his lips onto mine, I close my eyes and my insides melt away and my ears are filled with music, a beautiful, romantic melody all around us, ringing in the room, filling the space, joyous and triumphant, like . . .

'Is that your phone?' he says suddenly, pulling away.

I realize that the music I thought I was imagining was in fact the *Superman* theme, and it's coming from my handbag, informing me that I have received a text.

'Oh, yes, it is. Sorry.' We disengage and I rummage in my bag, eventually pulling out my mobile and pressing the 'Read now?' button. It says:

U r dumpd, Luv. Ur loss. Ur admirer Nigel No 15 xxx

THE END

THANKS FOR NOTHING, NICK MAXWELL
Debbie Carbin

'Mum says that you shouldn't judge a book by its cover, so I hope you're not going to base your decision whether or not to buy this book on what's written here, or on the picture on the front. Clearly that would be a big mistake. Mind you, if there had been a little summary or taster of what Nick Maxwell was going to be like on the back of *his* jacket (it could have just been a single word) then maybe I wouldn't be in the mess that I'm in now.

This is the story about how everything got started with me and Nick Maxwell and one other. There was chocolate cake, some wine, a little romance, and a lot of lust . . .'

'HILARIOUS . . . YOU'LL BE RACING THROUGH THE CHAPTERS SO QUICKLY YOU'LL FORGET TO EAT OR GO TO THE LOO'
Heat

9780552774161

BLACK SWAN

DIVING INTO LIGHT
Natasha Farrant

Every summer throughout her childhood, Florence
would return to her family home on the west coast
of France, where she would be joined by her exotic,
hopelessly glamorous cousins. Here life as she knew
it would begin under the benevolent eye of her
grandmother Mimi. It was a heady existence of
illicit drinking, stolen kisses and the
bittersweet pains of first love.

But now Florence is living completely alone with her
new baby. Haunted by nightmares, she cannot open
the letters from her grandmother accumulating on
her mantelpiece. What devastating truth do these
letters hold? Why has Florence turned her back
on her past? And will she and Mimi ever be able
to escape the guilt that is tearing them apart and
has shaken their family to its very core?

9780552774918

BLACK SWAN

COUNTRY PURSUITS
Jo Carnegie

The gorgeous women of Churchminster know exactly
what they want – a constant flow of champagne and
the love of a good man. But faced with the likes of
braying, beer-guzzling farmer Angus, foul-tempered
Sir Fraser and conceited banker Sebastian,
their attentions are increasingly drawn
to more *attractive* possibilities . . .

Meanwhile, when a part of their beloved village
comes under threat from a villainous property
developer and his bulldozer, the entire community
is united by a different kind of passion. Can
they raise enough money to save Churchminster?
Will Mick Jagger turn up to the charity ball?
Will good (sex) overcome bad?

Introducing a glamorous and unforgettable
cast, *Country Pursuits* is a raunchy, rip-roaring,
unashamedly romantic début.

'Pacy, racy and enormous fun!'
Tasmina Perry

'As sinfully English as a hot buttered crumpet!'
Tilly Bagshawe

9780552157063

BLACK SWAN

PLATINUM
Jo Rees

The Maid – Frankie Willis is a twenty-five-year-old blonde computer whizzkid, searching for adventure as a stewardess on board mega-yacht Pushkin;

The Hooker – Peaches Gold is a risk-taking, tough-talking, knockout brunette who's LA's most influential madam. At nearly forty, she's got a little black book that could bring Hollywood's A-list to its knees;

The Lady – Emma Harvey is a fiery red-headed aristocrat. She's a social mover and shaker, who at fifty is happily married to the most handsome man in England.

Three women who have every reason to distrust and despise each other. But their hatred for one man will unite them. For ever. He's

The Billionaire – Yuri Khordinsky, the ruthless Russian oligarch. He's on a mission to get recognition in polite society and will stop at nothing to get it.

But this time he's crossed the wrong women. And they're determined to get back on top.

'Packed with hot men, hotter sex, designer labels and oodles of scandal. Heaven sent for sunbathing'
Heat

'This is a blue-chip, classic bonkbuster and it makes contemporary chick-lit look down at heel. *Platinum* has all the branding and excess that we expect from page-turners of the Eighties and Nineties but the evil Ruskie storyline and the machinations of the world's super-rich gives it a thoroughly modern twist. It's genuinely exciting, extremely well crafted and long enough to be perfect beach reading'
Daily Express

9780552156073

CORGI BOOKS